"A dashing and dangerous hero
who is as likable as he is lethal."

"Surprisingly appealing."

"Readers will warm to Eisler's ruthless
protagonist...quite the accomplishment."

"A definite three-dimensional hit man."

"John Rain is a remarkable creation,
a multifaceted killer with the soul of a poet...
easily one of the most interesting characters
to come along in some time."

"Like Andrew Vachss's vigilante
and Lawrence Block's hit man...
an alienated loner living outside the law."

"A complex and most interesting hero."

RAIN FALL
by Barry Eisler

"*Rain Fall* is a hypnotically hip resurrection of the hit-man thriller. It's got it all: dazzling plot, deft characterization, beaucoup originality. You should dig."

—James Ellroy

"High-tech sparkle provides the pulpy fun in Eisler's thriller." —*Entertainment Weekly*

"Barry Eisler makes a terrific debut with *Rain Fall*, possibly the best cool-killer novel since *The Eiger Sanction*. . . . This is good fun, and Eisler's depiction of contemporary Japan is rich in detail and noir atmospherics. Best of all, he has created in John Rain a dashing and dangerous hero who is as likable as he is lethal. Rain's conflicted past only adds to his interest . . . cat-and-nouse action. . . . Rain's sardonic outlook and the novel's fast pace keep the pages flying by. Readers may find themselves deliberately rereading passages so as not to miss the many grace notes Eisler has sneaked into the narrative—snappy exchanges of dialogue, colorful background action, the intricacies of a judo match. John Rain is not a man you want mad at you. Let's hope there are plenty of bad guys in future installments who don't know this." —*San Francisco Chronicle*

"A crackling good yarn, well written, deftly plotted, and surprisingly appealing. Thomas Perry and Lawrence Block need not retire their hit men quite yet, but Eisler is clearly a challenger." —*The Boston Globe*

"Fast-paced. . . . Readers will warm to Eisler's ruthless protagonist . . . quite the accomplishment." —*New York Daily News*

"A quirky intellectual spin on the first-person hit man story." —*Dallas Morning News*

continued . . .

"Set in a memorable noir version of Tokyo (jazz clubs, whiskey bars, 'love hotels'), Eisler's rich and atmospheric debut thriller winds its way around the city. . . . The author, an American lawyer who has lived and worked in Japan, brings to live a complex and most interesting hero: John Rain, a hard and resourceful man in his forties with an American mother, a Japanese father, a childhood spent in both countries and a stretch with Special Operations in Vietnam that literally made him what he is today—a highly paid freelance assassin. . . . Excellent action scenes . . . an intriguing and intimate evocation of Japan's intense love-hate relationship with America." —*Publishers* Weekly (starred review)

"A James Bond-style secret agent cum hit man. . . . Eisler provides plenty of fascinating detail about the new technologies involved in secret-agent tracking and surveillance. A perfect subway read for spy-story addicts." —*Booklist*

"Rich atmosphere and believable politics . . . a distinguished debut thriller . . . pleasantly fast and polished, in the John Sandford style." —*Kirkus Review*

"*Rain Fall* is written with a firm and confident hand. The story's intriguing plot moves forward at a driving pace, but the author still has the skill and foresight to include some rich characterizations, along with enough of the right kind of details to make his writing authentic and engrossing. There is much to recommend about this book, not the least its compelling protagonist. John Rain is a remarkable creation, a multifaceted killer with the soul of a poet. He is easily one of the most interesting characters to come along in some time. One can only hope that Eisler is already hard at work on his return. *Rain Fall* is a tremendous debut, the best to come out so far this year." —*Mystery Ink*

RAIN
FALL

BARRY EISLER

A SIGNET BOOK

SIGNET
Published by New American Library, a division of
Penguin Putnam Inc., 375 Hudson Street, New York, New York 10014, U.S.A.
Penguin Books Ltd, 80 Strand, London WC2R 0RL, England
Penguin Books Australia Ltd, 250 Camberwell Road,
Camberwell, Victoria 3124, Australia
Penguin Books Canada Ltd, 10 Alcorn Avenue, Toronto, Ontario, Canada M4V 3B2
Penguin Books (N.Z.) Ltd, Cnr Rosedale and Airborne Roads,
Albany, Auckland 1310, New Zealand

Penguin Books Ltd, Registered Offices:
Harmondsworth, Middlesex, England

Published by Signet, an imprint of New American Library, a division of Penguin
Putnam Inc. This is an authorized reprint of a hardcover edition published by
G. P. Putnam's Sons. For information address G. P. Putnam's Sons, a division of
Penguin Putnam Inc., 375 Hudson Street, New York, NY 10014.

First Signet Printing, July 2003
10 9 8 7 6 5 4 3 2 1

 REGISTERED TRADEMARK—MARCA REGISTRADA

Printed in the United States of America

THIS NOVEL is for three people who are not here to read it.

For my father, Edgar, who gave me strength.
For my mother, Barbara, who gave me insight.
For my brother, Ian, who helped me climb the mountain, whose memory keeps me climbing still.

In the changing of the times, they were like autumn lightning, a thing out of season, an empty promise of rain that would fall unheeded on fields already bare.

— SHOSABURO ABE, *on the Meiji-era* samurai

PART ONE

Who is the third who walks always beside you?
When I count, there are only you and I together
But when I look ahead up the white road
There is always another one walking beside you
Gliding wrapt in a brown mantle, hooded
I do not know whether a man or a woman
—But who is that on the other side of you?

—T. S. Eliot, *The Waste Land*

PART ONE

1

HARRY CUT THROUGH the morning rush-hour crowd like a shark fin through water. I was following from twenty meters back on the opposite side of the street, sweating with everyone else in the unseasonable October Tokyo heat, and I couldn't help admiring how well the kid had learned what I'd taught him. He was like liquid the way he slipped through a space just before it closed, or drifted to the left to avoid an emerging bottleneck. The changes in Harry's cadence were accomplished so smoothly that no one would recognize he had altered his pace to narrow the gap on our target, who was now moving almost conspicuously quickly down Dogenzaka toward Shibuya Station.

The target's name was Yasuhiro Kawamura. He was a career bureaucrat connected with the Liberal Democratic Party, or LDP, the political coalition that has been running Japan almost without a break since the war. His current position was vice minister of land and infrastructure at the Kokudokotsusho, the successor to the old Construction Ministry and Transport Ministry, where he had obviously done something to seriously offend someone because serious offense is the only reason I ever get a call from a client.

I heard Harry's voice in my ear: "He's going into the Higashimura fruit store. I'll set up ahead." We were each sporting a Danish-made, microprocessor-controlled receiver small enough to nestle in the ear canal, where you'd need a flashlight to find it. A voice transmitter about the same size goes under the jacket lapel. The transmissions are burst UHF, which makes them very hard to pick up if you don't know exactly what you're looking for, and they're scrambled in case you do. The equipment freed us from having to maintain constant visual contact, and allowed us to keep moving for a while if the target stopped or changed direction. So even though I was too far back to see it, I knew where Kawamura had exited, and I could continue walking for some time before having to stop to keep my position behind him. Solo surveillance is difficult, and I was glad I had Harry with me.

About twenty meters from the Higashimura, I turned off into a drugstore, one of the dozens of open-façade structures that line Dogenzaka, catering to the Japanese obsession with health nostrums and germ fighting. Shibuya is home to many different *buzoku*, or tribes, and members of several were represented here this morning, united by a common need for one of the popular bottled energy tonics in which the drugstores specialize, tonics claiming to be bolstered with ginseng and other exotic ingredients but delivering instead with a more prosaic jolt of ordinary caffeine. Waiting in front of the register were several gray-suited *sarari-man*—"salary man," corporate rank and file—their faces set, cheap briefcases dangling from tired hands, fortifying themselves for another interchangeable day in the maw of the corporate machine. Behind them, two empty-faced teenage girls, their hair reduced to steel-wool brittleness by the dyes they used to turn it orange, noses pierced with oversized rings, their costumes meant to proclaim rejection of the traditional route chosen by the *sarariman* in front of them but offering no understanding of what they had chosen instead. And a gray-haired retiree, his skin sagging but his face oddly bright, probably in Shibuya to avail himself of one of the area's well-known sexual services, which he would pay for out of a pension account that he kept hidden from his wife, not realizing that she knew what he was up to and simply didn't care.

I wanted to give Kawamura about three minutes to get his fruit before I came out, so I examined a selection of bandages that gave me a view of the street. The way he had ducked into the store looked like a move calculated to flush surveillance, and I didn't like it. If we hadn't been hooked up the way we were, Harry would have had to stop abruptly to maintain his position behind the target. He might have had to do something ridiculous, like tie his shoe or stop to read a street sign, and Kawamura, probably peering out of the entranceway of the store, could have made him. Instead, I knew Harry would continue past the fruit store; he would stop about twenty meters ahead, give me his location, and fall in behind when I told him the parade was moving again.

The fruit store was a good spot to turn off, all right— too good for someone who knew the route to have chosen it by accident. But Harry and I weren't going to be flushed out by amateur moves out of some government antiterrorist primer. I've had that training, so I know how useful it is.

I left the drugstore and continued down Dogenzaka, more slowly than before because I had to give Kawamura time to come out of the store. Shorthand thoughts shot through my mind: Are there enough people between us to obscure his vision if he turns when he comes out? What shops am I passing if I need to duck off suddenly? Is anyone looking up the street at the people heading toward the station, maybe helping Kawamura spot surveillance? If I had already drawn any countersurveillance attention, they might notice me now, because before I was hurrying to keep up with the target and now I was taking my time, and people on their way to work don't change their pace that way. But Harry had been the one walking point, the more conspicuous position, and I hadn't done anything to arouse attention before stopping in the drugstore.

I heard Harry again: "I'm at one-oh-nine." Meaning he had turned into the landmark 109 Department Store, famous for its collection of 109 restaurants and trendy boutiques.

"No good," I told him. "The first floor is lingerie. You going to blend in with fifty teenage girls in blue sailor school uniforms picking out padded bras?"

"I was planning to wait outside," he replied, and I could imagine him blushing.

The front of 109 is a popular meeting place, typically crowded with a polyglot collection of pedestrians.

"Sorry, I thought you were going for the lingerie," I said, suppressing the urge to smile. "Just hang back and wait for my signal as we go past."

"Right."

The fruit store was only ten meters ahead, and still no sign of Kawamura. I was going to have to slow down. I was on the opposite side of the street, outside Kawamura's probable range of concern, so I could take a chance on just stopping, maybe to fiddle with a cell phone. Still, if he looked, he would spot me standing there, even though, with my father's Japanese features, I don't have a problem blending into the crowds. Harry, a pet name for Haruyoshi, being born of two Japanese parents, has never had to worry about sticking out.

When I returned to Tokyo in the early eighties, my brown hair, a legacy from my mother, worked for me the way a fluorescent vest does for a hunter, and I had to dye it black to develop the anonymity that protects me now. But in the last few years the country has gone mad for *chappatsu*, or tea-color dyed hair, and I don't have to be so vigilant about the dye anymore. I like to tell Harry he's going to have to go *chappatsu* if he wants to fit in, but Harry's too much of an *otaku*, a geek, to give much thought to issues like personal appearance. I guess he doesn't have that much to work with, anyway: an awkward smile that always looks like it's offered in anticipation of a blow, a tendency to blink rapidly when he's excited, a face that's never lost its baby fat, its pudginess accentuated by a shock of thick black hair that on bad days seems almost to float above it. But the same qualities that keep him off magazine covers confer the unobtrusiveness that makes for effective surveillance.

I had reached the point where I was sure I was going to have to stop when Kawamura popped out of the fruit store and reentered the flow. I hung back as much as possible to increase the space between us, watching his head bobbing as he moved down the street. He was tall for a Japanese and that helped, but he was wearing a dark suit like ninety percent of the other people in this crowd—including Harry and me, naturally, so I couldn't drop back too far.

Just as I'd redeveloped the right distance, he stopped and turned to light a cigarette. I continued moving slowly behind and to the right of the group of people that separated us, knowing he wouldn't be able to make me moving with the crowd. I kept my attention focused on the backs of the suits in front of me, just a bored morning commuter. After a moment he turned and started moving again.

I allowed myself the trace of a satisfied smile. Japanese don't stop to light cigarettes; if they did, they'd lose weeks over the course of their adult lives. Nor was there any reason, such as a strong headwind threatening to blow out a match, for him to turn and face the crowd behind him. Kawamura's obvious attempt at countersurveillance simply confirmed his guilt.

Guilt of what I don't know, and in fact I never ask. I insist on only a few questions. Is the target a man? I don't work against women or children. Have you retained anyone else to solve this problem? I don't want my operation getting tripped up by someone's idea of a B-team, and if you retain me, it's an exclusive. Is the target a principal? I solve problems directly, like the soldier I once was, not by sending messages through uninvolved third parties like a terrorist. The concerns behind the last question are why I like to see independent evidence of guilt: It confirms that the target is indeed the principal and not a clueless innocent.

Twice in eighteen years the absence of that evidence has stayed my hand. Once I was sent against the brother of a newspaper editor who was publishing stories on corruption in a certain politician's home district. The other time it was against the father of a bank reformer who showed excessive zeal in investigating the size and nature of his institution's bad debts. I would have been willing to act directly against the editor and the reformer, had I been retained to do so, but apparently the clients in question had reason to pursue a more circuitous route that involved misleading me. They are no longer clients, of course. Not at all.

I'm not a mercenary, although I was nothing more than that once upon a time. And although I do in a sense live a life of service, I am no longer samurai, either. The essence of samurai is not just service, but loyalty to his master, to a cause greater than himself. There was a time when I burned with loyalty, a time when, suffused with the samurai ethic I had absorbed from escapist novels and comics as a boy in Japan, I was prepared to die in the service of my adopted liege lord, the United States. But loves as uncritical and unrequited as that one can never last, and usually come to a dramatic end, as mine did. I am a realist now.

As I came to the 109 building I said, "Passing." Not

into my lapel or anything stupid like that; the transmitters are sensitive enough so that you don't need to make any subtle movements that are like billboards for a trained countersurveillance team. Not that one was out there, but you always assume the worst. Harry would know I was passing his position and would fall in after a moment.

Actually, the popularity of cell phones with earpieces makes this kind of work easier than it once was. It used to be that someone walking alone and talking under his breath was either demented or an intelligence or security agent. Today you see this sort of behavior all the time among Japan's *keitai*, or cell phone, generation.

The light at the bottom of Dogenzaka was red, and the crowd congealed as we approached the five-street intersection in front of the train station. Garish neon signs and massive video monitors flashed frantically on the buildings around us. A diesel-powered truck ground its gears as it slogged through the intersection, laborious as a barge in a muddy river, its bullhorns blaring distorted right-wing patriotic songs that momentarily drowned out the bells commuters on bicycles were ringing to warn pedestrians out of the way. A street hawker angled a pushcart through the crowds, sweat running down the sides of his face, the smell of steamed fish and rice following in his zigzagging wake. An ageless homeless man, probably a former *sarariman* who had lost his job and his moorings when the bubble burst in the late eighties, slept propped against the base of a streetlight, inured by alcohol or despair to the tempest around him.

The Dogenzaka intersection is like this night and day, and at rush hour, when the light turns green, over three hundred people step off the curb at the same instant, with another twenty-five thousand waiting in the crush. From here on, it was going to be shoulder to shoulder, chest to back. I would keep close to Kawamura now, no more than five meters, which would put about two hundred people between us. I knew he had a commuter pass and wouldn't need to go to the ticket machine. Harry and I had purchased our tickets in advance so we would be able to follow him right through the wickets. Not that the attendant would notice one way or the other. At rush hour, they're practically numbed by the hordes; you could flash anything, a baseball card, probably, and in you'd go.

The light changed, and the crowds swept into one another like a battle scene from some medieval epic. An invisible radar I'm convinced is possessed only by Tokyoites prevented a mass of collisions in the middle of the street. I watched Kawamura as he cut diagonally across to the station, and maneuvered in behind him as he passed. There were five people between us as we surged past the attendant's booth. I had to stay close now. It would be chaos when the train pulled in: five thousand people pouring out, five thousand people stacked fifteen deep waiting to get on, everyone jockeying for position. Foreigners who think of Japan as a polite society have never ridden the Yamanote at rush hour.

The river of people flowed up the stairs and onto the platform, and the sounds and smells of the station seemed to arouse an extra sense of urgency in the crowd. We were swimming upstream against the people who had just gotten off the train, and as we reached the platform the doors were already closing on handbags and the odd protruding elbow. By the time we had passed the kiosk midway down the platform, the last car had passed us and a moment later it was gone. The next train would arrive in two minutes.

Kawamura shuffled down the middle of the platform. I stayed behind him but hung back from the tracks, avoiding his wake. He was looking up and down the platform, but even if he had spotted Harry or me earlier, seeing us waiting for the train wasn't going to unnerve him. Half the people waiting had just walked down Dogenzaka.

I felt the rumble of the next train as Harry walked past me like a fighter jet buzzing a carrier control tower, the slightest nod of his head indicating that the rest was with me. I had told him I only needed his help until Kawamura was on the train, which is where he had always gone during our previous surveillance. Harry had done his usual good work in helping me get close to the target, and, per our script, he was now exiting the scene. I would contact him later, when I was done with the solo aspects of the job.

Harry thinks I'm a private investigator and that all I do is follow these people around collecting information. To avoid the suspicious appearance of a too-high mortality rate for the subjects we track, I often have him follow people in whom I have no interest, who of course then provide some measure of cover by continuing to live their happy and oblivious lives. Also, where possible, I avoid sharing the subject's name with Harry to minimize the chances that he'll come across too many coincidental obituaries. Still, some of our subjects do have a habit of dying at the end of surveillance, and I know Harry has a curious mind. So far he hasn't asked, which is good. I like Harry as an asset and wouldn't want him to become a liability.

I moved up close behind Kawamura, just another commuter trying to get a good position for boarding the train. This was the most delicate part of the operation. If I flubbed it, he would make me and it would be difficult to get sufficiently close to him for a second try.

My right hand dipped into my pants pocket and touched a microprocessor-controlled magnet, about the size and weight of a quarter. On one side the magnet was covered with blue worsted cloth, like that of the suit Kawamura was wearing. Had it been necessary, I could have stripped away the blue to expose a layer of gray, which was the other color Kawamura favored. On the opposite side of the magnet was an adhesive backing.

I withdrew the magnet from my pocket and protected it from view by cupping it in my hands. I would have to wait for the right moment, when Kawamura's attention was distracted. Mildly distracted would be enough. Maybe as we were boarding the train. I peeled off the wax paper covering the adhesive and crumbled it into my left pants pocket.

The train emerged at the end of the platform and hurtled toward us. Kawamura pulled a cell phone out of his breast pocket. Started to input a number.

Okay, do it now. I brushed past him, placing the magnet on his suit jacket just below the left shoulder blade, and moved several paces down the platform.

Kawamura spoke into the phone for only a few seconds, too softly for me to hear over the screeching brakes of the train slowing to a halt in front of us, and then slipped the phone back in his left breast pocket. I wondered whom he had called. It didn't matter. Two stations ahead, three at the most, and it would be done.

The train stopped and its doors opened, releasing a gush of human effluent. When the outflow slowed to a trickle, the lines waiting on either side of the doors collapsed inward and poured inside, as though someone had hit the reverse switch on a giant vacuum. People kept jamming themselves in despite the warnings that "The doors are closing," and the mass of commuters grew more swollen until we were all held firmly in place, with no need to grip the overhead handles because there was nowhere to fall. The doors shut, the car lurched forward, and we moved off.

I exhaled slowly and rotated my head from side to side, hearing the bones crack in my neck, feeling the last remnants of nervousness drain away as we reached the final moments. It has always been this way for me. When I was a teenager, I lived for a while near a town that had a network of gorges cutting through it, and at some of them you could jump from the cliffs into deep swimming holes. You could see the older kids doing it all the time—it didn't look so far up. The first time I climbed to the top and looked down, though, I couldn't believe how high I was, and I froze. But the other kids were watching. And right then, I knew that no matter how afraid I was, no matter what might happen, I was going to jump, and some instinctive part of me shut down my awareness of everything except the simple, muscular action of running forward. I had no other perceptions, no awareness of any future beyond the taking of those brisk steps. I remember thinking that it didn't even matter if I died.

Kawamura was standing in front of the door at one end of the car, about a meter from where I was positioned, his right hand holding one of the overhead bars. I needed to stay close now.

The word I had gotten was that this had to look natural: my specialty, and the reason my services are always in demand. Harry had obtained Kawamura's medical records from Jikei University Hospital, which showed that he had a condition called complete heart block and owed his continuing existence to a pacemaker installed five years earlier.

I twisted so that my back was to the doors—a slight breach of Tokyo's minimal train etiquette, but I didn't want anyone who might speak English to see the kinds of prompts that were going to appear on the screen of the PDA computer I was carrying. I had downloaded a cardiac interrogation program into it, the kind a doctor uses to adjust a patient's pacemaker. And I had rigged it so that the PDA fed infrared commands to the control magnet. The only difference between my setup and a cardiologist's was that mine was miniaturized and wireless. That, and I hadn't taken the Hippocratic oath.

The PDA was already turned on and in sleep mode, so it powered up instantly. I glanced down at the screen. It was flashing "pacing parameters." I hit the

Enter key and the screen changed, giving me an option of "threshold testing" and "sensing testing." I selected the former and was offered a range of parameters: rate, pulse width, amplitude. I chose rate and quickly set the pacemaker at its lowest rate limit of forty beats per minute, then returned to the previous screen and selected pulse width. The screen indicated that the pacemaker was set to deliver current at durations of .48 milliseconds. I decreased the pulse width as far as it would go, then changed to amplitude. The unit was preset at 8.5 volts, and I started dropping it a half volt at a time. When I had taken it down two full volts, the screen flashed, "You have now decreased unit amplitude by two volts. Are you sure you want to continue to decrease unit amplitude?" I entered, "Yes" and went on, repeating the sequence every time I took it down two volts.

When the train pulled into Yoyogi Station, Kawamura stepped off. Was he getting off here? That would be a problem: the unit's infrared had limited range, and it would be a challenge to operate it and follow him closely at the same time. *Damn, just a few more seconds,* I thought, bracing to follow him out. But he was only allowing the people behind him to leave the train, and stopped outside the doors. When the Yoyogi passengers had exited he got back on, followed closely by several people who had been waiting on the platform. The doors closed, and we moved off again.

At two volts, the screen warned me that I was nearing minimum output values and it would be dangerous to further decrease output. I overrode the warning and took the unit down another half volt,

glancing up at Kawamura as I did so. He hadn't
changed his position.

When I reached a single volt and tried to go further,
the screen flashed, "Your command will set the unit at
minimum output values. Are you certain that you wish
to enter this command?" I entered "Yes." It prompted
me one more time anyway: "You have programmed the
unit to minimum output values. Please confirm." Again
I entered, "Yes." There was a one-second delay, then the
screen started flashing bold-faced letters: **Unacceptable
output values. Unacceptable output values.**

I closed the cover, but left the PDA on. It would reset
automatically. There was always the chance that the
sequence hadn't worked the first time around, and I
wanted to be able to try again if I had to.

There wasn't any need. As the train pulled into Shinjuku Station and jerked to a stop, Kawamura stumbled
against the woman next to him. The doors opened and
the other passengers flowed out, but Kawamura remained, gripping one of the upright bars next to the
door with his right hand and clutching his package of
fruit with his left, commuters shoving past him. I
watched him rotate counterclockwise until his back hit
the wall next to the door. His mouth was open; he
looked slightly surprised. Then slowly, almost gently,
he slid to the floor. I saw one of the passengers who
had gotten on at Yoyogi stoop down to assist him. The
man, a mid-forties Westerner, tall and thin enough to
make me think of a javelin, somehow aristocratic in his
wireless glasses, shook Kawamura's shoulders, but
Kawamura was past noticing the stranger's efforts at
succor.

"Daijoubu desu ka?" I asked, my left hand moving to support Kawamura's back, feeling for the magnet. Is he all right? I used Japanese because it was likely that the Westerner wouldn't understand it and our interaction would be kept to a minimum.

"Wakaranai," the stranger muttered. I don't know. He patted Kawamura's increasingly bluish cheeks and shook him again—a bit roughly, I thought. So he did speak some Japanese. It didn't matter. I pinched the edge of the magnet and pulled it free. Kawamura was done.

I stepped past them onto the platform and the inflow immediately began surging onto the train behind me. Glancing through the window nearest the door as I walked past, I was stunned to see the stranger going through Kawamura's pockets. My first thought was that Kawamura was being robbed. I moved closer to the window for a better look, but the growing crush of passengers obscured my view.

I had an urge to get back on, but that would have been stupid. Anyway, it was too late. The doors were already sliding shut. I saw them close and catch on something, maybe a handbag or a foot. They opened slightly and closed again. It was an apple, falling to the tracks as the train pulled away.

FROM SHINJUKU I took the Maranouchi subway line to Ogikubo, the extreme west of the city and outside metropolitan Tokyo. I wanted to do a last SDR—surveillance detection run—before contacting my client to report the results of the Kawamura operation, and heading west took me against the incoming rush-hour train traffic, making the job of watching my back easier.

An SDR is just what it sounds like: a route designed to force anyone who's following you to show himself. Harry and I had of course taken full precautions en route to Shibuya and Kawamura that morning, but I never assume that because I was clean earlier I must be clean now. In Shinjuku, the crowds are so thick that you could have ten people following you and you'd never make a single one of them. By contrast, following someone unobtrusively across a long, deserted train platform with multiple entrances and exits is nearly impossible, and the trip to Ogikubo offered the kind of peace of mind I've come to require.

It used to be that, when an intelligence agent wanted

to communicate with an asset so sensitive that a meeting was impossible, they had to use a dead drop. The asset would drop microfiche in the hollow of a tree, or hide it in an obscure book in the public library, and later, the spy would come by and retrieve it. You could never put the two people together in the same place at the same time.

It's easier with the Internet, and more secure. The client posts an encrypted message on a bulletin board, the electronic equivalent of a tree hollow. I download it from an anonymous pay phone and decrypt it at my leisure. And vice versa.

The message traffic is pretty simple. A name, a photograph, personal and work contact information. A bank account number, transfer instructions. A reminder of my three no's: no women or children, no acts against nonprincipals, no other parties retained to solve the problem at hand. The phone is used only for the innocuous aftermath, which was the reason for my side trip to Ogikubo.

I used one of the pay phones on the station platform to call my contact within the Liberal Democratic Party—an LDP flunky I know only as Benny, maybe short for Benihana or something. Benny's English is fluent, so I know he's spent some time abroad. He prefers to use English with me, I think because it has a harder sound in some contexts and Benny fancies himself a hard guy. Probably he learned the lingo from a too-steady diet of Hollywood gangster movies.

We'd never met, of course, but talking to Benny on the phone had been enough for me to develop an antipathy. I had a vivid image of him as just another gov-

ernment seat-warmer, a guy who would try to manage
a weight problem by jogging a few ten-minute miles
three times a week on a treadmill in an overpriced
chrome-and-mirrors gym, where the air-conditioning
and soothing sounds of the television would prevent
any unnecessary discomfort. He'd splurge on items
like designer hair gel for a comb over because the little
things only cost a few bucks anyway, and would save
money by wearing no-iron shirts and ties with labels
proclaiming "Genuine Italian Silk!" that he'd selected
with care on a trip abroad from a sale bin at some dis-
count department store, congratulating himself on the
bargains for which he acquired such quality goods.
He'd sport a few Western extravagances like a Mont-
blanc fountain pen, talismans to reassure himself that
he was certainly more cosmopolitan than the people
who gave him orders. Yeah, I knew this guy. He was a
little order taker, a go-between, a cutout who'd never
gotten his hands dirty in his life, who couldn't tell the
difference between a real smile and the amused ric-
tuses of the hostesses who relieved him of his yen for
watered-down Suntory scotch while he bored them
with hints about the Big Things he was involved in but
of course couldn't really discuss.

After the usual exchange of innocuous, preestab-
lished codes to establish our bona fides, I told him,
"It's done."

"Glad to hear it," he said in his terse, false tough-
guy way. "Any problems?"

"Nothing worth mentioning," I responded after a
pause, thinking of the guy on the train.

"Nothing? You sure?"

I knew I wouldn't get anything this way. Better to say nothing, which I did.

"Okay," he said, breaking the silence. "You know to reach out to me if you need anything. Anything at all, okay?"

Benny tries to run me like an intelligence asset. Once he even suggested a face-to-face meeting. I told him if we met face-to-face I'd be there to kill him, so maybe we should skip it. He laughed, but we never did have that meeting.

"There's only one thing I need," I said, reminding him of the money.

"By tomorrow, like always."

"Good enough." I hung up, automatically wiping down the receiver and keys on the remote possibility that they had traced the call and would send someone to try for prints. If they had access to Vietnam-era military records, and I assumed they did, they would get a match for John Rain, and I didn't want them to know that the same guy they had known over twenty years ago when I first came back to Japan was now their mystery freelancer.

I was working with the CIA at the time, a legacy of my Vietnam contacts, making sure the agency's "support funds" were reaching the right recipients in the governing party, which even back then was the LDP. The agency was running a secret program to support conservative political elements, part of the U.S. government's anti-Communist policies and a natural extension of relationships that had developed during the postwar occupation, and the LDP was more than happy to play the role in exchange for the cash.

I was really just a bagman, but I had a nice rapport with one of the recipients of Uncle Sam's largesse, a fellow named Miyamoto. One of Miyamoto's associates, miffed at what he felt was a too-small share of the money, threatened to blow the whistle if he didn't receive more. Miyamoto was exasperated; the associate had used this tactic before and had gotten a bump-up as a result. Now he was just being greedy. Miyamoto asked me if I could do anything about this guy, for $50,000, "no questions asked."

The offer interested me, but I wanted to make sure I was protected. I told Miyamoto I couldn't do anything myself, but I could put him in touch with someone who might be able to help.

That someone became my alter ego, and over time, I took steps to erase the footprints of the real John Rain. Among other things, I no longer use my birth name or anything connected with it, and I've had surgery to give my somewhat stunted epicanthic folds a more complete Japanese appearance. I wear my hair longer now, as well, in contrast to the brush cut I favored back then. And wire-rim glasses, a concession to age and its consequences, give me a bookish air that is entirely unlike the intense soldier's countenance of my past. Today I look more like a Japanese academic than the half-breed warrior I once was. I haven't seen any of my contacts from my bagman days in over twenty years, and I steer scrupulously clear of the agency. After the number they did on me and Crazy Jake in Bu Dop, I was more than happy to shake them out of my life.

Miyamoto had put me in touch with Benny, who worked with people in the LDP who had problems like Miyamoto's, problems that I could solve. For a while I worked for both of them, but Miyamoto retired about ten years ago and died peacefully in his bed not long thereafter. Since then Benny's been my best client. I do three or four jobs a year for him and whoever in the LDP he fronts for, charging the yen equivalent of about $100k per. Sounds like a lot, I know, but there's overhead: equipment, multiple residences, a real but perpetually money-losing consulting operation that provides me with tax records and other means of legitimacy.

Benny. I wondered whether he knew anything about what had happened on the train. The image of the stranger rifling through the slumped Kawamura's pockets was as distracting as a small seed caught in my teeth, and I returned to it again and again, hoping for some insight. A coincidence? Maybe the guy had been looking for identification. Not the most productive treatment for someone who is going blue from lack of oxygen, but people without training don't always act rationally under stress, and the first time you see someone dying right in front of you it is stressful. Or he could have been Kawamura's contact, on the train for some kind of exchange. Maybe that was their arrangement, a moving exchange on a crowded train. Kawamura calls the contact from Shibuya just before boarding the train, says, "I'm in the third-to-last car, leaving the station now," and the contact knows where to board as the train pulls into Yoyogi Station. Sure, maybe.

Actually, the little coincidences happen frequently in my line of work. They start automatically when you become a student of human behavior—when you start following the average person as he goes about his average day, listening to his conversations, learning his habits. The smooth shapes you take for granted from a distance can look unconnected and bizarre under close scrutiny, like the fibers of cloth observed under a microscope.

Some of the targets I take on are involved in subterranean dealings, and the coincidence factor is especially high. I've followed subjects who turned out to be under simultaneous police surveillance: one of the reasons that my countersurveillance skills have to be as dead subtle as they are. Mistresses are a frequent theme, and sometimes even second families. One subject I was preparing to take out as I followed him down the subway platform surprised the hell out of me by throwing himself in front of the train, saving me the trouble. The client was delighted, and mystified at how I was able to get it to look like a suicide on a crowded train platform.

It felt like Benny knew something, though, and that feeling made it hard to put this little coincidence aside. If I had some way of confirming that he'd broken one of my three rules by putting a B-team on Kawamura, I'd find him and he would pay the price. But there was no obvious way to acquire that confirmation. I'd have to put this one aside, maybe mentally label it "pending" to make myself feel better.

The money appeared the next day, as Benny had promised, and the next nine days were quiet.

On the tenth day, I got a call from Harry. He told me it was my friend Koichiro, he was going to be at Galerie Coupe Chou in Shinjuku on Tuesday at eight with some friends, I should come by if I had time. I told him that sounded great and would try to make it. I knew to count back five listings in the restaurants section of the Tokyo City Source yellow pages, making our meeting place Las Chicas, and to subtract five days from the date and five hours from the time.

I like Las Chicas for meetings because almost everyone approaches it from Aoyama-dori, making the people coming from the other direction the ones to watch, and because people have to show themselves coming across a little patio before reaching the entrance. The place is surrounded by twisting alleys that snake off in a dozen different directions, offering no choke points where someone could set up and wait. I know those alleys well, as I make it my business to know the layout of any area where I spend a lot of time. I was confident that anyone unwanted would have a hard time getting close to me there.

The food and the ambience are good, too. Both the menu and the people represent a fusion of East and West: Indian *jeera* rice and Belgian chocolate, a raven-haired beauty of high-cheeked Mongolian ancestry next to a blonde straight out of the fjords, a polyglot of languages and accents. Somehow Las Chicas manages to be eternally hip and entirely comfortable with itself, both at the same time.

I got to the restaurant two hours early and waited, sipping one of the chai lattes for which the restaurant is justifiably celebrated. You never want to be the last one to arrive at a meeting. It's impolite. And it decreases your chances of being the one to leave.

At a little before three I spotted Harry coming up the street. He didn't see me until he was inside.

"Always sitting with your back to the wall," he said, walking over.

"I like the view," I answered, deadpan. Most people pay zero attention to these things, but I'd taught him that it's something to be aware of when you walk into a place. The people with their backs to the door are the civilians; the ones in the strategic seats could be people with some street sense or some training, people who might deserve a little more attention.

I had met Harry about five years earlier in Roppongi, where he'd found himself in a jam with a few drunken off-duty American Marines in a bar where I happened to be killing time before an appointment. Harry can come off as a bit of an oddball: sometimes his clothes are so ill fitting you might wonder if he stole them from a random clothesline, and he has a habit of staring unselfconsciously at anything that interests him. It was the staring that drew the attention of the jarheads, one of whom loudly threatened to stick those thick glasses up Harry's Jap ass if he didn't find somewhere else to look. Harry had immediately complied, but this apparent sign of weakness served only to encourage the Marines. When they followed Harry out, and I realized he hadn't even noticed what was going to happen, I left too. I have a problem with bullies—a legacy from my childhood.

Anyway, the jarheads got to mess with me instead of with Harry, and it didn't turn out the way they had planned. Harry was grateful.

It turned out that he had some useful skills. He was

born in the United States of Japanese parents and grew up bilingual, spending summers with his grandparents outside of Tokyo. He went to college and graduate school in the States, earning a degree in applied mathematics and cryptography. In graduate school he got in trouble for hacking into school files that one of his cryptography professors had bragged he had hack-proofed. There was also some unpleasantness with the FBI, which had managed to trace probes of the nation's Savings & Loan Administration and other financial institutions back to Harry. Some of the honorable men from deep within America's National Security Agency learned of these hijinks and arranged for Harry to work at Fort Meade in exchange for purging his growing record of computer offenses.

Harry stayed with the NSA for a few years, getting his new employer into secure government and corporate computer systems all over the world and learning the blackest of the NSA's computer black arts along the way. He came back to Japan in the mid-nineties, where he took a job as a computer security consultant with one of the big global consulting outfits. Of course they did a thorough background check, but his clean record and the magic of an NSA top-secret security clearance blinded Harry's new corporate sponsors to what was most fundamental about the shy, boyish-looking thirtysomething they had just hired.

Which was that Harry was an inveterate hacker. He had grown bored at the NSA because, despite the technical challenges of the work, it was all sanctioned by the government. In his corporate position, by contrast, there were rules, standards of ethics, which he was supposed to follow. Harry never did security work on a system without leaving a back door that he could use whenever the mood arose. He hacked his own firm's files to uncover the vulnerabilities of its clients, which he then exploited. Harry had the skills of a locksmith and the heart of a burglar.

Since we met I've been teaching him the relatively aboveboard aspects of my craft. He's enough of a misfit to be in awe of the fact that I've befriended him, and has a bit of a crush on me as a result. The resulting loyalty is useful.

"What's going on?" I asked him after he had sat down.

"Two things. One I think you'll know about; the other, I'm not sure."

"I'm listening."

"First, it seems Kawamura had a fatal heart attack the same morning we were tailing him."

I took a sip of my chai latte. "I know. It happened right in front of me on the train. Hell of a thing."

Was he watching my face more closely than usual? "I saw the obituary in the *Daily Yomiuri*," he said. "A surviving daughter placed it. The funeral was yesterday."

"Aren't you a little young to be reading the obituaries, Harry?" I asked, eyeing him over the edge of the mug.

He shrugged. "I read everything, you know that. It's part of what you pay me for."

That much was true. Harry kept his finger on the pulse, and had a knack for identifying patterns in chaos.

"What's the second thing?"

"During the funeral, someone broke into his apartment. I figured it might have been you, but wanted to tell you just in case."

I kept my face expressionless. "How did you find out about that?" I asked.

He took a folded piece of paper from his pants pocket and slid it toward me. "I hacked the Keisatsu-cho report." The Keisatsucho is Japan's National Police Agency, the Japanese FBI.

"Christ, Harry, what can't you get at? You're unbelievable."

He waved his hand as though it were nothing. "This is just the *Sosa*, the investigative section. Their security is pathetic."

I felt no particular urge to tell him that I agreed with his assessment of *Sosa* security—that in fact I had been an avid reader of their files for many years.

I unfolded the piece of paper and started to scan its contents. The first thing I noticed was the name of the person who had prepared the report: Ishikura Tatsuhiko. Tatsu. Somehow I wasn't surprised.

I had known Tatsu in Vietnam, where he was attached to Japan's Public Safety and Investigative Board, one of the precursors of the Keisatsucho. Hobbled by the restrictions placed on its military by Article Nine of the postwar constitution and unable to do more than send a few people on a "listen-and-learn" basis, the government sent Tatsu to Vietnam for six months to make wiring diagrams of the routes of KGB assistance to the Vietcong. Because I spoke Japanese, I was assigned to help him learn his way around.

Tatsu was a short man with the kind of stout build that rounds out with age, and a gentle face that masked an intensity beneath—an intensity that was revealed by a habit of jutting his torso and head forward in a way that made it look as though he was being restrained by an invisible leash. He was frustrated in postwar, neutered Japan, and admired the warrior's path I had taken. For my part, I was intrigued by a secret sorrow I saw in his eyes, a sorrow that, strangely, became more pronounced when he smiled and especially when he laughed. He spoke little of his family, of two young daughters in Japan, but when he did his pride was evident. Years later I learned from a mutual acquaintance that there had also been a son, the youngest, who had died in circumstances of which Tatsu would never speak, and I understood from whence that sorrowful countenance had come.

When I came back to Japan we spent some time together, but I had distanced myself since getting involved with Miyamoto and then Benny. I hadn't seen Tatsu since changing my appearance and moving underground.

Which was fortunate, because I knew from the reports I hacked that Tatsu had a pet theory: the LDP had an assassin on the payroll. In the late eighties Tatsu came to believe that too many key witnesses in corruption cases, too many financial reformers, too many young crusaders against the political status quo were dying of "natural causes." In his assessment there was a pattern here, and he profiled the shadowy shape at the center of it as having skills very much like mine.

Tatsu's colleagues thought the shape he saw was a ghost in his imagination, and his dogged insistence on investigating a conspiracy that others claimed was a mirage had done nothing to advance his career. On the other hand, that doggedness did afford him some protection from the powers he hoped to threaten, because no one wanted to lend credence to his theories by having him die suddenly of natural causes. On the contrary: I imagined that many of Tatsu's enemies hoped he would live a long and uneventful life. I also knew this attitude would change instantly if Tatsu ever got too close to the truth.

So far he hadn't. But I knew Tatsu. In Vietnam he had understood the fundamentals of counterintelligence at a time when even Agency higher-ups couldn't put together a simple wiring diagram of a typical V.C. unit. He had developed operational leads despite his "listen-and-learn-only" purview. He had refused the usual attaché's cushy life of writing reports from a villa, insisting instead on operating in the field.

His superiors had been horrified at his effectiveness, he had once told me bitterly over substantial quantities of sake, and they had studiously ignored the intelligence he had produced. In the end his persistence and courage had been wasted. I wish he could have learned from the experience.

But I supposed that was impossible. Tatsu was true samurai, and would continue serving the same master no matter how many times that master ignored or even abused him. Devoted service was the highest end he knew.

It was unusual for the Keisatsucho to be investigating a simple break-in. Something about Kawamura's death, and what he was doing before it, must have attracted Tatsu's attention. It wouldn't be the first time I had felt my old comrade in arms watching me as though through a one-way mirror, seeing a shape behind the glass but not knowing whose, and I was glad that I'd decided to drop off his radar so many years earlier.

"You don't have to tell me whether you knew about this," Harry said, interrupting my musings. "I know the rules."

I considered how much I should reveal. If I wanted to learn more, his skills would be helpful. On the other hand, I didn't like the idea of his getting any closer to the true nature of my work. He was getting uncomfortably close already. Tatsu's name on that report, for example. I had to assume that Harry would follow it like a link on the Internet, that he would tap into Tatsu's conspiracy theories, that he would sense a connection with me. Hardly proof beyond a reasonable doubt, of course, but between them Harry and Tatsu would have a significant number of puzzle pieces.

Sitting there in Las Chicas, sipping my chai latte, I had to admit that Harry could become a problem. The realization depressed me. *Christ,* I thought, *you're getting sentimental.*

Maybe it was time to get out of this shit. Maybe this time it really was.

"I didn't know about it," I said after a moment. "This is an unusual case." I saw no harm in telling him about the stranger on the train, and did so.

"If we were in New York, I'd tell you it was a pickpocket," he said when I was done.

"I thought the same thing when I first saw it. But

pickpocket would be a piss-poor career choice for a white boy in Tokyo. You have to blend."

"Target of opportunity?"

I shook my head. "Not too many people are that shameless and cold-blooded. I doubt one of them just happened to be standing next to Kawamura that morning. I think the guy was a Kawamura contact, there for some kind of exchange."

"Why do you suppose the Keisatsucho is investigating a simple break-in in a Tokyo apartment?" he asked.

"That I don't know," I said, although Tatsu's involvement made me wonder. "Maybe Kawamura's position in the government, the recency of his death, something like that. That's the theory I'd go on."

He looked at me. "Are you asking me to dig?"

I should have let it go. But I've been used before. The feeling that it had happened again would keep me awake at night. Had Benny put a B-team on Kawamura? I figured I might as well let Harry provide some clues.

"You will anyway, right?" I asked.

He blinked. "Can't help myself, I guess."

"Dig away, then. Let me know what else you find. And watch your back, hotshot. Don't get sloppy."

The warning was for both of us.

3

TELLING HARRY TO watch his back made me think of
Jimmy Calhoun, my best friend in high school, of who
Jimmy was before he became Crazy Jake.

Jimmy and I joined the Army together when we
were barely seventeen years old. I remember the recruiter telling us we would need parental permission
to join. "See that woman outside?" he had asked us.
"Give her this twenty, ask her if she'll sign as your
mother." She did. Later, I realized this woman was
making her living this way.

Jimmy and I had met, in a sense, through his younger
sister, Deirdre. She was a beautiful, black-haired Irish
rose, and one of the few people who was nice to the
awkward, out-of-place kid I was in Dryden. Some idiot
told Jimmy I liked her, which was true, of course, and
Jimmy decided he didn't like a guy with slanty eyes hitting on his sister. He was bigger than I was, but I fought
him to a standstill. After that, he respected me, and became my ally against the Dryden bullies, my first real
friend. Deirdre and I started dating, and woe to anyone
who gave Jimmy a hard time about it.

I told Deirdre before we left that I was going to marry her when I got back. She told me she'd be waiting. "Watch out for Jimmy, okay?" she asked me. "He's got too much to prove."

Jimmy and I had told the recruiter we wanted to serve together, and the guy said he would make it happen. I don't know if the recruiter had anything to do with it, in fact he was probably lying, but it worked out the way we asked. Jimmy and I did Special Forces training together at Fort Bragg, then wound up in the same unit, in a joint military-CIA program called the Studies and Observation Group, or SOG. The Studies and Observation moniker was a joke, some idiot bureaucrat's attempt to give the organization a low profile. You might as well name a pit bull Pansy.

SOG's mission was clandestine reconnaissance and sabotage missions into Cambodia and Laos, sometimes even into North Vietnam. The teams were composed of LURRPs, an acronym for men specializing in long-range reconnaissance patrols. Three Americans and nine Civilian Irregular Defense Group personnel, or CIDGs. The CIDGs were usually Khmer mercenaries recruited by the CIA, sometimes Montagnards. Three men would go into the bush for one, two, three weeks at a time, living off the land, no contact with MACV, the U.S. Military Assistance Command, Vietnam.

We were the elite of the elite, small and mobile, slipping like silent ghosts through the jungle. All the moving parts on the weapons were taped down for noise suppression. We operated so much at night that we could see in the dark. We didn't even use bug repellent because the V.C. could smell it. We were that serious.

We were operating in Cambodia at the same time Nixon was publicly pledging respect for Cambodia's neutrality. If our activities got out, Nixon would have had to admit that he'd been lying not just to the public, but to Congress as well. So our activities weren't just clandestine, they were outright denied, all the way to the top. For some of our missions we had to travel stripped, with no U.S.-issued weapons or other matériel. Other times we couldn't even get air support for fear that a pilot would be shot down and captured. When we lost a man, his family would get a telegram saying he had been killed "west of Dak To" or "near the border" or some other vague description like that.

We started out all right. Before we went, we talked about what we would and wouldn't do. We'd heard the stories. Everyone knew about My Lai. We were going to keep cool heads, stay professional. Keep our innocence, really. I can almost laugh, when I think about it now.

Jimmy became known as "Crazy Jake" because he fell asleep in the middle of our first firefight. Tracer rounds were coming at us from beyond the tree line, everyone was hunkered down, firing back at people we couldn't even see, and it went on for hours because we couldn't call in air support due to our illegal location. Jimmy said "fuck it" in the middle of things and took a nap. Everyone thought that was pretty cool. While they were saying, "you're crazy, man, you're crazy," Jimmy said, "well I knew everything was jake." So after that he was Crazy Jake. Outside the two of us, I don't think anyone ever knew his real name.

Jimmy didn't just act crazy; he looked it. A teenage

motorcycle accident had almost cost him an eye. The doctors got it back in, but couldn't get it to focus in line with his good eye, so Jimmy always looked as though he was watching something off to the side while he was talking to you. "Omnidirectional," he liked to say, with a smile, when he caught someone trying to steal a glance at it.

Jimmy had been social enough in high school but got quiet in Vietnam, training constantly, serious about his work. He wasn't a big guy, but people were afraid of him. Once, an MP with a German shepherd confronted Jimmy about some unruly behavior in a bar. Jimmy didn't look at him, acted like he wasn't even there. Instead, he stared at the dog. Something passed between them, some animal thing, and the dog whimpered and backed away. The MP got spooked and wisely decided to let the whole thing go, and the incident became part of the growing legend of Crazy Jake, that even guard dogs were afraid of him.

But there was nobody better in the woods. He was like an animal you could talk to. He made people uncomfortable with his omnidirectional eye, his long silences. But when the sound of the insert helicopters receded into the distance, everyone wanted him there.

Memories, crowding me like a battalion of suddenly reanimated corpses.

Waste 'em means waste 'em. Num suyn!

There's no home for us, John. Not after what we've done.

Let that shit go, I told myself, the refrain white noise familiar. *What's done is done.*

I needed a break, and decided to take in a jazz performance at Club Alfie. Jazz has been my haven

from the world since I was sixteen and heard my first
Bill Evans record, and a haven sounded good at the
moment.

Alfie is what's called a *raibu hausu*, or live house—a
small club hosting jazz trios and quartets and catering
to Tokyo's jazz aficionados. Alfie is the real deal: dark,
cramped, with a low ceiling and accidentally excellent
acoustics, accommodating only twenty-five people or
so and specializing in young artists on the cusp of
really being discovered. The place is always packed
and you need a reservation, a little luxury my life in
the shadows doesn't permit. But I knew Alfie's mama-
san, a roly-poly old woman with thick little fingers
and a waddle that had probably once been a swish.
She was past the age of flirting but flirted with me anyway, and loved me for flirting back. Alfie would be
crowded, but that wouldn't mean much to Mama if
she wanted to make a space for one more person.

That night I took the subway to Roppongi, Alfie's
home, running a medium-security SDR on the way. As
always I waited until the station platform had cleared
before exiting. No one was following me, and I walked
up the stairs into the Roppongi evening.

Roppongi is a cocktail composed of Tokyo's brash-
est foreign and domestic elements, with sex and
money giving the concoction its punch. It's full of
Western hostesses who came to Japan thinking they
were going to be models but who found themselves
trapped in something else, selling risqué conversation
and often more to their *sarariman* customers, striding
along in self-consciously stylish clothes and high heels
that accentuate their height, their haughtiness meant

to signify success and status but often indicating
something closer to desperation; stunning Japanese
girls, their skin perfectly salon-tanned, streaked hair
worn long and straight down their backs, like the
folded wings of some hungry bird of prey, on the make
for rich boyfriends who for the promise of sex or simply for the opportunity to be seen with such prizes in
public will give them Chanel suits and Vuitton bags
and the other objects that they crave; swarthy foreigners selling controlled substances that might or might
not be what they claim; preposterously elderly female
pimps tugging at the elbows of passersby, trying to get
them to choose a "companion" from a photo album;
people walking fast, as though they're going somewhere important, or posing nonchalantly, as though
they're waiting to meet a celebrity; everybody hungry
and on the make, a universe of well-adorned predators
and prey.

Alfie was to the left of the station, but I made a right
as I hit the street, figuring I'd circle around behind it.
The party animals were already out, pushing their
leaflets in front of me, trying to get my attention. I ignored them and made a right down Gaienhigashi-
dori, just in front of the Almond Cafe, then another
right down an alley that took me parallel to Roppongi-
dori and deposited me behind Alfie. A red Ferrari
growled by, a relic of the bubble years, when trophy
hunters gobbled up million-dollar impressionist originals of which they knew nothing and faraway proper-
ties like Pebble Beach that they had heard of but never
seen; when it was said that the land under Tokyo was
worth more than that of the continental United States;

when the newly minted rich celebrated their status in Ginza hostess bars by ordering thousand-dollar magnum after magnum of the best champagne, to be ruined with sugar cubes and consumed in flutes sprinkled with flakes of fourteen-karat gold.

I cut right on the street and took the elevator to the fifth floor, doing a last 180-degree sweep with my eyes before the doors closed.

Predictably, there was a crowd of people outside the club's door, which was papered over with posters, some new, some faded, advertising the acts that had appeared here over the years. There was a young guy in a cheap European-cut suit with his hair slicked back standing at the door and checking reservations. *"Ona-mae wa?"* he asked me, as I made my way forward across the short distance from the elevator. Your name? I told him I didn't have a reservation, and he looked pained. To spare him the anguish of explaining that I wouldn't be able to see the performance, I told him I was an old friend of Mama's and needed to see her, could he just get her? He bowed, stepped inside, and disappeared behind a curtain. Two seconds later Mama came out. Her posture was businesslike, no doubt in preparation for making an excruciatingly polite but firm Japanese apology, but when she saw me her eyes crinkled up in a smile.

"Jun-chan! Hisashiburi ne!" she greeted me, smoothing her skirt with her hands. *Jun* is Mama's pet name for Junichi, my Japanese first name, bastardized to John in English. I bowed to her formally but returned her welcoming smile. I explained that I just happened to be in the neighborhood and hadn't had a chance to

make a reservation. I could see that they were crowded and didn't want to be a bother . . .

"Tonde mo nai!" she interrupted me. Don't be ridiculous! She hustled me inside, dashed behind the bar, and whisked the bottle of Cao Lila I kept there off a shelf. Snatching a glass, she returned to where I was standing and motioned me to a seat at a table in the corner of the room.

She sat with me for a moment, poured me a drink, and asked me if I was with someone—I don't always come to Alfie alone. I told her it was just me, and she smiled. *"Un ga yokatta ne!"* she said. My good luck! Seeing Mama made me feel good. I hadn't been there in months, but she knew exactly where my bottle was; she still had her tricks.

My table was close to the small stage. The room was shadowy, but a light hanging from the ceiling illuminated a piano and the area just to the right of it. Not a great view of the entrance, but you can't have everything.

"I've missed you, Mama," I told her in Japanese, feeling myself unwind. "Tell me who's on tonight."

She patted my hand. "A young pianist. Kawamura Midori. She's going to be a star, she's already got a gig at the Blue Note this weekend, but you can say you saw her at Alfie in the early days."

Kawamura is a common Japanese name, and I didn't think anything of the coincidence. "I've heard of her, I think, but don't know her music. What's she like?"

"Wonderful—she plays like an angry Thelonious Monk. And completely professional, not like some of the young acts we book here. She lost her father only a week and a half ago, poor thing, but she kept her engagement tonight."

That's when the name struck me. "I'm sorry to hear that," I said slowly. "What happened?"

"Heart attack on Tuesday morning, right on the Yamanote. Kawamura-san told me it wasn't a complete surprise—her father had a heart condition. We have to be grateful for every moment we're given, *ne*? Oh, here she comes." She patted me on the hand again and slipped away.

I turned and saw Midori and her trio walking briskly, expressionless, toward the stage. I shook my head, trying to take it all in. I had come to Alfie to get away from Kawamura and everything associated with him, and instead here was his ghost. I would have gotten up and left, but that would have been conspicuous.

And at the same time there was an element of curiosity, as though I was driving back past the results of a car accident I had caused, unable to avert my eyes.

I watched Midori's face as she took up her post at the piano. She looked to be in her mid-thirties and had straight, shoulder-length hair so black it seemed to glisten in the overhead light. She was wearing a short-sleeved pullover, as black as her hair, the smooth white skin of her arms and neck appearing almost to float beside it. I tried to see her eyes but could catch only a glimpse in the shadows cast by the overhead light. She had framed them in eyeliner, I saw, but other than that she was unadorned. Confident enough not to trouble herself. Not that she needed to. She looked good and must have been aware of it.

I could feel a tension in the audience, a leaning forward. Midori raised her fingers over the keyboard, levitating them there for a second. Her voice came, quiet: "One, two, one two three four," and then her hands descended and brought the room to life.

It was "My Man's Gone," an old Bill Evans number, not one of her own. I like the piece and I liked the way she played it. She brought a vibrancy to it that made me want to watch as well as listen, but I found myself looking away.

I lost my own father just after I turned eight. He was killed by a rightist in the street demonstrations that rocked Tokyo when the Kishi administration ratified the 1960 U.S./Japan Security Pact. My father had always approached me as if from a great distance when he was alive, and I sensed that I was the source of some strain between him and my mother. But my understanding of all that came later. Meanwhile, I cried a small boy's nightly tears for a long time after he was gone.

My mother didn't make it easy for me afterward, although I believe she tried her best. She had been a State Department staff lawyer in Occupation Tokyo with MacArthur's Supreme Command of Allied Powers, part of the team MacArthur charged with drafting a new constitution to guide postwar Japan into the coming American Century. My father was part of Prime Minister Yoshida's staff, responsible for translating and negotiating the document on terms favorable to Japan.

Their romance, which became public shortly after the new constitution was signed into law in May 1947, scandalized both camps, each of which was convinced that its representative must have made concessions on the pillow that could never have been achieved at the negotiating table. My mother's future with the State Department was effectively ended, and she remained in Japan as my father's wife.

Her parents broke with her over the cross-cultural, cross-racial marriage, which she entered into against their command, and so my mother, in reaction to her *de facto* orphanage, adopted Japan, learning Japanese well enough to speak it at home with my father and with me. When she lost him, she lost her moorings to the new life she had built.

Had Midori been close with her father? Perhaps not. Perhaps there had been awkwardness, even fights, over what to him might have seemed a frivolous career choice. And if there had been fights, and painful silences, and struggling attempts at mutual comprehension, had they had a chance to reconcile? Or was she left with so many things she wished she could have told him?

What the hell is with you? I thought. *You've got nothing to do with her or her father. She's attractive, it's getting to you. Okay. But drop it.*

I looked around the room, and all the people seemed to be in pairs or larger groups.

I wanted to get out, to find a place that held no memories.

But where would that place be?

So I listened to the music. I felt the notes zigzagging playfully away from me, and I grabbed on and let them pull me from the mood that was rising around me like black waters. I hung on to the music, the taste of Cao Lila in my throat, the melody in my ears, until Midori's hands seemed to blur, until her profile was lost in her hair, until the heads I saw around me in the semidarkness and cigarette haze were rocking and hands were tapping tables and glasses, until her hands blurred faster and then stopped, leaving a moment of perfect silence to be filled with a burst of applause.

A moment later Midori and her trio made their way to a small table that was left open for them, and the room was filled with a low murmur of conversation and muffled laughter. Mama joined them. I knew I couldn't slip away without paying my respects to Mama, but didn't want to stop at Midori's table. Besides, an early departure would look odd no matter what. I realized I was going to have to stay put.

Admit it, I thought to myself. *You want to hear the second set.* And it was true. Midori's music had settled my roiled emotions, as jazz always does. I wasn't upset at the prospect of staying for more. I would enjoy the second set, leave quietly, and remember this as a bizarre evening that somehow had turned out all right.

That's fine. Just no more of that shit about her father, okay?

Out of the corner of my eye I saw Mama walking in my direction. I looked up and smiled as she sat down next to me.

"Well? What do you think?" she asked.

I picked up my bottle, which was considerably less full than it had been when I arrived, and poured us each a glass. "An angry Thelonious Monk, just like you said. You're right, she's going to be a star."

Her eyes twinkled. "Would you like to meet her?"

"That's nice, Mama, but I think I'm in more of a listening mood than a talking mood tonight."

"So? She can talk, and you can listen. Women like men who listen. They're such rare birds, *ne*?"

"I don't think she'd like me, Mama."

She leaned forward. "She asked about you."

Shit. "What did you tell her?"

"That if I were a little younger, I wouldn't tell her anything." She clapped a hand over her mouth and shook with silent laughter. "But since I'm too old, I told her that you are a jazz enthusiast and a big fan of hers, and that you came here tonight especially to hear her."

"That was good of you," I said, realizing that I was losing control of the situation, and not sure how to regain it.

She leaned back in her chair and smiled. "Well? Don't you think you should introduce yourself? She told me she wants to meet you."

"Mama, you're setting me up. She didn't say anything like that."

"No? She's expecting you—look." She turned and waved to Midori, who looked over and waved back.

"Mama, don't do this," I said, knowing that it was already over.

She leaned forward abruptly, the laugh disappearing like the sun behind a cloud. "Now don't embarrass me. Go say hello."

The hell with it. I had to take a leak anyway.

I got up and walked over to Midori's table. I sensed that she was aware of my approach, but she gave no sign until I was directly in front of her. Then she looked up from her seat, and I was struck by her eyes. Unreadable, even looking right at me, but not distant, and not cold. Instead they seemed to radiate a controlled heat, something that touched you but that you couldn't touch back.

I knew instantly that I had been right about Mama setting me up. Midori didn't have a clue who I was.

"Thank you for your music," I said to her, trying to think of something else to say. "It rescued me from something."

The bass player, super-cool in his head-to-toe black threads, long sideburns, and rectangular Euro glasses, snorted audibly, and I wondered whether there was anything between them. Midori conceded a small smile that said she'd heard it all before, and simply said, "Domo arigato," the politeness of her thanks a form of dismissal.

"No," I told her, "I mean it. Your music is honest, it's the perfect antidote for lies."

I wondered for a moment what the hell I was saying.

The bass player shook his head, as though disgusted. "We don't play to rescue people. We play because it pleases us to play."

Midori glanced at him, her eyes detached and registering the slightest disappointment, and I knew that these two were dancing steps they knew well, steps that had never led to the bass player's satisfaction.

But fuck him anyway. "But jazz is like sex, isn't it?" I said to him. "It takes two to really enjoy it."

I saw his eyes flare open as Midori pursed her lips in what might have been a tightly suppressed smile.

"We're happy to go on rescuing you, if that's what

we've been doing," she said in a tone as even as a flat-lined EKG. "Thank you."

I held her gaze for a moment, trying unsuccessfully to read it, then excused myself. I ducked into Alfie's washroom, which has about the same square footage as a telephone pole, where I reflected on the notion that I had survived some of the most brutal fighting in Southeast Asia, some of the world's worst mercenary conflicts, but still couldn't beat one of Mama's ambushes.

I emerged from the washroom, acknowledging Mama's satisfied grin as I did so, then returned to my seat. A moment later I heard the club's door open behind me and casually glanced back to see who would be walking through it. My head automatically returned to the front less than a second later, guided by years of training—the same training that prevented the attendant surprise from revealing itself in my expression.

It was the stranger from the train. The one I had seen searching Kawamura.

4

I KEEP A number of unusual items on my key chain, including several rudimentary lock picks that the uninitiated would mistake for toothpicks and a sawed-off dental mirror. The mirror can be held up to the eye unobtrusively, particularly if the user is leaning forward on an elbow and supporting his head with his hand.

From this posture I was able to watch the stranger arguing with a scowling Mama as the second set began. No doubt she was telling him he wouldn't be able to stay, that there weren't any more seats and the room was already overcrowded. I saw him reach into his jacket pocket and produce a wallet, which he then opened, revealing some aspect of its contents for Mama's inspection. She looked closely, then smiled and gestured magnanimously to the far wall. The stranger walked in the proffered direction and found a place to stand.

What could he have used to trump Mama? ID from Tokyo's liquor-licensing authority? A police badge? I watched him throughout the second set, but he gave no indication, leaning expressionless against the wall.

When the set ended, I had a decision to make. On the one hand, I assumed he was here for Midori, and wanted to watch him to confirm and to see what else I could learn. On the other hand, if he was connected with Kawamura, he might know that the heart attack had been induced, and he might recognize me from the train, where we had spoken briefly over Kawamura's prone form. The risk was small, but, as Crazy Jake once liked to put it, the penalty for missing was high. Someone could learn of my current appearance, and the cocoon of anonymity I had been so careful to build would be ruptured.

Also, if I did stay to watch his interaction with Midori, I wouldn't be able to follow him when he left. I'd have to share Alfie's five-person elevator with him for that, or hope but probably fail to beat him by using the stairs, and he'd make me. And if he got to the street first, by the time I caught up he would already have been carried away by the tides of pedestrians sweeping across Roppongi-dori.

Although it was frustrating, I had to leave first. When the applause for the second set had ended, I watched the stranger shove off in the direction of the stage. Several patrons stood and began milling about, and I placed them between us as I headed for the exit.

Keeping my back to the stage, I stopped to return the remnants of my Cao Lila. I thanked Mama again for letting me in without a reservation.

"I saw you talk to Kawamura-san," she said. "Was that so hard?"

I smiled. "No, Mama, it was fine."

"Why are you leaving so early? You don't come by nearly enough."

"I'll have to remedy that. But tonight I have other plans."

She shrugged, perhaps disappointed that her machinations had come to so little.

"By the way," I said to her, "who was that *gaijin* who came in during the second set? I saw you arguing with him."

"He's a reporter," she said, wiping a glass. "He's writing an article on Midori, so I let him stay."

"A reporter? That's great. With what publication?"

"Some Western magazine. I don't remember."

"Good for Midori. She really is going to be a star." I patted her on the hand. "Good night, Mama. See you again."

I took the stairs down to the street, then crossed Roppongi-dori and waited in the Meidi-ya supermarket across the street, pretending to examine their champagne selection. Ah, an '88 Moët—good, but hardly a bargain at 35,000 yen. I examined the label and watched the elevator to Alfie through the window.

Out of habit I scanned the other spots that would make sense as setup points if you were waiting for someone to emerge from Alfie. Cars parked along the street, maybe, but you could never count on getting a space, so low probability there. The phone booth just down from the Meidi-ya, where a crew-cut Japanese in a black leather jacket and wraparound shades had been on the phone as I emerged from the stairwell. He was still there, I could see, facing the entrance to Alfie.

The stranger emerged after about fifteen minutes

and made a right on Roppongi-dori. I stayed put for a moment, waiting for Telephone Man's reaction, and sure enough he hung up and started off down the street in the same direction.

I left the Meidi-ya and turned left onto the sidewalk. Telephone Man was already crossing to the stranger's side, not even waiting until he got to the crosswalk. His surveillance moves were blatant: hanging up the phone the instant the stranger had emerged, the constant visual contact with the exit before that, the sudden move across the street. He was following too closely, too, a mistake because it allowed me to fall in behind him. For a second I wondered if he might be working with the stranger, maybe as a bodyguard or something, but he wasn't close enough to have been effective in that capacity.

They turned right onto Gaienhigashi-dori in front of the Almond Cafe, Telephone Man following by less than ten paces. I crossed the street to follow, hurrying because the light had already changed.

This is stupid, I thought. *You are in the middle of someone else's surveillance. If there's more than one and they're using film, you could get your picture taken.*

I imagined Benny, putting a B-team on Kawamura, playing me for a fool, and I knew I would take the risk.

I followed them for several blocks, noting that neither exhibited any concern about what was going on behind him. From the stranger I saw no surveillance-detection behavior—no turns or stops that, however innocent seeming, would have forced a follower to reveal his position.

At the fringes of mad Roppongi, where the crowds

began to thin, the stranger turned into one of the Starbucks that are exterminating the traditional *kissaten*, the neighborhood coffee shops. Telephone Man, constant as the North Star, found a public booth a few meters farther on. I crossed the street and entered a place called the Freshness Burger, where I ordered their eponymous entrée and took a seat at the window. I watched the stranger order something inside Starbucks and then sit down at a table.

My guess was that Telephone Man was alone. If he had been part of a team, it would have made sense for him to peel off and change places at some point to avoid detection. Also, my periodic checks as we progressed down the street hadn't identified anyone behind me. If he had been with a team and they were as clueless as he appeared to be, I would have made them easily as we moved along.

I sat quietly, monitoring the street, watching the stranger sipping his Starbucks beverage and checking his watch. Either he was waiting for someone to meet him there, or he was killing time before a meeting somewhere else.

Turned out it was door number one. After about half an hour had gone by, I was surprised to see Midori heading down the street in our direction. She was checking storefronts as she walked, finally seeing the Starbucks sign and heading in.

Telephone Man pulled out a cell phone, pressed a key, and held the unit to his ear. Nice move for a guy standing in a public phone booth. He hadn't needed to input the whole number, I noted, so whomever he was calling was a speed dial, someone he would call frequently.

The stranger stood when he saw Midori approaching his table and bowed formally. The bow was good, and I knew this was someone who had been in Japan for some time, who would be comfortable with the language and culture. Midori returned his bow but at a lesser angle, uncertainty in her stance. I sensed that they were not well acquainted. My guess was that Alfie had been their first meeting.

I glanced over at Telephone Man and saw him put away his cell phone. He stayed where he was.

The stranger gestured for Midori to sit; she accepted, and he followed suit. He gestured to the counter, but Midori shook her head. She wasn't ready to break bread with this man.

I watched them for about ten minutes. As their conversation progressed, the stranger's gestures took on an air of entreaty, while Midori's posture grew increasingly rigid. Finally she stood up, bowed quickly, and began to back away. The stranger returned her bow, but much more deeply, and somehow awkwardly.

Which one to follow now? I decided to leave the decision to Telephone Man.

As Midori exited the Starbucks and headed back in the direction of Roppongi, Telephone Man watched her go but held his position. So it was the stranger he wanted, or wanted more.

The stranger left shortly after Midori, returning to Hibiya Station on Roppongi-dori. Telephone Man and I followed, maintaining our previous positions. I stayed with them down to the tracks, waiting a full car's length down from both until an Ebisu-bound train arrived and we all boarded. I kept my back to them, watching in the reflection of the glass, until the train stopped in Ebisu and I saw them exit.

I stepped off a moment later, hoping the stranger would be heading away, but he was coming toward me. Shit. I slowed my pace, then stopped in front of a station map, examining it at such an angle that neither would be able to see my face as he passed.

It was late, and there were only a half dozen people leaving the station with us. I kept a full riser of stairs between us as we left the bowels of the station, then let them pull a good twenty meters ahead before emerging from the station entrance to follow.

At the edge of Daikanyama, an upscale Tokyo suburb, the stranger turned into a large apartment complex. I watched him insert a key in the entrance door, which opened electronically and then closed behind him. Telephone Man also took obvious note, then continued for about twenty paces past the entrance, where he stopped, pulled out his cell phone, pressed a key, and spoke briefly. Then he pulled out a pack of cigarettes, lit one, and sat down on the curb.

No, this guy wasn't on the stranger's team, as I had briefly wondered. He was tailing him.

I moved into the shadows at the back of a small commercial parking lot and waited. Fifteen minutes later a scarlet racing-style motorcycle, its exhaust modified to produce the maximum Godzillalike rumble, roared onto the street. The driver, in matching scarlet racing leathers and full helmet, pulled up in front of Telephone Man. Telephone Man gestured to the stranger's building and got on the back of the bike, and they blasted off into the night.

A safe bet that the stranger lived here, but the building housed hundreds of units and I had no way of telling which was his or of checking for a name. There would be at least two points of egress, as well, so waiting would be useless. I stayed until the sound of the motorcycle had disappeared before getting up and checking the address. Then I headed back toward Ebisu Station.

5

FROM EBISU I took the Hibiya line to Hibiya Station, where I would change to the Mita line and home. I never change trains directly, though, and I emerged from the station first to run an SDR.

I stopped in a Tsutaya music shop and made my way past the teenyboppers in their grunge costumes listening to the latest Japanese pop sounds on the headphones the store provides, bobbing their heads to the music. Strolling to the back of the store, I paused now and then to look at CDs on shelves that faced the door, glancing up to see who might be coming in behind me.

I browsed for a bit in the classical section, then moved on to jazz. On impulse I checked to see whether Midori had a CD. She did: *Another Time*. The cover showed her standing under a streetlamp in what looked like one of the seedier parts of Shinjuku, her arms folded in front of her, her profile in shadows. I didn't recognize the label—something still small-time. She wasn't there yet, but I believed Mama was right, that she would be.

I started to return it to its place on the shelf, then thought, *Christ, it's just music. If you like it, buy it.* Still, a clerk might remember. So I also picked up a collection of someone else's jazz instrumentals and some Bach concertos on the way to the registers. Chose a long line, harassed-looking clerk. Paid cash. All the guy would remember was that someone bought a few CDs, maybe classical, maybe jazz. Not that anyone was going to ask him.

I finished the SDR and took the CDs back to my apartment in Sengoku. Sengoku is in the northeast of the city, near the remnants of old Tokyo, what the natives call *Shitamachi*, the downtown. The area is antique, much of it having survived both the Great Kanto quake of 1923 and the firebombing that came during the war. The neighborhood has no nightlife beyond the local *nomiya*, or watering holes, and no commercial district, so there aren't many transients. Most of its people are *Edoko*, the real Tokyoites, who live and work in its mom-and-pop shops and its tiny restaurants and bars. "Sengoku" means "the thousand stones." I don't know the origin of the name, but I've always liked it.

It's not home, but it's as close as anything I've ever had. After my father died, my mother took me back to the States. In the face of her loss and the accompanying upheavals in her life, I think my mother wanted to be close to her parents, who seemed equally eager for a reconciliation. We settled in a town called Dryden in upstate New York, where she took a job as a Japanese instructor at nearby Cornell University and I enrolled in public school.

Dryden was a predominantly white, working-class town, and my Asian features and nonnative English made me a favorite with the local bullies. I received my first practical lessons in guerilla warfare from the Dryden indigenous population: they hunted me in packs, and I struck back at them on my own terms when they were alone and vulnerable. I understood the guerrilla mentality years before I landed at Da Nang.

My mother was distraught over my constant bruises and scraped knuckles, but was too distracted with her new position at the university and with trying to mend fences with her parents to intervene. I spent most of those years homesick for Japan.

So I grew up sticking out, only afterwards learning the art of anonymity. In this sense, Sengoku is an anomaly for me. I chose the area before anonymity was an issue, and I stayed by rationalizing that the damage was already done. It's the kind of place where everyone knows your name, thinks they know your business. At first it made me uncomfortable, everyone recognizing me, pinpointing me. I thought about moving to the west of the city. The west feels exactly like Tokyo and nothing like Japan. It's brash and fast and new, swirling with caffeineated crowds, alienating and anonymous. I could go there, blend in, disappear.

But the old downtown has a magic to it, and it's hard for me to imagine leaving. I like the walk from the subway to my apartment in the evening, up the little merchant's street painted green and red so that it always feels festive, even in the early darkness of winter. There's the middle-aged couple that owns the corner five-and-dime, who greet me *"Okaeri nasai!"*—Welcome home!—when they see me at night, rather than the usual *"Kon ban wa,"* or good evening. There's the plump, laughing old woman who runs the video store with the big yellow sign out front and the windows plastered with posters of recent Hollywood releases, whose door is always left open when the weather is cool. She stocks everything from Disney to the most outrageous pornography, and from noon to ten at night, she sits like a jolly Buddha in her little store, watching her own wares on a TV next to the cash register. And there's the Octopus Woman, who sells *takoyaki*—fried octopus— from a streetside window in her ancient house, whose face, weary with the accumulated years and boredom of her labors, has come to resemble the creatures that go into her food. Every night she shuffles around her stove, pouring her potions in unconscious, repetitive motions, and sometimes when I walk by, I see giggling children running past, whispering, *"Tako onna! Ki o tsukete!"* The Octopus Woman! Be careful! And there's the house of Yamada, the piano teacher, from which, on summer evenings, when darkness comes late, soft notes drift lazily down the street, mingling with the shuffling slippers of bathers returning from the *sento*, the local public bath.

I listened to Midori's music a lot that weekend. I'd get home from my office, boil water for a dinner of *ramen* noodles, then sit with the lights down and the music playing, unwinding, following the notes. Listening to the music, looking out the balcony window onto the quiet, narrow streets of Sengoku, I sensed the presence of the past but felt that I was safe from it.

The neighborhood's rhythms and rituals, too subtle to appreciate at first, have steeped quietly over the years. They've grown on me, infected me, become part of me. Somehow a small step out of the shadows doesn't seem such a high price to pay for such indulgences. Besides, sticking out is a disadvantage in some ways, an asset in others. Sengoku doesn't have anonymous places where a stranger can sit and wait for a target to arrive. And until Mom and Pop pull their wares back into their shops at night and roll down the corrugated doors, they're always out there, watching over the street. If you don't belong in Sengoku people will notice, wonder what you're doing there. If you do belong—well, you get noticed in a different way.

I guess I can live with that.

6

THE FOLLOWING WEEK I arranged a lunch meeting with Harry at the Issan *sobaya*. I wasn't going to be able to let go of this little mystery, and I knew I would need his help to solve it.

Issan is in an old wooden house in Meguro, about fifty meters off Meguro-dori and a five-minute walk from Meguro Station. Utterly unpretentious, it serves some of the best *soba* noodles in Tokyo. I like Issan not just for the quality of its *soba*, but for its air of whimsy, too: there's a little lost-and-found cabinet by the front entrance, the contents of which haven't changed in the decade since I discovered the place. I sometimes wonder what the proprietors would say if a customer were to come in and exclaim, "At last! My tortoiseshell shoehorn—I've been looking for it for years!"

One of the restaurant's petite waitresses escorted me to a low table in a small tatami room, then knelt to take my order. I selected the day's *umeboshi*, pickled plums, to crunch on while I waited for Harry.

He rolled in about ten minutes later, led by the same waitress who had seated me. "I guess it was too much to hope that you would pick Las Chicas again," he said, looking around at the ancient walls and faded signs.

"I've decided it's time for you to experience more of traditional Japan," I told him. "I think you're spending too much time in the electronics stores in Akihabara. Why don't you try something classic? I recommend the *yuzukiri*." *Yuzukiri* are *soba* noodles flavored with the juice of a delicate Japanese citrus fruit called the *yuzu*, and an Issan house specialty.

The waitress came back and took our order: two *yuzukiri*. Harry told me he hadn't managed to unearth anything particularly revealing about Kawamura, just general biographical details.

"He was a Liberal Democratic Party lifer," Harry explained. "Graduated from the University of Tokyo in 1960, political science major, went straight to the government along with the rest of the cream of the crop."

"The States could learn something from this. There, the government gets the college rejects. Like sowing the smallest seeds of corn."

"I've worked with some of them," Harry said. "Anyway, Kawamura started out crafting administrative guidance for the Japanese consumer electronics industry at the Ministry of International Trade and Industry. MITI was working with companies like Panasonic and Sony to enhance Japan's position in the world economy, and Kawamura had a lot of power for a guy in his twenties. Steady promotions up the bureaucratic ladder, successful but not spectacular. High marks for architecting strategic domestic semiconductor guidance in the eighties."

"That's all discredited now," I said absently.

Harry shrugged. "He took the credit when he could. After MITI he was transferred to the Kensetsusho, the old Construction Ministry, and stayed with it as vice minister of land and infrastructure when Construction was merged into the Kokudokotsusho."

He paused and ran his fingers through his unruly hair, doing nothing to improve its appearance. "Look, mostly what I can tell you is basic bio stuff. I need to have a better idea of what I'm looking for, or I might not even recognize it if I see it."

"Harry, don't be so hard on yourself. Let's just keep working the problem, okay?" I paused, recognizing that this would be dangerous, knowing that, if I wanted to solve this mystery, I would take the risk.

I told him what I had seen at Alfie and afterward, of following the stranger to the apartment in Daikanyama.

He shook his head. "What are the chances that you would run into Kawamura's daughter like that? Unbelievable."

I looked at him closely, not sure that he believed me. *"Seken wa semai yo,"* I said. It's a small world.

"Or it could be karma," he said, his face unreadable. *Christ, how much does this kid know?* "I didn't know you believed in karma, Harry."

He shrugged. "You think there's a connection with the break-in at Kawamura's apartment?"

"Could be. The guy on the train was looking for something on Kawamura. Couldn't find it. So he breaks into Kawamura's apartment. Still can't find it. Now he thinks the daughter has it, I guess because she would have her father's things."

The waitress brought us the two *yuzukiri.* Without a sound she knelt on the *tatami,* placed each dish on the table, slightly repositioned them in accordance with some strict mental framework, stood, bowed, and departed.

When we were done eating, Harry leaned back against the wall and belched long and low. "It was good," he admitted.

"I know."

"I want to ask you a question," he said. "You don't have to answer if you don't want to."

"Okay."

"What's your angle on this? Why are you looking so hard? It's not like you."

I thought about telling him that I was doing it for a client, but I knew he wouldn't buy that.

"Some of what's been happening doesn't jibe with what the client told me," I said. "That makes me uncomfortable."

"This uncomfortable?"

I could see he was in a relentless mood today. "It reminds me of something that happened to me a long time ago," I said, telling him the truth. "Something I want to make sure never happens again. Let's leave it at that for now."

He held up his hands for a moment, palms forward in a gesture of supplication, then leaned forward and put his elbows on the table. "Okay, the guy you followed, we can assume he lives in the apartment building. A good number of foreigners live in Daikanyama, but I can't imagine there are more than a dozen or so in that one building. So we're already in decent shape."

"Good."

"The mama-san said he told her he was a reporter?"

"She did, but that doesn't mean much. I think he showed her a card, but it could have been fake."

"Maybe, but it's a start. I'll try to cross-check the foreigners I find at that apartment address against the declarations kept at the Nyukan, see if any of the people I identify are with the media." The Nyukan, or Nyukokukanrikyoku, is Japan's immigration bureau, part of the Ministry of Justice.

"Do that. And while you're at it, see if you can get me the girl's home address. I tried one-zero-four, but it's unlisted."

He scratched his cheek and looked down, as though trying to hide a smile.

"What," I said.

He looked up. "You like her."

"Oh, for Christ's sake, Harry . . ."

"You thought she was going to open up for you, and instead she blew you off. Now it's a challenge. You want another chance."

"Harry, you're dreaming."

"Is she pretty? Just tell me that."

"I'm not going to give you the satisfaction."

"So she's pretty. You like her."

"You've been reading too many *manga*," I said, referring to the thick, often lascivious pulp comic books that are so popular in Japan.

"Okay, sure," he said, and I thought, *Christ, he really does read that shit. I've hurt his feelings.*

"C'mon, Harry, I need your help to get to the bottom of this. That guy on the train was expecting Kawamura to be carrying something, which is why he patted him down. He didn't find it, though—otherwise, he wouldn't have been asking Midori questions. Now you tell me: Who currently has possession of all of Kawamura's belongings, including the clothes he was wearing and personal effects he was carrying when he died?"

"Midori, most likely," he allowed with a small shrug.

"Right. She's still the best lead we've got. Get me the information, and we'll go from there."

We talked about other matters for the duration of our lunch. I didn't tell him about the CD. He'd already leaped to enough conclusions.

7

THE NEXT DAY I got a page from Harry, who used a pre-set numeric code to tell me that he had uploaded something to a bulletin board we use. I figured it was Midori's address, and Harry didn't disappoint.

She lived in a small apartment complex called Hara-juku Badento Haitsu—Harajuku Verdent Heights—in the shadow of the graceful arches of Tange Kenzo's 1964 Tokyo Olympic Stadium. Cool Harajuku is the borderland that traverses the long silences and solemn cryptomeria trees of Yoyogi Park and its Meiji shrine; the frenetic, shopping-addled teen madness of Takeshita-dori; and the elegant boutiques and bistros of Omotesando.

Harry had confirmed that Midori did not have an automobile registered with the Tokyo Motor Vehicles Authority, which meant that she would rely on trains: either the JR, which she would pick up at Harajuku Station, or one of the subway lines, which she would access at Meijijingu-mae or Omotesando.

The problem was that the JR and subway stations were in opposite directions, and she was as likely to use one as the other. With no single chokepoint leading to both sets of stations, I had no basis for choosing either one. I would just have to find the best possible venue for waiting and watching and base my decision on that.

Omotesando-dori, where the subway stations were located, fit the bill. Known as the "Champs Elysées of Tokyo," albeit mostly among people who have never been to Paris, Omotesando-dori is a long shopping boulevard lined with elm trees whose narrow leaves provide first a crown and then a carpet of yellow for a few days every autumn. Its many bistros and coffee shops were designed with Paris-style people-watching in mind, and I would be able to spend an hour or two watching the street from various establishments without attracting attention.

Even so, absent a lot of luck, I would have been in for a very boring few days of waiting and watching. But Harry had an innovation that saved me: a way of remotely turning a phone into a microphone.

The trick only works with digital phones with a speakerphone feature, where a line can be established even though the handset is in the cradle. The reception is muffled, but you can hear. Anticipating my next move, Harry had tested Midori's line for me and had let me know that we were good to go.

At ten o'clock the following Saturday morning, I arrived at the Aoyama Blue Mountain coffee shop on Omotesando-dori, equipped with a small unit that would activate Midori's phone and a cell phone for listening in on whatever I connected to. I took a seat at one of the small tables facing the street, where I ordered

an espresso from a bored-looking waitress. Watching
the meager morning crowds drift past, I flipped the
switch on the unit and heard a slight hiss in the earpiece that told me the connection had been established.
Other than that, there was silence. Nothing to do
but wait.

A construction crew had set up a few meters down
from the Blue Mountain's entrance, where they were
repairing potholes in the road. Four workers busied
themselves mixing the gravel and measuring out the
right amounts—about two more men than were
needed, but the *yakuza*, the Japanese mob, works
closely with the construction industry and insists that
workers be provided with work. The government,
pleased at this additional avenue of job creation, is
complicit. Unemployment is kept at socially tolerable
levels. The machine rolls on.

As vice minister at the Kokudokotsusho, Midori's
father would have been in charge of construction and
most of the major public-works projects undertaken
throughout Japan. He would have been hip deep in a
lot of this. Not such a surprise that someone wanted
him to come to an untimely end.

Two middle-aged men in black suits and ties, modern
Japanese funeral attire, left the coffee shop, and the
aroma of hot gravel wafted over to my table. The smell
reminded me of my childhood in Japan, of the late summers when my mother would walk me to school for the
first day of the new term. The roads always seemed to
be in the process of being repaved at that time of year,
and to me this kind of construction still smells like a
portent of a fresh round of bullying and ostracism.

Sometimes I feel as though my life has been divided into segments. I would call these chapters, but the pieces are divided so abruptly that the whole lacks the kind of continuity that chapters would impart. The first segment ends when my father was killed, an event that shattered a world of predictability and security, replacing it with vulnerability and fear. There is another break when I receive the brief military telegram telling me that my mother has died, offering stateside leave for the funeral. Along with my mother I lost an emotional center of gravity, a faraway psychic governor on my behavior, and was left suffused with a new and awful sense of freedom. Cambodia was a further rupture, a deeper step into darkness.

Strangely, the time when my mother took me to the United States from our home in Japan does not represent a dividing line, then or now. I was an outsider in both places, and the move merely confirmed that status. Nor are any of my subsequent geographic ramblings particularly distinct. For a decade after Crazy Jake's funeral I wandered the earth a mercenary, daring the gods to kill me but surviving because part of me was already dead.

I was fighting alongside Lebanese Christians in Beirut when the CIA recruited me to train the Mujahideen guerrillas battling the Soviets in Afghanistan. I was perfect: combat experience, and a mercenary history that made possible maximum governmental deniability.

For me, there has always been a war, and the time before feels unreal, dreamlike. War is the basis from which I approach everything else. War is all I really know. You know the Buddhist parable? "A monk awoke from a dream that he was a butterfly, then wondered whether he was a butterfly dreaming that he was a man."

At a little after eleven, I heard sounds of movement within Midori's apartment. Footsteps, then running water, which I took to be a shower. She worked at night, I realized; of course she would be a late riser. Then, shortly before noon, I heard a closing exterior door and the mechanical click of a lock, and I knew she was finally on the move.

I paid for the two espressos I had drunk and walked out onto Omotesando-dori, where I began to amble in the direction of JR Harajuku station. I wanted to get to the pedestrian overpass at Harajuku. This would give me a panoramic view, but it would also leave me exposed, so I wouldn't be able to linger.

The timing was good. I only had to wait on the overpass for a minute before I caught sight of her. She was approaching from the direction of her apartment building and made a right onto Omotesando-dori when she reached it. It was easy for me to follow her from there.

Her hair was tied back in a ponytail, her dark eyes concealed by sunglasses. She was wearing snug black pants and a black V-necked sweater, and walked confidently, with purpose. I had to admit she looked good.

Enough of that, I told myself. *How she looks has nothing to do with this.*

She was carrying a shopping bag that I recognized from the distinctive maple color came from Mulberry, the English leather goods manufacturer. They had a store in Minami Aoyama, and I wondered if she was on her way to return something.

Midway to Aoyama-dori she turned into Paul Stuart. I could have followed her in, tried for our chance meeting there, but I was curious about where else she was going, and decided to wait. I set up in the Fouchet Gallery across the street, where I admired several paintings that afforded me a view of the street until she emerged, a Paul Stuart shopping bag in hand, twenty minutes later.

Her next stop was at Nicole Farhi London. This time I waited for her in the Aoyama Flower Market, on the ground floor of the La Mia building. From there, she continued onto a series of nameless Omotesando backstreets, periodically stopping to browse in one of the area's boutiques, until she emerged onto Koto-dori, where she made a right. I followed her, staying back and on the opposite side of the street, until I saw her duck into Le Ciel Bleu.

I turned into the Tokyo J. M. Weston shop, admiring the handmade shoes in the windows at an angle that afforded me a view of Le Ciel Bleu. I considered. Her taste was mostly European, it seemed. She eschewed the large stores, even the upscale ones. She seemed to be completing a circle that would take her back in the direction of her apartment. And she was carrying that Mulberry bag.

If she was indeed on her way to return something, I had a chance to be there first. It was a risk because if I set up there and she went the other way, I would lose her. But if I could anticipate her and be waiting at her next stop before she got there, the encounter would seem more like chance and less like the result of being followed.

I left the Weston store and moved quickly up Koto-dori, window-shopping as I walked so that my face was turned away from Midori's position. Once I was clear of Le Ciel Bleu, I cut across the street and ducked into Mulberry. I strolled over to the men's section, where I told the proprietress that I was just looking, and began to examine some of the briefcases on display.

Five minutes later she entered the store as I had hoped, removing her sunglasses and acknowledging the welcoming *irrashaimase* of the proprietress with a slight bow of her head. Keeping her at the limits of my peripheral vision, I picked up one of the briefcases, as though examining its heft. From this angle, I felt her gaze stop on me and linger longer than would have been warranted by a casual glance around the store. I gave the briefcase a last once-over, then set it down on its shelf and looked up. She was still watching me, her head cocked slightly to the right.

I blinked once, as though in surprise, and approached her. "Kawamura-san," I said in Japanese. "This is a nice surprise. I just saw you at Club Alfie last Friday. You were tremendous."

She evaluated me silently for a long moment before responding, and I was glad my gamble had worked. I sensed that this intelligent woman would be cynical about coincidences, and might have suspected, had I come in after her, that she had been followed.

"Yes, I remember," she said finally. "You're the one who thinks jazz is like sex." Before I could come up with a suitable response, she continued: "You didn't have to say that, you know. You could try to be more forgiving."

For the first time, I was in a position to notice her body. She was slender and long limbed, perhaps a legacy from her father, whose height had made him easy to follow down Dogenzaka. Her shoulders were broad, a lovely counterpart to a long and graceful neck. Her breasts were small, and, I couldn't help but notice, shapely beneath her sweater. The skin on the exposed portion of her chest was beautiful: smooth and white, framed by the contrast of the black V-neck.

I looked into her dark eyes, and felt my usual urge to spar dissipate. "You're right," I told her. "I'm sorry."

She closed her eyes briefly and shook her head. "You enjoyed the performance?"

"Immensely. I have your CD, and have been meaning to catch you and your trio for the longest time. I travel a lot, though, and this was my first chance."

"Where do you travel?"

"Mostly America and Europe. I'm a consultant," I said in a tone indicating that my work would be a boring topic for me. "Nothing as exciting as being a jazz pianist."

She smiled. "You think being a jazz pianist is exciting?"

She had a natural interrogator's habit of reflecting back the last thing the other party had said, encouraging the speaker to share more. It doesn't work with me. "Well, let me put it this way," I said. "I can't remember someone ever suggesting to me that consulting is like sex."

She threw back her head and laughed then, not bothering to cover her open mouth with her hand in the typical Japanese woman's unnecessarily dainty gesture, and again I was struck by the unusual confidence with which she carried herself.

"That's good," she said after a moment, folding her arms across her chest and conceding a small, lingering smile.

I smiled back. "What's today? A bit of shopping?"

"A bit. And you?"

"The same. It's past time for a new briefcase. We consultants have to maintain appearances, you know." I glanced down at the shopping bag she was carrying. "I see you're a fan of Paul Stuart. That was going to be my next stop."

"It's a good store. I know it from New York, and was glad when they opened a Tokyo branch."

I raised my eyebrows slightly. "Have you spent much time in New York?"

"Some," she said with a faint smile, looking into my eyes.

Damn, she's tough, I thought. *Challenge her.* "How's your English?" I asked, switching from Japanese.

"I get by," she said, without missing a beat.

"You want to get a cup of cawfee?" I asked, staying with English and using my best Brooklyn accent.

She smiled again. "That's pretty authentic."

"So is the suggestion."

"I thought you were going to Paul Stuart."

"I was. But now I'm thirsty. Do you know the Tsuta coffeehouse? It's great. And right around the corner, just off Koto-dori."

Her arms were still folded across her chest. "I don't know it."

"Then you've got to try it. Koyama-san serves the best coffee in Tokyo, and you can drink it listening to Bach or Chopin, looking out onto a wonderful secret garden."

"A secret garden?" she asked, playing for time, I knew. "What's the secret?"

I gave her a sober look. "Koyama-san says that if I tell you, I have to kill you. So it would be better if you were to see for yourself."

She laughed again, cornered but seeming not to mind. "I think I'd have to know your name first," she said.

"Fujiwara Junichi," I replied, bowing automatically. Fujiwara was my father's last name.

She returned the bow. "It's nice to meet you, Fuji-wara-san."

"Let me introduce you to Tsuta," I said, smiling, and we headed off.

The stroll over to Tsuta took less than five minutes, during which we made small talk about how the city had changed over the years, how we missed the days when the boulevard in front of Yoyogi Park was closed to automobile traffic on Sundays and host to a delirious outdoor party of costumed revelers, when the identity of Japanese jazz was being newly forged in a thousand basement bars and coffeehouses, when there was no gleaming new City Hall in Shinjuku and the area was alive with real yearning and romance and grit. I enjoyed talking with her, and knew at some level that this was strange, even undesirable.

We were in luck, and one of Tsuta's two tables, each of which overlooks the establishment's secret garden through a single oversized picture window, was open and waiting for us. Alone, I typically enjoy a seat at the counter, where a view of Koyama-san's reverential coffee preparations is always a wonder, but today I wanted an atmosphere more conducive to conversation. We each ordered the house demitasse, made with an intense dark roast, and sat at right angles to each other, so that we could both see the garden.

"How long have you lived in Tokyo?" I asked, when we were settled in.

"On and off for my whole life, really," she said, slowly stirring a spoonful of sugar crystals into her demitasse. "I lived abroad for a few years when I was little, but mostly I grew up in Chiba, one town over. I used to come to Tokyo all the time when I was a teenager, to try to sneak into the live houses and listen to jazz. Then I spent four years in New York, studying at Julliard. After that, I came back to Tokyo. And you?"

"Same as you—off and on for my whole life."

"And where did you learn to order coffee in an authentic New York accent?"

I took a sip of the bitter liquid before me and considered how to answer. It's rare for me to share biographical details. The things I have done, and continue to do, have marked me, just as Crazy Jake said they would, and, even if the mark is invisible to most of the wider world, I am always aware of its presence. Intimacy is no longer familiar to me. Probably, I sometimes realize with a measure of regret, it is no longer possible.

I haven't had a real relationship in Japan since my move into the shadows. There were some faltering dates, perfunctory on my part. Tatsu, and some other friends that I no longer see, sometimes tried to set me up with women they knew. But where were these relationships going to go, when the two subjects that most define me were unmentionable, taboo? Imagine the conversation: "I served in Vietnam." "How did you manage that?" "I'm half American, you see, a mongrel."

There are a few women from the *mizu shobai*, the water trade, as Japan calls its demimonde, whom I see from time to time. We've known each other long enough so that things are no longer conducted on a straight cash basis, expensive gifts instead providing the necessary currency and context, and there is even a certain degree of mutual affection. They all assume that I'm married, an assumption that makes it easy for me to explain the subtle security measures in which I engage as a matter of course. And the assumption also renders explainable the suspended, on-again, off-again nature of our relationship, and my reticence about personal details.

But Midori had a reticence about her, too, a reticence she had just breached in telling me a bit about her childhood. I knew that if I failed to reciprocate, I would learn nothing more from her.

"I grew up in both countries," I said after a long pause. "I never lived in New York, but I've spent some time there, and I know some of the region's accents."

Her eyes widened. "You grew up in Japan and the States?"

"Yes."

"How did you come to do that?"

"My mother was American."

I was aware of a slight intensification of her gaze, as she searched for the first time for the Caucasian in my features. You can still spot it, if you know what you're looking for.

"You don't look very . . . I mean, I think you must have inherited mostly your father's features."

"That bothers some people."

"What does?"

"That I look Japanese, but I'm really something else."

I remembered for a moment the first time I heard the word *ainoko*, half-breed. It happened at school, and I asked my father about it that night. He scowled and said only, *"Taishita koto nai."* It's nothing. But pretty soon I got to hear the word while the *ijimekko*, the school bullies, were busy trying to beat the shit out of me, and I put two and two together.

She smiled. "I don't know about other people. For me, the intersection of cultures is where things get most interesting."

"Yeah?"

"Sure. Look at jazz. Roots in black America, branches in Japan and all over the world."

"You're unusual. Japanese are typically racist." I realized that my tone was more bitter than I had intended.

"I don't know that the country is so racist. It's just been insular for so long, and we're always afraid of what's new or unknown."

Ordinarily I find such idealism in the face of all contrary facts irritating, but I recognized that Midori was simply projecting her own good sentiment onto everyone around her. Looking into her dark, earnest eyes, I couldn't help smiling. She smiled back, her full lips parting and lighting up her eyes, and I had to look away.

"What was it like to grow up that way, in two countries, two cultures?" she asked. "It must have been incredible."

"Pretty standard, really," I said, reflexively.

She paused, her demitasse halfway to her lips. "I don't see how something like that could really be 'standard.'"

Careful, John. "No. It was difficult, actually. I had a hard time fitting in either place."

The demitasse continued upward, and she took a sip. "Where did you spend more time?"

"I lived in Japan until I was about ten, then mostly in the States after that. I came back here in the early eighties."

"To be with your parents?"

I shook my head. "No. They were already gone."

My tone rendered unambiguous the word *gone*, and she nodded in sympathy. "Were you very young?"

"Early teens," I said, averaging things out, still trying to keep it vague when I could.

"That's terrible, to lose both parents so young. Were you close with them?"

Close? Although my face bore the stamp of his Asian features, and although he married an American, I believe my father had a typically outsized Japanese focus on race. The bullying I received in school both enraged and ashamed him.

"Fairly close, I suppose. They've been gone a long time."

"Do you think you'll go back to America?"

"I did at one point," I said, remembering how I'd gotten drawn into the work it now seemed like I'd been doing forever. "After returning as an adult, I spent ten years here always thinking I would stay just one more and then go back. Now I don't really dwell on it."

"Does Japan feel like home to you?"

I remembered what Crazy Jake told me, just before I did what he asked of me. *There's no home for us, John. Not after what we've done.*

"It's become my home, I guess," I said after a long time. "What about you? Would you want to live in America again?"

She was gently tapping on her demitasse, her fingers rippling up its sides from pinky to forefinger, and I thought, *She plays her moods. What would my hands do if I could do that?*

"I really loved New York," she said after a moment, smiling at some memory, "and I'd like to go back eventually, even to stay for a while. My manager thinks that the band isn't too far off. We've got a gig at the Vanguard in November; that'll really put us on the map."

The Village Vanguard, the Manhattan mecca of live jazz. "The Vanguard?" I said, impressed. "That's quite a pedigree. Coltrane, Miles Davis, Bill Evans, Thelonious Monk, the whole pantheon."

"It's a big opportunity," she said, nodding.

"You could leverage that, make New York your base, if you wanted to."

"We'll see. Don't forget, I've lived in New York before. It's a great place, maybe the most exciting place I've ever been. But it's like swimming underwater, you know? At first you feel as though you could go along forever, seeing everything from this new perspective, but eventually you have to come up for air. After four years, it was time for me to come home."

That was the opening. "You must have had indulgent parents, if they were willing to send you abroad for that long."

She smiled faintly. "My mother died when I was young—same as you. My father sent me to Julliard. He loved jazz and was thrilled that I wanted to be a jazz pianist."

"Mama told me you lost him recently," I said, hearing a flat echo of the words in my ears. "I'm sorry." She bowed her head in acknowledgment of my expression of sympathy, and I asked, "What did he do?"

"He was a bureaucrat." This is an honorable profession in Japan, and the Japanese word *kanryo* lacks the negative connotations of its English counterpart.

"With what ministry?"

"For most of his career, the Kensetsusho." The construction ministry.

We were making some progress. I noticed that the manipulation was making me uncomfortable. *Finish the interview,* I thought. *Then get the hell out. She puts you off your game; this is dangerous.*

"Construction must have been a stuffy place for a jazz enthusiast," I said.

"It was hard for him at times," she acknowledged, and suddenly I sensed guardedness. Her posture hadn't changed, her expression was the same, but somehow I knew she had been ready to say more and then had thought better of it. If I had touched a nerve, she had barely shown it. She wouldn't have expected me to notice.

I nodded, I hoped reassuringly. "I know a little bit about being uncomfortable in your environment. At least your father's daughter doesn't have any problems like that—doing gigs at Alfie makes a lot of sense for a jazz pianist."

I felt the odd tension for a second longer, then she laughed softly as though she had decided to let something go. I wasn't sure what I had brushed up against, and would consider it later.

"So, four years in New York," I said. "That's a long time. You must have had a very different perspective when you returned."

"I did. The person who returns from living abroad isn't the same person who left originally."

"How do you mean?"

"Your outlook changes. You don't take things for granted that you used to. For instance, I noticed in New York that when one cab cut off another, the driver who got cut off would always yell at the other driver and do this"—she did a perfect imitation of a New York cabbie flipping someone the bird—"and I realized this was because Americans assume that the other person intended to do what he did, so they want to teach the person a lesson. But you know, in Japan, people almost never get upset in those situations. Japanese look at other people's mistakes more as something arbitrary, like the weather, I think, not so much as something to get angry about. I hadn't thought about that before I lived in New York."

"I've noticed that difference, too. I like the Japanese way better. It's something to aspire to."

"But which are you? Japanese or American? The outlook, I mean," she added quickly, I knew for fear of insulting me by being too direct.

I looked at her, thinking for an instant of her father. I thought of other people I've worked with, and how much different my life might have been if I'd never known them. "I'm not sure," I said, finally, glancing away. "As you seem to have noticed at Alfie, I'm not a very forgiving person."

She paused. "Can I ask you a question?"

"Sure," I responded, not knowing what was coming.

"What did you mean, when you said we had 'rescued' you?"

"Just trying to strike up a conversation," I said. It sounded flip, and I saw immediately from her eyes that it was the wrong response.

You have to show her a little bit, I thought again, not sure whether I was compromising or rationalizing. I sighed. "I was talking about things I've done, things I knew, or thought I knew, were right," I said, switching to English, which was more comfortable for me on this subject. "But then later it turned out they weren't. At times those things haunt me."

"Haunt you?" she asked, not understanding.

"Borei no yo ni." Like a ghost.

"My music made the ghosts go away?"

I nodded and smiled, but the smile turned sad. "It did. I'll have to listen to it more often."

"Because they'll come back?"

Jesus, John, get off this. "It's more like they're always there. *Sugita koto wa, sugita koto da.*" The past is the past.

"You have regrets?"

"Doesn't everyone?"

"Probably. But are yours like everyone else's?"

"That I wouldn't know. I don't usually compare."

"But you just did."

I chuckled. "You're tough" was all I could say.

She shook her head. "I don't mean to be."

"I think you do. But you wear it well."

"What about the saying 'I only regret the things I haven't done'?"

I shook my head. "That's someone else's saying. Someone who must have spent a lot of time at home."

I knew I would learn nothing more about her father or the stranger today without questions that would betray my true intention in asking them. It was time to start winding things down.

"Any more shopping today?" I asked.

"I was going to, but I've got someone to meet in Jinbocho in less than an hour."

"A friend?" I asked, professionally curious.

She smiled. "My manager."

I paid the bill and walked back to Aoyama-dori. The crowds had thinned, and the air felt cold and heavy. The temperature had dropped in the two and a half weeks since I had taken out Kawamura. I looked up and saw unbroken clouds.

I had enjoyed myself much more than I had expected— more, really, than I had wanted. But the chill cut through my reverie, reviving my memories and doubts. I glanced over at Midori's face, thinking, *What have I done to her? What am I doing?*

"What is it?" she asked, seeing my eyes.

"Nothing. Just tired."

She looked to her right, then again at me. "It felt as though you were looking at someone else."

I shook my head. "It's just us."

We walked, our footsteps echoing softly. Then she asked, "Will you come see me play again?"

"I'd like that." Stupid thing to say. But I didn't have to follow through on it.

"I'm at the Blue Note Friday and Saturday."

"I know," I said, stupid again, and she smiled.

She flagged down a cab. I held the door for her as she went in, an annoying part of me wondering what it would be like to be getting in with her. As it pulled away from the curb, she rolled down the window and said, "Come alone."

8

THE NEXT FRIDAY I received another page from Harry telling me to check our bulletin board.

What he had found out was that the stranger on the train was indeed a reporter: Franklin Bulfinch, the Tokyo bureau chief for *Forbes* magazine. Bulfinch was one of only five male foreigners living in the Daikanyama apartment complex I had seen the stranger enter; all Harry had needed to do was cross-reference the names he found in the local ward directory against the main files kept by the Immigration Bureau. The latter kept information on all foreign residents in Japan, including age, birthplace, address, employer, fingerprints, and a photograph. Using this information, Harry had been able to quickly determine that the other foreigners failed to match the description I had provided. He had also obligingly hacked and uploaded Bulfinch's photo so I could confirm that we were talking about the same guy. We were.

Harry had recommended a look at forbes.com, where Bulfinch's articles were archived. I checked the site, and spent several hours reading Bulfinch's accounts of suspected alliances between the government and the *yakuza*, about how the Liberal Democratic Party uses threats, bribery, and intimidation to control the press, about the cost of all this corruption to the average Japanese.

Bulfinch's English-language articles had little impact in Japan, and the local media were obviously not following up on his efforts. I imagined this would be frustrating for him. On the other hand, it was probably the reason I hadn't been tasked with removing him.

My guess was that Kawamura was one of Bulfinch's sources, hence the reporter's presence on the train that morning and his quick search of Kawamura. I felt some abstract admiration for his doggedness: his source is having a heart attack right in front of him, and all he does is search the guy's pockets for a deliverable.

Someone must have found out about the connection, figured it was too risky to take out a foreign bureau chief, and decided to just plug the leak instead. It had to look natural, or they would have provided more grist for Bulfinch's mill. So they called me.

All right, then. There had been no B-team. I had been wrong about Benny. I could let this one go.

I looked at my watch. It was not quite 5:00. If I wanted to, I could easily get to the Blue Note by 7:00, when the first set would begin.

I liked her music and I liked her company. She was attractive, and, I sensed, attracted to me. Enticing combination.

Just go, I thought. *It'll be fun. Who knows what'll happen afterward? Could be a good night. The chemistry is there. Just a one-nighter. Could be good.*

But that was all bullshit. I couldn't say what would happen after her performance, but Midori didn't feel like a one-nighter. That was exactly why I wanted to see her, and exactly why I couldn't.

What's wrong with you? I thought. *You need to call one of your acquaintances. Maybe Keiko-chan, she's usually good for a few laughs. A late dinner, maybe that little Italian place in Hibiya, some wine, a hotel.*

For the moment, though, the prospect of a night with Keiko-chan was oddly depressing. Maybe a workout instead. I decided to head over to the Kodokan, one of the places where I practice judo.

The Kodokan, or "School for Studying the Way," was founded in 1882 by Kano Jigoro, the inventor of modern judo. A student of various schools of swordsmanship and hand-to-hand combat, Kano distilled a new system of fighting based on the principle of maximum efficiency in the application of physical and mental energy. Loosely speaking, judo is to Western wrestling what karate is to boxing. It is a system not of punches and kicks, but of throws and grappling, distinguished by an arsenal of brutal joint locks and deadly strangling techniques, all of which must of course be employed with great care in the practice hall. *Judo* literally means "the way of gentleness" or "the way of giving in." I wonder what Kano would make of my interpretation.

Today the Kodokan is housed in a surprisingly modern and bland eight-story building in Bunkyo-ku, southwest of Ueno Park and just a few kilometers from my neighborhood. I took the subway to Kasuga, the nearest station, changed in one of the locker rooms, then climbed the stairs to the *daidojo*, the main practice room, where the Tokyo University team was visiting. After I threw my first *uke* easily and made him tap out with a strangle, they all lined up to do battle with the seasoned warrior. They were young and tough but no match for old age and treachery; after about a half hour of nonstop *randori* I was still consistently coming out on top, especially when it went to groundwork.

A couple of times, as I returned to the *hajime* position after a throw, I noticed a Japanese *kurobi*, or black belt, stretching out in the corner of the tatami mats. His belt was tattered and more gray than black, which indicated that he'd been wearing it for a lot of years. It was hard to guess his age. His hair was full and black, but his face had the sort of lines that I associate with the passage of time and a certain amount of experience. His movements were certainly young; he was holding splits without apparent difficulty. Several times I sensed that he was intently aware of me, although I never actually saw him looking in my direction.

I needed a break and made my apologies to the college students who were lined up, still waiting to test their mettle against me. It felt good to beat *judoka* half my age, and I wondered how much longer I'd be able to do it.

I went over to the side of the mat and, while I was stretching, watched the guy with the tattered belt. He was practicing his *harai-goshi* entries with one of the college students, a stocky kid with a crew cut. His entry was so powerful that I caught the college kid wincing a couple of times as their torsos collided.

He finished and thanked the kid, then walked over to where I was stretching and bowed. "Will you join me for a round of *randori*?" he asked, in lightly accented English.

I looked up and noted an intense pair of eyes and strongly set jaw, neither of which his smile did anything to soften. I was right about his watching me, even if I hadn't caught him. Did he spot the Caucasian in my features? Maybe he did, and just wanted to take the *gaijin* test—although, in my experience, that was a game for *judoka* younger than he looked to be. And his English, or at least his pronunciation, was excellent. That was also odd. The Japanese who are most eager to pit themselves against foreigners have usually had the least experience with them, and their English will typically reflect that lack of contact.

"*Kochira koso onegai shimasu,*" I replied. My pleasure. I was annoyed that he had addressed me in English, and I stayed with Japanese. "*Nihongo wa dekimasu ka?*" Do you speak Japanese?

"*Ei, mochiron. Nihonjin desu kara,*" he responded, indignantly. Of course I do. I'm Japanese.

"*Kore wa shitsuri: shimasita. Watashi mo desu. Desu ga, hatsuon ga amari migoto datta no de . . .*" Forgive me. So am I. But your accent was so perfect that . . .

He laughed. "And so is yours. I expect your judo to be no less so." But by continuing to address me in English, he avoided having to concede the truth of his compliment.

I was still annoyed, and also wary. I speak Japanese as a native, as well as I speak English, so trying to compliment me on my facility with either language is inherently insulting. And I wanted to know why he would assume that I spoke English.

We found an empty spot on the tatami and bowed to each other, then began circling, each of us working for an advantageous grip. He was extremely relaxed and light on his feet. I feinted with *deashi-barai*, a foot sweep, intending to follow with *osoto-gari*, but he countered the feint with a sweep of his own and slammed me down to the mat.

Damn, he was fast. I rolled to my feet and we took up our positions again, this time circling the other way. His nostrils were flaring slightly with his breathing, but that was the only indication he gave of having exerted himself.

I had a solid grip on his right sleeve with my left hand, my fingers wrapped deeply into the cloth. A nice setup for *ippon seonagi*. But he'd be expecting that. Instead, I swept in hard for *sasae-tsurikomi-goshi*, spinning inside his grip and tensing for the throw. But he'd anticipated the move, popping his hips free before I'd cut off the opening and blocking my escape with his right leg. I was off balance and he hit me hard with *tai-otoshi*, powering me over his outstretched leg and drilling me into the mat.

He threw me twice more in the next five minutes. It was like fighting a waterfall.

I was getting tired. I faced him and said, "*Jaa, tsugi o saigo ni shimasho ka?*" Shall we make this the last one?

"*Ei, so shimasho,*" he said, bouncing on his toes. Let's do it.

Okay, you bastard, I thought. *I've got a little surprise for you. Let's see how you like it.*

Juji-gatame, which means "cross-lock," is an arm-bar that gets its name from the angle of its attack. Its classical execution leaves the attacker perpendicular to his opponent, with both players lying on their backs, forming the shape of a cross. One permutation—classicists would say mutation—is called flying *juji-gatame*, in which the attacker launches the lock directly from a standing position. Because it requires total commitment and fails as often as it succeeds, this variation is rarely attempted, and is not particularly well known.

If this guy wasn't familiar with it, he was about to receive an introduction.

I circled defensively, breathing hard, trying to look more tired than I was. Three times I shook off the grip he attempted and dodged around him as though I was reluctant to engage. Finally he got frustrated and took the bait, reaching a little too deeply with his left hand for my right lapel. As soon as he had the grip, I caught his arm and flung my head backward, launching my legs upward as though I were a diver doing a gainer. My head landed between his feet, my weight jerking him into a semicrouch, with my right foot jammed into his left armpit, destroying his balance. For a split second, before he went sailing over me, I saw complete surprise on his face. Then we were on the mat and I had trapped his arm, forcing it back against the elbow.

He somersaulted over onto his back and tried to twist away from me, but he couldn't get free. His arm was straightened to the limit of its natural movement. I applied a fraction more pressure but he refused to submit. I knew that we had about two more millimeters before his elbow hyperextended. Four more and his arm would break.

"*Maita ka*," I said, bending my head forward to look at him. Submit. He was grimacing in pain but he ignored me.

It's stupid to fight a solid armlock. Even in Olympic competition, *judoka* will submit rather than face a broken arm. This was getting dangerous.

"*Maita ka*," I said again, more sharply. But he kept struggling.

Another five seconds went by. I wasn't going to let him go without a submission, but I didn't want to break his arm. I wondered how long we could maintain our position.

Finally he tapped my leg with his free hand, the *judoka's* way of surrender. I released my grip instantly and pushed away from him. He rolled over and then kneeled in classic *seiza* posture, his back erect and his left arm held stiffly in front of him. He rubbed his elbow for several seconds and regarded me.

"*Subarashikatta*," he said. "Excellent. I would request a rematch, but I don't think my arm will allow that today."

"You should have tapped out earlier," I said. "There's no point resisting an armlock. Better to survive to fight another day."

He bowed his head in acknowledgment. "My foolish pride, I suppose."

"I don't like to tap out, either. But you won the first four rounds. I'd trade your record for mine." He was still using English; I was responding in Japanese.

I faced him in *seiza*, and we bowed. When we stood up he said, "Thank you for the lesson. I've never seen that variation of *juji-gatame* executed successfully in *randori*. Next time I'll know not to underestimate the risks you're willing to take to gain a submission."

I already knew that. "Where do you practice?" I asked him. "I haven't seen you here before."

"I practice with a private club," he said. "Perhaps you might join us sometime. We're always in search of *judoka* of *shibumi.*" *Shibumi* is a Japanese aesthetic concept. It's a kind of subtle power, an effortless authority. In the narrower, intellectual sense, it might be called wisdom.

"I'm not sure I'd be what you're looking for. Where is your club?"

"In Tokyo," he said. "I doubt that you would have heard of it. My . . . club is not generally open to foreigners." He recovered quickly. "But, of course, you are Japanese."

Probably I should have let it go. "Yes. But you approached me in English."

He paused. "Your features are primarily Japanese, if I may say so. I thought I detected some trace of Caucasian, and wanted to satisfy myself. I am usually very sensitive to such things. If I had been wrong, you simply wouldn't have understood me, and that would have been that."

Reconnaissance by fire, I thought. You shoot into the treeline; if someone shoots back, you know they're there. "You find satisfaction in that?" I asked, consciously controlling my annoyance.

For a moment, I thought he looked oddly uncomfortable. Then he said, "Would you mind if I were to speak frankly?"

"Have you not been?"

He smiled. "You are Japanese, but American also, yes?"

My expression was carefully neutral.

"Regardless, I think you can understand me. I know Americans admire frankness. It's one of their disagreeable characteristics, made doubly so because they congratulate themselves for it ceaselessly. And this disagreeable trait is now infecting even me! Do you see the threat America poses to Nippon?"

I regarded him, wondering if he was a crackpot rightist. You run into them from time to time—they profess to abhor America but they can't help being fascinated with it. "Americans are . . . causing too many frank conversations?" I asked.

"I know you are being facetious, but in a sense, yes. Americans are missionaries, like the Christians who came to Kyushu to convert us five hundred years ago. Only now, they proselytize not Christianity, but the American Way, which is America's official secular religion. Frankness is only one, relatively trivial, aspect."

Why not have some fun. "You feel that you're being converted?"

"Of course. Americans believe in two things: first, despite everyday experience and common sense, that 'all men are created equal'; and second, that complete trust in the market is the best way for a society to order its affairs. America has always needed such transcendental notions to bind together its citizens, who have come from different cultures all over the world. And Americans are then driven to prove the universality of these ideas, and so their validity, by aggressively converting other cultures to them. In a religious context, this behavior would be recognized as missionary in its origins and effect."

"It's an interesting theory," I allowed. "But an aggressive outlook toward other cultures has never been an American monopoly. How do you explain the Japanese colonial history in Korea and China? Attempts to save Asia from the tyranny of Western market forces?"

He smiled. "You are being facetious again, but your explanation is not so far from the truth. Because market forces—competition—are what drove the Japanese into their own imperial conquests. The Western nations had already taken their concessions in China—America had institutionalized the plunder of Asia with the 'Open Door.' What choice had we but to take our own concessions, lest the West encircle us and gain a chokehold on our supplies of raw materials?"

"Tell me the truth," I said, fascinated despite myself. "Do you really believe all this? That the Japanese never wanted war, that the West caused it all? Because the Japanese launched their first campaigns against Korea under Hideyoshi, over four hundred years ago. How did the West cause that?"

He faced me directly and leaned forward, his thumbs hooked into his *obi*, his toes taking his weight. "You are missing my larger point. Japanese conquest in the first half of this century was a reaction to Western aggression. In earlier times there were other causes, even such base ones as the lust for power and plunder. War is a part of human nature, and we Japanese are human, *ne*? But we have never fought, we have certainly never built weapons of mass destruction, to convince the world of the rightness of an idea. It took America and its bastard twin, communism, to do that."

He leaned closer. "War has always been with the world and always will be. But an intellectual Crusades? Fought on a global scale, backed by modern industrial economies, with the threat of a nuclear *auto-da-fé* for the unbelievers? Only America offers this."

Well, that confirmed the crackpot-rightist diagnosis. "I appreciate your speaking frankly with me," I said, bowing slightly. *"Ii benkyo ni narimashita."* It's been an education.

He returned my bow and started backing away. *"Kochira koso."* The same here. He smiled, again with some seeming discomfort. "Perhaps we will meet again."

I watched him leave. Then I walked over to one of the regulars, an old-timer named Yamaishi, and asked if he'd ever seen the guy who was walking off the tatami. *"Shiranai,"* he said with a shrug. *"Amari shiranai kao da. Da kedo, sugoku tsuyoku na. Randori, mita yo."* I don't know him. But his judo is very strong. I saw your fight.

I wanted to cool off before showering, so I went down to an empty *dojo* on the fifth floor. I left the fluorescent lights off when I went in. This room was best when it was lit only by Korakuen Amusement Park, which twinkled and hummed next door. I bowed to the picture of Kano Jigoro on the far wall, then did *ukemi* rolls until I reached the center of the room.

Standing in the quiet darkness, I looked out over Korakuen. Just barely, I could hear the roller coaster ratcheting slowly up to its apogee, then suspended silence, then the whoosh of its downward plunge and the screaming laughter of its passengers, the wind whipping away their cries.

I stretched in the center of the room, the *judogi* uniform wet against my skin. I came to the Kodokan because it's the premiere spot to study judo, but, like my neighborhood in Sengoku, the place has become much more to me than it was at first. I've seen things here: a grizzled old veteran who has been doing judo every day for half a century, patiently showing a child in an oversized *gi* that the proper placement of the hooking leg in *sankakujime* is at a slight angle to, not straight behind, one's opponent; a young *sandan*, third-degree black belt, who left his native Iran to practice at the Kodokan four years ago, hardly missing a day of practice since, drilling his *osoto-gari* in such precise and powerful repetitions that his movements come to resemble some vast natural force, the movement of tides, perhaps, the dancer becoming the dance; a college kid quietly crying after being choked out in a match, the crowd cheering for his victorious opponent and taking no heed of his dignified tears.

The roller coaster was making its familiar ratcheting sound, the last of the light fading from the sky above it. It was past seven, too late for me to get to the Blue Note. Just as well.

9

I HAD NO special plans the next day, so I decided to stop at an antiquarian bookstore I like in Jinbocho, a part of the city best known for its warren of densely packed bookshops, some specializing in Eastern fare, others in Western. The shop's proprietor had alerted me via pager a few days earlier that he had located and was holding for me an old tome on *shimewaza*— strangles—that I had been trying to find for a long while, to add to my modest collection on *bugei*, the warrior arts.

I picked up the Mita subway line at Sengoku Station. Sometimes I use the subway; other times I take the JR from Sugamo. It's good to be random. Today there was a priest in Shinto garb collecting donations outside the station. It seemed like these guys were everywhere lately, not just in front of parliament anymore. I took the train in the direction of Onarimon and got off at Jinbocho. I meant to leave the station at the exit nearest the Isseido Bookstore, but, distracted by thoughts of Midori and Kawamura, I wound up taking the wrong corridor. After turning a corner and then coming to a sign for the Hanzoman line, I realized my error, turned, and rounded the corner again.

A pudgy Japanese was moving quickly down the corridor, about ten meters away. I flashed his eyes as he approached but he ignored me, looking straight ahead. He was wearing a pinstriped suit and a striped shirt. Must have heard somewhere that stripes make you look taller.

I glanced down and saw why I hadn't heard him coming: cheap shoes with rubber soles. But he was carrying an expensive-looking black attaché case, a lid-over model, maybe an old Swain Adeney. A businessman who knew good attachés but assumed no one would notice his shoes? Maybe. But this wasn't really the place for business—Kasumigaseki or Akasaka would be more likely. I knew the shoes would make for comfortable attire on a long walk—if following someone were part of the likely itinerary, for example.

Aside from the attaché, his hands were empty, but I tensed anyway as we passed each other. Something about him bothered me. I slowed down a little as we passed each other, looked back over my shoulder, marked the way he walked. Faces are easy to disguise, clothes you can change in a minute, but not too many people can conceal their gait. It's something I look for. I watched this guy's walk—short stride, bit of an ex-aggerated, self-important arm swing, slight side-to-side swaying action of the head—until he turned the corner.

I cut back the other way, checking behind me before

I left the station. Probably it was nothing, but I'd re-member his face and gait, watch my back as always, see if he showed up again.

Principles of Strangles was in excellent condition, as promised, with a price to match, but I knew that I would greatly enjoy the slim volume. Although I was eager to depart, I waited patiently while the proprietor carefully, almost ceremoniously, wrapped the book in heavy brown paper and string. He knew it wasn't a gift, but this was his way of showing his appreciation for the sale and it would have been rude for me to hurry him. Finally, he proffered the package with ex-tended arms and a deep bow, and I accepted it from a similar posture, bowing again as I left.

I headed back to the Mita line. If I had really been concerned that someone was tailing me I would have caught a cab, but I wanted to see if I could spot At-taché Man again. I waited on the platform while two trains pulled in and departed. Anyone trying to fol-low me would have had to stay on the platform, also—incongruous behavior that makes a person stand out in sharp relief. But the platform was de-serted, and Attaché Man was gone. Probably it had been nothing.

I thought of Midori again. It was her second night at the Blue Note, and she'd be starting her first set in about an hour. I wondered what she would think when I didn't show for the second time. She was human; she would probably assume that I hadn't been interested, that maybe she had been a little too for-ward in inviting me. It was unlikely that I would ever see her again, or if we did by chance bump into each other, it would be slightly awkward but polite, two people who met and started an acquaintanceship that somehow didn't take off, certainly nothing out of the ordinary. She might ask Mama about me at some point, but all Mama knows is that I pop into Alfie from time to time without warning.

I wondered what it would have been like if we'd met under other circumstances. *It could have been good,* I thought again.

I almost laughed at the absurdity. There was no room for anything like that in my life, and I knew it.

Crazy Jake again: *There's no home for us, John. Not after what we've done.*

That was about the truest advice I'd ever been given. *Forget about her,* I thought. *You know you have to.*

My pager buzzed. I found a pay phone and dialed the number.

It was Benny. After the usual exchange of bona fides, he said, "There's another job for you, if you want it."

"Why are you contacting me this way?" I asked, meaning why not the bulletin board.

"Time-sensitive matter. You interested?"

"I'm not known for turning away work."

"You'd have to bend one of your rules on this one. If you do, there's a bonus."

"I'm listening."

"We're talking about a woman. Jazz musician."

Long pause.

"You there?" he said.

"Still listening."

"You want the details, you know where to find them."

"What's the name?"

"Not over the phone."

Another pause.

He cleared his throat. "All right. Same name as a recent job. Related matter. Is that important?"

"Not really."

"You want this?"

"Probably not."

"Significant bonus if you want it."

"What's significant?"

"You know where to find the details."

"I'll take a look."

"I need an answer within forty-eight hours, okay? This needs to be taken care of."

"Don't they all," I said, and hung up.

I stood there for a moment afterwards, looking around the station, watching people bustling back and forth.

Fucking Benny, telling me, "This needs to be taken care of," letting me know that someone else would be doing it if I didn't.

Why Midori? A connection with Bulfinch, the reporter. He had sought her out, I saw that at Alfie, along with Telephone Man. So whoever Telephone Man worked for would assume that Midori had learned something she wasn't supposed to, or maybe that her father had given her something, something Bulfinch was after. Something not worth taking any chances over.

You could do it, I thought. *If you don't, someone else will. You'd at least do it right, do it fast. She wouldn't feel anything.*

But they were just words. I wanted to feel that way

but couldn't. What I felt like instead was that her world should never have collided with mine.

A Mita-sen train pulled in, heading in the direction of Otemachi, the transfer point to Omotesando and the Blue Note. *An omen*, I thought, and got on it.

10

IF YOU WANT to survive as long as I have in the world I inhabit, you've got to think like the opposition. I learned that from the gangs that pursued me when I was a kid, and refined the lesson with SOG in Cambodia. You've got to ask: If I were trying to get at me, how would I go about it?

Predictability is the key, geographical and chronological. You need to know where a person will be and at what time. You learn this by surveillance, analyzing the routes to work, the times the target comes and goes, until you've identified a pattern, and choke points through which the target can almost always be counted on to pass at a certain time. You choose the most vulnerable of these, and that's where you lay the ambush.

And if that's what you're doing, you'd better not forget that all the time someone is running the same kind of operation on you. Thinking like this is what divides the hard targets from the soft ones.

The same principle works for crime prevention. If you wanted to grab some quick cash, where would you wait? Near an ATM, probably, and probably at night. You'd scout around for the right location, too, someplace with enough pedestrian traffic to save you a long wait, but not so much of a crowd that you'd be impeded from acting when you identified a good target. You'd look for a dark spot far enough from the machine so the target wouldn't notice you, but close enough so that you could move right in once the cash transaction was completed. Police stations close by would make you nervous, and you'd probably hunt for a better place. Etc. If you think this way, you'll know exactly where to look to spot someone lurking, and you'll know where you're vulnerable, where more alertness is required.

With Midori, extensive surveillance wasn't even necessary. Her schedule was publicly available. Presumably that was how Bulfinch knew to find her at Alfie. And that would be the easiest way for Benny's people to find her now.

From Otemachi I rode the Chiyoda-sen subway seven stops to Omotesando, where I exited and took the stairs to the street. I walked the short distance to the Yahoo Café, a coffee shop with Internet terminals. I went in, paid the fee, and logged on to one of the terminals. With the café's T1 line, it took just a few seconds to access the file Benny had posted. It included a few scanned publicity photos, Midori's home address, a concert schedule with tonight's appearance at the Blue Note, and parameters indicating that the job had to look natural. They were offering the yen equivalent of about $150,000—a substantial premium over our usual arrangement.

The reference to tonight's appearance at the Blue Note, first set at 7:00, was ominous. Predictability, time and place. If they wanted to take her out soon, tonight would be almost too good to pass up. On the other hand, Benny had told me I had forty-eight hours to get back to him, which would indicate that she would be safe for at least that long.

But even if she had that much time, I didn't see how I could parlay it into a reasonable life span. Warn her that someone had just put a contract out on her? I could try, but she had no reason to believe me. And even if she did, what then? Teach her how to improve her personal security? Sell her on the benefits of an anonymous life in the shadows?

Ludicrous. There was really only one thing I could do. Use the forty-eight hours to figure out why Benny's people had decided Midori was a liability and to eliminate the reasons behind that view.

I could have walked the kilometer or so to the Blue Note, but I wanted to do a drive-by first. I caught a cab and told the driver to take me down Koto-dori, then left to the Blue Note. I was counting on traffic to make the ride slow enough so that I could do a quick sneak-and-peek at some of the spots where I would wait if I were setting up surveillance outside.

Traffic was heavy as I had hoped, and I had a good chance to scope the area as we crawled past. In fact, the Blue Note isn't that easy a place to wait around un-obtrusively. It's surrounded mostly by stores that were now closed. The Caffe Idee restaurant across the street, with its outdoor balcony, would offer a clear-enough view, but the Idee has a long, narrow external staircase that would afford access sufficiently slow as to make the restaurant an unacceptable place to wait.

On the other hand, you wouldn't have to linger long. You can time the end of a Blue Note set to within about five minutes. The second set hadn't yet begun, so if anyone was planning on visiting Midori after the show tonight, they probably hadn't even arrived yet.

Or they could already be inside, just another appreciative audience member.

I had the cab stop before reaching Omotesando-dori, then got out and walked the four blocks back to the Blue Note. I was careful to scope the likely places, but things looked clear.

There was already a long line waiting for the second set. I walked up to the ticket window, where I was told that the second set was sold out unless I had a reservation.

Damn, I hadn't thought about that. But Midori would have, if she really had wanted me to come. "I'm a friend of Kawamura Midori's," I said. "Fujiwara Junichi . . . ?"

"Of course," the clerk responded immediately. "Kawamura-san told me you might be coming tonight. Please wait here—the second set will start in fifteen minutes, and we want to make certain that you have a good seat."

I nodded and stepped off to the side. As promised, the crowd from the first set started filing out five minutes later, and as soon as they were clear I was taken inside, down a wide, steep staircase, and shown to a table right in front of the still-empty stage.

No one would ever confuse the Blue Note with

Alfie. First, the Blue Note has a high ceiling that conveys a feeling of spaciousness totally unlike Alfie's almost cave-like intimacy. Also, the whole feel is higher-end: good carpeting, expensive-looking wood paneling, even some flat panel monitors in an antechamber for obsessive-compulsives who need to check their e-mail between sets. And the crowd is different at the Blue Note, too: first, because you can't even fit a crowd into Alfie, and second, because the people at Alfie are there only for the music, whereas, at the Blue Note, people also come to be seen.

I looked around the room as the second-set crowd flowed in, but nothing set off my radar.

If you wanted to get to her, and you had a choice of seats, where would you go? You'd stay close to one of the entrances to this floor. That would give you an escape route, if you needed one, and it would keep the entire room in front of you, so you could watch everyone else from behind, instead of the reverse.

I swiveled and looked behind me as though searching for an acquaintance. There was a Japanese man, mid-forties, sitting all the way in the left rear, near one of the exits. The people sitting next to him were all talking to one another; he was obviously alone. He was wearing a rumpled suit, dark blue or gray, which fit him like an afterthought. His expression was bland, too bland for my taste. This was a crowd composed of enthusiasts, sitting in twos and threes, waiting eagerly for the performance. Mr. Bland felt like he was deliberately trying to be unobtrusive. I filed him as a strong possible.

I swiveled in the other direction. Same seat, right

rear. Three young women who looked like office ladies on a night out. No apparent problem there.

Mr. Bland would be able to watch me throughout the performance, and I needed to avoid the mistake of conspicuous aloneness that he had made. I told the people around me that I was a friend of Midori's and was here at her invitation; they started asking me questions, and pretty soon we were shooting the shit like old friends.

A waitress came by and I ordered a twelve-year-old Cragganmore. The people around me all followed suit. I was a friend of Kawamura Midori's, so whatever I had ordered, it must be cool. They probably didn't know whether they had just ordered scotch, vodka, or a new kind of beer.

When Midori and her trio walked down the side of the room, everyone started clapping. Another thing about Alfie: There, when the musicians first appear, the room fills with reverential silence.

Midori took her place at the piano. She was wearing faded blue jeans and a black velvet blouse, low cut and clinging, her skin dazzling white next to it. She tilted her head forward and touched her fingers to the keys, and the audience grew silent, expectant. She spent a long moment frozen that way, staring at the piano, and then began.

She started slowly, with a coy rendering of Thelonious Monk's "Brilliant Corners," but overall she played harder than she had at Alfie, with more abandon, her notes sometimes struggling with the bass and the drums, but finding a harmony in the opposition. Her riffs were angry and she rode them longer, and when she came back the notes were sweet but you could still sense a frustration, a pacing beneath the surface.

The set lasted for ninety minutes, and the music alternated between a smoky, melodic sound, then elegiac sadness, then a giddy, laughing exuberance that shook the sadness away. Midori finished in a mad, exhilarated riff, and when it was over the applause was unrestrained. Midori stood to acknowledge it, bowing her head. The drummer and bass guitarist were laughing and wiping dripping sweat from their faces with handkerchiefs, and the applause went on and on. What Midori felt when she played, the place her music took her, she had taken the audience there, and the clapping was filled with real gratitude. When it finally faded, Midori and her trio left the stage, and people started to get up and move about.

A few minutes later she reappeared and squeezed in next to me. Her face was still flushed from the performance. "I thought I saw you here," she said, giving me a mild check with her shoulder. "Thank you for coming."

"Thank you for inviting me. They were expecting me at the ticket window."

She smiled. "If I hadn't told them, you wouldn't have gotten in, and you can't hear the music very well from the street, can you?"

"No, the reception is certainly better from where I'm sitting," I said, looking around as though taking in the grandeur of the Blue Note, but in fact scoping for Mr. Bland.

"Do you want to get something to eat?" she asked. "I'm going to grab something with the band."

I hesitated. I wasn't going to have a chance to probe for information with other people around, and I wasn't eager to broaden my always-small circle of acquaintances.

"Hey, this is your big night, your first gig at the Blue Note," I said. "You probably want to just enjoy it yourselves."

"No, no," she said, giving me another shoulder check. "I'd like you to come. And don't you want to meet the rest of the band? They were great tonight, weren't they?"

On the other hand, depending on how the evening progressed, you might have a chance to talk to her alone a bit later. "They really were. The audience loved you."

"We were thinking the Living Bar. Do you know it?"

Good choice, I thought. The Living Bar is an atmospheric place in Omotesando, absurdly named as only the Japanese can name them. It was close by, but we'd have to turn at least five corners to walk there, which would allow me to check our backs and see if Mr. Bland was following.

"Sure. It's a chain, isn't it?"

"Yes, but the one in Omotesando is nicer than all the others. They serve lots of interesting little dishes, and the bar is good, too. Good selection of single malts. Mama says you're a connoisseur."

"Mama flatters me," I said, thinking that if I weren't careful, Mama would put together a damn dossier and start handing it out. "Let me just pay for the drinks."

She smiled. "They're already paid for. Let's go."

"You paid for me?"

"I told the manager that the person sitting front center was my special guest." She switched to English: "So everything is on the house, *ne*?" She smiled, pleased at the chance to use the idiom.

"Okay, then," I said. "Thank you."

"Can you wait for just a few minutes? I've got a few things to take care of backstage first."

Getting to her backstage would be too difficult to bother trying. If they were going to make a move, they'd make it outside. "Sure," I said, getting up and shifting so that my back was to the stage and I could see the room. Too many people were now up and milling about, though, and I couldn't spot Mr. Bland. "Where do you want to meet?"

"Right here—five minutes." She turned and walked backstage.

Fifteen minutes later she reappeared through a curtain at the back of the stage. She had changed into a black turtleneck, silk or a fine cashmere, and black slacks. Her hair was loose over her shoulders, her face perfectly framed.

"Sorry to make you wait. I wanted to change—a performance is hard work."

"No problem," I said, taking her in. "You look great."

She smiled. "Let's go! The band is out front. I'm starving."

We headed out the front entrance, passing a number of lingering fans who thanked her on the way. *If you wanted to get to her and could time it right*, I thought, *you would wait at the bottom of the stairs of the Caffe Idee, where you would have a view of both the front and side entrances*. Sure enough, Mr. Bland was there, strolling away from us with studied nonchalance.

So much for Benny's forty-eight hours, I thought. It was probably just his version of "Act now—offer expires at midnight." Something he picked up in a sales course somewhere.

The bass guitarist and drummer were waiting for us, and we strolled over. "Tomo-chan, Ko-chan, this is Fujiwara Junichi, the gentleman I mentioned," Midori said, gesturing to me.

"*Hajimemashite,*" I said, bowing. "*Konya no enso wa saiko ni subarashikatta.*" It's good to meet you. Tonight's performance was a great pleasure.

"Hey, let's use English tonight," Midori said, switching over as she did so. "Fujiwara-san, these guys both spent years in New York. They can order a cab in Brooklyn as well as you can."

"In that case, please call me John," I said. I extended my hand to the drummer.

"You can call me Tom," he said, shaking my hand and bowing simultaneously. He had an open, almost quizzical expression, and was dressed unpretentiously in jeans, a white oxford-cloth shirt, and a blue blazer. There was something sincere in the way he had combined his Western and Japanese greetings, and I found I liked him immediately.

"I remember you from Alfie," the bassist said, extending his hand carefully. He was dressed predictably in black jeans, turtleneck, and blazer, the sideburns and rectangular glasses all trying a bit too hard for The Look.

"And I remember you," I said, taking his hand and consciously injecting some warmth into my grip. "You were all wonderful. Mama told me before the performance that you were all going to be stars, and I can see that she was right."

Maybe he knew I was soft-soaping him, but he must have felt too good after the performance to care. Or his personality was different in English. Either way, he gave me a small but genuine-looking smile and said, "Thank you for mentioning that. Call me Ken."

"And call me Midori," Midori cut in. "Now let's go, before I starve!"

During the ten-minute walk to *Za Ribingu Baa*, as the locals called it, we all chatted about jazz and how we had discovered it for ourselves. Although I was ten years older than the oldest of them, philosophically we were all purists of the Charlie Parker/Bill Evans/Miles Davis school, and conversation was easy enough.

Periodically I was able to glance behind us as we turned corners. On several of these occasions I spotted Mr. Bland in tow. I didn't expect him to move while Midori was with all these people, if that's what he had in mind.

Unless they were desperate, of course, in which case they would take chances, maybe even move sloppily. My ears were intensely focused on the sounds behind us as we walked.

The Living Bar announced its existence in the basement of the Scène Akira building with a discreet sign over the stairs. We walked down and into the entranceway, where we were greeted by a young Japanese man with a stylish brush cut and a well-tailored navy suit with three of its four buttons fastened. Midori, very much the leader of the group, told him we wanted a table for four; he answered *"Kashikomari-mashita"* in the most polite Japanese and murmured into a small microphone next to the register. By the time he had escorted us inside, a table had been prepared and a waitress was waiting to seat us.

The crowd wasn't too dense for a Saturday night. Several groups of glamorous-looking women were sitting in high-backed chairs at the black varnished tables, wearing expertly applied makeup and Chanel like it was made for them, their cheekbones in sharp relief in the subdued glow of the overhead incandescent illumination, their hair catching the light. Midori put them to shame.

I wanted the seat facing the entrance, but Tom moved too quickly and took it himself. I was left facing the bar.

As we ordered drinks and enough small appetizers to make for a reasonable meal, I saw the man who had escorted us inside walk Mr. Bland over to the bar. Mr. Bland sat with his back to us, but there was a mirror behind the bar, and I knew he had a good view of the room.

While we waited for our order to arrive, we continued our safe, comfortable conversation about jazz. Several times I considered the merits of removing Mr. Bland. He was part of a numerically superior enemy. If an opportunity presented itself to reduce that number by one, I would take it. If I did it right, his employers would never know of my involvement, and taking him out could buy me more time to get Midori out of this.

At some point, after much of the food had been consumed and we, along with Mr. Bland, were on our second round of drinks, one of them asked me what I did for a living.

"I'm a consultant," I told them. "I advise foreign companies on how to bring their goods and services into the Japanese market."

"That's good," Tom said. "It's too hard for foreigners to do business in Japan. Even today, liberalization is just cosmetic. In many ways it's the same Japan as during the Tokugawa *bakufu*, closed to the outside world."

"Yes, but that's good for John's business," Ken added. "Isn't it, John? Because, if Japan didn't have so many stupid regulations, if the ministries that inspect incoming food and products weren't so corrupt, you would need to find a different job, *ne?*"

"C'mon, Ken," Midori said. "We know how cynical you are. You don't have to prove it."

I wondered if Ken might have had too much to drink.

"You used to be cynical, too," he went on. He turned to me. "When Midori came back from Julliard in New York, she was a radical. She wanted to change everything about Japan. But I guess not anymore."

"I still want to change things," Midori said, her voice warm but firm. "It's just that I don't think a lot of angry slogans will make any difference. You have to be patient, you have to pick your battles."

"Which ones have you picked lately?" he asked.

Tom turned to me. "You have to understand, Ken feels like he sold out by doing gigs at established places like the Blue Note. Sometimes he takes it out on us."

Ken laughed. "We all sold out."

Midori rolled her eyes. "C'mon, Ken, give it a rest."

Ken looked at me. "What about you, John? What's the American expression: 'Either you're a part of the solution, or you're a part of the problem'?"

I smiled. "There's a third part, actually: 'Or you're a part of the landscape.'"

Ken nodded as though internally confirming something. "That's the worst of all."

I shrugged. He didn't matter to me, and it was easy to stay disengaged. "The truth is, I hadn't really thought of what I do in these terms. Some people have a problem exporting to Japan, I help them out. But you make some good points. I'll think about what you're saying."

He wanted to argue and didn't know what to do with my agreeable responses, which was fine. "Let's have another drink," he said.

"I think I've reached my limit," Midori said. "I'm ready to call it a night."

As she spoke I noticed Mr. Bland, who was studiously looking elsewhere, clicking a small device about the size of a disposable lighter that he was resting on one knee and pointing in our direction. *Fuck*, I thought. *A camera.*

He'd been taking Midori's picture, and I would be in the shots. This was the kind of risk I'd be taking if I stayed close to her now.

Okay. I'd have to leave with the three of them, then invent an excuse, maybe that I left something, double back to the bar and catch him as he was leaving to follow Midori again. I wasn't going to let him keep that camera, not with my pictures on the film in it.

But Mr. Bland gave me another option, instead. He got up and started walking in the direction of the rest room.

"I'm going to head home, too," I said, standing up, feeling my heart beginning to beat harder in my chest. "Just need to hit the rest room first." I eased away from the table.

I followed a few meters behind Mr. Bland as he maneuvered along the polished black floor. I kept my head down somewhat, avoiding eye contact with the patrons I was passing, hearing my heart thudding steadily in my ears. He opened the rest-room door and went inside. Before the door had quite swung closed, I opened it and followed him in.

Two stalls, two urinals. I could see in my peripheral vision that the stall doors were open a crack. We were alone. The thudding of my heart was loud enough to block out sound. I could feel the air flowing cleanly in and out of my nostrils, the blood pumping through the veins of my arms.

He turned to face me as I approached, perhaps recognizing me from his peripheral vision as one of the people who was with Midori, perhaps warned by some vestigial and now futile instinct that he was in danger. My eyes were centered on his upper torso, not focusing on any one part of him, taking in his whole body, the position of his hips and hands, absorbing the information, processing it.

Without pausing or in any way breaking my stride I

stepped in and blasted my left hand directly into his throat, catching his trachea in the V created by my thumb and index finger. His head snapped forward and his hands flew to his throat.

I stepped behind him and slipped my hands into his front pockets. From the left I retrieved the camera. The other was empty.

He was clawing ineffectually at his damaged throat, silent except for some clicking from his tongue and teeth. He started to stamp his left foot on the ground and contort his torso in what I recognized as the beginning of panic, the body moving of its own primitive accord to get air, *air*, through the broken trachea and into the convulsing lungs.

I knew it would take about thirty seconds for him to asphyxiate. No time for that. I took hold of his hair and chin in a sentry removal hold and broke his neck with a hard clockwise twist.

He collapsed backward into me and I dragged him into one of the empty stalls, sitting him on the toilet and adjusting his position so that the body would stay put. With the door closed, anyone coming in to use the bathroom would see his legs and just think the stall was occupied. With luck, the body wouldn't be discovered until closing time, long after we were gone.

I eased the door shut with my right hip and used my knee to close the latch. Then, gripping the upper edge of the stall divider, I pulled myself up and slid over to the stall on the other side. I pulled a length of toilet paper from the dispenser and used it to wipe the two spots that I had touched. I jammed the toilet paper in a pants pocket, took a deep breath, and walked back out into the bar.

"All set?" I asked, walking up to the table, controlling my breathing.

"Let's go," Midori said. The three of them stood up, and we headed toward the cashier and the exit.

Tom was holding the bill, but I took it from him gently and insisted that they all let me pay; it was my privilege after the pleasure of their performance. I didn't want to take a chance on anyone trying to use a credit card and leaving a record of our presence here tonight.

As I was paying, Tom said, "I'll be right back," and headed toward the rest room.

"Me, too," Ken added, and followed him.

I imagined vaguely that the body could slide off the toilet while they were in there. Or that Murphy's Law would make an appearance in some other way. The thoughts weren't unduly troubling. There was nothing I could do but relax and wait until they had returned.

"You want a walk home?" I asked Midori. She had mentioned during the evening that she lived in Harajuku, although of course I already knew that.

She smiled. "That would be nice."

Three minutes later, Tom and Ken returned. I saw them laughing about something as they approached us, and knew that Mr. Bland had gone undiscovered.

We stepped outside and walked up the steps into the cool Omotesando evening.

"My car's at the Blue Note," Ken said when we were outside. He looked at Midori. "Anyone need a ride?"

Midori shook her head. "No, I'm fine. Thanks."

"I'll take the subway," I told him. "But thanks."

"I'll go with you," Tom said, diffusing the slight tension I could feel brewing as Ken did the math. "John, it was nice meeting you tonight. Thank you again for coming, and for the dinner and drinks."

I bowed. "My pleasure, really. I hope I'll have another opportunity."

Ken nodded. "Sure," he said, with a demonstrable lack of enthusiasm. Tom took a step backward, his cue to Ken, I knew, and we said good night.

Midori and I strolled slowly in the direction of Omotesando-dori. "Was that okay?" she asked when Tom and Ken were out of earshot.

"I had a good time," I told her. "They're interesting people."

"Ken can be difficult."

I shrugged. "He was a little jealous that you had invited someone else to tag along, that's all."

"He's just young. Thanks for handling him gently tonight."

"No problem."

"You know, I don't usually invite people I've only just met to come to a performance, or to go out afterwards."

"Well, we'd met once before, so your guideline should be intact."

She laughed. "You feel like another single malt?"

I looked at her, trying to read her. "Always," I said. "And I've got a place I think you'll like."

I took her to Bar Satoh, a tiny second-story establishment nestled in a series of alleys that extend like a spider's web within the right angle formed by Omotesando-dori and Meiji-dori. The route we took gave me several opportunities to check behind us, and I saw that we were clean. Mr. Bland had been alone.

We took the elevator to the second floor of the building, then stepped through a door surrounded by a riot of gardenias and other flowers that Satoh-san's wife tends with reverence. A right turn, a step up, and there was Satoh-san, presiding over the solid cherry bar in the low light, dressed immaculately as always in a bow tie and vest.

"*Ah, Fujiwara-san,*" he said in his soft baritone, smiling a broad smile and bowing as he caught sight of us. "*Irrashaimase.*" Welcome.

"Satoh-san, it's good to see you," I said in Japanese. I looked around, noting that his small establishment was almost full. "Is there a possibility that we could be seated?"

"*Ei, mochiron,*" he replied. Yes, of course. Apologizing in formal Japanese, he had the six patrons at the bar all shift to their right, freeing up an additional seat at the far end and creating room for Midori and me.

Thanking Satoh-san and apologizing to the other patrons, we made our way to our seats. Midori's head was moving back and forth as she took in the décor: bottle after bottle of different whiskeys, many obscure and ancient, not just behind the bar but adorning shelves and furniture throughout the room, as well. Eclectic Americana like an old Schwinn bicycle suspended from the back wall, an ancient black rotary telephone that must have weighed ten pounds, a framed photograph of President Kennedy. As a complement to his whiskey-only policy, Satoh-san plays nothing but jazz, and the sounds of singer/poet Kurt Elling issued warm and wry from the Marantz vacuum-tube stereo in the back of the bar, accompanied by the low murmur of conversation and muffled laughter.

"I . . . love this place!" Midori whispered to me in English as we sat down.

"It's great, isn't it?" I said, pleased that she appreciated it. "Satoh-san is a former *sarariman* who got out of the rat race. He loves whiskey and jazz, and saved every yen he could until he was able to open this place ten years ago. I think it's the best bar in Japan."

Satoh-san strolled over, and I introduced Midori. "Ah, of course!" he exclaimed in Japanese. He reached under the bar, shuffling things around until he found what he was looking for: a copy of Midori's CD. Midori had to beg him not to play it.

"What do you recommend tonight?" I asked him. Satoh-san makes four pilgrimages a year to Scotland and has introduced me to malts that are available almost nowhere else in Japan.

"How many drinks?" he asked. If the answer were several, he would conduct a tasting, starting with something light from the Lowlands and progressing to the iodine tang of the Islay malts.

"Just one, I think," I responded. I glanced at Midori, who nodded her head.

"Subtle? Strong?"

I glanced at Midori again, who said, "Strong."

Satoh-san smiled. "Strong" was clearly the answer that he was hoping for, and I knew he had something special in mind. He turned and took a clear glass bottle from in front of the mirror behind the bar, then held it before us. "This is a forty-year-old Ardbeg," he explained. "From the south shore of Islay. Very rare. I keep it in a plain bottle because anyone who recognized it might try to steal it."

He took out two immaculate tumblers and placed them before us. "Straight?" he asked, not knowing Midori's preferences.

"*Hai*," she answered, to Satoh-san's relieved nod of approval. He carefully poured off two measures of the bronze liquid and recorked the bottle.

"What makes this malt special is the balance of flavors—flavors that would ordinarily compete with or override one another," he told us, his voice low and slightly grave. "There is peat, smoke, perfume, sherry, and the salt smell of the sea. It took forty years for this malt to realize the potential of its own character, just like a person. Please, enjoy." He bowed and moved to the other end of the bar.

"I'm almost afraid to drink it," Midori said, smiling and raising the glass before her, watching the light turn the liquid to amber.

"Satoh-san always provides a brief lecture on what you're about to experience. It's one of the best things about this place. He's a student of single malts."

"*Jaa, kanpai*," she said, and we touched glasses and drank. She paused for a moment afterward, then said, "Wow, that is good. Like a caress."

"Like what your music sounds like."

She smiled and gave me one of her shoulder checks. "I enjoyed our conversation the other day at Tsuta," she said. "I'd like to hear more about your experiences growing up in two worlds."

"I'm not sure how interesting a story that is."

"Tell it to me, and I'll tell you if it's interesting."

She was much more a listener than a talker, which would make my job of collecting operational intelligence more difficult. *Let's just see where this goes,* I thought.

"Home for me was a little town in upstate New York. My mother took me there after my father died so she could be close to her parents," I said.

"Did you spend any time in Japan after that?"

"Some. During my junior year in high school, my father's parents wrote to me about a new U.S./Japan high-school exchange program that would allow me to spend a semester at a Japanese high school. I was actually pretty homesick at the time and enrolled right away. So ultimately, I got to spend a semester at Saitama Gakuen."

"Just one semester? Your mother must have wanted you back."

"Part of her did. I think another part of her was relieved to have some time to focus on her own career. I was pretty wild at that age." This seemed an appropriate euphemism for constant fights and other discipline problems at school.

"How was the semester?"

I shrugged. Some of these memories were not particularly pleasant. "You know what it's like for returnees. It's bad enough if you're just an ordinary Japanese kid with an accent that's been Americanized by time abroad. If you're half-American on top of it, you're practically a freak."

I saw a deep sympathy in her eyes that made me feel I was worsening a betrayal. "I know what it's like to be a returnee child," she said. "And you had envisioned the semester as a homecoming. You must have felt so alienated."

I waved my hand as though it was nothing. "It's all in the past."

"Anyway, after high school?"

"After high school was Vietnam."

"You were in Vietnam? You look young for that."

I smiled. "I was a teenager when I joined the army, and when I got there the war was already well under way." I was aware that I was sharing more personal details than I should have. I didn't care.

"How long were you over there?"

"Three years."

"I thought that back then getting drafted meant only one year."

"It did. I wasn't drafted."

Her eyes widened. "You volunteered?"

It had been ages since I had talked about any of this, or even thought about it. "I know it sounds a little strange from this distance. But yes, I volunteered. I wanted to prove that I was American to the people who doubted it because of my eyes, my skin. And then, when I was over there, in a war against Asians, I had to prove it even more, so I stayed. I took dangerous assignments. I did some crazy things."

We were quiet for a moment. Then she said, "Can I ask, are those the things that you said 'haunt' you?"

"Some of them," I said evenly. But this would go no further. She may have had guidelines about inviting strangers to performances, but my rules regarding these matters are stricter still. We were getting close to places that even I can look at only obliquely.

Her fingers were resting lightly on the sides of her glass, and without thinking I reached out and took them into my hands, raised them before my face. "I bet I could tell from your hands that you play the piano," I said. "Your fingers are slender, but they look strong."

She twisted her hands around, so that now she was holding mine. "You can tell a lot from a person's hands," she said. "In mine you see the piano. In yours I see *bushido*. But on the joints, not the knuckles . . . what do you do, judo? Aikido?"

Bushido means the martial ways, the way of the warrior. She was talking about the calluses on the first and second joints of all my fingers, the result of years of gripping and twisting the heavy cotton *judogi*. She was holding my hands in a businesslike way, as though to examine them, but there was a gentleness in her touch and I felt electricity running all the way up my arms.

I withdrew my hands, afraid of what else she might read in them. "These days just judo. Grappling, throwing, strangles—it's the most practical martial art. And the Kodokan is the best place in the world for judo."

"I know the Kodokan. I studied aikido at a little *dojo* in Ochanomizu, one stop away on the Chuo line."

"What's a jazz pianist doing studying aikido?"

"It was before I got really serious about the piano, and I don't practice anymore because it's too hard on the hands. I did it because I got bullied in school for a while—my father once had a tour in the States. I told you I know what it's like to be a returnee."

"Did the aikido help?"

"Not at first. It took me awhile to get good. But the bullies gave me incentive to keep practicing. One day, one of them grabbed my arm, and I threw her with *san-kyo*. After that, they left me alone. Which was good, because *san-kyo* was actually the only throw I knew well enough to do."

I looked at her, imagining what it would be like to be on the *san-kyo* receiving end of the determination that was taking her to increasing renown, maybe to fame, in jazz circles.

She lifted her glass with the fingers of both hands, and I noticed an economy of movement to the simple act. It was graceful, pleasant to watch.

"You do *sado*," I said, almost thinking out loud. *Sado* is the Japanese tea ceremony. Its practitioners strive through the practice of refined, ritualized movements in the preparation and serving of tea to achieve *wabi* and *sabi*: a sort of effortless elegance in thought and movement, a paring down to the essentials to more elegantly represent a larger, more important concept that would otherwise be obscured.

"Not since I was a teenager," she answered, "and even then never well. I'm surprised that you can see it. Maybe if I have another drink it will disappear."

"No, I wouldn't want that," I said, fighting the feeling of being drawn into those dark eyes. "I like the *sado*."

She smiled. "What else do you like?"

Where is she going? "I don't know. Lots of things. I like watching you play."

"Tell me."

I sipped the Ardbeg, peat and smoke meandering across my tongue and throat. "I like the way you start calm, and build on it. I like the way you start playing the music, and then how, when you get going, it's as though the music is playing you. How you get caught up in it. Because when I feel that happening to you, I get caught up in it also. It pulls me outside myself. I can tell how alive it makes you feel, and it makes me feel that way, too."

"What else?"

I laughed. "What else? That's not enough?"

"Not if there's more."

I rolled the glass back and forth between my hands, watching the reflections of light inside.

"I always feel like you're looking for something while you're playing but that you can't find it. So you look harder, but it still eludes you, and the melody starts to get really edgy, but then you hit this point where it's as though you realize that you're not going to find it, you just can't, and then the edginess is gone and the music turns sad, but it's a beautiful sadness, a wise, accepting sadness."

I realized again that there was something about her that made me open up too much, reveal too much. I needed to control it.

"It means a lot to me that you recognize that in my music," she said after a moment. "Because it's something that I'm trying to express. Do you know *mono no aware*?"

"I think so. 'The pathos of things,' right?"

"That's the usual translation. I like 'the sadness of being human.'"

I was surprised to find myself moved by the idea. "I hadn't thought of it that way," I said quietly.

"I remember once, when I was living in Chiba, I took a walk on a winter night. It was warm for winter, and I took off my jacket and sat in the playground of the school where I had gone as a little girl, all by myself, and watched the silhouettes of the tree branches against the sky. I had such a strong awareness that one day, I was going to be gone, but the trees would still be here, the moon would still be above them, shining down, and it made me cry, but a good kind of crying, because I knew it had to be that way. I had to accept it because that's the way things are. Things end. That's *mono no aware*."

Things end. "Yes, it is," I said, thinking of her father.

We were quiet for a moment. Then I asked, "What did Ken mean when he said that you were a radical?"

She took a sip of her Ardbeg. "He's a romantic. I was hardly a radical. Just rebellious."

"Rebellious how?"

"Look around you, John. Japan is incredibly screwed up. The LDP, the bureaucrats, they're bleeding the country dry."

"There are problems," I allowed.

"Problems? The economy's going to hell, families can't pay their property taxes, there's no confidence in the banking system, and all the government can think to do to solve the problem is deficit spending and public works. And you know why? Payoffs to the construction industry. The whole country is covered in concrete, there's nowhere else to build, so the politicians vote for office parks that no one uses, bridges and roads that no one drives on, rivers lined with concrete. You know those ugly concrete 'tetrapods' that line the Japanese coast, supposedly protecting it from erosion? All the studies show those monstrosities speed erosion; they don't forestall it. So we're destroying our own ecosystem to keep the politicians fat and the construction industry rich. Is that what you call just 'problems'?"

"Hey, maybe Ken was right," I said, smiling. "You are pretty radical."

She shook her head. "This is just common sense. Tell me the truth, really. Don't you sometimes feel like you're being screwed by the status quo and all the people who profit from it? And doesn't that piss you off?"

"Sometimes, yes," I said, carefully.

"Well, it pisses me off a lot. That's all Ken meant."

"Forgive me for saying so, but wasn't your father a part of that status quo?"

A long pause. "We had our differences."

"That must have been hard."

"It was, sometimes. For a long time we were pretty alienated."

I nodded. "Were you ever able to mend fences?"

She laughed softly, but without mirth. "My father found out he had lung cancer just a few months before he died. The diagnosis made him reassess his life, but that didn't give us long to work things out."

The information caught me by surprise. "He had lung cancer? But . . . Mama mentioned a heart attack."

"He had a heart condition, but always smoked any-way. All his government cronies did, and he felt he needed to do it to fit in. He was so much a part of the system, in a way, he gave his life for it."

I took a sip of the smoky liquid and swallowed. "Lung cancer is a terrible way to go," I said. "At least, the way he died, he didn't suffer." The sentiment was weirdly heartfelt.

"That's true, and I'm grateful for it."

"Forgive me if I'm prying, but what do you mean when you say the diagnosis made him reassess his life?"

She was looking past me, her eyes unfocused. "In the end, he realized that he had spent his life being part of the problem, as Ken would say. He decided he wanted to be part of the solution."

"Did he have time to do that?"

"I don't think so. But he told me he wanted to do something, wanted to do something right, before he died. The main thing was that he felt that way."

"How do you know he didn't have time?"

"What do you mean?" she asked, her eyes coming back to me.

"Your father—he's diagnosed, suddenly face-to-face with his own mortality. He wants to do something to atone for the past. Could he have? In such a short time?"

"I'm not sure what you mean," she said, and instantly I knew I had bumped up against that defensive wall again.

"I'm thinking about what we talked about the other day. About regret. If there's something you regret, but you've only got a short time to do something about it, what do you do?"

"I imagine that would be different for everyone, depending on the nature of your regrets."

C'mon, Midori. Work with me. "What would your father have done? Was there anything that could have reversed the things he came to regret?"

"I wouldn't know."

But you do know, I thought. *A reporter he was meeting with contacted you. You know, but you're not telling me.*

"What I mean is, maybe he was trying to do something to be part of the solution, even if you couldn't see it. Maybe he talked to his colleagues, told them about his change of heart, tried to get them to change theirs. Who knows?"

She was quiet, and I thought, *That's it, that's as far as you can possibly push it, she's going to get suspicious and clam up on you now for sure.*

But after a moment she said, "Are you asking because of a regret of your own?"

I looked at her, simultaneously disturbed by the truth of her question and relieved at the cover it afforded me. "I'm not sure," I said.

"Why don't you just tell me?"

I felt like I'd been hit with an aikido throw. "No," I said, my voice low.

"Am I that hard to talk to?" she asked, her voice gentle.

"No," I said, smiling into her dark eyes. "You're easy. That's the problem."

She sighed. "You're a strange man, John. You're so obviously uncomfortable talking about yourself."

"I'm more interested in you."

"In my father."

"I thought there'd be a lesson there for me. That's all."

"Some lessons you have to learn for yourself."

"Probably true. But I try to learn them from others when I can. I'm sorry for pressing."

She gave me a small smile. "That's okay. This is all still a little recent."

"Of course it is," I said, recognizing the dead end. I looked at my watch. "I should get you home."

This was apt to be tricky. On the one hand, we had undeniable chemistry, and it wasn't inconceivable that she would invite me up for a drink or something. If she did, I'd get a chance to make sure her apartment was secure, although I would have to be careful once we were inside. I couldn't let anything stupid happen—more stupid than the time I had already spent with her and the things I had already said.

On the other hand, if she wanted to go home alone, it would be hard for me to escort her without seeming like I was angling for a way to get into her bed. It would be awkward. But I couldn't just turn her loose alone. They knew where she lived.

We thanked Satoh-san for his hospitality and for the delicious introduction to the rare Ardbeg. I paid the bill, and we took the stairs down into the now slightly chilly Omotesando night air. The streets were quiet.

"Which way are you heading?" Midori asked me. "From around here, I usually walk."

"I'll go with you. I'd like to see you all the way home."

"You don't have to."

I looked down for a moment, then back at her. "I'd

like to," I said again, thinking of Benny's write-up on the bulletin board.

She smiled. "Okay."

It was a fifteen-minute walk to her building. I didn't observe anyone behind us. Not a surprise, given Mr. Bland's departure from the scene.

When we reached the entranceway of her building, she took her keys out and turned to me. "*Jaa . . .*" Well, then . . .

It was a polite good night. But I had to see her inside. "You'll be okay from here?"

She looked at me knowingly, although she didn't really know. "I live here. I'm sure I'll be fine."

"Okay. Have you got a phone number?" I already knew it, of course, but I had to keep up appearances.

"No, I don't have a phone."

Wow. That bad. "Yeah, I'm a bit of a Luddite myself. If something comes up, send me a smoke signal, okay?"

She giggled. "Five, two, seven, five-six, four, five, six. I was only teasing."

"Right. Can I call you sometime?" In about five minutes, for example, to make sure there's no one waiting for you in your apartment.

"I hope you will."

I took out a pen and wrote the number down on my hand.

She was looking at me, half smiling. The kiss was there, if I wanted it.

I turned and walked back up the path toward the street.

She called out after me. "John?"

I turned.

"I think there's a radical in you trying to get out."

Several ripostes came quickly to mind. Instead: "Good night, Midori."

I turned and walked away, pausing at the sidewalk to look back. But she had already gone inside, and the glass doors were closing behind her.

I I

I SLIPPED INTO a parking area that faced the entrance. Hanging back beyond the perimeter of light cast from inside, I saw her waiting for an elevator to her right. From where I was standing I could see the doors open when it arrived but couldn't see inside it. I watched her step inside, and then the doors closed.

No one seemed to be lurking outside. Unless they were waiting in her apartment or nearby, she would be safe for the night.

I took out Harry's unit and activated her phone, then listened in on my cell phone. Silence.

A minute later, I heard her door being unlocked and opened, then closed. Muffled footsteps. Then the sound of more footsteps, from more than one person. A loud gasp.

Then a male voice: "Listen. Listen carefully. Don't be afraid. We're sorry to alarm you. We're investigating a matter of national security. We have to move with great circumspection. Please understand."

Midori's voice, not much more than a whisper: "Show me . . . Show me identification."

"We don't have time for that. We have some questions that we need to ask you, and then we'll leave."

"Show me some ID," I heard her say, her voice stronger now, "or I'm going to start making noise. And the walls in this building are really, really thin. People can probably already hear."

My heart leaped. She had instinct and she had guts.

"No noise, please," came the reply. Then the reverberation of a hard slap.

They were roughing her up. I was going to have to move.

I heard her breathing, ragged. "What the hell do you want?"

"Your father had something on his person around the time that he died. It is now in your possession. We need it."

"I don't know what you're talking about."

Another slap. Shit.

I couldn't get into the building without a key. Even if someone entered or exited right then so that I could slip inside, I would never be able to make it into her apartment to help her. Maybe I could kick the door down. And maybe there would be four guys with guns standing ten feet away who would drop me before I was half inside.

I broke the connection with the unit and input her number on the cell phone. Her phone rang three times, then an answering machine cut in.

I hung up and repeated the procedure using the redial key, then again. And again.

I wanted to make them nervous, to give them pause. If someone tried to get through enough times, maybe they would let her answer it to allay potential suspicions.

On the fifth try, she picked up. *"Moshi moshi,"* she said, her voice uncertain.

"Midori, this is John. I know you can't speak. I know there are men in your apartment. Say to me 'There isn't a man in my apartment, Grandma.'"

"What?"

"Say 'There isn't a man in my apartment, Grandma.' Just say it!"

"There isn't . . . There isn't a man in my apartment, Grandma."

"Good girl. Now say, 'No, I don't want you coming over now. There's no one here.'"

"No, I don't want you coming over now. There's no one here."

They'd be itching to get out of her apartment now. "Very good. Just keep arguing with your grandmother, okay? Those men are not the police; you know that. I can help you, but only if you get them out of your apartment. Tell them your father had some papers with him when he died, but that they're hidden in his apartment. Tell them you'll take them there and show them. Tell them you can't describe the hiding place; it's a place in the wall and you'll have to show them. Do you understand?"

"Grandma, you worry too much."

"I'll be waiting outside," I said, and broke the connection.

Which way are they likely to go? I thought, trying to decide where I could set up an ambush. But just then, an old woman, bent double at the waist from a childhood of poor nutrition and toil in the rice paddies, emerged from the elevator, carrying out her trash. The electronic doors parted for her as she shuffled outside, and I slipped into the building.

I knew Midori lived on the third floor. I bolted up the stairwell and paused outside the entrance to her floor, listening. After about half a minute of silence, I heard the sound of a door opening from somewhere down the corridor.

I opened the door part way, then took out my key chain and extended the dental mirror through the opening in the doorway until I had a view of a long, narrow hallway. A Japanese man was emerging from an apartment. He swept his head left and right, then nodded. A moment later Midori stepped out, followed closely by a second Japanese. The second one had his hand on her shoulder, not in a gentle way.

The one in the lead checked the corridor in both directions, then they started to move toward my position. I withdrew the mirror. There was a CO_2-type fire extinguisher on the wall, and I grabbed it and stepped to the right of the door, toward the side where it opened. I pulled the pin and aimed the nozzle face high.

Two seconds went by, then five. I heard their footsteps approaching, heard them right outside the door.

I breathed shallowly through my mouth, my fingers tense around the trigger of the unit.

For a split second, in my imagination, I saw the door start to open, but it didn't. They had continued past it, heading for the elevators.

Damn. I had thought they would take the stairs. I

eased the door open again and extended the mirror, adjusting its angle until I could see them. They had her sandwiched in tightly, the guy in the rear holding something against her back. I assumed a gun, but maybe a knife.

I couldn't follow them from there with any hope of surprising them. I wouldn't be able to close the distance before they heard me coming, and if they were armed, my chances would range from poor to nonexistent.

I turned and bolted down the stairs. When I got to the first floor I cut across the lobby, stopping behind a weight-bearing pillar that they'd have to walk past as they stepped off the elevator. I braced the extinguisher against my waist and eased the mirror past the corner of the pillar.

They emerged half a minute later, bunched up in a tight formation that you learn to avoid on day one in Special Forces because it makes your whole team vulnerable to an ambush or a mine. They were obviously afraid Midori was going to try to run.

I slipped the mirror and key chain back in my pocket, listening to their footsteps. When they sounded only a few centimeters away I bellowed a warrior's *kiyai* and leaped out, pulling the trigger and aiming face high.

Nothing happened. The extinguisher hiccupped, then made a disappointing hissing sound. But that was all.

The lead guy's mouth dropped open, and he started fumbling inside his coat. Feeling like I was moving in slow motion, sure I was going to be a second late, I brought the butt end of the extinguisher up. Saw his hand coming free, holding a short-barreled revolver. I stepped in hard and jammed the extinguisher into his face like a battering ram, getting my weight behind the blow. There was a satisfying thud and he spilled into Midori and the guy in the rear, his gun clattering to the floor.

The second guy stumbled backward, slipping clear of Midori, pinwheeling his left arm. He was holding a gun in his other hand and trying keep it in front of him.

I launched the extinguisher like a missile, catching him center mass. He went down and I was on him in an instant, catching hold of the gun and jerking it away. Before he could get his hands up to protect himself I smashed the butt into his mastoid process, behind the ear. There was a loud crack and he went limp.

I spun and brought the gun up, but his friend wasn't moving. His face looked like he'd run into a flagpole.

I turned back to Midori just in time to see a third goon emerge from the elevator, where he must have been positioned from the beginning. He grabbed Midori around the neck from behind with his left hand, trying to use her as a shield, while his right hand went to his jacket pocket, groping for a weapon. But before he could pull it free, Midori spun counterclockwise inside his grip, catching his left wrist in her hands and twisting his arm outward and back in a classic aikido *san-kyo* joint lock. His reaction showed training: he threw his body in the direction of the lock to save his arm from being broken, and landed with a smooth *ukemi* break fall. But before he could recover I had closed the distance, launching a field-goal-style kick at his head with enough force to lift his whole body from the ground.

Midori was looking at me, her eyes wide, her breath coming in shallow gasps.

"*Daijobu?*" I asked, taking her by the arm. "Are you okay? Did they hurt you?"

She shook her head. "They told me they were the police, but I knew they weren't: they wouldn't show me any identification and why were they waiting in my apartment anyway? Who are they? How did you know they were in there?"

Keeping my hand on her arm, I started moving us through the lobby toward the glass doors, my eyes sweeping back and forth for signs of danger outside.

"I saw them at the Blue Note," I said, urging her with the pressure on her arm to increase the pace. "When I realized they hadn't followed us back, I thought they might be waiting for you at your apartment. That's when I called."

"You saw them at the Blue Note? Who are they? Who the hell are you?"

"I'm someone who's stumbled onto something very bad and wants to protect you from it. I'll explain later. Right now, we've got to get you someplace safe."

"Safe? With you?" She stopped in front of the glass doors and looked back at the three men, their faces bloody masks, then back at me.

"I'll explain everything to you, but not now. For now, the only thing that matters is that you're in danger, and I can't help you if you don't believe me. Let me just get you somewhere safe and tell you what all this is about, okay?" The doors slid open, a hidden infrared eye having sensed our proximity.

"Where?"

"Someplace where no one would know to look for you, or wait for you. A hotel, something like that."

The goon I had kicked groaned and started to pull himself up onto all fours. I strode over and drop-kicked him in the face again, and he went down. "Midori, we don't have time to discuss this here. You're going to have to believe me. Please."

The doors slid shut.

I wanted to search the men on the floor for ID or some other way of identifying them, but I couldn't do that and get Midori moving at the same time.

"How do I know I can believe you?" she said, but she was moving again. The doors opened.

"Trust your instincts; that's all I can tell you. They'll tell you what's right."

We moved through the doors, and with the wider range of vision that our new position afforded me I was able to see a squat and ugly Japanese man standing about five meters back and to the left. He had a nose that looked like a U-turn—it must have been broken so many times he gave up having it set. He was watching the scene in the foyer, and seemed uncertain of what to do. Something about his posture, his appearance, told me he wasn't a civilian. Probably he was with the three on the floor.

I steered Midori to the right, keeping clear of the flat-nosed guy's position. "How could you know . . . how could you know that there were men in my apartment?" she asked. "How did you know what was happening?"

"I just knew, okay?" I said, turning my head, searching for danger, as we walked. "Midori, if I were with these people, what would I gain from this charade? They had you exactly where they wanted you. Please, let me help you. I don't want to see you get hurt. That's the only reason I'm here."

I saw the flat-nosed guy go inside as we moved away from the scene, I assumed to help his fallen comrades.

If they had been planning to take her somewhere, they would have had a car. I looked around, but there were too many vehicles parked in the area for me to be able to pinpoint theirs.

"Did they say where they were going to take you?" I asked. "Who they were with?"

"No," she said. "I told you, they only said they were with the police."

"Okay, I understand." Where the hell was their car? There might have been more of them. *All right, go, just keep on walking, they'll have to show themselves if they want to take you.*

We cut across the dark parking lot of the building across from hers, emerging onto Omotesando-dori, where we caught a cab. I told the driver to take us to the Seibu Department Store in Shibuya. I checked the side views as we drove. There were few cars on the road, and none seemed to be trying to tail us.

What I had in mind was a love hotel. The love hotel is a Japanese institution, born of the country's housing shortage. With families, sometimes extended ones, jammed into small apartments, Mom and Dad need to have somewhere to go to be alone. Hence the *rabu hoteru*—places with rates for either a "rest" or a "stay," famously discreet front desk, no credit card required for registration, and fake names the norm. Some of them are completely over-the-top, with theme rooms sporting Roman baths and Americana settings, like what you'd get if you turned the Disney Epcot Center into a bordello.

Beyond Japan's housing shortage, the hotels arose because inviting a stranger into your home tends to be a much more intimate act in Japan than it is in the States. There are plenty of Japanese women who will allow a man into their bodies before permitting him to enter their apartments, and the hotels serve this aspect of the market, as well.

The people we were up against weren't stupid, of course. They might guess that a love hotel would make an expedient safe house. That would be my guess, if the tables were turned. But with about ten thousand *rabu hoteru* in Tokyo, it would still take them awhile to track us down.

We got out of the cab and walked to Shibuya 2-chome, which is choked with small love hotels. I chose one at random, where we told the old woman standing inside at the front desk that we wanted a room with a bath, for a *yasumi*—a stay, not just a rest. I put cash on the counter and she reached underneath, then handed us a key.

We took the elevator to the fifth floor, and found our room at the end of a short hallway. I unlocked the door and Midori went in first. I followed her in, locking the door behind me. We left our shoes in the entranceway. There was only one bed—twins in a love hotel would be as out of place as a Bible—but there was a decent-sized couch in the room that I could curl up on.

Midori sat down on the edge of the bed and faced me. "Here's where we are," she said, her voice even. "Tonight three men were waiting for me in my apartment. They claimed to be police, but obviously weren't—or, if they were police, they were on some kind of private mission. I'd think you were with them, but I saw how badly you hurt them. You asked me to go somewhere safe with you so you could explain. I'm listening."

I nodded, trying to find the right words to begin. "You know this has to do with your father."

"Those men told me he had something they wanted."

"Yes, and they think you have it now."

"I don't know why they would think that."

I looked at her. "I think you do."

"Think what you want."

"You know what's wrong with this picture, Midori? Three men are waiting for you in your apartment, they rough you up a little, I appear out of nowhere and rough them up a lot, none of this exactly an average day in the life of a jazz pianist, and the whole time you've never once suggested that you want to go to the police."

She didn't answer.

"Do you want to? You can, you know."

She sat facing me, her nostrils flaring slightly, her fingers drumming along the edge of the bed. *God-damnit,* I thought, *what does she know that she hasn't been telling me?*

"Tell me about your father, Midori. Please. I can't help you if you don't."

She leaped off the bed and faced me squarely. "Tell you?" she spat. "No, you tell me! Tell me who the fuck you are, or I swear I will go to the police, and I don't care what happens after that!"

Progress, of a sort, I thought. "What do you want to know?"

"Everything!"

"Okay."

"Starting with, who were those men in my apartment?"

"Okay."

"Who are they?"

"I don't know who they are."

"But you knew they were there?"

She was going to pull hard at that loose thread until the entire fabric unraveled. I didn't know how to get around it. "Yes."

"How?"

"Because your apartment is bugged."

"Because my apartment is bugged . . . Are you with those men?"

"No."

"Would you please stop giving me one-word answers? Okay, my apartment is bugged, by who, by you?"

There it was. "Yes."

She looked at me for a long beat, then sat back down on the bed. "Who do you work for?" she asked, her voice flat.

"It doesn't matter."

Another long beat, and the same flat tone: "Then tell me what you want."

I looked at her, wanting her to see my eyes. "I want to make sure you don't get hurt."

Her face was expressionless. "And you're going to do that by . . ."

"These people are coming after you because they think you have something that could harm them. I don't know what. But as long as they think you have it, you're not going to be safe."

"But if I were to just give whatever it is to you . . ."

"Without knowing what the thing is, I don't even know if giving it to me would help. I told you, I'm not here for whatever it is. I just don't want you to get hurt."

"Can't you see what this looks like from my perspective? 'Just hand it over so I can help you.'"

"I understand that."

"I'm not sure you do."

"Doesn't matter. Tell me about your father."

There was a long pause. I knew what she was going to say, and she said it: "This is why you were asking all those questions before. You came to Alfie and, God, everything . . . You've just been using me from the beginning."

"Some of what you're saying is true. Not all of it. Now tell me about your father."

"No."

I felt a flush of anger in my neck. *Easy, John.* "The reporter was asking, too, wasn't he? Bulfinch? What did you tell him?"

She looked at me, trying to gauge just how much I knew. "I don't know what you're talking about."

I looked at the door and thought, *Walk away. Just walk away.*

But instead: "Listen to me, Midori. All I have to do is walk out that door. You're the one who won't be able to sleep in her own apartment, who's afraid to go to the police, who can't go back to her life. So you figure out a way to work with me on this, or you can damn well figure it all out on your own."

A long time, maybe a full minute, passed. Then she said, "Bulfinch told me my father was supposed to deliver something to him on the morning he died, but that Bulfinch never got it. He wanted to know if I had it, or if I knew where it was."

"What was it?"

"A computer disk. That's all he would tell me. He told me if he said more it would put me in danger."

"He had already compromised you just by talking to you. He was being followed outside of Alfie." I pressed my fingers to my eyes. "Do you know anything about this disk?"

"No."

I looked at her, trying to judge. "I don't think I have to tell you, the people who want it aren't particularly restrained about the methods they'll use to get it."

"I understand that."

"Okay, let's put together what we have. Everyone thinks your father told you something, or gave you something. Did he? Did he tell you anything, or give you some documents, maybe, anything that he said was important?"

"No. Nothing I remember."

"Try. A safe-deposit key? A locker key? Did he tell you that he had hidden something, or that he had important papers somewhere? Anything like that?"

"No," she said, after a moment. "Nothing."

She might be holding back, I knew. She certainly had reason not to trust me.

"But you know something," I said. "Otherwise, you'd go to the police."

She folded her arms across her chest and looked at me.

"For Christ's sake, Midori, tell me. Let me help you."

"It's not what you're hoping for," she said.

"I'm not hoping for anything. Just what pieces you can give me."

There was a long pause. Then she said, "I told you my father and I were . . . estranged for a long time. It started when I was a teenager, when I started to understand Japan's political system, and my father's place in it."

She got up and began to pace around the room, not looking at me. "He was part of the Liberal Democratic Party machine, working his way up the ladder in the old Kensetsusho, the Ministry of Construction. When the Kensetsusho became the Kokudokotsusho, he was made vice minister of land and infrastructure—of public works. Do you know what that means in Japan?"

"I know a little. The public-works program channels money from the politicians and construction firms to the *yakuza*."

"And the *yakuza* provide 'protection,' dispute resolution, and lobbying for the construction industry. The construction companies and *yakuza* are like twins separated at birth. Did you know that construction outfits in Japan are called *gumi*?"

Gumi means "gang," or "organization"—the same

moniker the *yakuza* gangs use for themselves. The original *gumi* were groups of men displaced by World War II who worked for a gang boss doing whatever dirty jobs they could to survive. Eventually these gangs morphed into today's *yakuza* and construction outfits.

"I know," I said.

"Then you know that, after the war, there were battles between construction companies that were so big the police were afraid to intervene. A bid-rigging system was established to stop these fights. The system still exists. My father ran it."

She laughed. "Remember in 1994 when Kansai International Airport was built in Osaka? The airport cost fourteen billion dollars, and everyone wanted a piece of it. Remember how Takumi Masaru, the Yamaguchi Gumi *yakuza* boss, was murdered that year? It was for not sharing enough of the profits from the airport construction. My father ordered his death to appease the other gang bosses."

"Christ, Midori," I said quietly. "Your father told you these things?"

"When he learned he was terminal. He needed to confess."

I waited for her to go on.

"The *yakuza* with tattoos and sunglasses, the ones you see in the bad sections of Shinjuku, they're just tools for people like my father," she said, continuing her slow pacing. "These people are part of a system. The politicians vote for useless public works that feed the construction companies. The construction companies allow politicians to use company staff as 'volunteers' during election campaigns. Construction Ministry bureaucrats are given postretirement 'advisor' jobs at construction companies—just a car and driver and other perks, but no work. Every year during budget season, officials from the Ministry of Finance and the Construction Ministry meet with politicians loyal to the industry to decide how to divvy up the pie."

She stopped pacing and looked at me. "Do you know that Japan has four percent of the land area and half the population of America, but spends a third more on public works? Some people think that in the last ten years ten *trillion* yen of government money have been paid to the *yakuza* through public works."

Ten trillion? I thought. That's maybe a hundred billion dollars. Bastards have been holding out on you.

"I know about some of this, sure," I told her. "Your father was going to blow the whistle?"

"Yes. When he was diagnosed, he called me. It was the first time we had talked in over a year. He told me he had to talk to me about something important, and he came over to my apartment. We hadn't talked in so long, I was thinking it was something about his health, about his heart. He looked older when I saw him and I knew I was right, or almost right.

"I made us tea, and we sat across from each other at the small table in my kitchen. I told him about the music I was working on, but of course I could never ask him about his work, and there was almost nothing for us to talk about. Finally I said, 'Papa, what is it?'

"'*Taishita koto jaa nai*,' he told me. 'Nothing big.' Then he looked at me and smiled, his eyes warm but sad, and for a second he looked to me the way he had when I was a little girl. 'I found out this week that I don't have very long to live,' he said to me, 'not very long at all. A month, maybe two. Longer if I choose to suffer from radiation and drugs, which I don't wish to do. The strange thing is that when I heard this news it didn't bother me, or even surprise me very much.' Then his eyes filled up, which I had never seen before. He said, 'What bothered me wasn't losing my life, but knowing that I had already lost my daughter.'"

With a quick, economical movement she raised her right hand and wiped the edge of one eye, then the other. "He told me about all the things he had been involved in, all the things he had done. He told me he wanted to do something to make it right, that he would have done something much sooner but he had been a coward, knowing he would be killed if he tried. He also said that he was afraid for me, that the people he was involved with wouldn't hesitate to attack someone's family to send a message. He was planning to do something now, something that would make things right, he told me, but if he did it I might be in danger."

"What was he going to do?"

"I don't know. But I told him I couldn't accept being a hostage to a corrupt system, that if we were going to reconcile he would have to act without regard to me."

I considered. "That was brave of you."

She looked at me, in full control again. "Not really. Don't forget, I'm a radical."

"Well, we know he was talking to that reporter, Bulfinch, that he was supposed to deliver a disk. We need to figure out what was supposed to be on it."

"How?"

"I think by contacting Bulfinch directly."

"And telling him what?"

"I haven't figured that part out yet."

We were quiet for a minute, and I started to feel exhaustion setting in.

"Why don't we get some sleep," I said. "I'll take the couch, all right? And we can talk more tomorrow. Things will seem clearer then."

I knew they couldn't become more murky.

12

I GOT UP early the next morning and went straight to Shibuya Station, telling Midori that I would call her later on her cell phone, after I picked up some things that I needed. I had a few items hidden in my place in Sengoku, among them an alias passport, which I'd want if I had to leave the country suddenly. I told her to go out only when she really had to, knowing that she would need to buy food and a change of clothes, and not to use plastic for any purchases. I also told her that, in case anyone had her cell phone number, we needed to keep our conversations brief, and that she should assume someone was listening to anything we said.

I took the Yamanote line to Ikebukuro, a crowded, anonymous commercial and entertainment center in the northwest of the city, then got off and flagged down a cab outside the station. I took the cab to Hakusan, a residential neighborhood about a ten-minute walk from my apartment, where I got out and dialed the voice-mail account that's attached to the phone in my apartment.

The phone has a few special features. I can call in

anytime from a remote location and silently activate the unit's speakerphone, essentially turning it into a transmitter. The unit is also sound activated: if there's a noise in the room, a human voice, for example, the unit's speakerphone feature is silently activated and it dials a voice-mail account that I keep in the States, where telco competition keeps the price of such things reasonable. Before I go home, I always call the voice-mail number. If someone has been in my apartment in my absence, I'll know.

The truth is, the phone is probably unnecessary. Not only has no one ever been in my apartment unannounced; no one even knows where I really live. I pay for a six-mat flat in Ochanomizu, but I never go there. The place in Sengoku is leased under a corporate name with no connection to me. If you're in this line of work, you'd better have an additional identity or two.

I looked up and down the street, listening to the beeps as the call snaked its way under the Pacific. When the connection went through, I punched in my code.

Every time I've done this, except for when I periodically test the system, I've listened to a mechanical woman's voice say, "You have no calls." I was expecting the same today.

Instead the message was "You have one call."

Son of a bitch. I was so startled I couldn't remember what button to press to hear the message, but the mechanical voice prompted me. Barely breathing, I pressed the "one" key.

I heard a man's voice, speaking Japanese. "Small place. Hard to catch him by surprise when he comes in."

Another man's voice, also in Japanese: "Wait here,

on the side of the *genkan*. When he arrives, use the pepper spray."

I knew that voice, but it took me a minute to place it—I was used to hearing it in English.

Benny.

"What if he doesn't want to talk?"

"He'll talk."

I was gripping the phone hard. *That piece of shit Benny. How did he track me down?*

When did this message get recorded? What was that special-functions button . . . Goddamnit, I should have run through this a few more times for practice before it really mattered. I'd gotten complacent. I hit six. That speeded up the message. Shit. I tried five. The mechanical woman informed me that this message was made by an outside caller at 2:00 P.M. That was California time, which meant that they entered my apartment at about 7:00 this morning, maybe an hour ago.

Okay, change of plan. I saved the message, hung up, and called Midori on her cell phone. I told her I had found out something important and would tell her about it when I got back, that she should wait for me even if I was late. Then I backtracked to Sugamo, once notorious as the site of a SCAP prison for Japanese war criminals, now better known for its red-light district and accompanying love hotels.

I picked the hotel that was closest to Sengoku. The room they gave me was dank. I didn't care. I just wanted a landline, so I wouldn't have to worry about my cell phone battery dying, and a place to wait.

I dialed the phone in my apartment. It didn't ring, but I could hear when the connection had gone through. I sat and waited, listening, but after a half hour there still wasn't any sound and I started to wonder if they'd left. Then I heard a chair sliding against the wood floor, footsteps, and the unmistakable sound of a man urinating in the toilet. They were still there.

I sat like that all day, listening in on nothing. The only consolation was that they must have been as bored as I was. I hoped they were as hungry.

At around 6:30, while I was doing some judo stretches to keep limber, I heard a phone ring on the other end of the line. Sounded like a cellular. Benny answered, grunted a few times, then said, "I have something to attend to in Shibakoen—shouldn't take more than a few hours."

I heard his buddy answer, "*Hai*," but I wasn't really listening anymore. If Benny was going to Shibakoen, he'd take the Mita line subway south from Sengoku Station. He wouldn't have driven; public transportation is lower profile, and there's nowhere for nonresidents to park in Sengoku anyway. From my apartment to the station, he could choose more or less randomly from a half dozen parallel and perpendicular streets— one of the reasons I had originally chosen the place. The station was too crowded; I couldn't intercept him there. Besides, I didn't know what he looked like. I had to catch him leaving the apartment or I was going to lose him.

I bolted out of the room and flew down the stairs. When I hit the sidewalk I cut straight across Hakusandori, then made a left on the artery that would take me to my street. I was running as fast as I could while trying to hug the buildings I passed—if I timed this wrong and Benny emerged at the wrong moment, he was going to see me coming. He knew where I lived, and I couldn't be certain any longer that he wouldn't know my face.

When I was about fifteen meters from my street I slowed to a walk, staying close to the exterior wall of an enclosed house, controlling my breathing. At the corner I crouched low and eased my head out, looking to the right. No sign of Benny. No more than four minutes had passed since I'd hung up the phone. I was pretty sure I hadn't missed him.

There was a streetlight directly overhead, but I had to wait where I was. I didn't know whether he'd make a right or left leaving the building, and I had to be able to see him when he exited. Once I'd gotten my hands on him, I could drag him into the shadows.

My breathing had slowed to normal when I heard the external door to the building slam shut. I smiled. The residents know the door slams and are careful to let it close slowly.

I crouched down again and peered past the edge of the wall. A pudgy Japanese was walking briskly in my direction. The same guy I had seen with the attaché case in the subway station at Jinbocho. Benny. I should have known.

I stood up and waited, listening to his footsteps getting louder. When he sounded like he was about a meter away, I stepped out into the intersection.

He pulled up short, his eyes bulging. He knew my face, all right. Before he could say anything I stepped in close, pumping two uppercuts into his abdomen. He dropped to the ground with a grunt. I stepped behind him, grabbed his right hand, and twisted his wrist in a pain-compliance hold. I gave it a sharp jerk and he yelped.

"On your feet, Benny. Move fast, or I'll break your arm." I gave his wrist another hard jerk to emphasize the point. He wheezed and hauled himself up, making sucking noises.

I shoved him around the corner, put him facefirst against the wall, and quickly patted him down. In his overcoat pocket I found a cell phone, which I took, but that was all.

I gave a last jerk on his arm, then spun him around and slammed him up against the wall. He grunted but still hadn't recovered enough wind to do more. I pinched his windpipe with the fingers of one hand and took an undergrip on his balls with the other.

"Benny. Listen very carefully." He started to struggle, and I pinched his windpipe harder. He got the message. "I want to know what's going on. I want names, and they better be names I know."

I relaxed both grips a little, and he sucked in his breath. "I can't tell you this stuff, you know that," he wheezed.

I took up the grip on his throat again. "Benny, I'm not going to hurt you if you tell me what I want to know. But if you don't tell me, I've got to blame you, understand? Tell me quick, no one's going to know." Again, a little more pressure on the throat—this time, cutting off all his oxygen for a few seconds. I told him to nod if he understood, and after a second or two with no air, he did. I waited another second anyway, and when the nodding got vigorous, I eased off the pressure.

"Holtzer, Holtzer," he rasped. "Bill Holtzer."

It was an effort, but I revealed no surprise at the sound of the name. "Who's Holtzer?"

He looked at me, his eyes wide. "You know him! From Vietnam, that's what he told me."

"What's he doing in Tokyo?"

"He's CIA. Tokyo chief of station."

Chief of station? Unbelievable. He obviously still knew just which asses to kiss.

"You're a damn CIA asset, Benny? You?"

"They pay me," he said, breathing hard. "I needed the money."

"Why is he coming after me?" I asked, searching his eyes. Holtzer and I had tangled when we were in Vietnam, but he'd come out on top in the end. I couldn't see how he'd still be carrying a grudge, even if I still carried mine.

"He said you know where to find a disk. I'm supposed to get it back."

"What disk?"

"I don't know. All I know is that in the wrong hands it would be detrimental to the national security of the United States."

"Try not to sound like the Stepford bureaucrat, Benny. Tell me what's on the disk."

"I don't know! Holtzer didn't tell me. It's need-to-know—you know that, why would he have told me? I'm just an asset, no one tells me these things."

"Who's the guy in my apartment with you?"

"What guy . . . ," he started to say, but I snapped his windpipe shut before he could finish. He tried to suck in air, tried to push me away, but he couldn't. After a few seconds, I eased off the pressure.

"If I have to ask you something twice again, or if you try to lie to me again, Benny, it's going to cost you. Who is the guy in my apartment?"

"I don't know him," he said, squeezing his eyes shut and swallowing. "He's with the Boeicho Boeikyoku. Holtzer handles the liaison. He just told me to take him to your apartment so we could question you."

The Boeicho Boeikyoku, or Bureau of Defense Policy, National Defense Agency, is Japan's CIA.

"Why were you following me in Jinbocho?" I asked.

"Surveillance. Trying to locate the disk."

"How did you find out where I live?"

"Holtzer gave me the address."

"How did he get it?"

"I don't know. He just gave it to me."

"What's your involvement?"

"Questions. Just questions. Finding the disk."

"What were you supposed to do with me after you were done asking me your questions?"

"Nothing. They just want the disk."

I pinched shut his windpipe again. "Bullshit, Benny, not even you could be that stupid. You knew what was going to happen afterwards, even if you wouldn't have the balls to do it yourself."

It was coming together. I could see it. Holtzer tells Benny to take this "Boeikyoku" guy to my apartment to "question" me. Benny figures out what's going to happen. The little bureaucrat is scared, but he's caught in the middle. Maybe he rationalizes that it's not really his affair. Besides, Mr. Boeikyoku would take care of the wet stuff; Benny wouldn't even have to watch.

The cowardly little weasel. I squeezed his balls suddenly and hard, and he would have cried out if I hadn't had the grip on his throat. Then I let go in both places and he spilled to the ground, retching.

"Okay, Benny, here's what you're going to do," I said. "You're going to call your buddy at my apartment. I know he has a cell phone. Tell him you're calling from the subway station. I've been spotted, and he needs to meet you at the station immediately. Use my exact words. If you use your own words or I hear you say anything that doesn't fit with that message, I'll kill you. Do it right, and you can go." Of course, it was always possible that these guys used an all-clear code, the absence of which indicated a problem, but I didn't think they were that smart. Besides, I hadn't heard anything like an all-clear code on the call Benny got in my apartment.

He looked up at me, his eyes pleading. "You'll let me go?"

"If you do this letter-perfect." I handed him his phone.

He did it, just like I told him to. His voice sounded pretty steady. I took the phone back when he was done. He was still looking up at me from his knees. "I can go now?" he said.

Then he saw my eyes. "You promised! You promised!" he panted. "Please, I was only following orders." He actually said it.

"Orders are a bitch," I said, looking down at him.

He was starting to hyperventilate. "Don't kill me! I have a wife and children!"

My hips were already swiveling into position. "I'll

have someone send flowers," I whispered, and blasted the knife edge of my hand into the back of his neck. I felt the vertebrae splinter and he spasmed, then slumped to the ground.

There was nothing I could do but leave him there. But my apartment was already blown. I was going to have to find another, anyway, so the heat the body would bring to Sengoku would be as irrelevant as it was unavoidable.

I stepped over the body and took a few steps back to the parking area I'd passed. I heard the door to my building slam shut.

The front of the parking area was roped off, and the ropes were strung across pylons that were planted in sand. I grabbed a fistful of sand from around one of the pylons and returned to my position at the corner of the wall, peeking out past the edge. I didn't see Benny's buddy. Shit, he'd made a right down the narrow alley connecting my street with the one parallel to it, about fifteen meters from my apartment. I had expected him to stick to the main roads.

This was a problem. He was ahead of me now, and there was nowhere I could set up for him and wait. Besides, I didn't even know what he looked like. If he made it to the main artery by the station, I wouldn't be able to separate him from all the other people. It had to be now.

I sprinted down my street, pulling up short at the alley. I flashed my head past the corner and saw a solitary figure walking away from me.

I scanned the ground, looking for a weapon. Nothing the right size for a club. Too bad.

I turned into the alley, about seven meters behind him. He was wearing a waist-length leather jacket and had a squat, powerful build. Even from behind, I could see that his neck was massive. He was carrying something with him—a cane, it looked like. Not good. The sand had better do the trick.

I had closed the gap to about three meters and was just getting ready to call out to him when he looked back over his shoulder. I hadn't made a sound, and I'd been keeping my eyes off him for the most part and diverting my attention. There's an old, animal part of you that can sense when you're being hunted. I'd learned that in the war. But I'd also learned not to give off the vibrations that set off a person's alarm bells. This guy had sensitive antennae.

He turned and faced me, and I could see the confusion in his expression. Benny had said I'd been spotted at the station. I was coming from the other direction. He was trying to clear the disparity with the central computer.

I saw his ears, puffed out like cauliflowers, disfigured from repeated blows. Japanese *judoka* and *kendoka* don't believe in protective gear; practitioners sometimes wear their scarred lobes, which they develop from head butts in judo and bamboo sword blows in kendo, like badges of honor. Awareness of his possible skills registered at some level of my consciousness.

I used everything I had to project that I was just Joe Pedestrian wanting to go around him, to buy myself the extra second. I moved to the left, took two more steps. Caught the recognition hardening on his face.

Saw the cane start to come up in slow motion, his left foot driving forward to add power to the blow.

I flung the sand in his face and leaped aside. His head recoiled but the cane kept coming up; a split second later it snapped down in a blur. Despite the power of the blow he brought it up short when it failed to connect with his target, and then, with the same fluid speed, he cut through the air horizontally. I moved back diagonally, off the line of attack, staying on my toes. I could see him grimacing, his eyes squeezed shut. The sand had hit him squarely. Keeping his hands from wiping his eyes showed a lot of training. But he couldn't see.

He took a cautious step forward, the cane on guard. Tears were streaming from his wounded eyes. He could tell I was in front of him but he didn't know where.

I had to wait until he was past me to make my move. I'd seen how fast he was with the cane.

He held his position, his nostrils flaring as though he was trying to catch my scent. *Jesus, how is he keeping himself from wiping his eyes?* I thought. *He must be in agony.*

With a loud *kiyai* he leapt forward, slashing horizontally at waist level. But he'd guessed wrong; I was farther back. Then, just as suddenly, he took two long steps backward, his left hand coming loose from the cane and desperately wiping at his eyes.

That's what I'd been waiting for. I plunged in, raising my right fist for a hammer blow to his clavicle. I brought it down hard but at the last instant he shifted slightly, his trapezius muscles taking the impact. I followed with a left elbow strike, trying for the sphenoid but connecting mostly with his ear.

Before I could get in another blow, he had whipped the cane around behind me and grabbed it with his free hand. Then he yanked me into him with a bear hug, the cane slicing into my back. He arched backward and my feet left the ground. My breath was driven out of me. Pain exploded in my kidneys.

I fought the urge to force myself away, knowing that I couldn't match his strength. Instead, I wrapped my arms around his neck and swung my legs up behind his back. The cane felt like it was going to cut through my spine.

The move surprised him and he lost his balance. He took a step backward, releasing the cane and pinwheeling his left arm. I crossed my legs behind his back and dropped my weight suddenly, forcing him to overcorrect and pitch forward onto me. We hit the ground hard. I was underneath and took most of the impact. But now we were in my parlor.

I grabbed a cross grip on the lapels of his jacket and slammed in *gyaku-jujime*, one of the first strangles a *judoka* learns. He reacted instantly, releasing the cane and going for my eyes. I whipped my head back and forth, trying to avoid his fingers, using my legs to control his torso. At one point he grabbed one of my ears but I yanked loose.

The choke wasn't perfect. I had more windpipe than carotid, and he fought for a long time, his groping getting more desperate. But there was nothing he could do. I kept the grip even after he had stopped struggling, rotating my head to see if anyone was coming. Nobody.

When I was sure that we were well past the point

where he could be playing dead, I released the grip and kicked out from under him. Christ, he was heavy. I slid away from him and stood up, my back screaming from the cane, my breath heaving in and out in ragged gasps.

I knew from long experience that he wasn't dead. People black out from strangles in the *dojo* with some regularity; it's not a serious thing. If the unconsciousness is deep, like this one was, then you need to sit them up and slap them on the back, do a little CPR to get them breathing again.

This guy was going to have to find someone else to jump-start his battery. I would have liked to have questioned him, but this was no Benny.

I squatted down, one hand on the ground to steady myself, and went through his pockets. Found a cell phone in the breast pocket of his jacket. Quickly went through his other pockets. Found the pepper spray. Other than that I came up empty.

I stood up, pulses of pain shooting through my back, and started walking toward my apartment. Two schoolgirls in their blue sailor uniforms were passing just as I emerged from the alley and turned left onto my street. Their mouths dropped when they saw me, but I ignored them. Why were they staring like that? I reached up with my hand, felt the wetness on my cheek. Shit, I was bleeding. He'd scratched the hell out of my face.

I walked to my building as quickly as I could, wincing as I went up the two flights of steps. I let myself in, then wet a washcloth at the bathroom sink and wiped some of the blood off my face. The image staring back at me from the mirror looked bad, and it was going to be awhile before it started to look better.

The apartment around me felt strange. It had always been a haven, an anonymous safe house. Now it had been exposed, by Holtzer and the Agency—two ghosts from a past I thought I'd left behind. I needed to know why they were after me. Professional? Personal? With Holtzer, probably both.

I grabbed the things I needed and shoved them into a bag, then headed for the door, turning once to glance around before leaving. Everything looked the same as always; there was no sign of the people who'd been here. I wondered when I would see the place again.

Outside I headed in the direction of Sugamo. From there I could catch the Yamanote line back to Shibuya, back to Midori. Maybe the cell phones would provide some clues.

13

BY THE TIME I reached the hotel, the pain in my back had become a dull throbbing. My left eye was swollen—he'd gotten a finger in there at one point—and my head ached, probably from when he'd tried to tear loose one of my ears.

I shuffled past the old woman at the front desk, flashing my keys as I went by so she'd know I was already registered. She glanced up and then went back to her reading. I tried to give her only my right profile, which was in better shape than the left. She didn't seem to notice my face.

I knocked on the door so Midori would know I was coming and then let myself in with the key.

She was sitting on the bed, and jumped when she saw my swollen eye and the scratches on my face. "What happened?" she gasped, and despite the pain the concern in her voice warmed me.

"Someone was waiting for me at my apartment," I said, locking the door behind me. I let my coat fall off my back and eased myself onto the couch. "It looks like we're both pretty popular lately."

She came over and knelt down next to me, her eyes searching my face. "Your eye looks bad. Let me get you some ice from the freezer."

I watched her walk away from me. She was wearing jeans and a navy sweatshirt that she must have picked up while I was out, and with her hair tied back I had a nice view of the proportions of her shoulders and waist, the curve of her hips. The next thing I knew I was wanting her so much I could almost have forgotten the pain in my back. There was nothing I could do about it. As any soldier who's really been through it can tell you, extreme horniness is a reaction to combat. One second you're fighting for your life, and then when it's over you've got a hard-on the size of Manhattan. I don't know why it happens, but it does.

She came back with some ice in a towel and I shifted on the couch, embarrassed. Electric pain jolted through my back but it didn't make a dent in my predicament. She knelt down again and held the ice against my eye, smoothing my hair back at the same time. Better if she'd just dumped the cubes in my lap.

She eased me back on the couch and I grimaced, intensely aware of how near she was. "Does that hurt?" she asked, her touch instantly becoming tentative.

"No, it's okay. The guy who cut up my face hit me in the back with a cane. It'll be okay."

Midori held the ice against my eye, her free hand warm on the side of my head, while I sat stiffly, afraid to move and embarrassed at my reaction, and the moment spun slowly out.

At one point she shifted the ice, and I reached to take it from her, but she continued to hold it and my hand wound up covering hers. The back of her hand was warm against my palm, the ice cold on my fingertips. "That feels good," I told her. She didn't ask whether I meant the ice or her hand. I wasn't sure myself.

"You were gone for a long time," she said after a while. "I didn't know what to do. I was going to call you, but then I was starting to think, maybe you and those men in my apartment set this up, like good cop, bad cop, to get me to trust you."

"I would have thought the same. I can imagine how this must all seem to you."

"It was starting to seem pretty unreal, actually. Until I saw you again."

I looked at the towel, now speckled red where it had been pressed against my face. "Nothing like a little blood to make things seem real."

"It's true. The thing I kept coming back to was how hard you kicked that man at my apartment—I saw blood shoot from his nose. If I hadn't seen that, I think I would have left while you were gone."

"Makes me glad I caught him in the head."

She laughed softly and pressed the towel against my face again. "Tell me what happened."

"You don't have anything to eat here, do you?" I asked. "I'm starving."

She reached for a bag next to the couch and opened it for me. "I brought back some *bento*. Just in case."

"Give me a few minutes," I said, and started wolfing down rice balls, eggs, and vegetables. I washed it all down with a can of mixed fruit juice. It tasted great.

When I was finished, I shifted on the couch so I

could see her better. "There were two of them at my apartment," I said. "I knew one—an LDP flunky I know only as Benny. Turns out he's connected to the CIA. Would that mean anything to you? Any connection to your father?"

She shook her head. "No. My father never said anything about a Benny or about the CIA."

"Okay. The other guy was a *kendoka*—he had a cane that he used like a sword. I don't know what the connection is. I managed to get both their cell phones. Maybe it'll give me a clue about who he is."

I took the ice from her with one hand and leaned across the couch to reach my coat, feeling angry bites of pain in my back as I did so. I pulled the coat over, reached into the inside breast pocket, and pulled out the phones. Both standard DoCoMo issue, small and sleek. "Benny told me the Agency is after the disk. I don't know why they're coming after me, though. Maybe they think . . . maybe they think I'm going to tell you something, put something together for you? That I can make use of what you've got? Figure out what it is? Prevent them from getting what they want?"

I flipped open the *kendoka*'s phone and pressed the recall button. A number lit up on the screen. "This is a start. We can do a reverse telephone number search. There might be some numbers preprogrammed, also. I've got a friend, someone I trust, who can help us with this."

I stood up, wincing at the pain in my back. "We're going to need to change hotels. Can't behave any differently than the other satisfied patrons."

She smiled. "I suppose that's true."

We changed to a nearby place called the Morocco, which seemed to be organized around some sort of Arabian Nights theme—Oriental rugs, hookahs, belly bracelets, and other harem gear for the woman to wear if she were so inclined. It was the picture of Bedouin luxury, but there was only one bed, and sleeping on the couch was going to be like a night on the rack.

"Why don't you take the bed tonight?" she said, as though reading my mind. "With your back like that, you can't very well sleep on this couch."

"No, that's okay," I told her, feeling strangely embarrassed. "The couch is fine."

"I'll take the couch," she said, with a smile that lingered.

I wound up accepting her offer, but my sleep was restless. I dreamed I was moving though dense jungle near Tchepone in southern Laos, hunted by an NVA counter-recon battalion. I had become separated from my team and was disoriented. I would sideslip and double back, but couldn't shake the NVA. They had me surrounded, and I knew I was going to be captured and tortured. Then Midori was there, trying to get me to take a side arm. "I don't want to be captured," she was saying. "Please, help me. Take the gun. Don't worry about me. Save my Yards."

I snapped upright, my body coiled like a spring. *Easy, John. Just a dream.* I tightened my abdomen and forced a long hiss of air out through my nostrils, feeling like Crazy Jake was right there in the room with me.

My face was wet and I thought it was bleeding

again, but when I put my hand to my cheek and looked at my fingers I realized that it was tears. *What the hell is this?* I thought.

The moon was low in the sky, its light flowing in through the window. Midori was sitting up on the couch, her knees drawn to her chest. "Bad dream?" she asked.

I flicked my thumb across the sides of my face. "How long have you been up?"

She shrugged. "Awhile. You were tossing and turning."

"I say anything?"

"No. Are you afraid of what you might say in your sleep?"

I looked at her, one side of her face illuminated by moonlight, the other hidden in shadow. "Yes," I said.

"What was the dream?" she asked.

"I don't know," I said, lying. "Mostly just images."

I could feel her looking at me. "You tell me to trust you," she said, "but you won't even tell me about a bad dream."

I started to answer, then all at once felt irritated with her. I slid off the bed and walked over to the bathroom.

I don't need her questions, I thought. *I don't need to take care of her. Fucking CIA, Holtzer, knows I'm in Tokyo, knows where I live. I've got enough problems.*

She was the key, I knew. Her father must have told her something. Or she had what whoever had broken into his apartment on the day of his funeral had been looking for. Why couldn't she just realize what the hell it was?

I walked back into the bedroom and stood facing

her. "Midori, you've got to try harder. You've got to remember. Your father must have told you something, or given you something."

I saw surprise on her face. "I told you, he didn't."

"Someone broke into his apartment after he died."

"I know. I got a call from the police when it happened."

"The point is, they couldn't find what they were looking for, and they think you have it."

"Look, if you want to take a look around my father's apartment, I can let you in. I haven't cleaned it out yet, and I still have the key."

The people who had broken in had come up empty, and my old friend Tatsu, as thorough a man as I have ever known, had been there afterward with the resources of the Keisatsucho. I knew another look would be a dead end, and her suggestion only served to increase my frustration.

"That's not going to help. What would these people think that you have? The disk? Something it's hidden in? A key? Are you sure you don't have anything?"

I saw her redden slightly. "I told you, I don't."

"Well, try to remember something, can't you?"

"No, I can't," she said, her voice angry. "How can I remember something if I don't have it?"

"How can you be sure you don't have it if you can't remember it?"

"Why are you saying this? Why don't you believe me?"

"Because nothing else makes sense! And I've got to tell you, I don't like the feeling of people trying to kill me when I don't even know why!"

She swung her feet to the floor and stood up. "Oh,

it's only you! Do you think I like it? I didn't do anything! And I don't know why these people are doing this, either!"

I exhaled slowly, trying to rein in my anger. "It's because they think you have the damn disk. Or you know where it is."

"Well, I don't! *Oai nikusama! Mattaku kokoroattari ga nai wa yo! Mo nan do mo so itteru ja nai yo!*" I don't know anything! I've already told you that!

We stood staring at each other at the foot of the bed, breathing hard. Then she said, "You don't give a shit about me. You're just after what they want, whatever it is."

"That's not true."

"It is true! *Mo ii! Dose anata ga doko no dare na no ka sae oshiete kurenain da kara!*" I've had enough! You won't even tell me who you are! She stalked over to the door and picked up a bag, started shoving her things into it.

"Midori, listen to me." I walked over and grabbed the bag. "Listen to me, goddamnit! I do care about you! Can't you see that?"

She tugged at the bag. "Why should I believe what you say when you don't believe me? I don't know anything! I don't know!"

I yanked the bag out of her hands. "All right, I believe you."

"Like hell you do. Give me my case. Give it to me!" She tried to grab it and I moved it behind my back.

She looked at me, her eyes briefly incredulous, then started hitting me in the chest. I dropped the bag and wrapped my arms around her to stop the blows.

Later, I couldn't remember exactly how it happened. She was fighting me and I was trying to hold her arms. I became very aware of the feel of her body and then we were kissing, and it seemed as though she was still trying to hit me but it was more that we were tearing at each other's clothes.

We made love on the floor at the foot of the bed. The sex was passionate, headlong. At times it was like we were still fighting. My back was throbbing, but the pain was almost sweet.

Afterwards I reached up and pulled the bedcovers over us. We sat with our backs against the edge of the bed.

"*Yokatta,*" she said, drawing out the last syllable. "That was good. Better than you deserved."

I felt a little dazed. It had been a long time for me, a connection like that. It was almost unnerving.

"But you don't trust me," she went on. "That hurts."

"It's not trust, Midori. It's . . . ," I said, then stopped. "I believe you. I'm sorry for pushing so hard."

"I'm talking about your dream."

I pressed my fingertips to my eyes. "Midori, I can't, I don't . . ." I didn't know what the hell to say. "I don't talk about these things. If you weren't there, you couldn't understand."

She reached over and gently pried my fingertips from my eyes, then held them without self-consciousness at her waist. Her skin and her breasts were beautiful in the diffused moonlight, the shadows pooled in the hollows above her clavicles. "You need to talk, I can feel that," she said. "I want you to tell me."

I looked down at the tangled sheets and blankets,

the shadows carving stark hills and valleys like some alien landscape in the moonlight. "My mother . . . she was Catholic. When I was a kid, she used to take me to church. My father hated it. I used to go to confession. I used to tell the priest about all my lascivious thoughts, all the fights I'd been in, the kids I hated and how I wanted to hurt them. At first it was like pulling teeth, but it got addictive.

"But that was all before the war. In the war, I did things . . . that are beyond confession."

"But if you keep them bottled up like this, they'll eat you like poison. They are eating you."

I wanted to talk to her. I wanted to let it out.

What's with you? I thought. *Do you want to drive her away?*

Yeah, maybe that was it. Maybe that would be best. I couldn't tell her about her father, but I could tell her something worse.

When I spoke, my voice was dry and steady. "Atrocities, Midori. I'm talking about atrocities."

Always a good conversation starter. But she stayed with me. "I don't know what you did," she said, "but I know it was a long time ago. In another world."

"It doesn't matter. I can't make you understand, not if you weren't over there." I pressed my fingertips to my eyes again, the reflex useless against the images playing in my mind.

"A part of me loved it, thrived on it. Operating in the NVA's backyard, not everybody could do that. Some guys, when they'd hear the insert helicopters going off into the distance and the jungle go quiet, they'd panic, they couldn't breathe. Not me. I had over twenty missions in Indian country. People would say I had used up all my luck, but I just kept going, and the missions kept getting crazier.

"I was one of the youngest One-Zeros—SOG team leaders—ever. My teammates and I were tight. We could be twelve guys against an NVA division, and I knew that not one of my people would run. And they knew I wouldn't, either. Do you know what that's like, for a kid who's been ostracized his whole life because he's a half-breed?"

I talked faster. "I don't care who you are. If you wade that deeply into the blood and muck, you won't stay clean. Some people are more susceptible than others, but eventually everyone goes over the edge. Two of your people are blown in half by a Bouncing Betty mine, their legs torn from their bodies. You're holding what's left of them in the last moments of their lives, telling them, 'Hey, it's going to be okay, you're going to be okay,' they're crying and you're crying and then they're dead. You walk away, you're covered with their insides.

"You lay your own booby traps for the enemy—that was one of our specialties, tit for tat—but there are only twelve of you and you can't win that kind of war of attrition no matter how much more you bleed them than they bleed you. You take more losses, and the frustration—the rage, the strangling, muscle-bunching rage—just builds and builds. And then one day, you're moving through a village with the power of life and death slung over your shoulder, sweeping back and forth, back and forth, muzzle forward. You're in a declared free-fire zone, meaning anyone who isn't a confirmed friendly is assumed to be Vietcong and treated accordingly. And intel tells you this village is a hotbed of V.C. activity, they're feeding half the sector, they're a conduit for arms that are flowing south down the Trail. The people are giving you sullen looks, and some mama-san says, 'Hey, Joe, you fuck mommie, you number ten,' some shit like that. I mean, you've got the intel. And two hours earlier you lost another buddy to a booby trap. Believe me, someone is going to pay."

I took two deep breaths. "Tell me to stop, or I'm going to keep going."

Midori was silent.

"The village was called Cu Lai. We herded all the people together, maybe forty or fifty people, including women and children. We burned their homes down right in front of them. We shot all their farm animals, massacred the pigs and cows. Effigy, you know? Catharsis. But it wasn't cathartic enough.

"Now what are we supposed to do with these people? I used the radio, even though you're not supposed to because the enemy can triangulate, they can find your position. But what were we supposed to do with these people? We had just destroyed their village.

"The guy on the other end of the radio, I still don't know who, says, 'Waste 'em.' This was the way we described killing back then—so and so got wasted, we wasted ten V.C.

"I'm quiet, and the guy says again, 'Waste 'em.' Now this is unnerving. It's one thing to be on the brink of hot-blooded murder. It's another to have the impulse coolly sanctioned higher up the chain of command. Suddenly I'm scared, realizing how close we had been. I say, 'Waste who?' He says, 'All of 'em. Everybody.' I say, 'We're talking about forty, fifty people here, some women and children, too. Do you understand that?' The guy says again, 'Just waste 'em.' 'Can I have your name and rank?' I say, because suddenly I'm not going to kill all these people just because a voice over the radio tells me to. 'Son,' the voice says, 'I assure you if I told you my rank you'd shit your pants for me. You are in a declared free-fire zone. Now do as I say.'

"I told him I wouldn't do it without being able to verify his authority. Then two more people, who claimed to be this guy's superiors, got on the radio. One of them says, 'You have been given a direct order under the authority of the Commander in Chief of the United States Armed Forces. Obey this order or suffer the consequences.'

"So I went back to the rest of the unit to talk this over. They were guarding the villagers. I told them what I had just heard. For most of the guys, it had the same effect it had on me: it cooled them down, scared them. But some of them it excited. 'No fucking way,' they were saying. 'They're *telling* us to waste 'em? Far out.' Still, everyone was hesitating.

"I had a friend, Jimmy Calhoun, who everyone called Crazy Jake. He hadn't been contributing much to the conversation. All of a sudden he says, 'Fucking pussies. Waste 'em means waste 'em.' He starts yelling at the villagers in Vietnamese. 'Get down, everybody on the ground! *Num suyn!*' And the villagers complied. We were fascinated, wondering what he was going to do. Jimmy doesn't even slow down, he just steps back, shoulders his rifle, then *ka-pop! ka-pop!* he starts shooting them. It was weird; no one tried to run away. Then one of the other guys yells 'Crazy fuckin' Jake!' and shoulders his rifle, too. The next thing I knew we were all unloading our clips into these people, just blowing them apart. Clip runs out, press, slide, click, you put in a new clip and fire some more."

My voice was still steady, my eyes fixed straight ahead, remembering. "If I could go back in time, I would try to stop it. I really would. I wouldn't participate. And the memories dog me. I've been running for twenty-five years, but in the end, it's like trying to lose a shadow."

There was a protracted silence, and I imagined her thinking, *I slept with a monster.*

"I wish you hadn't told me," she said, confirming my suspicions.

I shrugged, feeling empty. "Maybe it's better that you know."

She shook her head. "That's not what I meant. It's an upsetting story. Upsetting to hear what you've been through. I never thought of war as so . . . personal."

"Oh, it was personal. On both sides. There were special medals for NVA—North Vietnamese Army soldiers—who killed an American. A severed head was the proof. If it was a SOG man you killed, you'd get an extra ten thousand piastres—several months' pay."

She touched my face again, and I saw a deep sympathy in her eyes. "You were right. You've been through horrors. I didn't know."

I took her hands and gently moved them away. "Hey, I didn't even tell you the best part. The intel on the village being a V.C. stronghold? Bogus. No tunnel networks, no rice or weapons caches."

"*Sonna, sonna koto. . . ,*" she said. "You mean . . . but, John, you didn't know."

I shrugged. "Not even any telltale tire tracks, which, c'mon, we could have taken a second to check for before we started slaughtering people."

"But you were so young. You must have been out of your minds with fear, with anger."

I could feel her looking at me. It was okay. After all this time, the words sounded dead to me, just sounds without content.

"Is that what you meant that first night?" she asked. "About not being a forgiving person?"

I remembered saying it to her, remembered her looking like she was going to ask me about it, then seeming to decide not to. "It's not what I meant, actually. I was thinking of other people, not of myself. But I guess it applies to me, also."

She nodded slowly, then said, "I have a friend from Chiba named Mika. When I was in New York, she had a car accident. She hit a little girl who was playing in the street. Mika was driving at forty-five kilometers per hour, the speed limit, and the little girl drove her bicycle out right in front of the car. There was nothing she could do. It was bad luck. It would have happened to anyone who was driving the car right there and right then."

On a certain level, I understood what she was getting at. I'd known it all along, even before the psych evaluation they made me take at one point to see how I was handling the special stress of SOG. The shrink they made me talk to had said the same thing: "How can you blame yourself for circumstances that were beyond your control?"

I remember that conversation. I remember listening to his bullshit, half angry, half amused at his attempts to draw me out. Finally, I just said to him, "Have you ever killed anyone, Doc?" When he didn't answer, I walked out. I don't know what kind of evaluation he gave me. But they didn't turn me loose from SOG. That came later.

"Do you still work with these people?" she asked.

"There are connections," I responded.

"Why?" she asked after a moment. "Why stay attached to things that give you nightmares?"

I glanced over at the window. The moon had moved higher in the sky, its light slowly ebbing from the room. "It's a hard thing to explain," I said slowly. I watched her hair glistening in the pale light, like a vertical sheet of water. I ran my fingers through it, gathered it in my hand and let it fall free. "Some of what I was part of in Vietnam didn't sit well with me when I got back to the States. Some things belong only in a war zone, but then they want to follow you when you leave. After the war, I found I couldn't go back to the life I'd left behind. I wanted to come back to Asia, because Asia was where my ghosts were least restless, but it was more than just geography. All the things I'd done made sense in war, they were justified by war, I couldn't live with them outside of war. So I needed to stay at war."

Her eyes were pools of darkness. "But you can't stay at war forever, John."

I gave her a wan smile. "A shark can't stop swimming, or it dies."

"You're not a shark."

"I don't know what I am." I rubbed my temples with my fingers, trying to work through the images, past and present, that were colliding in my brain. "I don't know."

We were quiet for a while, and I felt a pleasant drowsiness descend. I was going to regret all this. Some lucid part of my mind saw that clearly. But sleep seemed so much more urgent, and anyway what was done was already done.

I slept, but the pain in my back kept the sleep fitful, and in those moments where consciousness briefly crested I would have doubted everything that had happened if she hadn't been lying next to me. Then I would slide down into sleep again, there to struggle with ghosts even more personal, more terrible, than those of which I could tell Midori.

PART TWO

When your sword meets that of your enemy, you can never waver, but must instead attack with the complete resolution of your whole body . . .

—MIYAMOTO MUSASHI, *A Book of Five Rings*

14

THE NEXT MORNING I was sitting with my back to the wall at my favorite vantage point in Las Chicas, waiting for Franklin Bulfinch to show himself.

It was a crisp, sunny morning, and between the bright light streaming through the windows and the overall hip atmosphere on which Las Chicas prides itself, I felt comfortable in my light-disguise knockoff Oakley shades, which I had picked up en route.

Midori was safely ensconced in the music section of the nearby Spiral Building on Aoyama-dori, close enough to meet Bulfinch quickly if necessary but far enough to be safe if things got hairy. She had called Bulfinch less than an hour earlier to arrange things. Most likely he was a legitimate reporter and would come to the meeting alone, but I saw no advantage in giving him time to deploy additional forces if I was mistaken.

Bulfinch was easy to spot as he approached the restaurant, the same tall, thin guy in wireless glasses I had seen on the train. He had a long stride and an erect, confident posture, and again struck me as having an aristocratic air. He was wearing jeans and tennis shoes, dressed up with a blue blazer. He crossed the patio and stepped inside the restaurant proper, pausing to look right, then left, searching for Midori. His eyes passed over me without recognition.

He wandered back in the direction of the rest room, presumably checking the separate dining space in the back of the building. I knew he'd be back in a moment, and used the time to watch the street a little longer. He'd been followed at Alfie, and it was possible that he was being followed now.

The street was still empty when Bulfinch returned to the front of the restaurant a minute later. His eyes swept the space again. When they were pointed in my direction, I said quietly, "Mr. Bulfinch."

He looked at me for a second before saying, "Do I know you?"

"I'm a friend of Midori Kawamura. She asked me to come in her stead."

"Where is she?"

"She's in some danger right now. She needs to take care in her movements."

"Is she coming here?"

"That depends."

"On what?"

"On whether I decide that it's safe."

"Who are you?"

"As I said, a friend, interested in the same thing you are."

"Which is?"

I looked at him through my shades. "The disk."

He paused before saying, "I don't know about a disk."

Right. "You were expecting Midori's father to deliver you a disk when he died on the Yamanote three weeks ago. He didn't have it with him, so you followed up with Midori after her performance at Alfie the following Friday. You met her in the Starbucks on Gaienhigashi-dori, near Almond in Roppongi. That's where you told her about the disk, because you hoped she might have it. You wouldn't tell her what's on the disk because you were afraid doing so would compromise her. Although you had already compromised her by showing up at Alfie, because you were followed. All of which will be sufficient, I hope, to establish my bona fides."

He made no move to sit. "You could have learned most of that without Midori telling you, and filled in the gaps by educated guessing—especially if you were the one following me."

I shrugged. "And then I imitated her voice and called you an hour ago?"

He hesitated, then walked over and sat, his back straight and his hands on the table. "All right. What can you tell me?"

"I was going to ask you the same question."

"Look, I'm a reporter. I write stories. Do you have information for me?"

"I need to know what's on that disk."

"You keep talking about a disk."

"Mr. Bulfinch," I said, focusing for an instant on the street, which was still empty, "the people who want that disk think that Midori has it, and they are more than willing to kill her to retrieve it. Your meeting her at Alfie while you were being watched is probably

what put her in the danger she's in. So let's stop fucking around, okay?"

He took off his glasses and sighed. "Assuming for a
moment there is a disk, I don't see how knowledge of
what's on it would help Midori."

"You're a reporter. I assume you would be interested
in publishing the hypothetical disk's contents?"

"You could assume that, yes."

"And I would also assume that certain people
would want to prevent that publication?"

"That would also be a safe assumption."

"Okay, then. It's the threat of publication that's making these people target Midori. Once the contents of
the disk are published, Midori would no longer be a
threat, is that right?"

"What you're saying makes sense."

"Then it seems we want the same thing. We both
want the contents of the disk published."

He shifted in his seat. "I see your point. But I'm not
going to be comfortable talking about this unless I see
Midori."

I considered for a moment. "Are you carrying a cell
phone?"

"Yes."

"Show it to me."

He reached into the left side of the blazer and withdrew a small flip-top unit.

"That's fine," I said. "Go ahead and put it back in
your pocket." As he did so, I pulled out a pen and
small sheet of paper from my own jacket pocket and
started jotting down instructions. My gut told me he
wasn't wired, but no one's gut is infallible.

"Until I say otherwise, under no circumstances do I want to see you reaching for that phone," my note read. "We'll walk out of the restaurant together. When we step outside, stop so I can pat you down for weapons. After that, go where I motion you to go. At some point I'll let you know that I want you to start walking ahead, and at some point I'll tell you where we're going. If you have questions now, write them down. If you don't, just hand back this note. Starting now, do not say a word unless I speak first."

I extended the note to him. He took it with one hand while slipping on his glasses with the other. When he was done reading, he pushed it across the table to me and nodded.

I folded the note up and put it back in my jacket pocket, followed by the pen. Then I placed a thousand-yen note on the table to cover the coffee I had been drinking and motioned him to leave.

We got up and walked outside. I patted him down and was unsurprised to find that he was clean. As we moved down the street I was careful to keep him slightly in front of me and to the side, a human shield if it came to that. I knew every good spot in the area for surveillance or an ambush, and my head swept back and forth, looking for someone out of place, someone who might have followed Bulfinch to the restaurant and then set up to wait outside it.

As we walked I called out "left" or "right" from behind him by way of directions, and we made our way to the Spiral Building. We walked through the glass doors and into the music section, where Midori was waiting.

"Kawamura-san," he said, bowing, when he saw her. "Thank you for your call."

"Thank you for coming to meet me," Midori replied. "I'm afraid I wasn't completely candid with you when we met for coffee. I'm not as ignorant of my father's affiliations as I led you to believe. But I don't know anything about the disk you mentioned. No more than you told me, anyway."

"I'm not sure what I can do for you, then," he said.

"Tell us what's on the disk," I replied.

"I don't see how that would help you."

"I don't see how it could hurt us," I answered. "Right now we're running blind. If we put our heads together, we've got a much better chance of retrieving the disk than we do if we work separately."

"Please, Mr. Bulfinch," Midori said. "I barely escaped being killed a few days ago by whoever is trying to find that disk. I need your help."

Bulfinch grimaced and looked at Midori and then at me, his eyes sweeping back and forth several times. "All right," he said after a moment. "Two months ago your father contacted me. He told me he read my column for *Forbes*. He told me who he was and said he wanted to help. A classic whistle-blower."

Midori turned to me. "That was about the time he was diagnosed."

"I'm sorry?" Bulfinch asked.

"Lung cancer. He had just learned that he had little time to live," Midori said.

Bulfinch nodded, understanding. "I see. I didn't know that. I'm sorry."

Midori bowed her head briefly, accepting his solicitude. "Please, go on."

"Over the course of the next month I had several clandestine meetings with your father, during which he briefed me extensively on corruption in the Construction Ministry and its role as broker between the Liberal Democratic Party and the *yakuza*. These briefings provided me with invaluable insight into the nature and extent of corruption in Japanese society. But I needed corroboration."

"What corroboration?" I asked. "Can't you just print it and attribute it to 'a senior source in the Construction Ministry'?"

"Ordinarily, yes," Bulfinch replied. "But there were two problems here. First, Kawamura's position in the Ministry gave him unique access to the information he was providing me. If we had published the information, we might as well have used his name in the byline."

"And the second problem?" Midori asked.

"Impact," Bulfinch answered. "We've already run a half dozen exposés on the kind of corruption Kawamura was involved in. The Japanese press resolutely refuses to pick them up. Why? Because the politicians and bureaucrats pass and interpret laws that can make or break domestic corporations. And the corporations provide over half the media's advertising revenues. So if, for example, a newspaper runs an article that offends a politician, the politician calls his contacts at the relevant corporations, who pull their advertising from the newspaper and transfer it to a rival publication, and the offending paper goes bankrupt. You see?

"If you have a reporter investigate a story from outside the government-sponsored *kisha* news clubs, you get shut down. If you play ball, the money keeps rolling in, licit and illicit. No one here takes chances; everyone treats the truth like a contagious disease. Christ, Japan's press is the most docile in the world."

"But with proof . . . ?" I asked.

"Hard proof would change everything. The papers would be forced to cover the story or else reveal that they are nothing but tools of the government. And flushing the corrupt kingpins out into the open would weaken them and embolden the press. We could start a virtuous cycle that would lead to a change in Japanese politics the likes of which the country hasn't seen since the Meiji restoration."

"I think you may be overestimating the zeal of domestic media," Midori said.

Bulfinch shook his head. "Not at all. I know some of these people well. They're good reporters, they want to publish. But they're realists, too."

"The proof," I said. "What was it?"

Bulfinch looked at me over the tops of his wireless glasses. "I don't know exactly. Only that it's hard evidence. Incontrovertible."

"It sounds like that disk should go to the Keisatsu-cho, not the press," Midori said, referring to Tatsu's investigative organization.

"Your father wouldn't have lasted a day if he'd handed that information over to the feds," I said, saving Bulfinch the trouble.

"That's right," Bulfinch said. "Your father wasn't the

first person to try to blow the whistle on corruption. Ever hear of Honma Tadayo?"

Ah, yes, Honma-san. A sad story.

Midori shook her head.

"When Nippon Credit Bank went bankrupt in 1998," Bulfinch went on, "at least thirty-six billion dollars, and probably much more, of its one-hundred-thirty-three-billion-dollar loan portfolio had gone bad. The bad loans were linked to the underworld, even to illegal payments to North Korea. To clean up the mess, a consortium of rescuers hired Honma Tadayo, the respected former director of the Bank of Japan. Honma-san became president of NCB in early September and started working through the bank's books, trying to bring to light the full extent of its bad debts and understand where and why they had been extended in the first place.

"Honma lasted two weeks. He was found hanged in an Osaka hotel room, with notes addressed to his family, company, and others nearby. His body was quickly cremated, without an autopsy, and the Osaka police ruled the death a suicide without even conducting an investigation.

"And Honma wasn't an isolated event. His death was the seventh 'suicide' among ranking Japanese either investigating financial irregularities or due to testify about irregularities since 1997, when the depth of bad loans affecting banks like Nippon Credit first started coming to light. There was also a member of parliament who was about to talk about irregular fund-raising activities, another Bank of Japan director who oversaw small financial institutions, an investigator at the Financial Supervision Agency, and the head of the small and medium financial institutions division at the Ministry of Finance. Not one of these seven cases resulted in so much as a homicide investigation. The powers that be in this country don't allow it."

I thought of Tatsu and his conspiracy theories, my eyes unblinking behind my shades.

"There are rumors of a special outfit within the *yakuza*," Bulfinch said, taking off his glasses and wiping the lenses on his shirt, "specialists in 'natural causes,' who visit victims at night in hotel rooms, force them to write wills at gunpoint, inject them with sedatives, then strangle them in a way that makes it appear that the victim committed suicide by hanging."

"Have you found any substance to the rumors?" I asked.

"Not yet. But where there's smoke, there's fire."

He held his glasses up above his head and examined them, then returned them to his face. "And I'll tell you something else. As bad as the problems are in the banks, the Construction Ministry is worse. Construction is the biggest employer in Japan—it puts the rice on one out of every six Japanese tables. The industry is by far the biggest contributor to the LDP. If you want to dig this country's corruption out by the roots, construction is the place to start. Your father was a brave man, Midori."

"I know," she said.

I wondered if she still assumed the heart attack had been from natural causes. The building was starting to feel warm.

"I've told you what I know," Bulfinch said. "Now it's your turn."

I looked at him through the shades. "Can you think of any reason that Kawamura would have gone to meet you that morning but not brought the disk?"

Bulfinch paused before saying "No."

"The plan that morning was definitely to do the handoff?"

"Yes. As I said, we'd had a number of previous deep background meetings. This was the morning Kawamura was going to deliver the goods."

"Maybe he couldn't get access to the disk, couldn't download whatever he was going to download that day, and that's why he was coming up empty-handed."

"No. He told me over the phone the day before that he had it. All he had to do was hand it over."

I felt a flash of insight. I turned to Midori. "Midori, where did your father live?" Of course I already knew, but couldn't let her know that.

"Shibuya."

"Which *chome*?" *Chome* are small subdivisions within Tokyo's various wards.

"San-chome."

"Top of Dogenzaka, then? Above the station?"

"Yes."

I turned to Bulfinch. "Where was Kawamura getting on the train that morning?"

"Shibuya JR Station."

"I've got a hunch I'm going to follow up on. I'll call you if it pans out."

"Wait just a minute . . . ," he started to say.

"I know this isn't comfortable for you," I said, "but you're going to have to trust me. I think I can find that disk."

"How?"

"As I said, I've got a hunch." I started to move toward the door.

"Wait," he said again. "I'll go with you."

I shook my head. "I work alone."

He took me by the arm and said again, "I'll go with you."

I looked at his hand on my arm. After a moment it drifted back to his side.

"I want you to walk out of here," I told him. "Head in the direction of Omotesando-dori. I'm going to get Midori someplace safe and follow up on my hunch. I'll be in touch."

He looked at Midori, clearly at a loss.

"It's all right," she said. "We want the same thing you do."

"I don't suppose I have much choice," he said, looking at me with a glare that was meant to convey resentment. But I saw what he was really thinking.

"Mr. Bulfinch," I said, my voice low, "don't try to follow me. I would spot you if you did. I would not react as a friend."

"For Christ's sake, tell me what you're thinking. I might be able to help."

"Remember," I said, gesturing to the street, "the direction of Omotesando-dori. I'll be in touch soon."

"You'd better be," he said. He took a step closer and looked through the shades and into my eyes, and I had to admire his balls. "You just better." He gave a nod to

Midori and walked through the glass doors of the Spiral Building and out onto the street.

Midori looked at me and asked, "What's your hunch?"

"Later," I said, watching him through the glass. "We need to move now, before he gets a chance to double back and follow one of us. Let's go."

We walked out and immediately flagged a cab heading in the direction of Shibuya. I could see Bulfinch, still walking in the other direction, as we got in and drove away.

We got out and separated at Shibuya JR Station. Midori headed back to the hotel while I made my way up Dogenzaka—where Harry and I had followed Kawamura that morning that now seemed like so long ago, where, if my hunch was right, Kawamura had ditched the disk the morning he died.

I was thinking about Kawamura, about his behavior that morning, about what must have been going on in his mind.

More than anything else he's scared. Today's the day; he's got the disk that's going to flush all the rats out in the open. It's right there in his pocket. It's small and almost weightless, of course, but he's intensely aware of its presence, this object that he knows will cost him his few remaining days if he's caught with it. In less than an hour he'll meet Bulfinch and unload the damn thing, and thank God for that.

What if I'm being followed right now? he would think. *What if they find me with the disk?* He starts looking over his shoulder. Stops to light a cigarette, turns and scans the street.

Someone behind him looks suspicious. Why not?

When you're hopped up on fear, the whole world is transformed. A tree looks like an NVA regular down to the details—the dark uniform, the Kalishnikov. Every guy in a suit looks like the government assassin who's going to reach into your pocket, take out the disk, and smile as he raises the gun to your forehead.

Get rid of the damn thing, and let Bulfinch retrieve it himself. Anywhere, anywhere at all . . . there, the Higashimura fruit store, that'll do.

I stopped outside the store's small door and looked at the sign over it. This was where he had ducked into that morning. If it wasn't here, it could be anywhere. But if he had unloaded it on his way to see Bulfinch, this was the place.

I walked in. The proprietor, a short man with defeated-looking eyes and skin the hue of a lifetime of tobacco, looked up and acknowledged me with a tired *"irrashaimase,"* then went back to reading his *manga*. The store was small and rectangular, and the proprietor had a view of the whole place. Kawamura would have been able to hide the disk only in places where a patron could acceptably put his hands. He would be moving quickly, too. As far as he was concerned, it would only need to stay hidden for an hour or so, anyway, so he didn't have to find an incredibly secure spot.

Which meant it was probably already gone, I realized. It wouldn't still be here. But I had nothing else to go on. It was worth a try.

Apples. I had seen an apple rolling out of the train car as the doors had closed.

There was a selection of Fujis, polished and beauti-

ful in their netted Styrofoam half blankets, at the farthest corner of the store. I imagined Kawamura
strolling over, examining the apples, slipping the disk
under them as he did so.

I walked over and looked. The bin was only a few
apples deep, and it was easy for me to search for the
disk simply by moving around the apples, as though I
was trying to select just the right one.

No disk. Shit.

I repeated the drill with the adjacent pears, then the
tangerines. Nothing.

Damn it. It had felt right. I had been so sure.

I was going to have to buy something to complete
the charade. I was obviously a discriminating buyer,
looking for something special.

"Could you put together a small selection as a gift?"
I asked the owner. "Maybe a half dozen pieces of fruit,
including a small musk melon."

"*Kashikomarimashita,*" he answered with a wan attempt at a smile. Right away.

As he went about carefully assembling the gift, I
continued my search. In the five minutes during which
the proprietor was preoccupied with my request, I was
able to check every place to which Kawamura would
have had access that morning. It was useless.

The proprietor was just about finished. He pulled
out a green moiré ribbon and wrapped it twice
around the box he had used, finishing it in a simple
bow. It was actually a nice gift. Maybe Midori would
enjoy it.

I took out some bills and handed them over. *What
were you hoping for, anyway?* I thought. *Kawamura*

wouldn't have had time to hide it well. Even if he tried to ditch it in here, someone would have found it by now.

Someone would have found it.

He was counting out my change with the same slow approach that he had employed in creating the fruit basket. Definitely a careful man. Methodical.

I waited for him to finish, then said in Japanese, "Excuse me. I know it's not likely, but a friend of mine lost a CD in here a week or so ago and asked me to check to see if anyone had found it. It's so unlikely that I hesitated to bring it up, but . . ."

"*Un,*" he grunted, kneeling down behind the counter. He stood up a moment later, a generic plastic jewel box in his hand. "I wondered whether anyone would claim this." He wiped it off with a few listless strokes of his apron and handed it to me.

"Thank you," I said, not a little bit surprised. "My friend will be happy."

"Good for him," he said, and his eyes filmed over again.

15

AT FIRST LIGHT the whole of Shibuya feels like a giant sleeping off a hangover. You can still sense the merriment, the heedless laughter of the night before, you can hear it echoed in the strange silences and deserted spaces of the area's twisting backstreets. The drunken voices of karaoke revelers, the unctuous pitches of the club touts, the secret whispers of lovers walking arm in arm, all are departed, but somehow, for just a few evanescent hours in the quiet of early morning, their shadows linger, like ghosts who refuse to believe that the night has ended, that there are no more parties to attend.

I walked, in the company of those ghosts, following a series of alleys that more or less paralleled Meiji-dori, the main artery connecting Shibuya and Aoyama. I had gotten up early, easing out of the bed as quietly as I could to let Midori sleep. She had awakened anyway.

I had taken the disk to Akihabara, Tokyo's electronics Mecca, where I tried to play it on a PC in one of the enormous, anonymous computer stores. No dice. It was encrypted.

Which meant that I needed Harry's help. The realization wasn't comfortable: given Bulfinch's description of the disk's contents—that it contained evidence of an assassin or assassins specializing in natural causes—I knew that what was on the disk could implicate me.

I called Harry from a pay phone in Nogizaka. He sounded groggy and I figured he'd been sleeping, but I could feel him become alert when I mentioned the construction work going on in Kokaigijidomae—our signal for an immediate, emergency meeting. I used our usual code to tell him that I wanted to meet at the Doutor coffee shop on Imoarai-zaka in Roppongi. It was near his apartment, so he would be able to get there fast.

He was already waiting when I arrived twenty minutes later, sitting at a table in back, reading a paper. His hair was matted down on one side of his head and he looked pale. "Sorry to get you up," I said, sitting across from him.

He shook his head. "What happened to your face?"

"Hey, you should see the other guy. Let's order some breakfast."

"I think I'll just have coffee."

"You don't want eggs or something?"

"No, just coffee is good."

"Sounds like it was a rough night," I said, imagining what that would consist of for Harry.

He looked at me. "You're scaring me with the small talk. I know you wouldn't have used the code unless it was something serious."

"You wouldn't forgive me for getting you up otherwise," I said.

We ordered coffee and breakfast and I filled him in

on everything that had happened since the last time I saw him, beginning with how I met Midori, through the attack outside her apartment and then mine, the meeting with Bulfinch, the disk. I didn't tell him about the previous night. I just told him we were using a love hotel as a safe house.

Looking at him there, feeling his concern, I realized I trusted him. Not just because I knew that, operationally, he had no way to hurt me, which was my usual reason for extending some minimal measure of trust, but because he was worthy of trust. And because I wanted to trust him.

"I'm in a bit of a tight spot here," I told him. "I could use your help. But . . . you're going to need to know some fairly deep background first. If that's not comfortable for you, all you need to do is say so."

He reddened slightly, and I knew that it would mean a lot to him that I would ask for his help, that I needed him. "It's comfortable," he said.

I told him about Holtzer and Benny, the apparent CIA connection.

"I wish you'd told me earlier," he said when I was done. "I might have been able to do more to help."

I shrugged. "The less you know, the less I have to worry about you."

He nodded. "Typical CIA outlook."

"Takes one to know one."

"No, no. Remember, I worked at the Puzzle Palace. It's the Agency types who turn paranoia into a point of pride. Anyway, why would I want to hurt you?"

"Just being careful, kid," I said. "It's nothing personal."

"You saved my butt that time in Roppongi, remember? You think I'd forget that?"

"You'd be surprised what people forget."

"Not me. Anyway, has it occurred to you how much I'm trusting you by letting you share this information with me, letting you make me a potential point of vulnerability? I know how careful you are, and I know what you're capable of."

"I'm not sure I understand what you mean," I said.

He looked at me for a long time before he responded. "I've kept your secrets for a long time. I'll continue to keep them. Fair enough?"

Never underestimate Harry, I thought, nodding.

"Fair enough?" he asked again.

"Yes," I said, not having anywhere else to go. "Now, enough of the I'm-okay-you're-okay routine. Let's work the problem. Start with Holtzer."

"Tell me more about how you know him."

"Not right after I've eaten."

"That bad, huh?"

I shrugged. "I knew him in Vietnam. He was with the Agency then, attached to SOG, a joint CIA-military Special Operations Group. He's got balls, I'll give him credit for that. He wasn't afraid to go into the field, unlike some of the other bean counters I worked with out there. I liked that about him when I first met him. But even then he was nothing but a careerist. The first time we locked horns was after an ARVN—Army of the Republic of Vietnam, the South's army—operation in Military Region Three. The ARVN had mortared the shit out of a suspected Vietcong base in Tay Ninh, based on intelligence from a source that Holtzer had developed. So we were involved in the body count, as a way of verifying the intelligence.

"The ARVN had really pounded the place, and it was hard to identify the bodies—there were pieces everywhere. But there were no weapons. I told Holtzer this didn't look like Vietcong activity to me. He says, What are you talking about? This is Tay Ninh, everyone here is Vietcong. I say, Come on, there aren't any weapons, your source was jerking you off. There was a mistake. He says no mistake, there must be two dozen enemy dead. But he's counting every blown-off limb as a separate body.

"Back at base, he writes up his report and asks me to verify it. I told him to fuck off. There were a couple officers nearby, out of earshot but close enough to see us. It got heated, and I wound up laying him out. The officers saw it, which is exactly what Holtzer had wanted, although I don't think he bargained for the rhinoplasty he needed afterward. Ordinarily that kind of thing wouldn't have aroused much attention, but at the time there was some sensitivity to the way Special Forces and the CIA were cooperating in the field, and Holtzer knew how to work the bureaucracy. He made it sound like I wouldn't verify his report because I had a personal problem with him. I wonder how many subsequent S&D operations were based on intelligence from his so-called fucking source."

I took a swallow of coffee. "He caused a lot of problems for me after that. He's the kind of guy who knows just which ears to whisper in, and I've never been good at that game. When I got back from the war I had some kind of black cloud over me, and I always knew he was the one behind it, even if I couldn't catch him pulling the strings."

"You never told me about what happened in the States after the war," Harry said after a moment. "Is that why you left?"

"Part of it." The terseness of my reply was meant to indicate that I didn't want to go there, and Harry understood.

"What about Benny?" he asked.

"All I know about him is that he was connected to the LDP—an errand boy, but trusted with some important errands. And that apparently he was also a mole for the CIA."

The word *mole* felt unpleasant in my mouth. It is still one of the foulest epithets I know.

For six years, SOG's operations in Laos, Cambodia, and North Vietnam were compromised by a mole. Time and again, a team would be inserted successfully, only to be picked up within minutes by North Vietnamese patrols. Some of these missions had been death traps, with entire SOG platoons wiped out. But others were successful, which meant that the mole had limited access. If an investigator could have compared dates and access, we could have quickly narrowed down the list of suspects.

But MACV—the U.S. Military Assistance Command, Vietnam—refused to investigate due to sensitivities about "counterpart relationships"—that is, they were afraid of insulting the South Vietnamese government by suggesting that a South Vietnamese national attached to MACV might have been less than reliable. Worse, SOG was ordered to continue to share its data with the ARVN. We tried to get around the command by issuing false insert coordinates to our Vietnamese counterparts, but MACV found out and there was hell to pay.

In 1972, a traitorous ARVN corporal was uncovered, but this single, low-level agent couldn't possibly have been the only source of damage for all those years. The real mole was never discovered.

I took Benny's and the *kendoka's* cell phones from my jacket pocket and handed them to Harry. "I need two things from you. Check out the numbers that have been called. They should be stored in the phones." I showed him which unit had belonged to the *kendoka*, and which to Benny. "See if there are any numbers speed-dial programmed, too, and try chasing them all down with a reverse directory. I want to know who these guys were talking to, how they were connected to each other and to the Agency."

"No problem," he said. "I'll get you something by the end of the day."

"Good. Now the second thing." I took out the disk and put it on the table. "What everybody is after is on this disk. Bulfinch says it's an exposé on corruption in the LDP and the Construction Ministry that could bring down the government."

He picked it up and held it up to the light.

"Why a disk?" he said.

"I was going to ask you the same question."

"Don't know. It would have been easier to move whatever's on here over the Net. Maybe a copy management program prevented that. I'll check it out." He slipped it inside his jacket.

"Could that be how they knew we were on to Kawamura?" I asked.

"What do you mean?"

"How they found out that he'd made the disk."

"Could be. There are copy management programs that will tell you if a copy has been made."

"It's encrypted, too. I tried to run it but couldn't. Why would Kawamura have encrypted it?"

"I doubt that he did. He probably wasn't supposed to have access. Someone else would have encrypted it, whoever he took it from."

That made sense. I still didn't understand why Benny had put me on Kawamura weeks earlier, though. They must have had some other way of knowing that he had been talking to Bulfinch. Maybe telephone taps, something like that.

"Okay," I said. "Page me when you're done. We'll meet back here—just input a time that's good for you. Use the usual code."

He nodded and got up to leave. "Harry," I said. "Don't be cocky now. There are people who, if they knew you had that disk, would kill you to get it back."

He nodded. "I'll be careful."

"Careful's not good enough. Be paranoid. You don't trust anyone."

"Almost anyone," he said with a slightly exasperated pursing of the lips that might have been a grin.

"No one," I said, thinking of Crazy Jake.

After he'd left I called Midori from a pay phone. We had switched to a new hotel that morning. She answered on the first ring.

"Just wanted to check in," I told her.

"Can your friend help us?" she asked. I had told her to watch what she said over the phone, and she was choosing her words carefully.

"Too early to tell. He's going to try."

"When are you coming?"

"I'm on my way now."

"Do me a favor, get me something to read. A novel, some magazines. I should have thought of it when I went out for something to eat before. There's nothing to do in this room and I'm going crazy."

"I'll stop someplace on the way. See you in a little bit."

Her tone was less strained than it had been when I first told her I had found the disk. She had wanted to know how, and I wouldn't tell her. Obviously couldn't.

"I was retained by a party that wanted it," I finally said. "I didn't know what was on it at the time. I obviously didn't know the lengths they would go to in trying to get it."

"Who was the party?" she had insisted.

"Doesn't matter" was my response. "All you need to know is that I'm trying to be part of the solution now, okay? Look, if I wanted to give it to the party that paid me to find it, I wouldn't be here with it right now, discussing it with you. That's all I'm going to say."

Not knowing my world, she had no reason to doubt that Kawamura's heart attack had been due to something other than natural causes. If it had been anything other than that—a bullet, even a fall from a building—I knew I would be suspect.

I headed to Suidobashi, where I began a thorough SDR by catching the JR line to Shinjuku. I changed trains at Yoyogi and watched to see who got off with me, then waited on the platform after the train left. I let two trains pass at Yoyogi before I got back on, and one stop later I exited at the east end of Shinjuku Station, the older, teeming counterpart to sanitized, government-occupied west Shinjuku. I was still wearing sunglasses to hide my swollen eye, and the dark tint gave the frenzied crowds a slightly ghostly look. I let the mob carry me through one of the mazelike underground shopping arcades until I was outside the Virgin Megastore, then fought my way across the arcade to the Isetan Department Store, feeling like a man trying to ford a strong river. I decided to buy Midori an oversized navy cashmere scarf and a pair of sunglasses with wraparound lenses that I thought would change the shape of her face. Paid for them at different registers so no one would think the guy in the sunglasses was buying a neat disguise for the woman in his life.

Finally, I stopped at Kinokuniya, about fifty meters down from Isetan, where I plunged into crowds so thick they made the arcade seem desolate by comparison. I picked up a couple of magazines and a novel from the Japanese best-seller section and walked over to the register to pay.

I was waiting in line, watching to see who was emerging from the stairway and escalator, when my pager starting vibrating in my pocket. I reached down and pulled it out, expecting to see a code from Harry. Instead the display showed an eight-digit number with a Tokyo prefix.

I paid for the magazines and the book and took the

stairs back to the first floor, then walked over to a pay phone on a side street near Shinjuku-dori. I inserted a hundred-yen coin and punched in the number, glancing over my shoulder while the connection went through.

I heard someone pick up on the other end. "John Rain," a voice said in English. I didn't respond at first, and the voice repeated my name.

"I think you've got the wrong number."

There was a pause. "My name is Lincoln."

"That's cute."

"The chief wants to meet with you."

I understood then that the caller was with the Agency, that the chief was Holtzer. I waited to see if Lincoln was going to add something, but he didn't. "You must be joking," I said.

"I'm not. There's been a mistake and he wants to explain. You can name the time and the place."

"I don't think so."

"You need to hear what he has to say. Things aren't what you think they are."

I glanced back in the direction of Kinokuniya, weighing the risks and possible advantages.

"He'll have to meet me right now," I said.

"Impossible. He's in a meeting. He can't get free before tonight, at the earliest."

"I don't care if he's having open-heart surgery. You tell him this, Abe. If he wants to meet me, I'll be waiting for him in Shinjuku in twenty minutes. If he's one minute late, I'm gone."

There was a long pause. Then he asked, "Where in Shinjuku?"

"Tell him to walk out the east exit of Shinjuku JR Station directly toward the Studio Alta sign. And tell him that if he's wearing anything besides pants, shoes, and a short-sleeved T-shirt, he'll never see me. Okay?" I wanted to make it as hard as possible for Holtzer to conceal a readily accessible weapon, if that's what he was planning to do.

"I understand."

"Exactly twenty minutes," I said, and hung up.

There were two possibilities. One, Holtzer might have something legitimate to say, the chances of which were remote. Two, this was just an attempt to reacquire me to finish the job they had botched outside my apartment. But either way, it was a chance for me to learn more. Not that I would count on Holtzer to be straight with me one way or the other, but I could read between the lines of his lies.

I had to assume there would be cameras. I'd keep him moving, but the risk would still be there. *But what the hell*, I thought. *They know where you live, bastards have probably got a damn photo album by now. You don't have a whole lot of anonymity to protect anymore.*

I crossed back to Shinjuku-dori and walked to the front of the Studio Alta building, where several cabs were waiting for fares. I strolled over to one of the drivers, a younger guy who looked like he might be willing to overlook a strange situation if the price were right, and told him I wanted him to pick up a passenger who would be coming out the east exit in about fifteen or twenty minutes, a *gaijin* wearing a T-shirt.

"Ask if he's the chief," I explained in Japanese, handing him a ten-thousand-yen note. "If he answers yes, I want you to drive him down Shinjuku-dori, then make a left on Meiji-dori, then go left again on Yasukuni-dori. Wait for me on the north side of Yasukuni-dori in front of the Daiwa Bank. I'll get there right after you do." I pulled out another ten-thousand-yen note and tore it in two pieces. I gave half to him, told him he would get the other half when he picked me up. He bowed in agreement.

"Do you have a card?" I asked him.

"*Hai*," he answered, and instantly produced a business card from his shirt pocket.

I took the card and thanked him, then walked around to the back of the Studio Alta building, where I took the stairs to the fifth floor. From there I had a good view of the east exit. I checked my watch: fourteen minutes to go. I wrote down an address in Ikebukuro on the back of the card and slipped it into my breast pocket.

Holtzer showed up one minute early. I watched him emerge from the east exit, then walk slowly toward the Studio Alta sign. Even from a distance I could recognize the fleshy lips, the prominent nose. For a brief, satisfying moment, I remembered breaking it. He still had all his hair, although now it was more steely gray than the dirty blond that I had known. I could tell from his carriage and build that he was keeping in shape. He looked cold in the short-sleeved shirt. Too bad.

I saw the cab driver approach him and say something. Holtzer nodded, then followed him to the cab, glancing left and right as they walked. He looked the cab over suspiciously before getting in, and then they moved off down Shinjuku-dori.

I hadn't given Holtzer's people time to set up a car or other mobile surveillance in the area, so anyone who was trying to keep up with him was going to have to scramble, most likely by hurrying to get a cab. I watched the area for four minutes, but there was no unusual activity. So far, so good.

I turned and headed back to the stairs, taking them three at a time until I got to the first floor. Then I cut across Yasukuni-dori to the Daiwa Bank, getting there just as the cab pulled up. I walked over to the passenger side, watching Holtzer's hands as I approached. The automatic door opened, and Holtzer leaned toward me.

"John . . . ," he started to say, in his reassuring voice.

"Hands, Holtzer," I said, cutting him off. "Let me see your hands. Palms forward, up in the air." I didn't really think he was going to try to just shoot me, but I wasn't going to give him the chance, either.

"I should ask the same thing of you."

"Just do it." He hesitated, then leaned back and raised his hands. "Now lace your fingers and put your hands on the back of your neck. Then turn around and look out the driver-side window."

"Oh, come on, Rain. . . ," he started to say.

"Do it. Or I'm gone." He glared at me for a second and then complied.

I slid in next to him and gave the driver the business card with the Ikebukuro address, telling him to drive us there. It didn't matter where he took us. I just didn't want to say anything out loud. Then I squeezed Holtzer's laced fingers together with my left hand while I patted him down with my right. After a minute

I moved away from him, satisfied that he wasn't carrying a weapon. But that was only half my worry.

"I hope you're happy now," he said. "Do you mind telling me where we're going?"

I thought he might ask. "You wearing a wire, Holtzer?" I said, watching his eyes. He didn't answer. *Where would it be?* I thought. I hadn't felt anything under his shirt.

"Take off your belt," I told him.

"Like hell, Rain. This is going too far."

"Take it off, Holtzer. I'm not playing games with you. I'm about halfway to deciding that the way to solve all my problems is just to break your neck right here."

"Go ahead and try."

"*Sayonara*, asshole." I leaned toward the driver. "*Tomatte kudasai.*" Stop here.

"Okay, okay, you win," he said, raising his hands as if in surrender. "There's a transmitter in the belt. It's just a precaution. After Benny's unfortunate accident."

Was he telling me not to worry, that Benny didn't even matter? "*Iya, sumimasen,*" I said to the driver. "*Itte kudasai.*" Sorry. Keep going.

"Good to see that you've still got the same high regard for your people," I said to Holtzer. "Give me the belt."

"Benny wasn't my people," he said, shaking his head at my obvious obtuseness. "He was fucking us just like he tried to fuck you." He slipped off the belt and handed it to me. I held it up. Sure enough, there was a tiny microphone under the buckle.

"Where's the battery?" I asked.

"The buckle is the battery. Nickel hydride."

I nodded, impressed. "You guys do nice work." I rolled down the window and pitched the belt out into the street.

He lunged for it, a second late. "Goddamnit, Rain, you didn't have to do that. You could have just disabled it."

"Let me see your shoes."

"Not if you're planning on throwing them out the window."

"I will if they're wired. Take them off." He handed them over. They were black loafers—soft leather and rubber soles. No place for a microphone. The insides were warm and damp from perspiration, which indicated that he'd been wearing them for a while, and there were indentations from his toes. Obviously not something that the lab boys put together for a special occasion. I gave them back.

"All right?" he asked.

"Say what you've got to say," I told him. "I don't have much time."

He sighed. "The incident outside your apartment was a mistake. It never should have happened, and I want to personally apologize."

It was disgusting, how sincere he could sound. "I'm listening."

"I'm going out on a limb here, Rain," he said in a low voice. "What I'm about to tell you is classified . . ."

"It better be classified. If all you've got to tell me is what I can read in the paper, then you're wasting my time."

He scowled. "For the last five years, we've been developing an asset in the Japanese government. An insider, someone with access to everything. Someone who knows where all the bodies are buried—and I'm not just being figurative here."

If he was hoping for a reaction, he didn't get one, and he went on. "We've gotten more and more from this guy over time, but never anything that went beyond deep background. Never anything we could use as leverage. You following me?"

I nodded. Leverage in the business means blackmail.

"It's like a Catholic schoolgirl, you know? She keeps saying no, you've just got to find another way, because hey, in the end, you know she wants it." He grinned, the fleshy lips lurid. "Well, we kept at him, getting in deeper an inch at a time. Finally, six months ago, the nature of his refusals started to change. Instead of 'No, I won't do that,' we started hearing, 'No, that's too dangerous, I'd be at risk.' You know, practical objections."

I did know. Good salesmen, good negotiators, and good intelligence officers all relish practical objections. They signal a shift from whether to how, from principle to price.

"It took us five more months to close him. We were going to give him a one-time cash payment big enough so he'd never have to worry again, plus an annual stipend. False papers, settlement in a tropical locale where he'd blend in—the Agency equivalent of the witness-protection program, but deluxe.

"In exchange, he was going to give us the goods on the Liberal Democratic Party—the payoffs, the bribery, the *yakuza* ties, the killings of whistle-blowers. And this is hard evidence we're talking about: phone taps, photographs, tape-recorded conversations, the kind of stuff that would stand up in court."

"What were you going to do with all that?"

"The fuck you think we were going to do with it? With that kind of information, the U.S. government would own the LDP. We'd have every Japanese pol in our pocket. Think we'd ever get any grief again about military bases on Okinawa or at Atsugi? Think we'd have any trouble exporting as much rice or as many semiconductors or cars as we wanted? The LDP is the power here, and we would have been the power behind the power. Japan would have been Uncle Sam's favorite prison fuckboy for the rest of the century."

"I gather from your tone that Uncle Sam has been disappointed in love," I said.

His smile was more like a sneer. "Not disappointed. Just postponed. We'll still get what we want."

"What was your connection with Benny?"

"Poor Benny. He was a great source on LDP slime. He knew the players, but he didn't have the access, you know? The asset had the access."

"But you sent him to my apartment."

"Yeah, we sent him. Alone, to question you."

"How did you find out what happened to him?"

"C'mon Rain, the guy's neck was snapped clean in half right outside your apartment. Who else would have done it, one of your neighbors on a pension? Besides, we had him wired for sound. SOP for this kind of thing. So we heard everything, heard him blaming me, the little prick."

"And the other guy?"

"We don't know anything about him, other than that he turned up dead a hundred meters from where the Tokyo police found Benny's body."

"Benny told me he was *Boeicho Boeikyoku*. That you handled the liaison."

"He was right that I handled the *Boeikyoku* liaison, but he was full of shit that I knew his friend. Anyway, you can bet we did some checking, and Benny's pal wasn't with Japanese Intelligence. When Benny took him to your apartment, he was on a private mission, getting paid by someone else. You know you can't trust these moles, Rain. You remember the problems we had with our ARVN counterparts in Vietnam?"

I looked up at the rearview and saw the driver looking at us, his face suspicious. The chances that he could follow our conversation in English were nil, but I could see that he sensed something was amiss, that it was unnerving him.

"They take money from you, they'll take it from anyone," he went on. "I'll tell you what, I'm not going to miss Benny. You get paid by both sides, someone finds out, hey, you get what you had coming anyway."

Or at least you should. "Right," I said.

"But let me finish the part about the asset. Three weeks ago he's on his way to deliver the information, downloaded to a disk, he's actually carrying the fucking crown jewels, and—can you believe this? He has a heart attack on the Yamanote and dies. We send people to the hospital, but the disk is gone."

"How can you be so sure he was carrying the disk when he died?"

"Oh we're sure, Rain, we've got our ways, you know that. Sources and methods, though, nothing I can talk about. But the missing disk, that's not even the best part. You want to hear the best part?"

"I can't wait."

"Okay, then," he said, leaning closer to me and smiling his grotesque smile again. "The best part is that it wasn't really a heart attack . . . someone iced this fucker, someone who knew how to make it look like natural causes."

"I don't know, Holtzer. It sounds pretty far-fetched."

"It does, doesn't it? Especially because there are so few people in the whole world, let alone Japan, who could pull something like that off. Hell, the only one I know of is you."

"This is what you wanted to meet me for?" I said. "To suggest that I was mixed up in this kind of bullshit?"

"C'mon, Rain. Enough fucking around. I know exactly what you're mixed up in."

"I'm not following you."

"No? I've got news for you, then. Half the jobs you've done over the last ten years, you've done for us."

What the hell?

He leaned closer and whispered the names of various prominent politicians, bankers, and bureaucrats who had met untimely but natural ends. They were all my work.

"You can read those names in the paper," I said, but I knew he had more.

He told me the particulars of the bulletin board system I had been using with Benny, the numbers of the relevant Swiss accounts.

Goddamn, I thought, feeling sick. *You've been nothing but a fool for these people. It's never stopped. Goddamn.*

"I know this is a shock for you, Rain," he said, leaning back in his seat. "All these years you've thought you've been working freelance and in fact the agency has been paying the bills. But look on the bright side, okay? You're great at what you do! Christ, you're a fucking magician, making these people disappear without a trace, without a sign that there was any foul play. I wish I knew how you do it. I really do."

I looked at him, my eyes expressionless. "Maybe I'll get a chance to show you sometime."

"Dream on, pal. Now look, we had access to the autopsy report. Kawamura had a pacemaker that somehow managed to shut itself off. The coroner attributed it to a defect. But you know what? We did a little research and found out that a defect like that is just about impossible. Someone shut that pacemaker off, Rain. Your kind of job exactly. I want to know who hired you."

"It doesn't make sense," I said.

"What doesn't?"

"Why go to such lengths just to retrieve the disk?"

His eyes narrowed. "I was hoping you could tell me."

"I can't. I can only tell you that if I had wanted that disk, I could have found a lot of easier ways to take it."

"Maybe it wasn't up to you," he said. "Maybe whoever hired you on this one told you to retrieve it. I know you're not in the habit of asking a lot of questions about these assignments."

"And have I ever been in the habit of being an errand boy on these jobs? 'Retrieving' requested items?"

He crossed his arms and looked at me. "Not that I know of."

"Then it sounds like you're barking up the wrong tree."

"You did him, Rain. You were the last one with him. You have to understand, it doesn't look good."

"My reputation will have to suffer."

He massaged his chin for a moment while he looked at me. "You know that the Agency is the least of your worries among the people who are trying to get the disk back."

"What people?"

"Who do you think? The people who it implicates. The politicians, the *yakuza*, the muscle behind the whole Japanese power structure."

I considered for a moment, then said, "How did you find out about me? About me in Japan?"

He shook his head. "Sorry, that would fall under sources and methods again, nothing I can discuss here. But I'll tell you what." He leaned forward again. "Come on in, and we can talk about anything you want."

It was such a non sequitur that I thought I heard wrong. "Did you say, 'Come on in'?"

"Yes, I did. If you look at your situation, you'll see that you need our help."

"I didn't know you were such a humanitarian, Holtzer."

"Cut the shit, Rain. We're not doing this for humanity. We want your cooperation. Either you've got that disk, or because you were hunting Kawamura you've probably got information that might help us find it. We'll help you in exchange. It's as simple as that."

But I knew these people, and I knew Holtzer. Nothing was ever simple with them—and the simpler it looked, the harder they were about to nail you.

"I'm in an uncomfortable spot," I said. "No sense denying it. Maybe I've got to trust someone. But it's not going to be you."

"Look, if this is about the war, you're being ridiculous. It was a long time ago. This is another time, another place."

"But the people are the same."

He waved his hand as though trying to dispel an offensive odor. "It doesn't matter what you think of me, Rain. Because this isn't about us. The situation is what matters, and the situation is this: The police want you. The LDP wants you. The *yakuza* wants you. And they're going to find you because your cover is fucking blown. Now let us help you."

What to do. Take him out right here? They knew where I lived, which made me newly vulnerable, and taking out the station chief could lead to retribution.

The car behind us made a right. I glanced back and saw the car that was following it, a black sedan with three or four Japanese in it, slow down instead of taking up the space that had developed. Not an effective strategy for driving in Tokyo traffic.

I waited until we were almost at the next light, then told the driver to make a left. He just had time to brake and make the turn. The sedan changed lanes with us.

I told the driver I was mistaken, that he should get back on Meiji-dori. He looked back at me, clearly annoyed, wondering what the hell this was all about.

The sedan stayed with us as we made the turns.

Oh, shit.

"You bring some people with you, Holtzer? I thought I told you to come alone."

"They're here to bring you inside. For your protection."

"Fine, they can follow us back to the embassy," I said, suddenly scared and trying to think of a way out.

"I'm not going to have a cab drive the two of us into the embassy compound together. It's enough of a breach of security that I've met with you at all. They'll bring you in. It's safer."

How could they have followed him? Even if he were wearing a transmitter in a body cavity, they couldn't have pinpointed the location in this traffic.

Then I realized. They had played me beautifully. They knew when "Lincoln" called that I was going to demand an immediate meeting. They didn't know where, but they had people mobile and ready to move the second they found out the place. They had twenty minutes to get to Shinjuku, and they could stay close enough to react to what they heard through the wire without my seeing them. Holtzer must have given them the name of the cab company, the car's description, the license-plate number, and updated them about its progress until I got in. By then they were already in position. All while I was congratulating myself for thinking so well on my feet and taking control of the situation, while I was relaxing after getting rid of the wire.

I hoped I would live to enjoy the lesson. "Who are they?" I asked.

"People we can trust. Working with the embassy."

The light at the Kanda River overpass turned red. The cab started to slow down.

I snapped my head right, then left, searching for an avenue of escape.

The sedan crept closer, stopping a car length away.

Holtzer looked at me, trying to gauge what I was going to do. For a split instant our eyes locked. Then he lunged at me.

"It's for your own good!" he yelled, trying to get his arms around my waist. I saw the back doors of the sedan open, a pair of burly Japanese in sunglasses stepping out on either side.

I tried to push Holtzer away, but his hands were locked behind my back. The driver turned around and started yelling something. I didn't really hear what.

The two Japanese had closed their doors and were carefully approaching the taxi. Shit.

I wrapped my right arm around Holtzer's neck, holding his head in place against my chest, and slipped my left between my body and his neck, the ridge of my hand searching for his carotid. *"Aum da! Aum Shinrikyo da!"* I yelled at the driver. *"Sarin!"* Aum was the cult that gassed the Tokyo subway in 1995, and memories of the sarin attack can still cause panic.

Holtzer yelled something against my chest. I leaned forward, using my torso and legs like a walnut cracker. I felt him go limp.

"Ei? Nan da tte?" the driver asked, his eyes wide. What do you mean?

One of the Japanese tapped on the passenger-side window. *"Aitsu! Aum da! Sarin da! Boku no tomodachi— ishiki ga nai! Ike! Kuruma o dase!"* Those men! They're

Aum—they have sarin! My friend is unconscious! Drive! Drive! Getting the right note of terror in my voice wasn't a reach.

He might have thought it was bullshit or that I was crazy, but sarin wasn't worth the chance. He snapped the car into gear and hauled the steering wheel to the right, doing a burning-rubber U-turn on Meiji-dori and cutting off oncoming traffic in the process. I saw the Japanese hurrying back to their car.

"Isoide! Isoide! Byoin ni tanomu!" Hurry! We need a hospital!

At the intersection of Meiji-dori and Waseda-dori, the driver ripped through a light that had just turned red, braking into a sliding lefthand turn in the direction of the National Medical Center. The G-force ripped Holtzer away from me. The flow of traffic on Waseda-dori closed in behind us a second later, and I knew the sedan would be stuck for a minute, maybe more.

Tozai Waseda Station was just ahead. Time for me to bail. I told the driver to pull over. Holtzer was slumped against the driver-side door, unconscious but breathing. I wanted to put the strangle back in—one less adversary to worry about. But there was no time.

The driver started to protest, saying that we had to get my friend to a hospital, that we needed to call the police, but I insisted again that he pull over. He stopped and I took out the half of the ten-thousand-yen note I owed him, then threw in one more.

I grabbed the package I had bought for Midori, jumped out of the cab, and bolted down the steps to the subway. If I had to wait for a train I was going to use an alternate exit and stay on foot, but my timing was good—the Tozai was just pulling in. I took it to Nihonbashi Station, switched to the Ginza line, and then changed at Shinbashi to the Yamanote. I did a careful SDR on the way, and by the time I surged through the station turnstiles at Shibuya, I knew I was safe for the moment. But they'd flushed me into the open, and the moment wouldn't last.

16

AN HOUR LATER I got Harry's page, and we met at the Doutor coffee shop per our previous arrangement. He was waiting for me when I got there.

"Tell me what you've got," I said.

"Well, it's strange."

"Explain 'strange.'"

"Well, the first thing is, this disk has some pretty advanced copy management protection built into it."

"Can you break it?"

"That's not what I'm talking about. Copy management is different than encryption. The disk can't be copied, can't be distributed electronically, can't be sent over the Internet."

"You mean you can make only one copy from the source?"

"One copy or many copies, I'm not sure, but the point is you can't make copies of copies. No grandchildren in this family."

"And there's no way to send the contents of the disk over the Internet, upload to a bulletin board, anything like that?"

"No. If you try, the data will get corrupted. You won't be able to read it."

"Well, that explains a few things," I said.

"Like what?"

"Like why they were messing with disks in the first place. Like why they're so eager to get this one back. They know it hasn't been copied or uploaded, so they know their potential damage is still limited to this one disk."

"That's right."

"Now tell me this. Why would whoever controls the data that got copied onto that disk permit even a single copy to be made? Why not no copies? Wouldn't that be more secure?"

"Probably more secure, but risky, too. If something happened to the master, all your records would be gone. You'd want some kind of backup."

I considered. "What else is there?"

"Well, as you know, it's encrypted."

"Yes."

"The encryption is strange."

"You keep saying that."

"Ever hear of a lattice reduction?"

"I don't think so."

"It's a kind of code. The cryptographer encodes a message in a pattern, a pattern like the flowers in a symmetrical wallpaper design. But wallpaper patterns are simple—only one image in two dimensions. A more complex code uses a pattern that repeats itself at various levels of detail, in multiple mathematical dimensions. To break the code, you have to find the most basic way the lattice repeats itself—the origin of the pattern, in a way."

"I get the picture. Can you break it?"

"I'm not sure. I did some work with lattice reductions at Fort Meade, but this one is strange."

"Harry, if you say that one more time . . ."

"Sorry, sorry. It's strange because the lattice seems to be a musical pattern, not a physical one."

"Now I'm not following you."

"There's an overlay of what look like musical notes—in fact, my optical drive recognized it as a music disk, not a data disk. The pattern is bizarre, but highly symmetrical."

"Can you crack it?"

"I've been trying to, so far without luck. I've got to tell you, John, I'm a little out of my element on this one."

"Out of your element? All those years with the NSA, what could be out of your element?"

He blushed. "It's not the encryption. It's the music. I need a musician to walk me through it."

"A musician," I said.

"Yeah, a musician. You know, someone who reads music, preferably someone who writes it."

I didn't say anything.

"I could really use her help on this," he said.

"Let me think about it," I told him, uncomfortable.

"Okay."

"What about the cell phones? Anything there?"

He smiled. "I was hoping you would ask. Ever hear of the Shinnento?"

"Not sure," I said, trying to place the name. "New Year something?"

"*Shinnen,* like faith or conviction, not New Year," he said, drawing the appropriate *kanji* in the air with a finger to distinguish one of the homonyms that pervade the language. "It's a political party. The last call the *kendoka* made was to their headquarters in Shibakoen, and the number was speed-coded into both of the phones' memories." He smiled, obviously relishing what he was about to say next. "And just in case that's not enough to establish the connection, Conviction was paying the phone bill for the *kendoka*."

"Harry, you will never cease to amaze. Tell me more."

"Okay. Conviction was established in 1978 by a fellow named Yamaoto Toshi, who is still the head of the party. Yamaoto was born in 1949. He's the only son of a prominent family that traces its lines back to the samurai clans. His father was an officer in the Imperial Army, military occupational specialty communications, who after the war started a company that made portable communications devices. The father got started in business by trading on his family's connections with the remnants of the *zaibatsu*, and then got rich during the Korean War, when the American army bought his company's equipment."

Zaibatsu were the prewar industrial conglomerates, run by Japan's most powerful families. After the war MacArthur cut down the tree, but he couldn't dig out the roots.

"Yamaoto started out in the arts—he spent some years as a teenager in Europe for classical piano training, I think at his mother's insistence. Apparently he was a bit of a child prodigy. But his father yanked him out of all that when Yamaoto turned twenty, and sent him to the States to complete his education as a prelude to taking over the family business. Yamaoto got a master's in business from Harvard, and was running the company's U.S. operations when his old man died. At which point Yamaoto returned to Japan, sold the business, and used the money to establish Conviction and run for parliament."

"The piano training. Is there a connection with the way the disk is encrypted?"

"Don't know for sure. There could be."

"Sorry. Keep going."

"Apparently the father's former position in the Imperial Army and the long samurai lineage made an impression on the son's politics. Conviction was a platform for Yamaoto's right-wing ideas. He was elected in 1985 to a seat in Nagano-ken, which he promptly lost in the next election."

"Yeah, you don't get elected in Japan because of your ideas," I said. "It's pork that pays."

"That's exactly the lesson Yamaoto learned from his defeat. After he was elected, he spent all his time and political capital arguing for abolishing Article Nine of the Constitution so that Japan could build up its military, kicking the U.S. out of Japan, teaching Shinto in the schools—the usual positions. But after his defeat, he ran again—this time focusing on the roads and bridges he would build for his constituents, the rice subsidies and tariffs he would impose. Very different politician. The nationalistic stuff was back-burnered. He got his seat back in eighty-seven, and has held on to it ever since."

"But Conviction is a marginal player. I've never even read about the LDP using them to form a coalition.

Outside Nagano-ken, I doubt anyone has heard of them."

"But Yamaoto has a few things going for him. One, Conviction is very well funded. That's his father's legacy. Two, he knows how to dole out the pork. Nagano has a number of farming districts, and Yamaoto keeps the subsidies rolling in and is a vocal opponent of any relaxation of Japan's refusal to allow foreign rice into the country. And three, he has a lot of support in the Shinto community."

"Shinto," I said, musing. Shinto is a nature-worshiping religion that Japan's nationalists turned into an ideology of Japaneseness before the war. Unlike Christianity and Buddhism, Shinto is native to Japan and isn't practiced anywhere else. There was something about the connection that was bothering me, something I should have known. Then I realized.

"That's how they found out where I live," I said. "No wonder I've been seeing priests begging for alms outside of stations on the Mita-sen. They blanketed me with static surveillance, traced me back to my neighborhood one step at a time. Goddamnit, how could I have missed it? I almost gave one of them a hundred yen the other day."

His eyes were worried. "How would they know to focus on the Mita line?"

"They probably didn't, for sure. But with a little luck, a little coincidence, a little Holtzer feeding them a dossier, maybe even military-era photographs, it could be done. If they placed me at the Kodokan, they would have assumed that I wouldn't live too far from it. And there are only three train lines with stops within a reasonable distance from the building, so all they had to do was commit enough manpower at enough places for enough time. Shit, they really nailed me."

I had to give them credit; it was nicely done. Static surveillance is almost impossible to spot. Unlike the moving variety, you can't get the person behind you to do something unnatural to give himself away. It's more like a zone defense in basketball: no matter where the guy with the ball goes, there's always someone new in the next zone to pick him up. If you can put enough people in place to make it work, it's deadly.

"What's the basis for the Shinto connection?" I asked.

"Shinto is a huge organization, with priests running shrines at the national, local, even neighborhood levels. As a result, the shrines take in a lot of donations and are well funded—so they're in a position to dispense patronage to the politicians they favor. And Yamaoto wants a much bigger role for Shinto in Japan, which means more power for the priests."

"So the shrines are part of his funding?"

"Yes, but it's more than that. Shinto is part of Conviction's program. The party wants it taught in schools; it wants to form an anticrime alliance between the police and the local shrines. Don't forget, Shinto was at the center of prewar Japanese nationalism. It's unique to Japan, and can easily be bent—has been bent—to foster the xenophobic cult of the *Yamato Gokoro*, the Japanese soul. And it's on the rise in Japan today, although not many people realize it outside the country."

"You said their headquarters is in Shibakoen," I said.

"That's right."

"Okay, then. While you're having a crack at the lattice, I'm going to need some surveillance equipment—infrared and laser. And video. Also a transmitter in case I can get inside. I want to listen in on our friends at Conviction."

"Why?"

"I need more information. Whose disk was this? Who's trying to get it back? Why? Without that information, there's not much I can do to protect myself. Or Midori."

"You need to get pretty close to the building to use that kind of equipment, never mind placing a transmitter. It'll be dangerous. Why don't you just give me some time with the lattice? Maybe everything you need is already in it."

"I don't have time. It might take you a week to crack the code, or you might not be able to crack it at all. In the meantime, I'm up against the Agency, the *yakuza*, and an army of Shinto priests. They know where I live, and I've been flushed out into the open. Time is running against me—I've got to end this soon."

"Well, why don't you just get out of the country? At least until I'm done with the lattice. What's keeping you here?"

"For one thing, I've got to take care of Midori, and she can't leave. I don't like the idea of her traveling under her own passport, and I doubt she's got false papers handy."

He nodded as though he understood, then looked at me closely. "Is something going on between you two?"

I didn't answer.

"I knew it," he said, blushing.

"I should have known I couldn't put one over on you."

He shook his head. "Is this why you don't want to let her help me with the lattice?"

"Am I that transparent?"

"Not usually."

"All right, I'll ask her," I said, not seeing an alternative.

"I could use her help."

"I know. Don't worry. I didn't really expect you to be able to decrypt something as complex as this without help."

For a half second his mouth started to drop in indignation. Then he saw my smile.

"Had you there," I told him.

17

HARRY RENTED ME a van from a place in Roppongi, using alias ID just in case, while I waited at his apartment to keep my exposure down. His apartment is a strange place, crammed with arcane electronic equipment, but nothing to make his life more comfortable. He'd told me a few years earlier that he'd read how the police had caught some indoor marijuana farmers by monitoring their electric bills—seems that hydroponic equipment sucks down a lot more electricity than average—and now Harry thinks his electronic signature might lead the police to him. So he doesn't use any electrical appliances that aren't absolutely necessary: a category that, in Harry's world, doesn't include a refrigerator, heat, or air-conditioning.

When he came back, we loaded the equipment into the back of the van. It's sophisticated stuff. The laser reads the vibrations on windows that are caused by conversation inside, then feeds the resulting data into a computer, which breaks down the patterns into words. And the infrared can read minutely different temperatures on glass—the kind caused by body heat in an otherwise cool room.

When we were done, I parked the van and made my way back to Shibuya, of course conducting a solid SDR en route.

I got to the hotel at a little past one o'clock. I had picked up some sandwiches at a stand I found on one of the nameless streets that snake off Dogenzaka, and Midori and I ate them sitting on the floor while I filled her in on what was going on. I gave her the package I had brought, told her that she should wear the scarf and sunglasses when she went out. I gave her Harry's address, told her to put her things together and meet me there in two hours.

When I arrived at Harry's, he was already running Kawamura's disk. A half hour later the buzzer rang; Harry walked over to the intercom, pressed a button, and said, *"Hai."*

"Watashi desu" came the response. It's me. I nodded, getting up to check the window, and Harry pressed the button to open the front entrance. Then he walked over to his door, opened it, and peered out. Better to see who's coming before they get to your position, while you still have time to react.

A minute later he opened the door wide and motioned Midori to come inside.

I said to her in Japanese, "This is Harry, the friend I told you about. He's a little shy around people because he spends all his time with computers. Just be nice to him and he'll open up after a while."

"Hajimemashite," Midori said, turning to Harry and bowing. Nice to meet you.

"It's nice to meet you," Harry responded in Japanese. He was blinking rapidly, and I could see that he was nervous. "Please don't listen to my friend. The government used him to test experimental drugs during the war, and it's led to premature senility."

Harry? I thought, impressed with his sudden gumption.

Midori made a face of perfect innocence and said, "It was caused by drugs?"

She had a light touch with him, I was glad to see. Harry looked at me with a radiant smile, feeling he'd finally gotten the better of me, and maybe had found an ally, too.

"Okay, I can see you're both going to get along," I said, cutting them off before Harry used his newfound courage to escalate to who knows what. "We don't have much time. This is the plan." I explained to Midori what I was going to do.

"I don't like it," she said, when I was done. "They could see you. It could be dangerous."

"No one's going to see me."

"You should give Harry and me some time with the musical code."

"I've already been over this with Harry. You both do your jobs; I'll do mine. It's more efficient. I'll be fine."

I DROVE THE van to the Conviction facility in Shibakoen, just south of the government district in Kasumigaseki. Conviction occupied part of the second floor of a building on Hibiya-dori, across from Shiba Park. I would use the laser to pick up the locus of conversation in their offices, and then, based on Harry's analysis of what we picked up, I'd be able to guess which room or rooms would be the best candidates for a transmitter. The same equipment would tell me when the offices had emptied out, probably well after dark, and that's when I'd go in to place the bug. The video might help us identify anyone else who was involved with the Agency and Conviction, and give us some clues about the nature of the connection between the two.

I parked across the street from the building. The spot was in a no-parking zone, but it was a good enough location to risk a ticket from a bored meter maid.

I had just finished setting up the equipment and targeting it at the appropriate windows when I heard a tap on the van's passenger-side window. I looked up and saw a uniformed cop. He was rapping the glass with his nightstick.

Oh, shit. I made a conciliatory gesture, as though I was going to just drive away, but he shook his head and said, *"Dete yo."* Get out.

The equipment was pointing out the back driver-side window, and wasn't visible from the cop's vantage point. I would have to take a chance. I slid across to the passenger side and opened the door, then stepped down onto the curb.

There were three men waiting on the blind side of the van, where I couldn't see them until I was outside. They were armed with matching Beretta 92 Compacts and wore sunglasses and bulky coats—light disguise to change the shape of the face and the build. I took this to mean that they would shoot me if I resisted, counting on the disguises to confuse potential witnesses. They all had the classic *kendoka's* ears. I recognized the one standing closest to me from outside Midori's apartment—the guy with the flat nose who had gone in after I had ambushed Midori's would-be abductors. One of them thanked the cop, who turned and walked away.

They motioned me across the street, and there wasn't much I could do except comply. At least this solved the problem of how I was going to get into the building. I had an earpiece in my pocket, as well as one of Harry's custom adhesive-backed microtransmitters. If I saw the chance, I'd put the transmitter in place.

They brought me in the front entrance, their hands staying steady in their coat pockets. We took the stairs to the second floor, the three of them crowding me on the way up, taking away any room to maneuver. When we got to the landing at the top of the stairs, Flatnose shoved me up against the wall, pushing his gun against my neck. One of his partners patted me down. He was looking for a weapon and didn't notice the small transmitter in my pocket.

When he was done, Flatnose took a step back and suddenly kneed me in the balls. I doubled over and he kicked me in the stomach, then twice again in the ribs. I dropped down to my knees, sucking wind, pain shooting through my torso. I was trying to get my arms up in anticipation of another blow when one of them stepped between Flatnose and me, saying "*Iya, sono kurai ni shite oke.*" That's enough. I wondered distantly if I was in for a game of good cop, bad cop.

We stayed like that for a few minutes, Flatnose's friend restraining him while I tried to catch my breath. When I was able I stood up, and they took me down a short hallway with closed doors on both sides. We stopped outside the last door on the right. Flatnose knocked, and a voice answered, *"Dozo."* Come in.

They brought me into a room that was spacious by Japanese standards, furnished in the traditional minimalist fashion. Lots of light-hued wood, expensive-looking ceramics on the shelves. The walls were decorated with *hanga*, wood-block prints. Probably originals. A small leather couch and armchairs in one corner of the room, arranged around a spotless glass coffee table. The overall appearance was clean and prosperous, which I guessed was the impression these people wanted to project. Maybe they hid Flatnose and his pals when they had guests.

There was a wooden desk on the far side of the room. It took me a second to recognize the guy sitting behind it. I hadn't seen him in a suit before.

It was the *judoka* from the Kodokan. The one I'd fought in *randori*.

"Hello, John Rain," he said, with a small smile. *"Hisashiburi desu ne."* It's been awhile.

I returned his gaze. "Hello, Yamaoto."

He stood up and circled to the front of the desk with the strong, graceful movements that I had first noticed at the Kodokan. "Thank you for coming today," he said. "I was expecting you."

That much was clear. "Sorry I didn't call first," I told him.

"No, no, not at all. That I would never expect. But I did anticipate that you would find a way to take the initiative—after all, as a *judoka* you are more comfortable on the offensive, using defense merely as a feint."

He nodded to his men, told them in Japanese to wait outside. I watched them file out quietly, Flatnose eyeing me as he closed the door behind them.

"Did I do something to offend the ugly one?" I asked, rubbing my ribs. "I get the feeling he doesn't like me."

"Was he rough with you? I told him not to be, but he has trouble controlling his temper. Ishikawa, the man you killed outside your apartment, was a friend of his."

"Sorry to hear that."

He shook his head as though it was all a misunderstanding. "*Dozo, suwatte kudasai,*" he said. "Please, sit. Would you like something to drink?"

"No, thank you. I'm not thirsty. And I'm more comfortable standing."

He nodded. "I know what you are thinking, Rainsan. Don't forget, I've seen how fast you are. That is why there are three armed men outside the door—in case you manage to get past me." He smiled, a supremely confident smile, and remembering how things went at the Kodokan, I knew his confidence was justified. "That would be an interesting contest, but now is not the time. Please, why don't you make yourself comfortable, and we can think of a way to solve our mutual problem."

"'Mutual problem'?"

"Yes, the problem is mutual. You have something that I want, or you know where it is. Once I have it, you will no longer be a liability, and we can 'live and let live.' But if I don't have it, the situation becomes more difficult."

I was silent, waiting to see if he would say more. After a moment he said, "I really would like to talk with you. *Dozo kakete kudasai.*" Please sit.

I bowed my head and walked over to one of the chairs facing the couch, putting my hands in my pockets as I did so, affecting an air of resignation. I switched on the transmitter. Regardless of how this turned out, Harry would at least hear everything. I sat down and waited.

"Thank you," he said, sitting opposite me on the couch. "Now tell me, how did you find me?"

I shrugged. "Your man Ishikawa broke into my apartment and tried to kill me. I got his cell phone and used it to find out he's connected to you. The rest was just taking the initiative, as you say—the best defense is a good offense."

"Ishikawa wasn't at your apartment to kill you. He was there to question you."

"If that was Ishikawa's idea of 'questioning,'" I said, "you should send him to Dale Carnegie."

"Regardless. We are not after you—only the disk."

"Disk?"

"Please don't insult my intelligence. You're protecting Kawamura Midori."

That caught me by surprise. But then I realized—the men who were waiting for her at her apartment. They must have been Yamaoto's people. They'd been focusing on her, thinking that if she had her father's things she might have the disk, and then I walked into the picture. It was only after I ambushed them and Midori went underground that they started coming at me.

"What does she have to do with this?"

"I know that her father had the disk when he died. It is therefore likely that she has it now. And she is in hiding."

"Of course she's in hiding. She had the same kind of welcome party at her apartment that I had at mine. She knows she's in danger but doesn't understand why."

"Ordinarily a person in her position would go to the police. She has not done so."

"I wouldn't know anything about that. I don't trust the police myself."

"Where is she?"

"I don't know. She took off after the ambush at her apartment. She thought I was with your people."

"Really? She hasn't resurfaced."

"Maybe she's staying with friends—in the country or something. She looked pretty scared to me."

"I see," he said, steepling his fingers. "You understand, Rain-san, there is information on that disk that would be harmful to Japan, useful to her enemies, if revealed. These enemies are looking for the disk, too."

I thought of Holtzer, how he wanted to turn the Japanese government into a "fuckboy," as only Holtzer could put it.

One thing I didn't understand. "Why the contact at the Kodokan?" I asked.

"Curiosity," he said, his posture contemplative. "I wanted to know what would drive a man with a history like yours. If I had known then of the way you would soon be involved in this matter, I would of course have avoided the contact."

"What do mean, 'history'?"

"A man of two such opposed countries and cultures."

"I think I'm missing something. Other than the fact that I inadvertently showed up at the same time as your men at Midori's apartment, I didn't know we were acquainted."

"Ah, of course. You wouldn't know, but I have retained you for your services from time to time."

Through Benny, then. Christ, the little bastard really slept around. Probably reselling my services at a markup. *Not any more, though.*

"So you see, until recently, your interests and mine have always been aligned. If we can just clear up this one matter, we can return to the *status quo ante bellum.*"

He wanted that disk badly. I hoped Harry's algorithms were up to speed.

"The problem, as I've said, is that I don't know where this disk is, or even what it is," I told him. "If I did, I'd give it to you. But I don't."

He frowned. "I am sorry to hear that. And Kawamura's daughter, she doesn't know, either?"

"How would I know?"

He nodded his head gravely. "This is a problem. You see, until I have what I am looking for, Kawamura's daughter is a liability. It would be much safer for her if the item were returned to me."

In that moment I was tempted to believe that there was some truth to what he was saying. If he had the disk back, Midori wouldn't be a liability.

But there were other parties after it, too, and they would have no way of knowing that Midori didn't have it anymore. Besides, the logistics were impossible. Yamaoto would never let me leave on the strength of a promise to return with the disk, and I wasn't going to tell him where to find Midori and Harry. Besides, there was no guarantee that he wouldn't go on cleaning up loose ends even after the disk had been returned.

"For what it's worth, I don't think she has what you're looking for," I said. "Why would Kawamura have given her anything, anyway? He would have known it would have put her in danger, right?"

"He may have given it to her inadvertently. Besides, as I have said already, the fact that she has not gone to the police is telling."

I said nothing, waiting for him.

"Enough games," he said finally. He stood and walked over to a coat rack, where he took a suit jacket off a hanger. "I have an appointment elsewhere and have no more time to try to persuade you. Tell me where I can find the disk, or tell me where to find Kawamura Midori."

"I told you I don't know."

"Unfortunately, there is only one way to confirm your ignorance. I think you know what it is."

Neither of us said anything more for about a full minute. I heard him exhale, as though he had been holding his breath. "Rain-san, you are in a difficult position, and I am sympathetic. But you must understand that I will have what I want. If you tell me now, as a friend, then I can trust you. You will be free to leave. But if my men have to acquire the information from you by other means, I may not be able to let you go afterwards. In fact, you may not be in a condition to go. Do you understand? If I don't have the disk, I am forced to do the next best thing: systematically eliminate every risk associated with it. So you see, it would be much better if you tell me now."

I folded my arms across my chest and regarded him. My look was impassive, but inside my head I was playing a map of the hallway, the staircase, trying to find a way out.

He must have really been hoping I would crack—he waited a long time. Finally he called for his men. The door opened, and I was surrounded and pulled to my feet. He barked some orders at them in Japanese. Find out where the disk is. And Midori. Whatever it takes.

They hauled me out of the room. Behind me, Yamaoto was saying, "I am very disappointed." I barely heard it. I was too busy looking for a way out.

18

THEY TOOK ME back down the hallway. I noted the entrance as we went past double glass doors, a dead bolt visibly locked in place in the small gap between them. The doors had opened outward when we came in. If I hit them dead center, on the fly, the lock might give. If it didn't, and I had time to back up and try again, I could try to go through the glass, hope not to get cut too badly. Lousy options, but they beat being tortured to death by Flatnose and his handsome friends.

They were pretty rough shoving me down the hallway ahead of them, and I tried to emanate waves of fear and helplessness so their confidence would build. I wanted them to feel in control, to believe that I was cowed by their size and their numbers. That might give me some small chance at surprise. Beyond that, I had only one advantage, the same one SOG always had against the North Vietnamese, even when we were operating in their backyard: Considering what was coming, I was more motivated to escape than they were to hold me.

They took me to a room at the farthest end of the

corridor. It was small, only about three meters square. The door had a window of frosted glass in its center and opened inward, to the left, at the back of the room. To the right was a small rectangular table with two chairs on either side of it. They pushed me into one of the chairs, my back to the door. I put my hands on my knees, under the table.

Flatnose disappeared for a few minutes. When he returned, he was carrying a large wooden truncheon. He took a seat on the other side of the table, facing me. I heard the other two take up positions behind me, to either side.

There was about a meter of empty space between Flatnose's back and the wall. Good.

They hadn't locked the door. Why bother? There were three of them, and they were big bastards. This was their place. They knew they were in control.

I lifted the table a fraction with my knees, getting a feel for its weight. Despite its size, it was satisfyingly heavy. My heart was thudding in my ears, my neck.

Flatnose started to say something. I didn't hear what. As soon as the words began I sprang up, my arms catching the table from underneath, driving it up and into him. The force of it slammed him backward into the wall. I felt the impact jolt through my arms.

The other two leaped forward. I shot my leg out into the guy coming in on my right. It caught him squarely in the gut, so hard his momentum continued to carry his feet forward. He went down and then the other one was on me.

He grabbed me from behind and tried for *hadaka jime*, a sleeper hold, but I turtled my neck in and his forearm closed across my mouth. Still, his grip was so strong it felt like he was going to unhinge my jaw. I opened my mouth and the leading edge of his arm jammed between my teeth. Before he could twist free I bit down hard. I felt my teeth sinking into muscle and heard him howl.

The grip loosened and I spun inside it, pumping uppercuts into his abdomen. He dropped his arms to protect his body and I caught him with a solid palm-heel under the nose. He didn't fall, but he was dazed. I shoved him to the right and scrambled for the door.

The guy I'd kicked grabbed my leg from the ground but I shook free. I gripped the doorknob hard and twisted it, flung the door open. It rocketed into the wall, the frosted glass exploding.

I stumbled into the hallway, running and almost falling like a man tearing out of control down a steep hill. It took me only a second to reach the entrance doors. I hit them hard, not holding anything back, and they burst open at the center. I spilled out into the hallway, rolled to my feet, and bolted for the stairwell. When I reached the outer door I wrenched it open and plunged down the stairs four at a time, my hand on the railing for balance. Just as I cleared the first riser, I heard the door slam open. They were already after me—not quite the head start I'd hoped for.

I had to get out of there before reinforcements started pouring in. Shibakoen subway station was on the opposite side of Hibiya-dori. I bolted across the street, trying to flow diagonally into the traffic, tires screeching as I jumped in front of cars.

Thick crowds of pedestrians were exiting at the top

of the steps to the station—a train must have just come in. I glanced back as I hit the entrance and saw two of Yamaoto's boys sprinting after me.

I could hear the chimes of another train pulling in. Maybe I could make it. I had no doubt that they would shoot me now if they could. In this crowd, no one would know where the shots had come from. I fought frantically for space, ducking past three slow-moving old women who were blocking the stairway, and spun left at the bottom of the stairs. There was a concession stand in front of the ticket windows and as I dodged past it I grabbed a palm-sized canned coffee. Hundred and ninety grams. Hard metal edges.

I shoved my way through the wickets and onto the platform. I was too late—the doors had already closed, and the train was starting to move.

The platform was crowded, but there was a clear passage alongside the train. I maneuvered into it, glanced back and saw one of Yamaoto's goons pass the wickets and burst through the crowd into the clear space next to the train.

I turned and measured the distance. About five meters, closing fast.

I threw the can like a fastball, aiming for center mass. It went a little high and caught him in the sternum with a thud I could hear even over the noise of the crowd. He went down hard. But his buddy was right behind him, his gun out.

I spun around. The train was picking up speed.

I dropped my head and sprinted after it, my breath hammering in and out. I heard a gunshot. Then another.

Two meters. One.

I was close enough to reach out and touch the vertical bar at the back corner of the car, but I couldn't get any closer. For an instant, my speed was perfectly synchronized with the train. Then it started to slip away.

I gave a wild yell and leaped forward, my fingers outstretched for the bar. For one bad second I thought I'd come up short and felt myself falling—then my hand closed around cold metal.

My body fell forward and my knees smacked into the back of the train. My feet were dangling just over the tracks. My fingers were slipping off the bar. I looked up, saw a kid in a school uniform staring at me out the back window, his mouth open. Then the train entered the tunnel and I lost my grip.

I twisted instinctively, getting my left arm under and across my body so I could roll with the impact. Still, I hit the tracks so hard that I actually bounced instead of rolling. There was one enormous shock all down my left side, then a brief sensation of flight. An instant later I felt a dull *whump!* and came to a sudden stop.

I was on my back, looking up at the ceiling of the subway tunnel. I lay there for a moment, the wind knocked out of me, wiggling my toes, flexing my fingers. Everything seemed to be working.

Five seconds went by, then another five. I drew in a few hitching breaths.

What the hell, I thought. *What the hell did I land on?*

I grunted and sat up. I was on a large sand pile to the left of the tracks. Beside it were two hard-hatted Japanese construction workers, looking at me, their mouths slightly agape.

Next to the sand pile was a concrete floor that the

workers were repairing. They were using the sand to mix cement. I realized that if I had let go of the train even a half second later, I would have landed on concrete instead of a soft pile of sand.

I slid over to the ground, stood, and began brushing myself off. The shape of my body was imprinted in the sand like something from an over-the-top cartoon.

The construction workers hadn't changed their posture. They were still looking at me, mouths still agape, and I realized they were in mild shock at what they had just seen.

"*Ah, sumimasen,*" I began, not knowing what else to say. "*Etto, otearae wa arimasu ka?*" Excuse me, do you have a bathroom?

They maintained their frozen postures, and I realized that my question had discombobulated them further. Just as well. I saw that I was only a few meters inside the tunnel and started walking out.

I considered what had happened. Yamaoto's men must have seen me go into the tunnel hanging on to the back of the train, but not seen me slip, and I was going too fast for them to expect that I'd let go deliberately. So they were figuring that, in three minutes, I would be deposited at Mita station, the end of the line. They must have bolted out of the station to Mita to try to intercept me.

I had a wild idea.

I reached into my pocket and pulled out the earpiece I had pocketed before Flatnose and his crew had caught me in the van, slipped it into place. I felt in my pocket for the adhesive-backed transmitter. Still there. But was it still transmitting?

"Harry? Can you hear me? Talk to me," I said.

There was a long pause, and just as I started to try again the earpiece came to life.

"John! What the hell is going on? Where are you?"

It felt great to hear the kid. "Relax, I'm okay. But I need your help."

"What's going on? I've been listening to everything. Are you in a train station? Are you all right?"

I hauled myself up onto the platform. Some people stared at me but I ignored them, walking past them as though it was perfectly natural that I had just emerged filthy and bruised from the depths of one of Tokyo's subway tunnels. "I've been better, but we can talk about that later. Is the equipment still up and running?"

"Yes, I'm still getting a feed on all the rooms in the building."

"Okay, that's what I need to know. Who's still in the building?"

"Infrared says just one guy. Everyone else left right after you."

"Yamaoto, too?"

"Yes."

"Where's the guy who stayed behind?"

"Very last room on the right as you face the building—where the three men took you. He's been there since you got out."

That would be Flatnose or one of his boys—must not have been in condition to come after me. It felt good to know.

"Okay, here's the situation. They all think I'm on the back of a subway to Mita, and that's where they're going to converge in about four minutes. It'll take them maybe another five to figure out that I'm not there and that they've lost me, and another five after that to get back to the Conviction building. So I've got fourteen minutes to get back in there and plant the bug."

"What? You don't know where they are. What if they didn't all go to Mita? They could come back while you're still in there!"

"I'm counting on you to let me know if that's going to happen. You're still getting a video feed from the van, right?"

"Yeah, it's still broadcasting."

"Look, I'm practically at the building now—still all clear?"

"Still all clear, but this is crazy."

"I'm never going to get a better chance. They're all out of the building, nothing's going to be locked, and when they get back, we'll be able to hear everything they say. I'm going in."

"Okay, I can see you now. Do it fast."

That advice I didn't need. I went through the stairway doors and turned right, then jogged down the hallway to the entrance. As I expected, they had left in a hurry and it was wide open.

Yamaoto's office was three doors down to the right. I was going to be in and out in no time.

The door was closed. I reached out for the knob, tried to turn it.

"Oh, fuck," I breathed.

"What is it?"

"It's locked."

"Forget it—put the bug somewhere else."

"I can't—this is where we need to listen." I examined the lock, and could see that it was only a regular five-pin tumbler. Not a big deal. "Hang on a minute. I think I can get in."

"John, get out of there. They could come back at any time."

I didn't answer. I slipped out my keys and detached one of my homemade picks and the dental mirror. The latter's long, slim handle made for a nice field-expedient tension wrench. I slipped the handle into the lock and gently rotated it clockwise. When the slack in the cylinder was gone, I eased in the pick and started working the fifth tumbler.

"Don't try to pick the lock! You're no good at it! Just put it somewhere else and get out!"

"What do you mean I'm no good at it? I taught you how to do it, didn't I?"

"Yeah, that's how I know you're no good." He stopped. Probably figured it was useless to try to stop me so he might as well let me concentrate.

I felt the fifth tumbler click, then lost it. Damn. I turned the dental mirror another fraction, tightening the cylinder against the pins. "Harry? I miss your voice. . . ." Another tumbler slipped.

"Don't talk to me. Concentrate."

"I am, but it's so hard. . . ." I felt the fifth pin click and hold. The next three were easy. Just one more.

The last pin was damaged. I couldn't feel the click. I worked the pick up and down, but couldn't get anything.

"C'mon, sweetheart, where are you?" I breathed. I held my breath and jiggled the pick.

I never felt the tumbler click into place. But the knob was suddenly free. It twisted to the right and I was in.

The office was the same as when I'd left it. Even the lights were still on. I knelt down next to the leather couch and felt its underside. It was covered with some kind of cloth. The edges were stapled to what felt like wood. Good backing to attach the bug.

I pulled the adhesive covering off the transmitter and pressed it into place. Anyone talking in this room was going to come through loud and clear.

Harry's voice in my ear: "John, two of them just got back. They're coming up the walkway. Get out right now. Use the side exit—the one at the left side of building as you face it."

"Shit, the transmitter's already in place. I'm not going to be able to respond to you once I leave this room. Keep talking to me."

"They just stopped at the end of the walkway to the front entrance. Maybe they're waiting for the others. Go down to the side entrance and stay there until I tell you you're clear."

"Okay. I'm gone." I relocked the door from the inside, then backed out and closed it behind me. Turned and started to move in the direction of the exterior corridor.

Flatnose was coming down the hallway. His shirt was covered with blood. The table must have caught him in the face and broken his nose again. It hadn't improved his appearance. Hoarse animal sounds were rumbling up out of his chest.

He was standing between me and the entrance. Nowhere to go but through him.

Harry again, a second late: "There's one right in front of you! And the others are coming up the walk!"

Flatnose dropped his head, his neck and shoulders bunching, looking like a bull about to charge.

All he wanted was to get his hands on me. He was going to come at me hard, crazed with rage, not thinking.

He launched himself at me, closing the gap fast. As he lunged for my neck, I grabbed his wet shirt and dropped to the floor in modified *tomo-nage*, my right foot catching him in the balls and hurling him over me. He landed on his back with a thud I could feel through the floor. Using the momentum of the throw I rolled to my feet, took two long steps over to him, and leaped into the air like a pissed-off bronco, coming down with both feet as hard as I could on his prone torso. I felt bones breaking inside him and all the air being driven from his body. He made a sound like a balloon deflating in a puddle of water and I knew he was done.

I lurched toward the corridor, then stopped. If they found him like this in the middle of the hallway, they would know I'd been back here, maybe figure out why. They might look for a bug. I had to get him back to the room at the other end of the hallway, where it would look like he'd died by a freak shot from the table.

His legs were pointing in the right direction. I squatted between them, facing away from him, grabbed him around the knees and stood. He was heavier than he looked. I leaned forward and dragged him, feeling like a horse yoked to a wagon with square wheels. There were bursts of pain in my back.

Harry's voice in my ear again: "What are you doing? They're coming in the front entrance. You've got maybe twelve seconds to get clear of the corridor."

I dumped him in the room at the end of the hallway and raced out into the corridor, sprinting toward the side exit.

I reached the entrance to the side stairwell and heard the door on the opposite side of the corridor opening. I yanked open the door and threw myself through it, pulling it shut behind me but stopping it before it closed completely.

I squatted on the landing, fighting the screaming need to breathe, holding the door open a crack and watching as three of Yamaoto's men walked into the corridor. One of them was doubled over—the guy I had nailed with the can of coffee. They walked into Conviction's offices and out of my field of vision.

Immediately, I heard Harry: "They're back in the office. The front of the building is clear. Walk out the side exit now and head east across the park toward Sakurada-dori."

I went down the stairs quietly but fast. Stuck my head out the exit door at the bottom, looked both ways. All clear. I shuffled down an alley connecting Hibiya-dori and Chuo-dori and cut across the park. The sun felt good on my face.

PART THREE

Now . . . they resolved to go back to their own land;
because the years have a kind of emptiness when we
spend too many of them on a foreign shore. But . . . if
we do return, we find that the native air has lost its
invigorating quality, and that life has shifted its
reality to the spot where we have deemed ourselves
only temporary residents.

Thus, between two countries, we have none at all . . .

—NATHANIEL HAWTHORNE, *The Marble Faun*

19

"YOU ARE A maniac with a death wish, and I'm never working with you again," Harry told me when I got to his apartment.

"I'm never working with me again, either," I said. "Have you been getting anything from the transmitter?"

"Yes, everything that went on while you were there and a short meeting that just ended. It's stored on the hard drive."

"They say anything about the guy I ran into on my way out?"

"What do you mean?"

"I had a little encounter with one of Yamaoto's men just after I put the transmitter in place. They must have figured it had happened earlier, or you would have heard them say something."

"Oh, that. Yes, they thought it happened when you busted out of interrogation. They didn't know you'd been back. You know, the guy is dead."

"Yeah, he didn't look too good when I left him."

He was watching me closely, but I couldn't read his

eyes. "That was fast. You can do something like that, that fast, with just your hands?"

I looked at him, deadpan. "No, I needed my feet, too. Where's Midori?"

"She went out to get an electronic piano keyboard. We're going to try playing what's on the disk for the computer—it's the only way to discern the patterns in the lattice."

I frowned. "She shouldn't be going out if we can avoid it."

"We couldn't avoid it. Someone had to monitor the laser and infrared and save your ass before, and she isn't familiar with the equipment. That didn't leave a lot of alternatives."

"I see what you mean."

"She knows to be careful. She's wearing light disguise. I don't think there's going to be a problem."

"Okay. Let's listen to what you got from the transmitter."

"Just a second—tell me you didn't leave the van."

"What do you think, I went back for it? I'm crazy, but not that crazy."

He looked like a kid who'd been told that his dog just died. "Do you have any idea how much that equipment cost?"

I suppressed a smile and patted him on the shoulder. "You know I'm good for it," I said, which was true. I sat down in front of a computer monitor and picked up a pair of headphones. "Play it," I said.

A few mouse clicks later I was listening to Yamaoto excoriating his men in Japanese. They must have called him with the bad news when I got away. "One

man! One unarmed man! And you let him get away!
Useless, incompetent idiots!"

I couldn't tell who or how many he was talking to
because they were suffering his tirade in silence. There
was a long pause, during which I assumed he was collecting himself, and afterward he said, "It doesn't matter. He may not know where the disk is, and even if he
does I'm not confident that you would have been able
to extract the information from him. He's obviously
tougher than any of you."

After another long pause, someone spoke up: "What
would you have us do, *toushu?*"

"What indeed," Yamaoto said, his voice slightly
hoarse from shouting. "Focus on the girl. She is still
our most promising lead."

"But she's underground now," the voice said.

"Yes, but she's unaccustomed to such a life," Yamaoto answered. "She went into hiding suddenly,
presumably having left much of the ordinary business of her life suspended. We can count on her to return to that business presently. Put men in all the
vital spots of her life—where she lives, where she
works, her known acquaintances, her family. Work
with Holtzer on this as necessary. He has the technical means."

Holtzer? Work with *him?*

"And the man?"

There was a long pause, then Yamaoto said, "The
man is a different story. He lives in shadows like a fish
in water. Unless we are extraordinarily lucky, I expect
you have lost him."

I could imagine heads bowed collectively in shame

in the Japanese fashion. After a while one of the men spoke up: "We may spot him with the girl."

"Yes, that's possible. He's obviously protecting her. We know he saved her from Ishikura's men outside her apartment. And his reaction to my questions about her whereabouts was defensive. He may have feelings for her." I heard him chuckle. "A strange basis for a romance."

Ishikura? I thought.

"In any event, Rain's loss is not fatal," Yamaoto continued. "The girl poses much more of a danger: she is the one Ishikura Tatsuhiko will be looking for, and he has as good a chance of finding her as we do—perhaps better, judging from his speed in preempting us at her apartment. And if he finds the disk, Ishikura will know what to do with it."

Tatsu? Tatsu is looking for the damn disk, too? Those were his men at her apartment?

"No more chances," Yamaoto went on. "No more loose ends. When the girl resurfaces, eliminate her immediately."

"Hai," several voices replied in chorus.

"Unfortunately, in the absence of the disk's return or certification of its destruction, eliminating the girl will no longer provide us with complete security. It's time to remove Ishikura Tatsuhiko from the equation, as well."

"But, *toushu,*" one of the voices said, "Ishikura is a Keisatsucho department head. Not an easy man to eliminate without causing collateral problems. Moreover . . ."

"Yes, moreover, Ishikura's death will make him a martyr in certain circles by providing elegant supporting evidence for all his conspiracy theories. But we have no choice. Better to have evidence of such theories than what's on the disk, which is proof itself. Do your utmost to make Ishikura's demise seem natural. Ironic, that at the moment we need him most, the man supremely capable of such art is unavailable to us. Well, take what inspiration you can from him. Dismissed."

That was it. I removed the headphones and looked at Harry. "It's still transmitting?"

"Until the battery runs out—about three weeks. I'll keep monitoring it."

I nodded, realizing that Harry was almost certainly going to hear things from that room that would lead back to me. Hell, Yamaoto's comments were already damning if you were smart and had context: the reference to the "strange basis" of my attachment to Midori, and to the irony of having lost the services of the man "supremely capable" of effecting death by natural causes.

"I don't think Midori should hear what's on that tape," I said. "She knows enough. I don't want to . . . compromise her further."

Harry bowed his head and said, "I completely understand."

All at once, I knew that he knew.

"It's good that I can trust you," I said. "Thank you."

He shook his head. "*Kochira koso*," he said. The same here.

The buzzer rang. Harry pressed the intercom button, and Midori said, "It's me."

Harry hit the entrance buzzer, and we took up our

positions, this time with me at the door and Harry at the window. A minute later I saw Midori walking down the hallway with a rectangular cardboard box in her arms. Her face broke into a smile when she saw me, and she covered the distance quickly, stepped inside the *genkan*, and gave me a quick hug.

"Every time I see you, you look worse," she told me, stepping back after a moment and setting the box on the floor. It was true: my face was still smudged with dirt from my tumble on the subway tracks, and I knew I looked exhausted.

"I feel worse, too," I said, but smiling to let her know she made me feel good.

"What happened?"

"I'll give you the details in a little while. First, Harry tells me you're going to give us a piano recital."

"That's right," she said, reaching down and stripping tape off the box. She popped open the end and slid out an electronic keyboard. "Will this work?" she said, holding it up to Harry.

Harry took it and examined the jack. "I think I've got an adapter here somewhere. Hang on." He walked over to the desk, pulled open a drawer filled with electronic components, and tried several units before finding one that satisfied him. He set the keyboard down on the desk, plugged it into the computer, and brought the scanned image of the notes up onto the monitor.

"The problem is that I can't play music and Midori can't run the computer. I think the shortcut will be to get the computer to apply the patterns of sounds to the representation of notes on the page. Once it's got enough data to work with, the computer will interpret the musical notes as coordinates in the lattice, then use fractal analysis until it can discern the most basic way the pattern repeats itself. Then it will apply the pattern to standard Japanese through a code-breaking algorithm I've set up, and we'll be in."

"Right," I said. "That's just what I was thinking."

Harry gave me his trademark "you-are-a-complete-knuckle-dragger" look, then said, "Midori, try playing the score on the monitor and let's see what the computer can do with the data."

Midori sat down at the desk and lifted her fingers over the keyboard. "Wait," Harry said. "You've got to play it perfectly. If you add or delete a note, or play one out of order, you'll create a new pattern, and the computer will get confused. You have to play exactly what appears on the screen. Can you do that?"

"I could if this were an ordinary song. But this composition is unusual. I'll need to run through it a few times first. Can you disconnect me from the computer?"

"Sure." He dragged and clicked the mouse. "Go ahead. Tell me when you're ready."

Midori looked at the screen for a few moments, her head straight and motionless, her fingers rippling ever so slightly in the air, reflecting the sounds she could hear in her mind. Then she brought her hands down gently to the keys, and for the first time we heard the eerie melody of the information that had cost Kawamura his life.

I listened uncomfortably while Midori played. After a few minutes, she said to Harry, "Okay, I'm ready. Plug me in."

Harry worked the mouse. "You're in. Let it hear you."

Again, Midori's fingers floated over the keys, and the room was filled with the strange requiem. When she reached the end of the score, she stopped and looked at Harry, her eyebrows raised in a question.

"It's got the data," he said. "Let's see what it can do with it."

We watched the screen, waiting for the results, none of us speaking.

After a half minute or so, a strange, disembodied series of notes emanated from the computer speakers, shadows of what I had heard Midori play a moment earlier.

"It's factoring the sounds," Harry said. "It's trying to find the most basic pattern."

We waited silently for several minutes. Finally Harry said, "I don't see any progress. I might not have the computing power here."

"Where can you get it?" Midori asked.

Harry shrugged. "I can try hacking into Livermore to gain access to their supercomputer. Their security has been getting better, though—it could take some time."

"Would a supercomputer do the trick?" I asked.

"It might," he said. "Actually, any reasonable amount of processing power is enough. It's a question of time, though—the more processing power, the more possibilities the computer can try in a shorter time."

"So a supercomputer would speed things up," Midori said, "but we don't know by how much."

He nodded. "That's right."

There was a moment of frustrated quiet. Then Harry said, "Let's think for a moment. How much do we even need to decrypt this?"

I knew where he was going: the same tempting thought I had at Conviction headquarters when Yamaoto was asking for the disk.

"What do you mean?" Midori asked.

"Well, what are our objectives here? The disk is like dynamite; we just want to render it safe. The owners know that it can't be copied or electronically transmitted. For starters, we could render it safe by just giving it back to them."

"No!" Midori said, standing up from in front of the monitor and facing Harry. "My father risked his life for what's on that disk. It's going where he wanted it to go!"

Harry held up his hands in an "I-surrender" gesture. "Okay, okay, I'm just trying to think outside the box. Just trying to be helpful."

"It's a logical idea, Harry," I said, "but Midori's right. Not only because her father risked his life to acquire the disk. We know now that there are multiple parties seeking its return—not just Yamaoto, but also the Agency, the Keisatsucho. Maybe more. Even if we were to give it back to one of them, it wouldn't solve our problems with the others."

"I see your point," Harry conceded.

"But I like your dynamite analogy. How do you render dynamite safe?"

"You detonate it somewhere safe," Midori said, still looking at Harry.

"Exactly," I said.

"Bulfinch," Midori said. "Bulfinch publishes it, and that's what makes it safe. And it's what my father wanted."

"Do we give it to him without even knowing for sure what's on it?" Harry asked.

"We know well enough," I said. "Based on what Bulfinch told us, corroborated by Holtzer. I don't see an alternative."

He frowned. "We don't even know if he has the resources to decrypt it."

I suppressed a smile at the slight hint of resentment I detected: someone was going to take away his toy, maybe solve the technopuzzle without him.

"We can assume that *Forbes* can access the right resources. We know how much they want what's on that disk."

"I'd still like a better chance at decrypting it first."

"So would I. But we don't know how long that would take. In the meantime we've got forces arrayed against us and we're not going to be able to go on eluding them for much longer. The sooner Bulfinch publishes the damn thing, the sooner we can breathe easy again."

Midori, not taking any chances, said, "I'll call him."

20

I HAD TOLD Bulfinch to meet me in Akasaka Mitsuke, one of the city's entertainment districts, second only to Ginza in its profusion of hostess bars. The area is intersected by a myriad of alleyways, some so narrow they can only be traversed sideways, all of which offer multiple means of access and escape.

It was raining and cold as I finished an SDR and exited Akasaka Mitsuke subway station in front of the Belle Vie department store. Across the street, bizarrely pink amidst the gray rain and sky, was the battleship bulk of the Akasaka Tokyu Hotel. I paused to open the black umbrella I was carrying, then turned right onto Sotobori-dori. After a right turn into an alley by the local Citibank, I emerged onto the red crenellated brick of the Esplanade Akasaka-dori.

I was over an hour early and decided to grab a quick lunch at the Tenkaichi ramen restaurant on the Esplanade. Tenkaichi, "First Under Heaven," is a chain, but the one on the Esplanade has character. The proprietors accept foreign currency, and the notes and coins of dozens of countries are taped to the establishment's brown wooden walls. They also play a continuous stream of jazz compilations, occasionally interspersed by some soft American pop. And the cushioned stools, some discreetly set off in corners, offer a good view of the street in front of the restaurant.

I ordered the *chukadon*—Chinese vegetables over rice—and ate while I watched the street through the window. Two *sarariman,* taking a late lunch break, also supped alone and in silence.

I had told Bulfinch that, at 2:00, he should start circling the block counterclockwise at 19-3 Akasaka Mitsuke san-chome. There were more than a dozen alleys accessing that particular block, each with multiple tributaries, so he wouldn't know where I'd be waiting until I made my presence known. It didn't matter if he came early. He'd just have to keep circling the block in the rain. He didn't know where I'd be.

I finished at 1:50, paid the check, and left. Keeping the canopy of the umbrella low over my head, I crossed the Esplanade to Misuji-dori, then cut into an alley opposite the Buon Appetito restaurant on the 19-3 block and waited under the overhang of some rusting corrugated roofing. Because of the hour and the weather, the area was quiet. I waited and watched sad drops of water falling in a slow rhythm from the rusted roof onto the tops of dilapidated plastic refuse containers beneath.

After about ten minutes I heard footsteps on the wet brick behind me, and a moment later Bulfinch appeared. He was wearing an olive trench coat and hunkering down under a large black umbrella. From where I was standing he couldn't see me, and I waited until he had passed before speaking.

"Bulfinch. Over here," I said quietly.

"Shit!" he said, turning to face me. "Don't do that. You scared me."

"You're alone?"

"Of course. You brought the disk?"

I stepped out from under the roofing and observed the alley in both directions. All clear. "It's nearby. Tell me what you plan to do with it."

"You know what I plan to do. I'm a reporter. I'm going to write a series of stories with whatever's on there as corroboration."

"How long will that take?"

"How long? Hell, the stories are already written. All I need is the proof."

I considered. "Let me tell you a few things about the disk," I said, and explained about the encryption.

"Not a problem," he said when I was done. "*Forbes* has a relationship with Lawrence Livermore. They'll help us. As soon as it's cracked, we publish."

"You know that every day that goes by without that publication, Midori's life is in danger."

"Is that why you're giving it to me? The people who want it would have paid you for it. Quite a lot, you know."

"I want you to understand something," I said. "If you were to fail to publish what's on that disk, your failure might cost Midori her life. If that were to happen, I would find you, and I would kill you."

"I believe you."

I looked at him a moment longer, then reached into

my breast pocket and took out the disk. I handed it to him and walked back to the station.

I ran an SDR to Shinbashi, thinking about Tatsu on the way. Until the contents of the disk were published, it wasn't just Midori who was in danger, I knew; it was also Tatsu. And while Tatsu was no soft target, he wasn't bulletproof, either. It had been a lot of years since I had seen him, but we had covered each other's backs once. I owed him a heads-up at least.

I called the Keisatsucho from a pay phone at Shinbashi Station. "Do you know who this is?" I asked in English after they had put me through to him.

There was a long pause. *"Ei, hisashiburi desu ne."* Yes, it's been a long time. Then he switched to English—a good sign, because it meant he didn't want the people around him to understand. "Do you know that the Keisatsucho found two bodies in Sengoku? One of them had been carrying a cane. Your fingerprints were on it. I've wondered from time to time whether you were still in Tokyo."

Damn, I thought, *must have grabbed the cane at some point without even realizing it.* My fingerprints were on file from the time I returned to Japan after the war—I was technically a foreigner, and all foreigners in Japan get fingerprinted.

"We tried to locate you," he went on, "but you seemed to have vanished. So I think I understand why you're calling, but there is nothing I can do for you. The best thing you can do now is to come to the Keisatsucho. If you do, you know I will do everything I can do to help you. You make yourself look guilty by running."

"That's why I'm calling, Tatsu. I've got information about this matter that I want to give to you."

"In exchange for what?"

"For you doing something about it. Listen to what I'm saying, Tatsu. This isn't about me. If you act on the information I've got, I'll turn myself in afterwards. I'll have nothing to be afraid of."

"Where and when?" he asked.

"Are we alone on this line?" I asked.

"Are you suggesting that this line could be tapped?" he asked, and I recognized the old subversive sarcasm in his voice. He was telling me to assume that it was.

"Okay, good," I said. "Lobby of the Hotel Okura, next Saturday, noon sharp." The Okura was a ridiculously public place to meet, and Tatsu would know that I would never seriously suggest it.

"Ah, that's a good place," he answered, telling me he understood. "I'll see you then."

"You know, Tatsu, it sounds crazy, but sometimes I miss the times we had in Vietnam. I miss those useless weekly briefings we used to have to go to—do you remember?"

The CIA head of the task force that ran the briefings invariably scheduled them for 16:30, leaving him plenty of time afterwards to chase prostitutes through Saigon. Tatsu rightly thought the guy was a joke, and wasn't shy about pointing it out publicly.

"Yes, I remember," he said.

"For some reason I was especially missing them just now," I said, getting ready to give him the day to add to the time. "Wished I had one to attend tomorrow, in fact. Isn't that strange? I'm getting nostalgic in my old age."

"That happens."

"Yeah, well. It's been a long time. I'm sorry we lost touch the way we did. Tokyo's changed so much since I first got here. We had some pretty good times back then, didn't we? I used to love that one place we used to go to, the one where the mama-san made pottery that she used to serve the drinks in. Remember it? It's probably not even there anymore."

The place was in Ebisu. "It's gone," he said, telling me he understood.

"Well, *shoganai, ne*?" That's life. "It was a good place. I think of it sometimes."

"I strongly advise you to come in. If you do, I promise to do everything I can to help."

"I'll think about it. Thanks for the advice." I hung up then, my hand lingering on the receiver, willing him to understand my cryptic message. I didn't know what I was going to do if he didn't.

21

THE PLACE I'D mentioned in Ebisu was a classic Japanese *izakaya* that Tatsu had introduced me to when I came to Japan after the war. *Izakaya* are tiny bars in old wooden buildings, usually run by an ageless man or woman, or a couple, who lives over the store, with only a red lantern outside the entrance to advertise their existence. Offering refuge from a demanding boss or a tedious marriage, from the tumult of the subways and the noise of the streets, *izakaya* serve beer and sake long into the night, as an endless procession of customers take and abandon seats at the bar, always to be replaced by another tired man coming in from the cold.

Tatsu and I had spent a lot of time at the place in Ebisu, but I had stopped going there once we lost touch. I kept meaning to drop by and check in on the mama-san, but the months had turned to years and somehow it just never happened. And now, according to Tatsu, the place wasn't even there anymore. Probably it had been torn down. No room for a little place like that in brash, modern Tokyo.

But I remembered where it had been, and that's where I would wait for Tatsu.

I got to Ebisu early to give myself a chance to look around. Things had really changed. So many of the wooden buildings were gone. There was a sparkling new shopping mall near the station—used to be a rice field. It made it a little hard to get my bearings.

I headed east from the station. It was a wet day, the wind blowing mist from an overcast sky.

I found the place where the *izakaya* had been. The dilapidated but cozy building was gone, replaced by an antiseptic-looking convenience store. I strolled past it slowly. It was empty, the sole occupant a bored-looking clerk reading a magazine under the store's fluorescent lights. No sign of Tatsu, but I was nearly an hour early.

I wouldn't have come back, if I'd had an alternative, once I knew the place was gone. Hell, the whole neighborhood was gone. It reminded me of the last time I'd been in the States, about five years before. I'd gone back to Dryden, the closest thing I had to a hometown. I hadn't been back in almost twenty years, and some part of me wanted to connect again, with something.

It was a four-hour drive north from New York City. I got there, and about the only thing that was the same was the layout of the streets. I drove up the main drag, and instead of the things I remembered I saw a McDonald's, a Benetton, a Kinko's Copies, a Subway sandwich shop, all in gleaming new buildings. A couple of places I recognized. They were like the ruins of a lost civilization poking through dense jungle overgrowth.

I walked on, marveling at how once-pleasant memories always seemed to be rendered painful by an alchemy I could never quite comprehend.

I turned onto a side street. A small park was wedged between two nondescript buildings. A couple of young mothers were standing by one of the benches, strollers in front of them, chatting. Probably about goings-on in the neighborhood, how the kids were going to be in school soon.

I circled around behind the new shopping mall, then came back through it, along a wide outdoor esplanade bright with chrome and glass. It was a pretty structure, I had to admit. A couple of high-school kids passed me, laughing. They looked comfortable, like they belonged there.

I saw a figure in an old gray trench coat coming toward me from the other end of the plaza, and although I couldn't make out the face I recognized the gait, the posture. It was Tatsu, sucking a little warmth from a cigarette, otherwise ignoring the damp day.

He saw me and waved, tossing away the cigarette. As he came closer I saw that his face was more deeply lined than I remembered, a weariness somehow closer to the surface.

"*Honto ni, shibaraku buri da na,*" I said, offering him a bow. It has been a long time. He extended his hand, and I shook it.

He was looking at me closely, no doubt seeing the same lines on my face that I saw on his, and perhaps something more. This was the first time Tatsu had seen me since my plastic surgery. He must have been wondering at how age seemed to have hidden the Caucasian in my features. I wondered if he suspected something besides the passage of time behind my changed appearance.

"Rain-san, *ittai*, what have you done this time?" he asked, still looking at me. "Do you know how much trouble it will mean if someone finds out that I've met you without arresting you? You are a suspect in a double murder. In which one of the victims was well connected in the LDP. I am under substantial pressure to solve this, you know."

"Tatsu, aren't you even going to tell me it's good to see me? I have feelings, you know."

He smiled his sorrowful smile. "You know it's good to see you. But I would wish for different circumstances."

"How are your daughters?"

The smile broadened, and he nodded his head proudly. "Very fine. One doctor. One lawyer. Luckily they have their mother's brains, *ne*?"

"Married?"

"The older is engaged."

"Congratulations. Sounds like you'll be a grandfather soon."

"Not too soon," he said, the smile evaporating, and I thought *I'd hate to be the kid Tatsu caught fooling around with one of his daughters.*

We headed back across the mall, past a perfect reproduction French château that looked homesick in its current surroundings.

The small talk done, I got to the point. "Yamaoto Toshi, head of Conviction, has put a contract out on your life," I told him.

He stopped walking and looked at me. "How do you know this?"

"Sorry, no questions about how."

He nodded. "Your source must be credible, or you wouldn't be telling me."

"Yes."

We started walking again. "You know, Rain-san, there are a lot of people who would like to see me dead. Sometimes I wonder how I've managed to keep breathing for all this time."

"Maybe you've got a guardian angel."

He laughed. "I wish that were so. Actually, the explanation is simpler. My death would establish my credibility. Alive, I can be dismissed as a fool, a chaser of phantoms."

"I'm afraid circumstances have changed."

He stopped again and looked at me closely. "I didn't know you were mixed up with Yamaoto."

"I'm not."

He was nodding his head, and I knew that he was adding this bit of data to his profile of the mysterious assassin.

He started walking again. "You were saying. 'Circumstances have changed.'"

"There's a disk. My understanding is that it contains information implicating various politicians in massive corruption. Yamaoto is trying to get it."

He knew something about the disk—I'd heard Yamaoto saying on the transmitter that Tatsu had sent men to Midori's apartment, after all—yet he said nothing.

"You know anything about this, Tatsu?" I asked.

He shrugged. "I'm a cop. I know a little about everything."

"Yamaoto thinks you know a lot. He knows you're after that disk. He's having trouble getting it back, so he's trying to eliminate loose ends."

"Why is he having trouble getting the disk back?"

"He doesn't know where it is."

"Do you?"

"I don't have it."

"That is not what I asked you."

"Tatsu, this isn't about the disk. I came here because I learned that you're in danger. I wanted to warn you."

"But the missing disk is the reason I'm in danger, is it not?" he said, affecting a puzzled, innocent look that would have fooled someone who didn't know him. "Find the disk; remove the danger."

"Ease up on the *inakamono* routine," I said, telling him I knew he wasn't a country bumpkin. "I'll tell you this much. The person who has the disk is in a position to publish what's on it. That should remove the danger, as you put it."

He stopped and grabbed my arm. "*Masaka*, tell me you didn't give that fucking disk to Bulfinch."

Alarm bells started going off in my head.

"Why do you ask that?"

"Because Franklin Bulfinch was murdered yesterday in Akasaka Mitsuke, outside the Akasaka Tokyu Hotel."

"Fuck!" I said, momentarily forgetting myself.

"*Komatta*," he swore again. "You gave it to him, didn't you?"

"Yes."

"Damn it! Did he have it with him when he was killed?"

Outside the Akasaka Tokyu—a hundred meters from where I gave it to him. "What time did it happen?" I asked.

"Early afternoon. Maybe two o'clock. Did he have it with him?"

"Almost certainly," I told him.

His shoulders slumped, and I knew he wasn't play-acting.

"Damn it, Tatsu. How do you know about the disk?"

There was a long pause before he answered. "Because Kawamura was supposed to give the disk to me."

I raised my eyebrows in surprise.

"Yes," he went on, "I had been developing Kawamura for quite some time. I had strongly encouraged him to provide me with the information that is now on that disk. It seems that, in the end, everyone trusts a reporter more than a cop. Kawamura decided to give the disk to Bulfinch instead."

"How do you know?"

"Kawamura called me the morning he died."

"What did he say?"

He looked at me, deadpan. "'Fuck off. I'm giving the disk to the Western media.' It's my fault, really. In my eagerness, I'd been putting too much pressure on him. I'm sure he found it unpleasant."

"How did you know it was Bulfinch?"

"If you wanted to give this kind of information to someone in the 'Western media,' who would you go to? Bulfinch is well known for his reporting on corruption. But I couldn't be sure until this morning, when I learned of his murder. And I wasn't completely certain until just now."

"So this is why you've been following Midori."

"Of course." Tatsu has a dry way of saying "of course" that always seems to emphasize some lack of mental acuity on the part of the listener. "Kawamura died almost immediately after he called me, meaning it was likely that he was unable to deliver the disk to the 'Western media' as planned. His daughter had his things. She was a logical target."

"That's why you were investigating the break-in at her father's apartment."

He looked at me disapprovingly. "My men performed that break-in. We were looking for the disk."

"Two chances to look for it—the break-in, and then the investigation," I said, admiring his efficiency. "Convenient."

"Not convenient enough. We couldn't find it. This is why we turned our attention to the daughter."

"You and everyone else."

"You know, Rain-san," he said, "I had a man following her in Omotesando. He had a most unlikely accident in the bathroom of a local bar. His neck was broken."

Christ, that was Tatsu's man. So maybe Benny had been serious about giving me forty-eight hours to accept the Midori assignment. Not that it mattered anymore. "Really," I said.

"On the same night I had men waiting at the daughter's apartment. Despite being armed, they were ambushed and overcome by a single man."

"Embarrassing," I said, waiting for more.

He took out a cigarette, studied it for a moment,

then placed it in his mouth and lit it. "Academic," he said, exhaling a cloud of gray smoke. "It's over. The CIA has the disk now."

"Why do you say that? What about Yamaoto?"

"I have means of knowing that Yamaoto is still searching for the disk. There is only one other player in this drama, besides me. That player must have taken the disk from Bulfinch."

"If you're talking about Holtzer, he's working with Yamaoto."

He smiled the sad smile. "Holtzer isn't working with Yamaoto, he's Yamaoto's slave. And, like most slaves, he's looking for a way to escape."

"I don't follow you."

"Yamaoto controls Holtzer through blackmail, as he controls all his puppets. But Holtzer is playing a double game. He plans to use that disk to bring Yamaoto down, to cut the puppet master's strings."

"So Holtzer hasn't told Yamaoto that the Agency has the disk."

He shrugged. "As I said, Yamaoto is still looking for it."

"Tatsu," I said quietly, "what's on that disk?"

He took a tired pull on his cigarette, then blew the smoke skyward. "Videos of extramarital sexual acts, audio of bribes and payoffs, numbers of secret accounts, records of illegal real estate transactions and money laundering."

"Implicating Yamaoto?"

He looked at me as though wondering how I could be so slow. "Rain-san, you were a great soldier, but you would make a very shitty cop. Implicating everyone *but* Yamaoto."

I was silent for a moment while I tried to connect the dots. "Yamaoto uses this information as blackmail?"

"Of course," he replied in his dry way. "Why do you think we have had nothing but failed administration after failed administration? Eleven prime ministers in as many years? Every one of them has either been an LDP flunky or a reformer who is immediately co-opted and defused. This is Yamaoto, governing from the shadows."

"But he's not even part of the LDP."

"He doesn't want to be. He is much more effective governing as he does. When a politician displeases him, incriminating information is released, the media is instructed to magnify it, and the offending politician is disgraced. The scandal reflects only on the LDP, not on Conviction."

"How does he get his information?"

"An extensive system of wiretaps, video surveillance, and accomplices. Every time he traps someone new, the victim becomes complicit and assists him in furthering his network of blackmail."

"Why would they help him?"

"Carrot and stick. Yamaoto of course has on his payroll a number of young women sufficiently beautiful to make even the most faithfully married politician temporarily forget himself. Say he has one of his people videotape a member of Parliament engaging in an embarrassing sexual act with one of these women. The politician is then shown the videotape and told that it will be kept in confidence in exchange for his vote on certain measures, typically affecting public-works spending, and for his cooperation in entrapping his colleagues. If the politician has a conscience, he won't want to vote in favor of these ridiculous public projects, but his fear of exposure is now a much more significant motivator than his conscience would ever have been. As for entrapping his colleagues, there is some psychology at work: by making others dirty, he feels less dirty by comparison. And because elections are decided in Japan not by a politician's voting record but by his access to money, Yamaoto offers an enormous slush fund that the politician can use to fund his next election campaign. Yamaoto gives generously: once a politician is part of his network, it is in his interest to see that person reelected, to advance the politician's career. Yamaoto's influence runs so deep that, if you're not part of his network, you can't get anything done and anyway you'll be defeated in the next election by being outspent by one of his puppets."

"With all that power, why have I never heard of him?"

"Yamaoto does not reveal the source of the pressure being applied. His victims know only that they are being blackmailed, not by whom. Most of them believe it is the work of one or another LDP faction. And why not? Every time Yamaoto determines that a scandal is in his interest, the LDP becomes the focus of the country's attention. Ironic, isn't it? Yamaoto manages things so that even the LDP believes the LDP is the power. But there is a power behind the power."

I thought of the reports I'd been tracking, of Tatsu's conspiracy theories. "But you've been focusing on corruption in the LDP yourself, Tatsu."

His eyes narrowed. "How would you know that?"

I smiled. "Just because we've fallen out of touch doesn't mean I've lost interest."

He took another drag on the cigarette. "Yes, I focus on corruption in the LDP," he said, the smoke jetting down from his nostrils. "Yamaoto is amused by this. He believes it serves his ends. And it would, if any of my reports were taken seriously. But only Yamaoto decides when corruption is to be prosecuted." There was a bitter set to his mouth as he said it.

I couldn't help but smile at him—the same wily bastard I knew in Vietnam. "But you've been playing possum. Your real goal is Yamaoto."

He shrugged.

"Now I understand why you wanted that disk," I said.

"You knew of my involvement, Rain-san. Why didn't you contact me?"

"I had reason not to."

"Yes?"

"Midori," I said. "If I'd given it to you, Yamaoto would still think it was missing, and he would keep coming after Midori. Publication was the only way to make her safe."

"Is this the only reason you were reluctant to contact me?"

I looked at him, wary. "I can't think of anything else. Can you?"

His only response was the sad smile.

We walked for a moment in silence, then I asked, "How did Yamaoto get to Holtzer?"

"By offering him what every man wants."

"Which is?"

"Power, of course. How do you think that Holtzer

rose so quickly through the ranks to become chief of Tokyo Station?"

"Yamaoto's been feeding him information?"

"Of course. It is my understanding that Mr. Holtzer has been notably successful at developing assets in Japan. And as chief of station in Tokyo, he has been responsible for producing certain critical intelligence reports—particularly regarding corruption in the Japanese government, on which Yamaoto is of course an expert."

"Christ, Tatsu, the quality of your information is almost scary."

"What is scary is how useless the information has always been to me."

"Holtzer knows that he's being played?"

He shrugged. "At first, he thought he was developing Yamaoto. Once he realized that the opposite was true, what were his options? Tell the CIA that the assets he had developed were plants, the reports all fabricated? That would have meant the end of his career. The alternative was much more pleasant: work for Yamaoto, who continues to feed him the 'intelligence' that makes Holtzer a star. And Yamaoto has his mole inside the CIA."

Holtzer, a mole, I thought, disgusted. *I should have known.*

"Holtzer told me that the CIA had been developing Kawamura, that Kawamura was on his way to deliver the disk to the Agency when he died."

He shrugged. "Kawamura screwed me. He might have screwed the Agency, as well. Impossible to say, and irrelevant."

"What about Bulfinch," I asked. "How did Holtzer get to him?"

"By having him followed until you handed over the disk, of course. Bulfinch was a soft target, Rain-san." I heard the soft note of criticism in his voice—telling me it was stupid to give the disk to a civilian.

We walked silently again for a few minutes. Then he said, "Rain-san. What have you been doing in Japan all this time? Since the last time we met."

With Tatsu, it was a mistake to assume that anything was small talk. A small warning bell went off somewhere in my consciousness.

"Nothing terribly new," I said. "The same consulting work as before."

"What was that, again?"

"You know. Helping a few U.S. companies find ways to import their products into Japan. Get around the red tape, find the right partners, that sort of thing."

"It sounds interesting. What sort of products?"

Tatsu ought to have known better than to think a few simple questions would crack my cover story. The consulting business, the clients, they're all real, albeit not exactly Fortune 500 stuff.

"Why don't you check out my Web site?" I asked him. "There's a section full of client references on it."

He waved his hand in a "don't-be-silly" gesture. "What I mean is, What are you still doing in Japan? Why are you still here?"

"What difference does it make, Tatsu?"

"I don't understand. I would like to."

What could I tell him? *I needed to stay at war. A shark can't stop swimming, or it dies.*

But it was more than that, I had to admit to myself. Sometimes I hate living here. Even after twenty-five years, I'm still an outsider, and I resent it. And it's not just my profession that militates a life in shadows. It's also that, despite my native features, my native linguistic level, what matters in the end is that inside I am half *gaijin*. A cruel teacher once said to me when I was a kid, "What do you get when you mix clean water with dirty water? Dirty water." It took several additional years of slights and rejection before I figured out what she meant: that I'm marked by an indelible stain that the shadows can conceal but never wash away.

"You've been here for over two decades," Tatsu said, gently. "Maybe it's time for you to go home."

He knows, I thought. *Or he's on the verge.* "I wonder where that is," I said.

He spoke slowly. "There is a risk that, if you stay, we could learn we have opposing interests."

"Let's not learn that, then."

I saw the sad smile. "We can try."

We walked again, the sky brooding above us.

Something occurred to me. I stopped walking and looked at him. "It might not be over," I said.

"What do you mean?"

"The disk. Maybe we can still get it back."

"How?"

"It can't be copied or transmitted electronically. And it's encrypted. Holtzer is going to need expertise to decrypt it. Either he has to take the disk to the experts, or the experts will have to come to him."

He paused for only a second before taking out his

cell phone. He input a number, raised the unit to his ear, and waited.

"I need a schedule for visiting American government personnel," he said in curt Japanese into the phone. "Particularly anyone declared from the NSA or CIA. For the next week, particularly the next few days. Right away. Yes, I'll wait."

The U.S. and Japanese governments declare their high-level spooks to each other as part of their security treaty and general intelligence cooperation. It was a long shot, but it was something.

And I knew Holtzer. He was a grandstander. He'd be billing the disk as the intelligence coup of the century. He'd be sure to hand it over himself to ensure that he received full credit.

We waited silently for a few minutes, then Tatsu said, "Yes. Yes. Yes. Understood. Wait a minute."

He held the phone against his chest and said, "NSA software cryptography specialist, declared to the Japanese government. And the CIA director of East Asian Affairs. Both arriving from Washington tonight at Narita. I don't believe this is a coincidence. Holtzer must have had them moving as soon as he got the disk."

"Where are they going? The embassy?"

"Hold on." He put the phone back to his ear. "Find out whether they've requested a diplomatic escort, and if so where they're going. I'll wait."

He put the phone back to his chest. "The Keisatsu-cho receives many requests for escorts of U.S. government personnel," he said. "The government people don't have the budget to pay for sedan service, so they use us on the pretext of diplomatic security. This may be the first time I won't find this habit annoying."

He put the phone back to his ear, and we waited. After a few minutes he said, "Good. Good. Wait." The phone went back to his chest. "Yokosuka U.S. Naval Base. Thursday morning, straight from the Narita Airport Hilton."

"We've got him, then."

His expression was grim. "How, exactly?"

"Hell, stop Holtzer's car, take the disk, declare him *persona non grata* for all I care."

"On what evidence, exactly? The prosecutors would want to know."

"Hell, I don't know. Tell them it was an anonymous source."

"You're missing the point. What you've told me is not evidence. It's hearsay."

"Christ, Tatsu," I said, exasperated, "when did you turn into such a damn bureaucrat?"

"It isn't a matter of bureaucracy," he said sharply, and I wished I hadn't let my temper flare. "It's a question of using the proper tools to get the job done. What you are suggesting would be useless."

I reddened. Somehow, Tatsu could always make me feel like a lumbering, thickheaded *gaijin*. "Well, if we can't go through channels, what do you propose instead?"

"I can get the disk and protect Midori. But you will need to be involved."

"What do you propose?"

"I will arrange to have Holtzer's car stopped outside the naval facility, perhaps on the pretext of needing to examine its undercarriage for explosive devices." He looked at me dryly. "Perhaps an anonymous call could warn us of such an attempt."

"Really," I said.

He shrugged and intoned a phone number, which I wrote down on my hand, reversing the last four numbers and subtracting two from each of them. When I was done, he said, "An officer will of course have to ask the driver to lower his window to explain."

I nodded, seeing where he was going. "Here's my pager number," I said, and gave it to him. "Use it to contact me when you've acquired the information on Holtzer's movements. Input a phone number, then five-five-five, so I'll know it's you. I'm going to need some equipment, too—a flashbang." Flashbang grenades are just what they sound like: no shrapnel, just a big noise and a flash of light, so they temporarily disorient, rather than kill and maim. Antiterrorist units use them to stun the occupants of a room before kicking down the door and shooting the bad guys.

I didn't have to tell him what the flashbang was for. "How can I get it to you?" he asked.

"The fountain at Hibiya Park," I answered, improvising. "Drop it in on the side facing Hibiya-dori. Right up at the edge, like this." I drew a diagram on my hand to ensure that he understood. "Page me when you emplace it so it doesn't stay insecure for too long."

"All right."

"One more thing," I said.

"Yes?"

"Warn your people. I don't want anyone shooting at me by mistake."

"I will do my best."

"Do better than your best. It's my ass that's going to get shot at."

"It's both our asses," he said, his voice level. "If you are unsuccessful, I can assure you that there will be an inquiry into who ordered that the car be stopped, and under what pretext. If I am lucky, under such circumstances, I will merely have to take early retirement. If I am less than lucky, I will go to prison."

He had a point, although I didn't think he would have accepted an offer to trade my risk for his. Not that it was worth arguing over.

"You just stop the car," I told him. "I'll take care of the rest."

He nodded, then bowed with unsettling formality.

"Good luck, Rain-san," he said, and walked off into the gathering darkness.

22

I LOVE TOKYO at night. It's the lights, I think: more than
the architecture, more, even, than its sounds and
scents, the lights are what animate the city's nocturnal
spirit. There is brightness: streets alight with neon,
with the urgent blinking of constellations of pachinko
parlors, streets where the store windows and the head-
lights of a thousand passing cars illuminate the pave-
ment as brightly as the halogen lamps of a night
baseball game. And there is gloom: alleys lit by nothing more than the fluorescent glow of a lonely vending
machine, left leaning against the worn brick like an old
man who's given up on everything and wants only to
catch his breath, streets lit only by the yellowish pall of
lamplights spaced so widely that a passing figure and
his shadow seem to evaporate in the dim spaces between.

I walked the gloomy backstreets of Ebisu after Tatsu
departed, heading toward the Imperial Hotel in Hibiya, where I would stay until this thing was over. For
near-suicidal audacity, what I was about to do would
rank with any of the missions I had undertaken during

my days with SOG, or with those of the mercenary conflicts that came after. I wondered if Tatsu's bow was some kind of epitaph.

Well, you've survived missions before that ought to have been your last, I thought, letting loose a memory.

After our rampage in Cambodia, things started going bad for my unit. Up until then the killing had been pretty impersonal. You get into a firefight, you're just aiming at tracer rounds, you can't even see the people who are firing back at you. Maybe later you'll find blood or brains, maybe some bodies. Or we'd hear one of the claymore booby traps we'd laid go off a klik or two away, and know we'd nailed someone. But the thing we did at Cu Lai was different. It affected us.

I knew what we had done was wrong, but I rationalized by saying hey, we're at war; wrong things happen in wars. Some of the other guys got morose, guilt making them gun-shy. Crazy Jake—Jimmy—went the opposite way. He locked himself even tighter into the war's embrace.

Crazy Jake was fanatically loyal to his Yards—short for Montagnards—and they responded to that. When a Yard was lost in a firefight, Jake would deliver the bad news personally to the village chief. He eschewed army barracks, preferring to sleep in the Yard quarters. He learned their language and their customs, participated in their ceremonies and rituals. Plus, the Yards believed in magic—the villages had their own sorcerers—and a man with Jake's killing record walked with a powerful aura.

All this made the brass uncomfortable, because they

didn't command the Yards' respect. The problem got worse when we were assigned to beef up the fortified hamlets at Bu Dop, on the Cambodian border, because it exposed Crazy Jake to more of the indigenous population.

Frustrated with the rules of engagement set by the Military Assistance Command, Vietnam, and with MACV's inability to root out the mole who was compromising SOG's operations, Jake started using Bu Dop as a staging ground for independent missions against the Vietcong in Cambodia. The Yards hated the Vietnamese because the Vietnamese had been shitting on them throughout history, and they were happy to follow Crazy Jake on his lethal forays. But SOG was being disbanded, and Vietnamization—that is, turning the war over to the Vietnamese so that America could back out—was the order of the day. MACV told him to shut off the Cambodian ops, but Jake refused—said it was just part of defending his hamlets.

So MACV recalled him to Saigon. Jake ignored them. A detachment was sent in to retrieve him, and never returned. This was even more spooky than if they had been slaughtered, their severed heads run up on pikes. Did they turn and join Crazy Jake? Did he have that much magic? Did he just disappear them into thin air?

So they cut off his supplies. No more weapons, no more materiel. But Jake wouldn't cease and desist. MACV figured out that he was selling poppy to finance his operation. Jake had become his own universe. He had a self-sustaining, highly effective, fanatically loyal private army.

MACV knew about Jimmy and me; they had the personnel files. They brought me in one day. "You're going to have to go in there and get him," they told me. "He's selling drugs now, he's going unauthorized into Cambodia, he's out of control. This is a public-relations fiasco if it gets out."

"I don't think I can get him out. He's not listening to anyone," I said.

"We didn't say, 'get him out.' We just said, 'get him,'" they told me.

There were three of them. Two MACV, one CIA. I was shaking my head. The guy from the agency spoke up.

"Do what· we're asking, and you've got a ticket home."

"I'll get home when I get home," I said, but I wondered.

He shrugged. "We've got two choices here. One is, we carpet-bomb every hamlet in Bu Dop. That's about a thousand friendlies, plus Calhoun. We'll just emulsify everyone. It's not a problem.

"Two is, you do what's right and save all those people, and you're on a plane the next day. Personally, I don't give a shit." He turned and walked out.

I told them I would do it. They were going to grease him anyway. Even if they didn't, I saw what he had become. I had seen it happen to a lot of guys, although Jimmy was the worst. They went over there, and found out that killing was what they were best at. Do you tell people? Do you put on your resume, "Ninety confirmed kills. Large collection of human ears. Ran private army"? C'mon, you're never going to fit in the real world again. You're marked forever, you can't go back.

I went in, told the Yards that I wanted to see Crazy Jake. I was known from the missions we had run together, so they took me to him. I didn't have a weapon; it was okay.

"Hey, Jimmy," I said when I saw him. "Long time no see."

"John John," he greeted me. He had always called me that. "You come in here to join me? It's about time. We're the only outfit in this fucking war that the V.C. is actually afraid of. We don't have to fight with one arm tied behind our balls by a bunch of no-load politicians."

We spent some time catching up. By the time I told him they were going to bomb him it was already night.

"I figured they would, sooner or later," he said. "I can't fight that. Yeah, I figured this was coming."

"What are you going to do?"

"Don't know. But I can't make the Yards my hostages. Even if I could, fuckers'd bomb them anyway."

"Why don't you just walk out?"

He gave me a sly look. "I don't fancy going to jail, John John. Not after leading the good life here in the Central Highlands."

"Well, you're in a tight spot. I don't know what to tell you."

He nodded his head, then said, "You supposed to kill me, man?"

"Yeah," I told him.

"So do it."

I didn't say anything.

"I've got no way out. They're going to vaporize my people otherwise, I know that. And I'd rather it be you than some guy I don't know, dropping a seven hundred and fifty-pound bomb from thirty-thousand feet up. You're my blood brother, man."

I still didn't say anything.

"I love these people," he said. "I really love them. Do you know how many of them have died for me? Because they know I would die for them."

These were not just words. It's hard for a civilian to understand the depth of trust, the depth of love, that can develop between men in combat.

"My Yards won't be happy with you. They really love me, the crazy fucks. Think I'm a magic man. But you're pretty slippery. You'll get away."

"I just want to go home," I said.

He laughed. "There's no home for us, John. Not after what we've done. It doesn't work that way. Here." He handed me a side arm. "Don't worry about me. Save my Yards."

I thought of the recruiter, the one who'd given us twenty bucks to pay some woman to sign us into the army as our mother.

"Save my Yards," Jimmy said again.

I thought of Deirdre saying, *Watch out for Jimmy, okay?*

He picked up a CAR-15, a submachine gun version of the ubiquitous M-16 with a folding stock and shortened barrel, and popped in a magazine. Clicked off the safety so I could see him do it.

"C'mon, John John. I'm not going to keep asking so nicely."

I remembered him putting out his hand after I had fought him to a standstill, saying *You're all right. What's your name?*

John Rain, fuckface, I had answered, and we had fought again.

The CAR-15 was swinging toward me.

I thought of the swimming hole near Dryden, how you had to just forget about everything else and jump.

"Last chance," Jimmy was saying. "Last chance."

Do what we're asking and you've got a ticket home.

There's no home for us, John. Not after what we've done.

I raised the pistol quickly, smoothly, chest level, double-tapping the trigger in the same motion. The two slugs slammed through his chest and blew out his back. Jimmy was dead before he hit the floor.

Two Yards burst into Jimmy's hooch but I had already picked up the CAR. I cut them down and ran.

Their security was outward facing. They weren't well prepared to stop someone going from the inside out. And they were shocked, demoralized, at losing Jimmy.

I took some shrapnel from an exploding claymore. The wounds were minor, but back at base they told me, "Okay, soldier, that's your million-dollar wound. You're going home now." They put me on a plane, and seventy-two hours later I was back in Dryden.

The body came back two days later. There was a funeral. Jimmy's parents were crying, Deirdre was crying. "Oh God, John, I knew, I knew he wasn't going to make it back. Oh God," she was saying.

Everyone wanted to know how Jimmy had died. I

told them he died in a firefight. That was all I knew. Near the border.

I left town a day later. Didn't say good-bye to any of them. Jimmy was right, there was no home after what we had done. "After such knowledge, what forgiveness?" I think some poet said.

I tell myself it's karma, the great wheels of the universe grinding on. A lifetime ago I killed my girl's brother. Now I take out a guy, next thing I know I'm involved with his daughter. If it were happening to someone else, I'd think it was funny.

I had called the Imperial before the meeting with Tatsu and made a reservation. I keep a few things stored at the hotel in case of a rainy day: a couple of suits, identity papers, currency, concealed weapons. The hotel people think I'm an expat Japanese who visits Japan frequently, and I pay them to keep my things so I don't have to carry them back and forth every time I travel. I even stay there periodically to back up the story.

The Imperial is centrally located and has a great bar. More important, it's big enough to be as anonymous as a love hotel, if you know how to play it.

I had just reached Hibiya Station on the Hibiya line when my pager went off. I pulled it from my belt and saw a number I didn't recognize, but followed by the 5-5-5 that told me it was Tatsu.

I found a pay phone and input the number. The other side picked up on the first ring. "Secure line?" Tatsu's voice asked.

"Secure enough."

"The two visitors are leaving Narita at oh-nine-hundred tomorrow. It's a ninety-minute ride to where they're going. Our man might get there before them, though, so you'll need to be in position early, just outside."

"Okay. The package?"

"Being emplaced right now. You can pick it up in an hour."

"Will do."

Silence. Then: "Good luck."

Dead line.

I reinserted the phone card and called the number Tatsu had given me in Ebisu. Whispering to disguise my voice, I warned the person on the other end of the line that there would be a bomb on the undercarriage of a diplomatic vehicle visiting the Yokosuka Naval Base tomorrow. That should slow things up in front of the guardhouse.

I had showered at Harry's before going to meet Tatsu, but I still looked pretty rough when I checked in at the hotel. No one seemed to notice my sleeve, wet from fishing Tatsu's package out of the fountain at the park. Anyway, I had just flown in from the East Coast of the United States—long trip, anything can happen. The attendant at the front desk laughed when I told him I was getting too old for this shit.

My things were already waiting for me in the room, the shirts pressed and the suits hung neatly. I bolted the door and sat down on the bed, then checked a false compartment in the suitcase they had brought up, where I saw the dull gleam of the Glock. I opened up the toiletry kit, took out the rounds I wanted from a dummy can of deodorant, loaded the gun, and slipped it between the mattress and the box spring.

At nine o'clock the phone rang. I picked it up, recognized Midori's voice, and told her the room number.

A minute later there was a quiet knock at the door. I got up and looked through the peephole. The light in the room was off, so the person on the other side wouldn't know whether the occupant was checking to see who was out there. Leaving the light on can make you a nice target for a shotgun blast.

It was Midori, as expected. I let her in and bolted the door behind her. When I turned toward her, she was looking around the room. "Hey, it's about time we stayed in a place like this," she said. "Those love hotels can get old."

"But they have their advantages," I said, putting my arms around her.

We ordered a dinner of sashimi and hot sake from the room-service menu, and while we waited for it to arrive I filled Midori in on my meeting with Tatsu, told her the bad news about Bulfinch.

The food arrived, and, when the hotel employee who brought it had left, Midori said, "I have to ask you something a little . . . silly. Is that okay?"

I looked at her, and felt my gut twist at the honesty in her eyes. "Sure."

"I've been thinking about these people. They killed Bulfinch. They tried to kill you and me. They must have wanted to kill my father. Do you think . . . did he really have a heart attack?"

I poured sake from the ceramic flask into two small matching cups, watching wisps of steam rise from the surface. My hands were steady. "Your question isn't silly. There are ways of killing someone that make it look like an accident, or like natural causes. And I agree that, based on what they learned of your father's activities, they certainly would have wanted him dead."

"He was afraid they were going to kill him. He told me."

"Yes."

She was drumming her fingers on the table, playing a furious tune on an imaginary piano. There was a cold fire in her eyes. "I think they killed him," she said, nodding.

There's no home for us, John. Not after what we've done. "You may be right," I said, quietly.

Did she know? Or did her mind refuse to go where instinct wanted to take her? I couldn't tell.

"What matters is that your father was a brave man," I said, my voice slightly thick. "And that, regardless of how he died, he shouldn't have died in vain. That's why I have to get that disk back. Why I have to finish what your father started. I really . . ." I wasn't sure what I was going to say. "I really want to do that. I need to do it."

Warring emotions crossed her face like the shadows of fast-moving clouds. "I don't want you to," she said. "It's too dangerous."

"It's less dangerous than it seems. My friend is going to make sure that the police who are there know what's going on, so no one is going to take a shot at me." I hoped.

"What about the CIA people? You can't control them."

I thought about that. Tatsu had probably already figured that if I got killed on the way in, he would use it as an excuse to order everyone out of the car, search for weapons, and find the disk that way. He was a practical guy.

"Nobody's going to shoot me. The way I've got it set up, they won't even know what's going on until it's too late."

"I thought that, in war, nothing goes according to plan."

I laughed. "That's true. I've made it this far by being a good improviser."

I took a swallow of sake. "Anyway, we're about out of alternatives," I said, enjoying the feeling of the hot liquid spreading through my abdomen. "Yamaoto doesn't know that Holtzer has the disk, so he's going to keep coming after you if we don't get it back. And after me, too."

We ate for a few minutes in silence. Then she looked at me and said, "It makes sense, but it's still terrible." Her voice was bitter.

I wanted to tell her that eventually you get used to terrible things that make sense. But I said nothing.

She stood up and wandered over to the window. Her back was to me, the glow through the window silhouetting her. I watched her for a moment, then got up and walked over, feeling the carpet taking the weight of my feet. I stopped close enough to smell the clean smell of her hair, and some other, more exotic scent, and slowly, slowly let my hands rise so that my fingertips were just touching her shoulders and arms.

Then my fingertips gave way to my hands, and when my hands made their way to her hips she eased back into me. Her hands found mine and together they rose up, covering her belly and stroking it in such a way that I couldn't tell who was initiating the movement.

Standing there with her, looking out the window over Tokyo, I felt the weight of what I would face in the morning drift slowly away from me. I had the exhilarating realization that there was nowhere, nowhere on the whole planet, that I would rather have been right then. The city around us was a living thing: the million lights were its eyes; the laughter of lovers its voice; the expressways and factories its muscles and sinews. And I was there at its pulsing heart.

Just a little more time, I thought, kissing her neck, her ear. A little more time at an anonymous hotel where we could float untethered from the past, free of all the things that I knew would soon end my fragile bond with this woman.

I became increasingly aware of the sound of her breathing, the taste of her skin, and my languid sense of the city and our place in it faded. She turned and kissed me, softly, then harder, her hands on my face, under my shirt, the heat from her touch spreading through my torso like ripples on water.

We tumbled onto the bed, stripping off each other's clothes, tossing them helter-skelter to the floor. Her back was arched upward and I was kissing her breasts, her belly, and she said, "No, now, I want you now," and I moved up, feeling her legs on either side of me, and into her. She made a sound like the wind picking up, and we moved against each other, with each other, slowly at first, then more urgently. We were fused together, breathing the breath from each other's lungs, the sensation arcing from my head to my groin to my toes and back again until I couldn't tell where my body ended and hers began. I felt a rumbling between us and in us like storm clouds rolling in and when I came it was like a thunderclap from everywhere, her body and my body and all the places where we were joined.

We lay there afterward, still entwined, exhausted as though we had done battle but had failed to vanquish each other with our last and mightiest blows. "*Sugoi*," she said. "What did they put in the sake?"

I smiled at her. "You want to get another bottle?"

"A lot of bottles," she said, drowsily. And that was the last thing either of us said before I drifted off into a sleep that was mercifully untroubled by memories and only slightly marred by dread of what was still to come.

23

I GOT UP just before dawn, and stood looking out the window as the lights came on in Tokyo and the city slowly emerged from its slumber, dreamily stretching its fingers and toes. Midori was still sleeping.

I showered and dressed in one of the suits I keep at the Imperial, an eleven-ounce gray flannel from Paul Stuart. A white Sea Island cotton shirt, conservative blue tie. The shoes were bench made, the well-seasoned attaché from a tragically defunct British leather-goods manufacturer called W. H. Gidden. I was dressed better than most people who are supposed to look the part—again, the details are what make the disguise, or give you away. *And who knows?* I thought. *If this doesn't go well, you could be buried in this outfit. You might as well look good.*

Midori had gotten up while I was in the shower. She was wearing a white terry-cloth hotel robe and sat on the bed silently while I dressed. "I like you in a suit," she told me when I was done. "You look good."

"Just a *sarariman* on his way to work," I said, trying to keep it light.

I slipped the Glock into a custom holster at the small

of my back, where it would be concealed by the nice drape of the flannel. Then I eased the flashbang up under my armpit above the sleeve of the suit, where the natural compression of my arm held it in place. I moved my arm out a few centimeters and jiggled it hard, and the device slid down into my waiting hand. Satisfied, I put it back in position.

I rotated my head and heard the joints in my neck crack. "Okay. I've got to go. I'll be back sometime in the evening. Will you wait for me?"

She nodded, her face set. "I'll be here. Just come back."

"I will." I picked up the attaché and left.

The hotel lobby was relatively empty of the visiting businessmen who would soon arise and meet for over-priced power breakfasts. I walked out through the front doors and shook my head at the bellman's offer to assist me with a cab, preferring instead an indirect walk to Tokyo Station, which would give me the chance to ensure that I wasn't being followed. From the station I would catch the train to Shinbashi, and from Shinbashi to the station at Yokosuka. I could have gone directly from Tokyo Station, but preferred a more circuitous route for my usual reasons.

It was a brisk, clear morning: rare weather for Tokyo, and the kind I've always liked best. As I cut across Hibiya Park I saw a small *asagao*, a morning glory, blooming improbably in the cold spray of one of the fountains. It was a summer flower, and looked sad to me, as though it knew it would die soon in the autumn chill.

At Tokyo Station I bought a ticket to Shinbashi,

where I transferred to the Yokosuka line, checking my back on the way. I bought a two-way ticket to Yokosuka, although a one-way would have been marginally more secure. All soldiers are superstitious, as Crazy Jake had liked to say, and old habits die hard.

I got on the train at 7:00, and it eased out of the station four minutes later, precisely on time. Seventy-four minutes after that we pulled into Yokusuka Station, across the harbor from the naval base. I stepped out onto the platform, attaché case in hand, and busied myself making an ostensible phone call from a public booth while the other passengers who had gotten off the train departed.

From the station I walked along the esplanade that follows the waterline of Yokosuka Harbor. A cold wind sliced across the water into my face, smelling faintly of the sea. The sky was dark, in contrast to the clear weather in Tokyo. *Too good to last,* I thought.

The harbor surface was as gray and foreboding as the sky. I paused on a wooden walkway overlooking the harbor, watching the brooding U.S. warships at rest, the clumps of hills behind them startlingly green against the gray of everything else. The detritus of the military was rhythmically washing up against the seawall below me: empty bottles, cigarette packs, plastic bags like some bizarre and decaying species of sea creature that had been wounded in the deep and come to the surface to die.

The harbor reminded me of Yokohama, and the long-ago Sunday mornings when my mother would take me there. Yokohama was where she went to church, and she was going to raise me as a Catholic.

Back then we left from Shibuya Station, and the trip took over an hour, not the twenty minutes in which the distance can be covered today.

I remember the long train rides, on which my mother would always take my hand, literally leading me away from my father's displeasure at the imposition of this primitive Western ritual on his impressionable young son. The church was an insidiously sensory experience: the settled, wooden smells of old paper and seat cushions; the erect pews, rigid as body casts; the glittering light of stained-glass angels; the ominous echoes of the liturgy; the bland taste of the Eucharist. All catalyzed by a dawning sense that the experience took place through a window that my father, the other half of my cultural heritage, would have preferred to keep closed.

People like to say that the West is a guilt-based culture, while that of Japan is based on shame, with the chief distinction being that the former is an internalized emotion while the latter depends on the presence of a group.

But I can tell you as the Tiresias of these two worlds that the distinction is less important than people would have you believe. Guilt is what happens when there isn't a group to shame you. Regret, horror, atrocity: if the group doesn't care, we simply invent a God who does. A God who might be swayed by the subsequent good acts, or at least efforts, of an erstwhile wrongdoer.

I heard tires crunching gravel, and turned toward the parking lot behind me just in time to see the first of three black sedans brake to a stop a few meters from where I was standing. The rear doors flew open and a man got out on each side. All Caucasians. *Holtzer*, I thought.

The follow-on cars stopped to the left and right of the lead; with my back to the water, I was encircled. Two more men got out of each of the additional cars. All of them were brandishing compact Berettas.

"Get in," the one closest to me growled, gesturing to the lead car with his gun.

"I don't think so," I said evenly. If they were going to kill me, I'd make them do it here.

Six of them stood around me in a semicircle. If they closed in a little tighter, I could try to blast through one of the guys at the outer edge—his opposite number would be afraid to shoot, lest he hit his comrade.

But they were well disciplined and resisted the urge to close. Probably they'd been briefed on the dangers of getting too near.

Instead, one of them reached under his jacket and pulled out what I instantly recognized as a taser—a stun gun.

Which meant they wanted to take me, not kill me. I pivoted to launch myself at the nearest man, but too late. I heard the pop of the taser firing its twin electrical darts, felt them sink into my thigh, current surging through my body. I went down, jerking helplessly, willing my hand to pull out the darts but getting no response from my twitching limbs.

They let the current surge for longer than they had to, standing around me while I spasmed like a fish on a deck. Finally it stopped, but I still had no control over my limbs and couldn't draw a breath. I felt them doing a pat-down—ankles, thighs, lower back. Hands pushed up the back of the suit jacket and I felt the Glock being taken from its holster. I waited for the pat-down to continue but it didn't. They must have been satisfied that they had found my weapon, and searched no further—an amateur mistake that saved the flashbang, which had stayed in place.

Someone knelt on my neck and handcuffed my arms behind my back. A hood was pulled over my head. Someone else moved in and I felt them pick me up, limp as a burlap sack, and dump me onto the floor in the back of one of the cars. Then knees were pressing down on my back, doors were slamming, and the car jerked into motion.

We drove for less than five minutes. From our speed and the absence of turns, I knew we were still on National Highway 16 and that we had passed the base. During the ride I tested my fingers, wiggled my toes. Control was coming back, but my nervous system was still scrambled from the electric jolt I had received, and I felt sick to my stomach.

I felt the car slow down and turn right, heard gravel crunching beneath the tires. We stopped. Doors opened, and a pair of hands took me by each ankle and dragged me out of the car. My head smacked the bottom edge of the door on the way out and I saw stars.

They pulled me to my feet and shoved me forward. I heard footsteps all around me and knew I was surrounded. Then they were pushing me up a short flight of stairs. I heard a door open, then slam shut with a hollow aluminum bang. I was shoved into a chair and the hood was pulled off my head.

I was inside a construction trailer. Dim light came through a single sliding window. A figure sat with his back to it.

"Hi, John. It's good to see you." It was Holtzer, of course.

"Fuck," I said, deliberately radiating an air of defeat and despondency. Not so hard, under the circumstances. "How did you get to me?"

"I knew you'd hear about Bulfinch, that you'd make another play for the disk. I know you've got sources, that you might be able to put together enough of the pieces to track me. As a precaution, we set up checkpoints around the likely staging areas near the base. You walked right into one of them."

"Fuck," I said again, meaning it.

"Don't be so hard on yourself. You got pretty close. But you should have known you were going to come up short, John. You always do, when you're up against me."

"Right," I said, trying to see how I was going to get out of this. Without the handcuffs, I might be able to get past Holtzer and the two men at the door, although I didn't know who was still outside. With the handcuffs, I wasn't going anywhere.

"You don't even know what I mean by that, do you?" he went on. "Christ, you've always been so blind."

"What are you talking about?"

His fleshy lips twisted into a loathsome smile and he silently mouthed four words. I couldn't catch them at first, so he kept mouthing them until I did.

I was the mole. I was the mole.

I dropped my head and fought for control. "Fuck you, Holtzer. You never had the access. It was someone on the ARVN side."

"You think so?" he said, his face close to mine and his voice low and obscenely intimate so his men couldn't hear. "Remember Cu Lai?"

The Cambodian village. I felt a sick feeling creeping in that had nothing to do with the aftereffects of the electric shock they had administered. .

"What about it?" I said.

"Remember 'Waste 'em'? Remember 'Son, I assure you if I told you my rank you'd shit your pants for me'? You were tough, John! I had to use three sets of voices to convince you."

Keep control, John. Focus on the problem. How do you get out of this.

"Why?" I asked.

"I had a source, a guy who could do a lot for me. I had to show him what I could do for him. Someone in the village had lent him a lot of money, was causing some problems about it. I wanted to show him how I could make those kinds of problems go away."

"So you massacred an entire village to get to one guy?"

"Had to. You all look alike, you know." He laughed at his joke.

"Bullshit. Why not just give the source money to pay back the loan?"

He threw back his head and laughed. "C'mon, Rain, the bean counters were paying much more attention to the money being expended than they were to the bullets. Some dead villagers? Just a few more V.C. to add to the body count. Christ, it was easier to do it that way than it would have been to requisition funds, fill out the paperwork, all that shit."

For the first time since some of the nightmares of the war, I could feel real despair starting to drill its way into my mind. I began to understand bone deep that in a very few minutes I would be dead, that Holtzer would have won, as he'd been winning all along. And while the thought of my own death no longer particularly fascinated me, the knowledge that I had failed to stop him, at the same moment that I came to understand what he had caused me to do so long ago, was overwhelming.

"I don't believe you," I said, playing for time. "What were they giving you that would have been worth it? I know it wasn't money—you're still a government bean counter in a cheap suit, thirty-five years later."

He made a face of exaggerated sympathy. "You're such a farmer, Rain. There's the way of the world, and you just don't get it. You trade intel for intel, that's the game. I had a source who was passing me information on NVA movements—information that was critical for the Arc Light raids that we used to disrupt the Ho Chi Minh Trail supply chain. And even though SOG's missions weren't doing any real operational damage, the North had a bug up its ass about you cowboys because you made them look like they couldn't control their own backyard. So they wanted intel on SOG, and were willing to pay a lot for it with intel of their own. I was bartering pigshit for gold."

I knew he was telling the truth. There was nothing I could say.

"Oh, and let me share just one more tidbit before these men take you outside, shoot you in the back of the head, and dump your body in the harbor," he went on. "I know all about 'Crazy Jake.' I volunteered you for the mission to get rid of him."

My throat constricted. I couldn't speak. It was like being raped.

"It's true, it was just good luck that the problem of his little Montagnard army came to my attention. But I knew just the guy to handle it—his old high-school pal, John Rain. No one else could get close enough."

It was over. I was going to die. My mind started to drift, and a strange calmness descended.

"I got the word out afterward. It was supposed to be confidential, but I made sure people knew. 'Just between you and me,' don't you love that phrase? You might as well say, 'make sure it gets in the papers.' It's great."

I found myself remembering the time I had first climbed Mount Fuji. I was with my father, and neither of us had dressed properly for the cold. We took turns wanting to go back, but somehow the other always insisted on going on, and eventually we made it to the top. We always laughed about it afterward, and he had loved to tell the story.

"I'll tell you, it made people uncomfortable, John. What kind of man can off his own best friend? Just sneak up on him and cap him? Not someone you could ever trust afterwards, I'll tell you that. Not someone you could promote, whose career you could advance. I guess that bit of 'just between you and me' info pretty much ruined your career in the military, didn't it? You've been nothing but a murderous little half-breed errand boy for your betters ever since."

The old man had always liked to tell that story. And how glad he was that we had managed to take turns convincing each other to go on until we had made it.

"Cat got your tongue, Rain?"

Yeah, it was a good memory. Not a bad one to have with you on your way out.

He stood up and turned to the two men at the door. "Don't kill him here—it's too close to the naval base. The military still has his dental records, and might ID the body. We don't want anyone to make any connection between him and the U.S. government—or with me. Take him somewhere else and dump him when you're done."

One of the men opened the door for him, and he walked out.

I heard car doors opening and closing, then two sets of tires crunching the gravel as they drove off. We had arrived in three cars, so only one was left. I didn't know if there were other men outside.

The two men remained at the door, their faces impassive.

Some deep part of me welled up, insisting on going out fighting.

"These cuffs are starting to hurt," I said, standing up slowly. "Can you do anything?"

One of them laughed. "Don't worry, we'll take care of the pain in a few minutes."

"But my arms hurt," I said again, making a face of near-tears and lifting my elbows to create space between my upper arms and my torso. I saw one of them sneer with disgust.

"Oh God, I think I'm losing circulation," I moaned. I worked my shoulders in circles until the flashbang was poised over my sleeve, then raised my elbows and started jiggling my arms violently. I felt the device ease into the upper part of the jacket sleeve.

The flashbang wouldn't slide as easily because of the pressure of my handcuffed arms against my sides. I realized I should have tried to force it out onto my back, where it would have dropped down more easily into my handcuffed hands. Too late.

I lowered my wrists, straightening my arms, and started bouncing on my toes as though I had to urinate. "I need to take a leak," I said.

The men at the door looked at each other, their expressions indicating that they found me pathetic.

Each bounce brought the device down another crucial centimeter. When it got past my elbow, I felt it slide smoothly down my sleeve and into my waiting hand.

The device had a five-second timer. If I rolled it out too early, they might make it out the door before it went off. If I waited too long, I would probably lose a hand. Not exactly how I was hoping to get the cuffs off.

I pulled the spoon free and counted. *One-one thousand . . .*

The man at the left of the door reached inside his jacket, started to slide out his gun.

Two-one thousand.

"Wait a second, wait a second," I said, my throat tight. *Three-one thousand.*

They looked at each other, expressions disgusted.

They were thinking, *This is the hard case we'd been warned would be so dangerous?*

Four-one thousand. I squeezed my eyes shut and spun so that my back was to them, simultaneously shoveling the flashbang at them with a flick of my wrists. I heard it hit the floor, followed by a huge bang that concussed my entire body. My breath was knocked out of me and I collapsed onto the floor.

I rolled left, then right, trying to take a breath, feeling like I was moving underwater. I couldn't hear anything but a huge roaring inside my head.

Holtzer's men were rolling on the floor, too, blinded, their hands gripping the sides of their heads. I drew a hitching, agonized breath and forced myself to my knees, then pitched onto my side, my balance ruined.

One of them pulled himself onto all fours and started feeling his way along the floor, trying to recover his gun.

I rolled onto my knees again, concentrating on balancing. One of the men was groping in a pattern of concentric circles that I saw would lead him momentarily to his weapon.

I planted a wobbly left foot forward and tried to stand, but fell over again. I needed my arms for balance.

The man's groping fingers moved closer to the gun.

I rolled onto my back and plunged my hands downward as hard as I could, forcing my cuffed wrists below the curve of my hips and buttocks and onto the backs of my thighs. I wriggled frantically from left to right, sliding my wrists down the backs of my legs, slipping one foot, then the other, through the opening, and got my hands in front of me.

I rolled onto all fours. Saw the man's fingers clutching the barrel of the gun.

Somehow I managed to stand. I closed the distance just as he was picking up the gun and kicked him soccer style in the face. The force of the kick sent him spinning away and knocked me over backward.

I lurched to my feet again just as the second man regained his own footing. He was still blinking rapidly from the flash, but he could see me coming. He reached inside his jacket, going for a weapon.

I stumbled over to his position just as he pulled free a pistol. Before he could raise it, I thrust the fingers of my cuffed hands hard into his throat, disrupting his phrenic and laryngeal nerves. Then I slipped my hands behind his neck and used the short space of chain between them to jerk his face down into my rising knee, again and again. He went limp and I tossed him to the side.

I turned toward the door and saw that the other one had gotten to his feet. One hand was extended and I flash-checked it, saw the knife. Before I could react by picking something up and getting it between us, he charged.

If he had stopped and collected himself he would have had a better chance, but he had decided to trade balance for speed. He thrust with the knife, but without focus. I had already taken a half step to the right, earlier than would have been ideal, but he couldn't adjust. The blade just missed me. I spun counterclockwise, clamping onto his knife wrist with both hands. I tried to rotate him to the ground, aikido style, but he recovered his balance too quickly. We grappled like that for a second, and I had the sick knowledge that I was about to lose the knife hand.

I yanked his wrist in the other direction and popped my right elbow into his nose. Then I spun in fast, crudely with no setup, taking a headlock with my right arm and grabbing the lapel of my jacket under his chin as though it was a *judogi*. The knife hand came loose and I hip-threw him with the headlock, my left hand coming in to strengthen the grip on his neck as his body sailed over me. When his torso had reached the extreme circumference of the throw, I jerked his neck hard in the other direction. A crack reverberated up my arms as his neck snapped where my forearm was pressed against it. The knife clattered to the ground and I released my grip.

I sank to my knees, light-headed, and tried to think. *Which one of them had the handcuff keys?* I thought. I frisked the first guy, whose blue skin and swollen, protruding tongue told me the cartilage fracture had proven fatal, and found a set of car keys but not the handcuff keys. With the other guy I hit pay dirt. I pulled out what I was looking for, and a second later I was free. A quick search on the floor, and I was armed with one of their Berettas.

I stumbled out the door and into the parking lot. As I had expected, there was one car left. I got in, slid the key into the ignition, fired up the engine, and raced out into the street.

I knew where I was—just off the national highway, five or six kilometers from the entrance to the naval base. Standard operating procedure would be to stop Holtzer's sedan before it could enter the grounds.

Holtzer had left less than five minutes earlier. Given the traffic and the number of lights between here and the base, there might still be time.

I knew the odds were massively against me, but I had one important advantage: I didn't give a shit whether I lived or died. I just wanted to watch Holtzer go first.

I wheeled left onto National Highway 16, flashing the high beams and working the horn to warn cars out of my way. I hit three red lights but forced my way through all of them, cars screeching to a halt on either side of me. Across from the local NTT building I saw that a red light ahead had created an opening in the oncoming traffic lane and I shot into it. I accelerated madly into oncoming traffic, leaning on the horn, then swung back into the correct lane just as the light changed so I could charge ahead of the cars that had been in front of me. I managed to buckle the seat belt as I drove, and noted with grim satisfaction that the car was equipped with an air bag. I had originally planned on tossing the flashbang into Holtzer's car as a means of gaining entry. As I had told Midori, I was going to have to improvise.

I was ten meters from the main gate when I saw the sedan turning right onto the access road to the base. A Marine guard in camouflage uniform was approaching, holding up his hands, and the driver-side window was coming down. There were a lot of guards, I saw, and they were doing the checks several meters ahead of the guard gate—the results of the anonymous bomb tip.

There were too many cars in front of me. I wasn't going to make it.

The sedan's driver-side window was down.

I leaned on the horn, but no one moved.

The guard looked up to see where the commotion was coming from.

I hit a button and my window began to lower automatically.

The guard was still looking around.

I pulled out onto the sidewalk, knocking down trash cans and mauling parked bicycles. A pedestrian dove out of the way. A few meters from the base access road I hauled the steering wheel to the right and accelerated diagonally across the meridian, driving over plantings and aiming for Holtzer's vehicle. The guard turned, saw me bearing down at high speed, and leaped clear just in time to save himself. I rammed the sedan full force into the driver-side rear door, spinning the car away from the impact and forming a two-car wreck shaped like the letter V. I was braced for the impact, and the seat belt and air bag, which deployed and deflated in a nanosecond as advertised, got me through.

I released the seat belt and tried the door, but it was jammed shut. I swiveled onto my back and shot my feet through the open window, grabbing the handle at the top of the door and using it to propel myself through.

It was only two steps to the sedan. I grabbed the steering wheel through the open window and hauled myself inside, my knees slamming into the door frame on the way in. I launched myself across the driver's lap, scrambled to get my feet under me, then dove into the back. Holtzer was in the left seat, leaning forward, obviously disoriented from the impact. A young guy I took to be one of Holtzer's aides sat next to him, a metal Halliburton attaché case between them.

I grabbed Holtzer around the head with my left arm, pressing the barrel of the Beretta against his temple with my right. I saw one of the Marine guards outside the driver's window, his gun drawn, looking for an opening. I pulled Holtzer's head closer.

"Get back, or I'll blow his fucking head off!" I bellowed at him.

His expression was uncertain, but he kept the gun up. "Everyone out of the car!" I shouted. "Now!"

I reached all the way around Holtzer's neck with my hand and took hold of my own lapel. We were cheek to cheek, and the Marine with the gun would have to have a hell of a lot of confidence in his marksmanship to try to get a shot off now.

"Out of the car!" I shouted again. "Now! You!" I yelled at the driver. "Roll up that fucking window! Roll it up!"

The driver pressed a switch and his window went up. I yelled at him again to get out and then to close the door. He stumbled out, slamming the door as he exited. "You!" I yelled at the aide. "Get out! Close the door behind you!"

Holtzer started to protest, but I squeezed his neck tighter, choking off the words. The aide glanced once at Holtzer, then tried the door.

"It's jammed," he said, obviously stunned and unable to take it all in.

"Climb across to the front!" I shouted. "Now!"

He scrambled forward and got out, taking the attaché case with him.

"All right, asshole, us too," I said to Holtzer, letting go of his neck. "But first give me that disk."

"Okay, okay. Take it easy," he said. "It's in my left breast pocket."

"Take it out. Slowly."

He reached over with his right hand and carefully took out the disk.

"Set it on my knee," I said, and he did so. "Now lace your fingers together, turn toward the window, and put your hands behind your head." I didn't want him to try to make a play for the gun while I was picking up the disk.

I picked it up and slipped it into one of my jacket pockets. "Now we're going to get out. But slowly. Or your head is going to be all over the upholstery."

He turned to me, his eyes hard. "Rain, you don't understand what you're doing. Put the gun down before the guards outside blow you away."

"If you're not on your way out of this vehicle in the next three seconds," I snarled, leveling the Beretta, "I will shoot you in the balls. Whether I leave it at that, I can't say."

Something was nagging at me, something about the way he had turned over the disk. Too readily.

Then I realized: It was a decoy. A disposable. He would never have given me the real disk so easily.

The attaché, I thought.

"Now!" I yelled, and he reached for the door handle. I pressed the gun barrel against his face.

We eased out of the car and were immediately surrounded by a phalanx of six Marine guards, all with drawn guns and deadly serious faces.

"Stay back or I'll blow his head off!" I yelled, shoving the gun up under his jaw. I saw the aide standing behind the guards, the attaché case set at his feet. "You, over there! Open up that case!" He looked at me uncomprehendingly. "Yes, you! Open up that attaché case right now!"

He looked bewildered. "I can't. It's locked."

"Give him the key," I growled to Holtzer.

He laughed. "Like hell."

Six people had the drop on me. I yanked Holtzer to the left so they would have to re-aim, giving myself a split second to pull the gun away from his head and crack him in the temple with the butt. He sank to his knees, stunned, and I went down with him, staying close to his body for what cover it could provide. I patted his left pants pocket, heard a jingling. Reached inside and pulled out a set of keys.

"Bring the case over here!" I yelled at the aide. "Bring it or he's dead!"

The aide hesitated for a second, then picked up the case and carried it over. He set it down in front of us.

I tossed him the keys. "Now open it."

"Don't listen to him!" Holtzer yelled, struggling to his feet. "Don't open it!"

"Open it!" I shouted again. "Or I'll blow him away!"

"I order you not to open that case!" Holtzer screamed. "It's the U.S. diplomatic pouch!" The aide was frozen, his face uncertain. "Goddamnit, listen to me! He's bluffing!"

"Shut up!" I yelled, digging the barrel of the gun in under his chin. "Listen. You think he's willing to take a chance on dying over the diplomatic pouch? What could be in there that's so important? Open it!"

"Shoot him!" Holtzer screamed suddenly at the guards. "Shoot him!"

"Open that case or you'll be wearing his fucking brains!"

The aide's eyes went from the case to Holtzer, then back. It seemed that everyone was frozen.

It happened suddenly. The aide dropped to his knees, fumbling with the key. Holtzer started to protest, and I cracked him in the head with the pistol again. He sagged against me.

The case popped open.

Inside, clearly visible between two protective layers of foam, was Kawamura's disk.

A long second passed, then I heard a familiar voice from behind me.

"Arrest this man."

I turned and saw Tatsu walking toward me, three Japanese cops behind him.

The cops converged on me, one of them unclipping a set of handcuffs from his equipment belt.

One of the Marine guards started to protest.

"We are outside the base," Tatsu explained in fluent English. "You have no jurisdiction. This is a Japanese domestic matter."

My arms were bent behind my back, and I felt the handcuffs clicking into place. Tatstu held my eyes long enough for me to see the sadness in his, then turned and walked away.

24

THEY PUT ME in a squad car and drove me to Keisatsucho headquarters. I was photographed, fingerprinted, and put in a concrete cell. No one mentioned what I was being charged with, or offered to allow me to contact a lawyer. What the hell, I don't know too many lawyers anyway.

The cell wasn't bad. There was no window, and I kept time by counting the meals they brought me. Three times a day a taciturn guard dropped off a tray with rice and vinegared fish, some vegetables, and picked up the tray from the previous meal. The food was okay. After every third meal I was allowed to shower.

I was waiting for my sixteenth meal, trying not to worry about Midori, when two guards came for me and told me to follow them. They took me to a small room with a table and two chairs. A naked bulb hung over the table from the ceiling. *Looks like it's time for your interrogation*, I thought.

I stood with my back against the wall. After a few minutes the door opened and Tatsu walked in, alone.

His face was serious, but after five days of solitary, it felt good to see someone I knew.

"*Konnichi wa,*" I said.

He nodded. "Hello, Rain-san," he said in Japanese. "It's good to see you. I'm tired. Let's sit."

We sat down with the table between us. He was silent for a long time, and I waited for him to speak. I didn't find his reticence encouraging.

"I hope you will forgive your recent incarceration, which I know must have been unexpected."

"I did think a pat on the back would have been more in order after I dove through that car window."

I saw the trademark sad smile, and somehow it made me feel good. "Appearances had to be maintained until I could straighten things out," he said.

"It took you awhile."

"Yes. I worked as quickly as possible. You see, to arrange for your release I first had to have Kawamura's disk decrypted. After that, various phone calls had to be made, meetings arranged, levers pulled to secure your release. There was a great deal of evidence of your existence that needed to be purged from Keisatsucho files. All this took time."

"You managed to decrypt the disk?" I asked.

"Yes."

"And its contents met your expectations?"

"Exceeded them."

He was holding something back. I could sense it in his demeanor. I waited for him to continue.

"William Holtzer has been declared *persona non grata* and has been returned to Washington," he said.

"Your ambassador has informed us that he will be resigning from the CIA."

"Just resigning? He's not being charged with anything? He's been a mole for Yamaoto, feeding false intel to the U.S. government. Doesn't the disk implicate him?"

He bowed his head and sighed. "The information on the disk is not the kind of evidence that will be used in court. And there is a desire on both sides to avoid a public scandal."

"And Yamaoto?" I asked.

"The matter of Yamaoto Toshi is . . . complicated," he said.

"'Complicated' doesn't sound good."

"Yamaoto is a powerful enemy. To be fought obliquely, with stealth, over time."

"I don't understand. What about the disk? I thought you said it was the key to his power?"

"It is."

It hit me then. "You're not going to publish it."

"No."

I was silent for a long moment as the implications set in. "Then Yamaoto still thinks it's out there," I said. "And you've signed Midori's death warrant."

"Yamaoto has been given to understand that the disk was destroyed by corrupt elements of the Keisatsucho. His interest in Kawamura Midori is thus substantially reduced. She will be safe for now in the United States, where Yamaoto's power does not extend."

"What? You can't just exile her to America, Tatsu. She has a life here."

"She has already left."

I couldn't take it all in.

"You may be tempted to contact her," he continued. "I would advise against this. She believes you are dead."

"Why would she believe that?"

"Because I told her."

"Tatsu," I said, my voice dangerously flat, "explain yourself."

His voice stayed matter-of-fact. "Although I knew you were concerned for her, I didn't know, when I told her of your death, what had happened between you," he said. "From her reaction, I realized."

He paused for a long moment, then looked at me squarely, his eyes resigned. "I deeply regret the pain you feel now. However, I am more convinced even than before that I did the right thing in telling her. Your situation was impossible. It is much better that she know nothing of your involvement in her father's death. Think of what such knowledge would do to her after what had happened between you."

I wasn't even surprised that Tatsu had put together all the pieces. "She didn't have to know," I heard myself say.

"At some level, I believe she already did. Your presence would eventually have confirmed her suspicions. Instead, she is left with memories of the hero's death you died in completing her father's last wishes."

I realized, but somehow could not grasp, that Midori had already been made part of my past. It was like a magic trick. Now you see it; now you don't. Now it's real; now it's just a memory.

"If I may say so," he said, "her affair with you was brief. There is no reason to expect that her grief over your loss will be prolonged."

"Thanks, Tatsu," I managed to say. "That's a comfort."

He bowed his head. It would be unseemly for him to give voice to his conflicted feelings, and anyway he would still do what he had to. *Giri* and *ninjo*. Duty, and human feeling. In Japan, the first is always primary.

"I still don't understand," I said after a minute. "I thought you wanted to publish what's on the disk. It would vindicate all your theories about conspiracies and corruption."

"Ending the conspiracies and corruption is more important than vindicating my theories about them."

"Aren't they one and the same? Bulfinch said that if the contents of the disk were public, the Japanese media would have no choice but to follow up, that Yamaoto's power would be extinguished."

He nodded slowly. "There is some truth to that. But publishing the disk is like launching a nuclear missile. You only get to do it once, and it results in complete destruction."

"So? Launch the missile. Destroy the corruption. Let the society breathe again."

He sighed, his sympathy for the shock I had just experienced perhaps ameliorating the impatience he usually felt in having to spell everything out for me. "In Japan, the corruption is the society. The rust has penetrated so deep that the superstructure is made of it. You cannot simply rip it all out without precipitating a collapse of the society that rests on it."

"Bullshit," I said. "If it's that corrupt, let it go. Get in there and rip."

"Rain-san," he said, a tiny note of impatience in his voice, "have you considered what would rise from the ashes?"

"What do you mean?"

"Put yourself in Yamaoto's place. Plan A is to use the threat of the disk to control the LDP from the shadows. Plan B is to detonate the disk—to publish it—to destroy the LDP and put Conviction in power."

"Because the tape implicates only the LDP," I said, beginning to understand.

"Of course. Conviction seems a model of probity by comparison. Yamaoto would have to step out of the shadows, but he would finally have a platform from which to move the nation to the right. In fact, I believe this is his ultimate hope."

"Why do you say that?

"There are signs. Certain public figures have been praising some of the prewar Imperial rescripts on education, the notion of the Japanese as a 'divine people,' and other matters. Mainstream politicians are openly visiting shrines like Yasukuni and its interred World War II soldiers, despite the costs incurred abroad by such visits. I believe Yamaoto orchestrates these events from the shadows."

"I didn't know you were so liberal on these things, Tatsu."

"I am pragmatic. It matters little to me which way the country moves, as long as the move is not accompanied by Yamaoto's means of control."

I considered. "After what's happened to Bulfinch

and Holtzer, Yamaoto is going to figure out that the disk wasn't destroyed, that you have it. He was already coming after you. It's only going to get worse."

"I am not such an easy man to get to, as you know."

"You're taking a lot of chances."

"I am playing for stakes."

"I guess you know what you're doing," I said, not caring anymore.

He looked at me, his face impassive. "There is another reason I must be careful with the disk's contents. It implicates you."

I had to smile at that. "Really?" I asked, imitating his country-bumpkin routine.

"I had been looking for the assassin for a long time, Rain-san—there have been so many convenient deaths of 'natural causes.' I always knew he was out there, although everyone else believed I was chasing a phantom. And now that I have found him, I realize he is you."

"What are you going to do about it?"

"That is for you to decide."

"Meaning?"

"As I have told you, I have deleted all evidence of your activities, even of your existence, from the Keisatsucho's databases."

"But there's still the disk. Is this your way of telling me that you're going to have leverage over me?"

He shook his head, and I saw the momentary disappointment at my characteristic American lack of subtlety. "I am uninterested in such leverage. It is not the way I would treat a friend. Moreover, knowing your character and your capabilities, I recognize that the exertion of such leverage would be futile, and possibly dangerous."

Amazing. The guy had just put me in jail, failed to publish the disk as he had implied he would, sent Midori to America, and told her I was dead, and yet I felt ashamed that I had insulted him.

"You are therefore free to return to your life in the shadows," he went on. "But I must ask you, Rain-san, is this really the life you want?"

I didn't answer.

"May I say that I had never seen you more . . . complete than you were in Vietnam. And I believe I know why. Because at heart you are samurai. In Vietnam you thought you had found your master, your cause larger than yourself."

What he said hit a nerve.

"You were not the same man when we met again in Japan after the war. Your master must have disappointed you terribly for you to have become *ronin*." A *ronin* is literally a floater on the waves, a person with no direction. A masterless samurai.

He waited for me to answer, but I didn't. Finally he said, "Is what I am saying inaccurate?"

"No," I admitted, thinking of Crazy Jake.

"You are samurai, Rain-san. But samurai cannot be samurai without a master. The master is yin to the samurai's yang. One cannot properly exist without the other."

"What are you trying to tell me, Tatsu?"

"My battle with what plagues Japan is far from over. My acquisition of the disk provides me with an important weapon in that battle. But it is not enough. I need you with me."

"You don't understand, Tatsu. You don't get burned by one master and just find another. The scars go too deep."

"What is your alternative?"

"The alternative is to be my own master. As I have been."

He waved his hand as if to dismiss such nonsense. "This is not possible for human beings. Any more than reproduction is possible through masturbation."

His uncharacteristic crudeness surprised me, and I laughed. "I don't know, Tatsu. I don't know if I can trust you. You're a manipulative bastard. Look what you've been up to while I've been in jail."

"Whether I am manipulative and whether you can trust me are two different matters," he said, easily able to compartmentalize such things because he was Japanese.

"I'll think about it," I told him.

"That is all I would ask."

"Now let me out of here."

He motioned to the door. "You have been free to go since I came in."

I gave him a small smile. "I wish you'd said so sooner. We could have done this over coffee."

25

I TOOK MY time getting back to Tatsu. There were a few things I needed to settle first.

Harry, for one. He had hacked the Keisatsucho files the same day I ambushed Holtzer at Yokosuka, so he knew I'd been arrested and "detained." Several days later, he told me, all references to me had been deleted from their files.

"When I saw those files had been deleted," he said, "I thought they had disappeared you. I figured you were dead."

"That's what people are supposed to believe," I said.

"Why?"

"They want my help with certain matters."

"That's why they let you go?"

"Nothing for nothing, Harry. You know that." I told him about Midori.

"Maybe that's for the best," he said.

He had most of the pieces, I knew. But what would be the use of either of us acknowledging any of that?

"What are you going to do now?" he asked me.

"I haven't figured all that out yet."

"If you ever need a good hacker, you know where to find me."

"I don't know, Harry. You had a lot of trouble with that music lattice reduction or whatever the hell it was. The Keisatsucho cracked it no problem."

"Hey, those guys have access to supercomputers at Japanese universities!" he sputtered, before noticing my grin. Then: "Very funny."

"I'll be in touch," I told him. "I'm just going to take a little vacation first."

I FLEW OUT to Washington, D.C., where Tatsu said they had shipped Holtzer. Processing his "retirement" would take a few days, even weeks, and in the meantime he'd be in the Langley area.

I thought I'd be able to find him by calling all the hotels listed in the suburban Virginia Yellow Pages. I worked my way outward from Langley in concentric circles, but there was no guest named William Holtzer at any of them. Probably he had checked in somewhere under an assumed name, using cash and no credit cards, afraid I might be coming after him.

What about a car, though? I started phoning the 800 numbers of the major rent-a-car companies. It was William Holtzer calling, wanting to extend his service contract. Avis didn't have a record of a William Holtzer. Hertz did. The clerk was kind enough to tell me the license plate number of the car, which I told him I needed for some supplementary insurance I wanted to get through my credit card company. I was ready for him to ask why I didn't just get the information from the key chain or the car itself, but he never did. After that, all I had to do was search a DMV database to learn that Holtzer was driving a white Ford Taurus.

Back to concentric circles. That night I drove through the parking lots of the major hotels closest to Langley, slowing to examine the license plate of every white Ford Taurus I passed.

At about two o'clock that morning I found Holtzer's car in the parking garage of the Ritz Carlton, Tyson's Corner. After confirming the license plate, I drove over to the nearby Marriott, where I took the license plates from a parked car. At the edge of the deserted parking lot of the Tyson's Corner Galleria, I switched the plates over to the rental van I was driving. The new plates and the light disguise I was wearing would be enough to beat any unforeseen witnesses or security cameras.

I drove back to the Ritz. The spaces adjacent to the Taurus were taken, but there was an empty spot behind it to one side. It was better not to park alongside him anyway. If you're savvy about the ways of my world, or even just sensitive to where and how you're likely to be mugged, you'll get nervous if you see a van parked right next to your car—especially a model with darkened rear windows, like mine. I pulled in, nose forward so the van's sliding door would be facing Holtzer.

I checked my equipment. A 250,000-volt "Thunder Blaster" guaranteed to cause disorientation upon contact and unconsciousness in less than five seconds. A medium-sized pink rubber "Super Ball," available for eighty-nine cents at pretty much any drugstore. A portable defibrillation kit like the ones some airlines are beginning to keep on their commercial jets, small enough to tote around in an ordinary briefcase and considerably more expensive than the Super Ball.

Shocking someone out of a ventricular fibrillation is tricky business. Three hundred and sixty joules is a massive dose of electricity. If a shock like that is applied at the top of the heart's T wave—that is, between beats—you'll induce a lethal arrhythmia. Modern defibrillators, therefore, have sensors that automatically detect the QRS complex of the heartbeat, which is the only instant at which the shock can safely be applied.

Of course, the same software that is designed to avoid the T wave can be reconfigured to initiate it.

I reclined the electronic seat a few degrees and relaxed. It was a safe bet that Holtzer would be heading over to the CIA's campus sometime in the morning, so I expected to have to wait only a few more hours.

At six-thirty, about a half hour before it would get light outside, I walked over to the far end of the garage and urinated into some potted hedges. I limbered up for a few minutes, then headed back to the van, where I enjoyed a breakfast of cold coffee and Chicken McNuggets, left over from the previous evening. The culinary joys of surveillance.

Holtzer showed an hour later. I watched him emerge from the elevator and head toward me. He was dressed in a gray suit, white shirt, dark tie. Standard Beltway attire, practically Agency issue.

His mind was elsewhere. I could see it in his expression, his posture, the way he failed to check the likely hot spots in the garage, especially around his car.

Shame on him, being so careless in a potential crime zone like a parking garage.

I slipped on a pair of black cowhide gloves. A click of the switch on the Thunder Blaster produced a sharp arc of blue sparks and an electric crackle. I was ready to go.

I scanned the garage, satisfying myself that for the moment it was empty. Then I slipped to the back of the van and watched him move to the driver's side of the Taurus, where he paused to remove his suit jacket. *Good,* I thought. *Let's not get any wrinkles on your funeral suit.*

I waited until the jacket was just past his shoulders, the spot that would make effective reaction most awkward for him, then swung the van's side door open and moved in on him. He looked up when he heard the door open, but had no chance to do anything but drop his mouth open in surprise. Then I was on him, my right hand jamming the Thunder Blaster into his belly, my left propping him up by the throat while the shock scrambled his central nervous system.

It took less than six seconds to drag his dazed form into the van and slide the door shut behind us. I pushed him onto the ample backseat, then gave him another hit with the Thunder Blaster to make sure he was incapacitated long enough for me to finish.

The moves were routine and it didn't take long. I buckled him in with the lap and shoulder belt, pulling the latter all the way out and then letting it retract fully until it was locked in place. The hardest part was getting his shirt open and his tie out of the way so I could apply the paddles directly to his torso, where the conducting jelly would prevent any telltale burn marks. The seat belt and shoulder restraint kept him in place while I worked.

As I applied the second paddle, his eyes fluttered open. He glanced down at his exposed chest, then looked up at me.

"Way . . . way . . . ," he stammered.

"Wait?" I asked.

He grunted, I guessed to affirm.

"Sorry, can't do that," I said, affixing the second paddle with medical tape.

He opened his mouth to say something else and I shoved the Super Ball into it. I didn't want him to bite his tongue from the force of the shock—it could look suspicious.

I shifted to the side of the van to make sure I wasn't touching him when the shock was delivered. He watched me as I moved, his eyes wide.

I flicked the switch on the unit.

His body jerked forward to the limit of the automatically locking shoulder belt and his head arched backward into the anti-whiplash head restraint. Cars are amazingly safe these days.

I waited for a minute, then checked his pulse to be sure he was finished. Satisfied, I removed the ball and the paddles, wiped off the residue of the conducting jelly with an alcohol swab, and fixed his clothes. I looked into his dead eyes and was surprised at how little I felt. Relieved, maybe. Not much more.

I opened the door of the Taurus with his key, then placed it in the car's ignition. I scanned the garage again. A woman in a business suit, probably on her way to an early meeting, came out of the elevator. I waited for her to get in her car and drive off.

Using a modified fireman's carry, I scooped up the body, walked it over to the car, and dumped it into the driver's seat. I closed the door, then paused for a moment to examine my work.

That's for Jimmy, I thought. *And Cu Lai. They've all been waiting for you in hell.*

And waiting for me. I wondered if Holtzer would be enough to satisfy them. I got into the van and drove away.

26

I HAD ONE more stop to make. Manhattan, 178 Seventh Avenue South. The Village Vanguard.

I had checked the Vanguard's Web site, and knew that the Midori Kawamura trio was appearing at the club from the first Tuesday in November through the following Sunday. I called and made a reservation for the 1:00 A.M. set on Friday night. I didn't need to use a credit card, although I knew they'd give away my seat if I didn't show up at least fifteen minutes before the set, so I was easily able to use an alias: Watanabe, a common Japanese name.

I headed up Interstate 95, crossing from Maryland to Delaware and then to New Jersey. From the turnpike I could have picked up I-80 and gone on to Dryden, two hundred miles and someone else's lifetime away.

Instead I left the turnpike for the Holland Tunnel, where I entered the city and drove the quarter mile to the Soho Grand Hotel on West Broadway. Mr. Watanabe had reserved a suite for Friday night. He arrived before six o'clock to ensure that the hotel didn't give away his reservation, and paid cash for the suite, counting out fourteen hundred dollar bills for the night. The staff, to their credit, evinced no surprise, probably guessing that the wealthy man with a passion for anonymity would be meeting his mistress.

The early arrival gave me time to shower, sleep for three hours, and enjoy an excellent room service dinner of Paillard of Veal and an '82 Mouton from the hotel's Canal House Restaurant. With another hour to kill before I left for the Vanguard, I repaired to the visually spectacular Grand Bar, where the ambience of the high ceilings, warm lighting, and wonderfully symmetrical black glass tables made up for an unimaginative selection of single malts and the annoying house music. Still, there's no quarreling with a twenty-five-year-old Macallan.

I walked the mile or so from the hotel to the Vanguard. It was cold, and I was glad for the charcoal gabardine trousers, black cashmere mock turtleneck, and navy blazer I was wearing. The charcoal trilby I was wearing low across my forehead also provided some warmth, while obscuring my features.

I picked up my ticket at 12:35, then continued walking until almost 1:00 sharp. I didn't want to take a chance on Midori or anyone else in her trio walking past me at the back of the wedge-shaped room before the set began.

I passed under the trademark red awning and neon sign and through the mahogany doors, taking a seat at one of the small round white tables in back. Midori was already at the piano, wearing black like the first time I saw her. It felt good to watch her for the moment, unobserved, separated by a sadness that I knew she must have shared. She looked beautiful, and it hurt.

The lights dimmed, the murmur of conversation died away, and Midori brought the piano to life with a vengeance, her fingers ripping into the keys. I watched intently, trying to lock in the memory of the way she moved her hands and swayed her body, the expressions of her face. I knew I'd be listening to her music forever, but this would be the last time I would watch her play.

I had always heard a frustration in her music, and loved the way it would at times be replaced by a deep, accepting sadness. But there was no acceptance in her music tonight. It was raw and angry, sometimes mournful, but never resigned. I watched and listened, feeling the notes and the minutes slipping away from me, trying to find some solace in the thought that perhaps what had passed between us was now part of her music.

I thought about Tatsu. I knew he had done right in telling Midori I was dead. As he said, she would have figured out the truth eventually, or it would have found its own way of forcing itself into her consciousness.

He was right, too, about my loss not being a long-term issue for her. She was young and had a brilliant career opening up right in front of her. When you've known someone only briefly, even if intensely, death comes as a shock, but not a particularly long or deep one. After all, there was no time for the person in question to become woven tightly into the fabric of your life. It's surprising, even a little disillusioning, how quickly you get over it, how quickly the memory of what you might have shared with someone comes to seem distant, improbable, like something that might have happened to someone you know but not to you yourself.

The set lasted an hour. When it was done, I stood up and eased out the back, exiting through the wooden doors and pausing for a moment under a moonless sky. I closed my eyes and inhaled the smells of Manhattan's night air, at once strange and yet, connected to that long-ago life, still disturbingly familiar.

"Excuse me," a woman's voice came from behind me.

I turned, thinking *Midori*. But it was only the coat-check girl. "You left this behind," she said, holding out the trilby. I had placed it on the seat next to me after the lights had gone down and had then forgotten it.

I took the hat wordlessly and walked off into the night.

Midori. There were moments with her when I would forget everything I had done, everything I had become. But those moments would never have lasted. I am the product of the things I have done, and I know I will always wake up to this conclusion, no matter how beguiling the reverie that precedes the awakening.

What I needed to do was not deny what I was, but to find a way to channel it. Maybe, for the first time, into something worthwhile. Maybe something with Tatsu. I'd have to think about that.

Midori. I still listen to her music. I hang on hard to the notes, trying to keep them from vanishing into the air, but they are elusive and ungraspable and each one dies in the dark around me like a tracer in a treeline.

Sometimes I catch myself saying her name. I like its texture on my lips, something tenuous but still tangible to give substance to my memories. I say it slowly, several times in succession, like a chant or a prayer.

Does she ever think of you? I sometimes wonder.

Probably not, is the inevitable reply.

It doesn't matter. It feels good to know she's out there. I'll keep listening to her from the shadows. Like it was before. Like it's always going to be.

ACKNOWLEDGMENTS

TO MY AGENT, Nat Sobel, and his wife, Judith, for believing in me all the way back to the first iteration. At times Nat knew John Rain better than I did (this could be a little unsettling), and Rain would never have emerged as the complex character he is without Nat's insight and guidance.

To Walter LaFeber of Cornell University, for being a great teacher and friend, and for writing *The Clash: A History of U.S.-Japan Diplomatic Relations,* the definitive study of its subject, which provided some of the historical foundations for the birth of John Rain.

To my instructors, formal and informal, and *randori* partners at the Kodokan in Tokyo, the beating heart of world judo, for imparting to me some of the skills that make their home in John Rain's deadly toolbox.

To Benjamin Fulford, *Forbes* Tokyo Bureau Chief, for his courageous and unrelenting reporting of the corruption that plagues Japan—corruption that acts as an underpinning for this story and that should be more widely heeded by the people it most directly affects.

To Koichiro Fukasawa, a diplomat with the soul of an artist and the most bicultural person I have ever known, for sharing his insights about all things Japanese, and for introducing me to so many of the marvels of Tokyo.

To Dave Lowry, for his sublime *Autumn Lightning: The Education of an American Samurai,* which influenced my own understanding of *shibumi* and the warrior arts, and which provided, therefore, part of the education of John Rain.

To the omnidirectional Carl, veteran of the secret wars, for teaching me to hit first, soon, early, and often, whose very presence got me thinking in the right direction.

Most of all to my wife, Laura, for putting up with my writing and other obsessions and for doing so many other things to support and encourage the creation of this book. Through countless discussions on walks, long drives, and sometimes late at night over a single malt, Laura helped me as no one else ever could to find the story, the characters, the words, the will.

AUTHOR'S NOTE

WITH TWO EXCEPTIONS, I have depicted the Tokyo in this book as accurately as I could. Tokyoites familiar with Shibuya will know that there is no Higashimura fruit store midway up Dogenzaka. The real fruit store is at the bottom of the street, closer to the station. And seekers after Bar Satoh in Omotesando, although they will come across a number of fine whiskey bars in the area, will find Satoh-san's establishment only in Miyakojima-ku, Osaka. It is the best whiskey bar in Japan and worth the trip.

Read on
for a special abridged
excerpt of Barry Eisler's
new novel

HARD RAIN

Now on sale from Putnam

Once you get past the overall irony of the situation, you realize that killing a guy in the middle of his own health club has a lot to recommend it.

The target was a yakuza, an iron freak named Ishihara who worked out every day in a gym he owned in Roppongi, one of Tokyo's entertainment districts. Tatsu had told me the hit had to look like natural causes, like they always do, so I was glad to be working in a venue where it was far from unthinkable that someone might keel over from a fatal aneurism induced by exertion, or suffer an unlucky fall onto a steel bar, or undergo some other tragic mishap while using one of the complicated exercise machines.

The health club was also convenient because I wouldn't have to worry about fingerprints. In Japan, where costumes are a national pastime, a weightlifter wouldn't pump iron without wearing stylish padded gloves any more than a politician would take a bribe in his underwear. It was a warm early spring for Tokyo, portending, they said, a fine cherry blossom season, and where else but at a gym could a man in gloves have gone unnoticed?

In my business, going unnoticed is half the game. People put out signals—body language, gait, clothes, facial expressions, posture, attitude, speech, mannerisms—that can tell you where they're from, what they do, who they are. Most importantly, *do they fit in.* Because if you don't fit in, the target will spot you, and after that you won't be able to get close enough to do it right. Or the rare uncorrupt cop will spot you, and you'll have some explaining to do. Or a countersurveillance team will spot you, and then—congratulations!—the target will be you.

But if you're attentive, you begin to understand that the identifying signals are a science, not an art. You watch, you imitate, you acquire. Eventually, you can shadow different targets through different societal ecosystems, remaining anonymous in all of them.

The story my signals would tell the yakuza was simple. He'd only begun seeing me at his gym recently, but I was already obviously in shape. So I wasn't some middle-aged guy who'd decided to take up weightlifting to try to regain a lost college-era physique. The more likely explanation would be that I worked for a company that had transferred me to Tokyo, and, if they had sprung for digs near Roppongi, maybe in Minami-Aoyama or Azabu, I must be someone reasonably important and well compensated. That I was apparently into body building at all at this stage in my life probably meant affairs with young women, for whom a youthful physique might ameliorate the unavoidable emotional consequences of sleeping with an older man in what at root would be little more than an exchange of sex and the illusion of immortality for Ferragamo handbags and the other implicit currencies of such arrangements. All of which the yakuza would understand, and even respect.

In fact, my recent appearance at the yakuza's gym had nothing to do with a company transfer—it was more like a business trip. After all, I was in Tokyo just to do a job. When the job was finished, I would leave. I'd done some things to generate animosity when I'd been living here, and the relevant parties might still be looking for me, even after I'd been away for a year, so a short stay was all I could sensibly afford.

Tatsu had given me a dossier on the yakuza a month earlier, when he'd found me and persuaded me to take the job. From the contents, I would have concluded that the target was just mob muscle, but I knew he must be more than that if Tatsu wanted him eliminated. I didn't ask. I only wanted the particulars that would help me get close. The rest was irrelevant.

The dossier had included the yakuza's cell phone number. I had fed it to Harry, who, compulsive hacker that he was, had long since penetrated the cellular network control centers of Japan's three telco providers. Harry's computers were monitoring the movements of the yakuza's cell phone within the network. Any time the phone got picked up by the tower that covered the area around the yakuza's health club, Harry paged me.

Tonight, the page had come at just after eight o'clock, while I was reading in my room at the New Otani hotel in Akasaka Mitsuke. The club closed at eight, I knew, so there was a good possibility that I'd find the yakuza working out there alone. What I'd been waiting for.

My workout gear was already in a bag, and I was out the door within minutes after getting the page. I caught a cab a slight distance from the hotel, not wanting a doorman to hear or remember where I might be going, and five minutes later I exited at the corner of Roppongi-dori and Gaienhigashi-dori in Roppongi. I hated to use such a direct route because doing so afforded me limited opportunity to ensure that I wasn't being followed, but I had only a little time to pull this off the way I'd planned and decided it was worth the risk.

I had been watching the yakuza for over a month now, and knew his routines. I'd learned that he liked to vary the times of his workouts, sometimes arriving at the gym early in the morning, sometimes at night. Probably he assumed the resulting unpredictability would make him hard to get to.

He was half right. Unpredictability is the key to being a hard target, but the concept applies to both time and place. Half measures like this guy's will protect you from some of the people some of the time, but they won't save you for long from someone like me.

Strange, how people can take adequate, even strong security measures in some respects, while leaving themselves vulnerable in others. Like double locking the front door and leaving the windows wide open.

The yakuza's weakness was his addiction to weights. Who knows what fueled it—a history of childhood bullying that made him want to appear visibly strong afterward, an attempt to overcome a feeling of inadequacy born of being naturally slighter of build than Caucasians, some suppressed homoeroticism like the one that drove Mishima. Maybe some of the same impulses that had led him to become a gangster to being with.

His obsession had nothing to do with health, of course. In fact, the guy was an obvious steroid abuser. His neck was so thick it looked as though he could slide a tie up over his head without having to loosen the knot, and he sported acne so severe that the club's stark incandescent lighting, designed to show off to maximum effect the rips and cuts its members had developed in their bodies, cast small shadows over the pocked landscape of his face. His testicles were probably the size of raisins, his blood pressure likely rampaging through an overworked heart.

I'd also seen him explode into the kind of abrupt, unprovoked violence that is another symptom of steroid abuse.

* * *

I moved quickly down Gaienhigashi-dori, easing past pedestrians on the crowded sidewalk, ignoring the cacophony of traffic and sound trucks and touts, using the chrome and glass façades around me to gauge whether there was anyone to my rear trying to keep up. I turned right just before the Roi Roppongi building, then right again onto the club's street, where I paused behind a thicket of parked bicycles, my back to the incongruous pink façade of a Starbucks coffee shop, waiting to see who might be trailing in my wake. A few groups of young partygoers drifted by, caught up in the urgent business of entertaining themselves and failing to notice the man standing quietly in the shadows. No one set off my radar. After a few minutes, I made my way to the club.

The facility occupied the ground floor of a gray commercial building hemmed in by rusting fire escapes and choked with high-tension wires that clung to the structure's façade like rotting vegetation. Across from it was a parking lot crowded by Mercedes with darked-out windows and high-performance tires, the status symbols of the country's elite and of its criminals, each aping the other, comfortably sharing the pleasure of the night in Roppongi's tawdry demimonde. The street itself was illuminated only by the indifferent glow of a single arched lamplight, its base festooned with flyers advertising the area's innumerable sexual services in the shadows of its own luminescence, looking like the elongated neck of some antediluvian bird shedding diseased and curling feathers.

The shades were drawn behind the club's plate glass windows, but I spotted the yakuza's anodized aluminum Harley-Davidson V-Rod parked in front, surrounded by commuter bicycles like a shark amidst pilot fish. Just past the windows was the entrance to the building. I tried the door, but it was locked.

I backed up a few steps to the club windows and tapped on the glass. A moment later the lights went off inside. *Nice,* I thought. He had cut the lights so he could peek through the shades without being seen from outside. I waited, knowing he was watching me and checking the street.

The lights went back on, and a moment later the yakuza appeared in the entranceway to the building. He was wearing gray sweatpants and a black cut-away A-shirt, along with the obligatory weightlifting gloves. Obviously in the middle of a workout.

He opened the door, his eyes searching the street for danger, failing to spot it right there in front of him.

"Shimatteru," he told me. Club's closed.

"I know," I said in Japanese, my hands up, palms forward in a placating gesture. "I was hoping someone might be here. I was going to come by earlier but got held up. You think I could squeeze in a quick one? Just while you're here, no longer than that."

He hesitated, then shrugged and turned to go back inside. I followed him into the hallway, then into the club.

"How much longer have you got to go?" I asked, dropping my gear bag and changing out of my unobtrusive khakis, blue oxford cloth shirt, and navy blazer. I had already slipped on the gloves, as I always did before coming to the club, but the yakuza hadn't noticed this detail. "So I can time my workout."

He walked over to the squat station. "Forty-five minutes, maybe an hour," he said, getting into position under the weight.

Squats. What he usually did when he was finished bench pressing. *Shit.*

I slipped into shorts and a sweatshirt, then warmed up with some push-ups and other calisthenics while he did his sets of squats. The warm-up might actually be useful, I realized, depending on the extent of his struggles. A small advantage, but I don't give anything away for free.

When he was through, I asked, "Already done benching?"

"So da." Yeah.

"How much you put up tonight?"

He shrugged, but I detected a slight puffing of his chest that told me his vanity had been kindled.

"Not so much. Hundred and forty kilos. Could have done more, but with that much weight, it's better to have someone spot you."

Perfect. "Hey, I'll spot you."

"Nah, I'm already done."

"C'mon, do another set. It inspires me. What are you putting up, twice your body weight?" My underestimate was deliberate.

"More."

"Shit, *more* than twice your body weight? That's what I'm talking about, I'm not even close to that. Do me a favor, do one more set, it'll motivate me. I'll spot you, fair enough?"

He hesitated, then shrugged and started walking over to the bench press station.

The bar was already set up with the hundred and forty kilos he'd been using earlier. "Think you can handle a hundred and sixty?" I asked, my tone doubtful.

He looked at me, as though bored by such a question. "I can handle it."

"Okay, this I've got to see," I said, pulling two ten-kilo plates off the weight tree and sliding them onto the ends of the bar. I stood behind the bench and gripped the bar at about shoulder width with both hands. "Let me know when you're ready."

He sat at the foot of the bench, his shoulders hunched forward, and rotated his neck from side to side. He swung his arms back and forth and I heard a series of short, forceful exhalations. Then he lay back and took hold of the bar.

"Give me a lift on three," he said.

I nodded.

There were several additional sharp exhalations. Then: "One . . . two . . . three!"

I helped him get the bar into the air and steady it over his chest. He was staring at the bar as though enraged by it, his chin sunk into his neck in preparation for the effort.

Then he let it drop, controlling its descent but allowing enough momentum to ensure a good bounce off his massive chest. Two thirds of the way up, the bar almost stopped, suspended between the drag of gravity and the power of his steroid-fueled muscles, but it continued its shaky ascent until his elbows were straightened. His arms were trembling from the effort. There was no way he had another one in him.

"One more, one more," I urged. "C'mon, you can do it."

There was a pause, and I prepared to try some fresh exhortations. But he was only mentally preparing for the effort. He took three quick breaths, then dropped the bar to his chest. It rose a few centimeters from the impact, then a few more from the northward shove that followed, but a second later it stopped and began to move inexorably downward.

"Tetsudate kure," he grunted. Help. But calmly, expecting my immediate assistance.

The bar continued downward and settled against his chest. *"Tetsudate kure yo,"* he said again, more sharply this time.

I pushed downward instead.

His eyes popped open, searching for mine.

Between the weight of the bar and plates and the pressure I was delivering, he was now struggling with almost two hundred kilos.

I focused on the bar and his torso, but in my peripheral vision I saw his eyes bulging in confusion, then fear. He made no sound. I continued to concentrate on the clinical downward pressure.

With his teeth clenched shut, his chin almost buried in his neck, he threw everything he had into moving the bar. In this extremis he was actually able to get the weight off his chest. I hooked a foot under the horizontal supports at the bottom of the bench and used the leverage to add additional pressure to the bar, and again it settled against his chest.

I felt a tremor in the weights as his arms began to shake with exertion. Again the bar moved slightly north.

Suddenly I was struck by the reek of feces. His sympathetic nervous system, in desperation, was shutting down nonessential bodily activities, including sphincter control, and diverting all available energy to his muscles.

The rally lasted only another moment. Then his arms began to shake more violently, and I felt the bar moving downward, more deeply into his chest. There was a slight hissing as his breath was driven out through his nostrils and pursed lips. I felt his eyes on my face but kept my attention on his torso and the bar. Still he made no sound.

Seconds went by, then more. His position didn't change. I waited. His skin began to blue. I waited longer.

Finally, I eased off the pressure I had been putting on the bar and released my grip.

His eyes were still on me, but they no longer perceived. I stepped back, out of their sightless ambit, and paused to observe the scene. It looked like what it almost was: a weightlifting addict, alone and late at night, tries to handle more than he can, gets caught under the bar, suffocates, and dies there. A bizarre accident.

I changed back into my street clothes. Picked up my bag, moved to the door. A series of cracks rang out behind me, like the snaps of dried tinder. I turned to look one last time, realizing as I did that the sound was of his ribs giving way. No question, he was done. Only his convulsive grip on the bar remained, as though the fingers refused to believe what the body had already accepted.

I stepped into the dark hallway and waited until the street was clear. Then I eased out onto the sidewalk and into the shadows around me.